THE *Lady* AND THE OUTLAW

THE KINCAID FAMILY SERIES

JOYCE BRANDON

DIVERSIONBOOKS

Also by Joyce Brandon

After Eden

The Kincaid Family Series
The Lady and the Lawman
The Lady and the Robber Baron
Adobe Palace

Diversion Books
A Division of Diversion Publishing Corp.
443 Park Avenue South, Suite 1008
New York, New York 10016
www.DiversionBooks.com

For more information, email info@diversionbooks.com

First Diversion Books edition July 2015.
Print ISBN: 978-1-68230-247-7
eBook ISBN: 978-1-62681-905-4

This book is dedicated to my spiritual teacher, Huzur Maharaj Charan Singh Ji, and his successor, Baba Gurinder Singh Ji, who taught me how to make the best use of this human life, guiding and supporting me as I struggled to change my focus from the tumult and chaos of family life to one more centered on love for God, resulting in greater emotional and mental comfort and contentment, worthwhile service, and a fruitful and satisfying spiritual life.

CHAPTER ONE

August 3, 1888

"Why are we slowing down here?" Leslie Powers demanded of the conductor who paused, frowning, beside their seat. He was a tall man, paunchy, black-garbed, with the inevitable mustache and serviceable watch on a long gold chain hanging across his vest. He peered out the half-open window of the passenger coach, mopping his perspiring brow with a dingy handkerchief, and squinted at the endless expanse of desert that baked under the midday sun.

"Don't rightly know, ma'am," he mumbled, scratching his balding head. "Never stopped here before."

Brakes screeched as they were applied with a heavy hand. Annette muttered something in French and clutched frantically at the yarn ball that tumbled off her lap. A woman at the front of the long passenger car stood up and threw off the *rebozo* that had covered her long black hair and dark, smoldering features. She whirled, brandishing the gun she held. A man in the back of the car, who had risen slowly, leveled his gun and shouted over the noise of the brakes.

"Keep looking straight ahead! Hands on your heads! Keep it slow and easy, and nobody gets hurt. Do it!" His tone demanded compliance. Leslie could feel her arms going up of their own volition.

"Well, I'll be dang blasted!" the man in front of Leslie muttered as he slowly complied with the order. "A holdup." There was a volley of darkly uttered oaths as other men followed his example. Women gasped at the language.

The bandit started up the aisle, and Leslie turned to look in spite of the warning. The bottom half of his face was hidden beneath a red bandana, and his eyes were shaded by a dark hat pulled low on his forehead. Tawny wheat-colored hair curled crisply along the nape of his sun-bronzed neck. His lean, straight form was clad in dusty brown trousers and shirt, half covered by a vest that had long ago faded. Like her mother, Leslie usually saw colors first, because they were the tools of her trade, but in this bandit she saw motion and resolute masculine aggressiveness. His body telegraphed a clear message that no disobedience would be tolerated.

Spurs jingled when the bandit moved. "Howdy, Ben, Sam, Three Fingers," he said amiably, nodding as if he were meeting them on the street, his voice low and richly masculine. He took each weapon, ignoring the looks of chagrin and disgust. He dropped them into a sack he had pulled out of his back pants pocket and started to move on, but the one he had called Ben spoke in a voice loud enough for all to hear.

"You overstepped yourself this time, mister. We were expecting you."

The gunman chuckled softly. "I see you were," he said dryly. Now his eyes, a clear cornflower blue so intense in color that they reminded Leslie of mother-of-pearl, fairly danced with mischief.

"I can't imagine Kincaid's making much money in the train business when half the passengers are hired guns, riding the train free. Me and my men had a helluva time finding hotel rooms in Tucson with all the special agents around. Had a hard time getting a good night's rest with you fellows stomping in and out all the time."

Ben shrugged, ignoring the gunman's contempt for their ineptitude as railroad detectives. He was listening for gunfire that would announce to this cocky bandit that the posse hidden in the closed boxcar had made its move. He grimaced. What was taking them so long?

"Kincaid has authorized me to make you a proposition," he said tersely, "if you'll listen for a minute."

The bandit's blue eyes narrowed into wicked slits. "Like what?" he demanded, obviously skeptical.

"There's a job waiting for you if you want to come work with us instead of against us."

The bandit laughed, a rich husky baritone that sounded completely relaxed, unhurried. "Stretching a rope?" he demanded, his smooth, low-pitched words taunting the suddenly uncomfortable detective. "Tell Mr. Kincaid I'm satisfied with our present arrangement," he said firmly, starting to move forward again.

"Wait!" Ben made a move to reach out but thought better of it as the gunman pointed the heavy revolver point blank at his forehead. Leslie could feel herself tensing, as if that would somehow help the man called Ben withstand the force of a bullet slamming into his forehead.

"Wait!" Ben said again, nervously. "The offer is serious. Kincaid can arrange a pardon."

"Now why would Kincaid want to do that?"

Ben, thankful to still be alive, dragged his arm across his perspiring brow. "Maybe he thinks that if you're working for the railroad, he'll get more silver to the bank."

The gunman shook his head, chuckling softly, but when he spoke there was no doubt that he meant every word. "Tell your Mr. Kincaid I'm *particular* about who I work for. There are some things he can't buy."

Leslie was watching his eyes. The dancing lights she had seen before were gone, replaced by something almost tangible in its intensity. Was it bitterness? Hate? Irony? There was no way to tell from his coolly drawled words. Before she could decide, Ben called after the gunman. "You better think it over! This may be your last chance…"

The outlaw didn't look like he considered it very seriously. He had turned his attention back to the other occupants, moving up the aisle toward Leslie, gathering guns from the unprotesting men. Neither of the bandits had done anything threatening to the passengers, but Leslie could feel her heart beating a wild staccato of fear against her throat and temples.

"Don't move, *señor!*"

Leslie's attention was drawn back to the woman at the front of the coach. Now she was pointing her pistol menacingly at one of the men seated across from Leslie. Caught in the act of pulling his own revolver, he cursed and raised his hands slowly, and the woman, who looked no more than a slip of a girl, relaxed the snarl of defiance that had come over her pretty face. She looked too young to be robbing trains, almost childlike, with a soft golden complexion, brown eyes, and full red lips. Very Spanish-looking, with mother-of-pearl combs holding back her abundant hair. She was like one of those highly romanticized creatures from the pulp magazines Leslie had read because her father lived in what everyone called the Wild West.

"Nice and easy," the gunman said smoothly as he came even with her seat. Annette's cold fingers bit into Leslie's wrist as the poor woman sucked in a ragged breath. In self-defense, to keep her circulation from being cut off, she took Annette's hand in her own.

"Everybody does what they're told and nobody gets hurt. Just relax. This won't take long," the bandit said, starting to move past her seat.

"How very thoughtful of you!" Leslie said caustically.

The bandit looked at her for the first time, catching her reproachful glance and holding it. His eyes, close up, were the pale blue of the noonday sky and filled with the same diffuse intensity. Now they flicked over her appraisingly, taking in the slender curves beneath her very proper traveling gown. The bandana flattened slightly, as if he were smiling, and he winked, his eyes filled with appreciation or amusement. Caught off guard, she flushed with heat. His eyes darted from her eyes to her mouth. She wanted to reject his bold scrutiny with a haughty shrug of indifference, but her hand moved up to fidget with the very proper traveling bonnet that temporarily contained the heavy black mass of her hair, keeping it chastely away from the creamy white oval of her face.

The sudden heat in his eyes brought the realization to her that she was practically flirting with him—flirting with an outlaw in the midst of a holdup. Angry sparks kindled and flared in her long-lashed green eyes. She lifted her skirts and pulled them back as if she feared contamination. Now the gunman's eyes fairly danced. Tiny pinpricks of light shimmered in their depths before he touched the brim of his hat and moved past her to continue his trip to the front of the coach.

At some point in that almost wordless exchange Leslie had stood up. She didn't know she had shrugged off Annette's hand and was following the bandit's lithe form with her eyes, feeling somehow bested or rejected, until the Mexican girl's voice suddenly jarred her.

"Keep your eyes to yourself, you *gringa puta!*" she snapped, her dark eyes filled with feral heat. The female trainrobber looked like a tawny gold puma set to attack; but Leslie, who had been hot, tired, and frustrated on this train for five days, felt no instinct to withdraw from the challenge in the other woman's eyes, even if she did have a gun.

"Don't tell me what to do, you female cretin! You're not exactly a magnolia blossom!" Leslie snapped, her eyes exchanging sudden hatred with the young woman. That slur would have withered any female at Wellesley College, but it was hardly devastating enough for a young savage who consorted with train robbers. It did earn Leslie a startled look from the gunman, though, before he moved forward again, tossing the sack of guns over his shoulder. He grabbed his girlfriend around the waist with one arm to keep her from leaping on top of Leslie.

The girl squirmed wildly in his embrace. "We aren't here so you can cat-fight with the passengers," he reminded her, his voice firm. Chastised by the grimness of his husky voice, she became still, and the outlaw lowered her onto her feet so she could stand.

"That *gringa puta*..." she snarled, switching to rapid-fire Spanish, her dark eyes spitting fury at Leslie.

"Enough." The gunman cut her off with the increasing pressure of his arm around her rib cage and the suddenly cold finality of that one quietly uttered word. If that hadn't stopped her, Leslie felt sure that the look in his suddenly cold eyes, which had taken on the flat, unyielding quality of new steel, would have, had the girl turned to look.

Going limp suddenly, the *bandita* said something submissive and conciliatory in Spanish, and Leslie saw him relax his grip on her. The girl stepped slightly away from him, rearranging her garments and casting a haughty, scornful look at Leslie.

"What did that milk-faced daughter of a brood sow call me?" she asked sullenly, switching to English.

The twinkle was back in his blue eyes. "Relax. She just returned your compliment in kind," he said. His eyes found Leslie's, and he winked at her again, sending that furious heat back into her cheeks.

The Mexican girl straightened her blouse where the bandit's hands had rumpled it and began to unbutton the waistband of her skirt. Her bold eyes swept the room, and she let the skirt drop to reveal a pair of boy's pants. She smiled with pride and defiance, clearly enjoying the chagrin of the women, whose eyes plainly showed their outrage. She gave Leslie, whose face had remained coldly impassive, a deliberately sultry look, and smoothed her left hand over her slender hip, straightening some imaginary wrinkle in the tight fabric. Without waiting for a response, she stooped gracefully, lithe and catlike, retrieved the skirt, and tossed it carelessly over her shoulder, flashing a contemptuous smile at Leslie.

Three gunshots rent the sudden stillness, and the outlaw became all business again. "Let's go," he said, swinging the sackful of guns over his broad shoulder. His brown hand closed over the girl's, and they turned to leap down the steps.

Leslie leaned across Annette, whose usually ruddy face had turned quite pale. She saw masked bandits leaving the other coaches, the locomotive, and the mail car. They ran purposefully, converging on a man who was leading a string of horses. Leslie saw the bandit boost the girl up onto a small red mustang, then leap gracefully into the saddle of a big black horse. The animal stretched out its long powerful neck, with the man leaning forward on its back, and she could see horse and rider, like one, stretching into the long, easy strides that would carry them away from pursuit. She watched until he was only a cloud of gray dust in the distance, blending into the monotony of the Arizona desert.

"Well, it's over," she said, more to herself than to Annette. Still dazed, she glanced around at the other occupants of the passenger car and noticed that she and Annette were practically alone. The men had all rushed outside and were milling around like lost children.

"Ohhh!" With that, Annette, who was usually entirely unflappable, swooned.

CHAPTER TWO

"Oh, no!" Leslie said under her breath as she moved quickly to catch Annette before she slid off the hard wooden seat and onto the soot-covered floor.

"Here, miss. Allow me, please." The young man who had rushed forward to help fished a tiny bottle of smelling salts out of his pants pocket and held it under Annette's nose.

She revived almost instantly and pushed his hand away. *"Non!* I can't breathe!"

"Sorry, ma'am, but you fainted."

"Oh, *non, mademoiselle!* How could I? How ashamed I am!" she moaned, covering her pale cheeks with shaking hands.

Now that the danger was past, Leslie could feel tremors in her own midriff and rushed to reassure her lady's maid. "Nonsense, Annette. There is nothing to be ashamed of. If I'd thought of it first, I would have swooned too! It was very exciting, wasn't it?"

"Oui! Terrifying! Exciting!"

"What's happening now? Why are all those men running around out there?" she asked.

But the young man was gazing shyly into Annette's eyes and seemed oblivious to everything else. "Excuse me," Leslie said, waving her dainty hand in front of him.

Caught, he blushed and pretended to peer out the window past Annette, as if searching for the answer to her question while he composed himself. "They're looking for our guns," he said, his gray eyes narrowed against the glare of the sun.

"Our guns?" she asked, frowning at the men outside who looked like they were participants in a wild and hurried Easter egg hunt.

"They wouldn't leave us out here without our guns. Too much danger from marauding bandits or escaped Indians."

"I didn't realize that outlaws care what happens to their victims," she said, lifting an expressive black brow.

"Some don't, I suppose. But that was the Devil's Canyon Gang. Their style is easy to recognize. They take control of the whole train—every boxcar, Pullman coach, mail car, locomotive, everything—disarm the passengers, clean out the safe, and dump the guns in the bushes, then disappear into the mountains. I've read about them, but I never thought I would actually get to see them in action," he said, his voice filled with awe.

"The Devil's Canyon Gang?" she asked, frowning out the window. "How did they get that name?"

"Because the one and only time they were seriously pursued, they disappeared into Devil's Canyon, and no one could find them."

Leslie noticed the interest in Annette's eyes for the young man and decided to draw him out. "My, you sound very knowledgeable about this Devil's Canyon Gang." He had nice eyes, and she could see him beginning to color. He looked young, probably only a few years older than her nineteen years, but he appeared to be the sort of gentleman that two women on a train could talk to without getting into trouble. She relaxed a little, smiling at the way his eyes kept slipping back to Annette's flushed face.

"I've followed their activities," he admitted. "The newspapers print stories about the Devil's Canyon Gang. Seems people love to read about them." He colored suddenly, his chipmunk cheeks turning pink. "Oh, excuse me, ma'am. I entreat you to forgive my lack of manners. Would—would I be too forward if I introduced myself?"

"Please do," Leslie said, smiling.

"John Loving, at your service." The warm glow from their smiles made him bold, but not bold enough to speak directly to the young Frenchwoman. "You were magnificent against those bandits, miss. I had the feeling that if you were one of the detectives we would have seen an entirely different show," he ended gallantly.

Leslie laughed, a golden tinkle of notes climbing a scale. "Leslie Powers. And this is Annette Guillet. Thank you for your concern. And for being there with the smelling salts. Are you the official swoon control officer aboard this train?"

"He ees very good at it, no?" Annette asked, beaming at him. John Loving blushed from neck to hairline, and Leslie decided that she liked him. He looked very stern and proper, until he smiled, and then he looked mischievous in a sort of quiet way.

He shrugged. "I work in the Texas and Pacific's main office—or I will—as soon as we get to Phoenix. I'm going to be Mr. Summers's assistant. He's right under Mr. Kincaid."

"Sounds like a very important position, *monsieur.*"

The pink in his fat, muscular cheeks darkened again, and Leslie decided it was time to change the subject before John Loving, who looked very earnest, crawled under one of those hard wooden seats in embarrassment. "Tell me about this gang," she said quickly. "Why are you so sure they left the guns?"

"See those men using crowbars on the boxcar?"

She leaned across Annette to peer out the window. "Yes." She couldn't actually see what they were doing, but assumed Loving was correct.

"The bandits nailed the boxcar shut sometime before they stopped the train. There's a posse inside. The gang always seems to know the important things ahead of time—as if they have inside information..."

"Over here!" a masculine voice yelled from outside. By the stampede that followed, Leslie could tell they had found the guns.

"What are they going to do now?" she asked, watching armed men on horseback jumping from the boxcar onto the ground.

"Follow them, but they won't catch them."

"How do you know that?" she asked, noting that John Loving had considerable admiration for the bandits.

He shrugged. "The gang has too many friends. They don't rob ordinary people, seldom hurt anyone, not even posses. They're sort of looked up to—like modern-day Robin Hoods—especially by the Mexicans."

"Does the Texas and Pacific know you speak so highly of the bandits who rob their trains?" she asked, teasing him.

Loving sneaked another look at Annette and nodded, his young face solemn. "Mr. Kincaid talks the same way, and he *is* the Texas and Pacific."

"Is he the one they were talking about? The one who offered that bandit a pardon and a job?"

"Yes. The same."

"But why would he do that?"

"Kincaid's probably one of the richest men in the United States. I guess he considers it good business. He knows that some people resent the railroads for taking all the best land and that most ordinary folks admire men who can take some small part of it back."

"Do railroads really take land away from people?"

"No, not really. Congress grants the railroad one square mile of land for every mile of track the company lays if they complete a stretch of track tying two towns together.

"Kincaid built a line all the way from San Diego to El Paso. The company owns millions of acres of land now. And sometimes the land is occupied by a homesteader or a squatter who doesn't want to move when the railroad takes possession. The railroad usually does what it can to help the people relocate, but sometimes nothing helps, and it ends badly. Some say the leader of the gang may have been one of the squatters who used to ranch around here."

"You sound like quite an admirer of Mr. Kincaid's railroad."

"It's hard not to admire such a visionary. I'm learning everything I can from him."

"I thought for a moment that you wanted to be just like that outlaw." She laughed, completely recovered now from her earlier fright. "Who do you think is the gang's leader?"

"Some folks think it's Clay Allison, a big, sandy-haired fellow with a loud, booming voice. This chap was more like Sam Bass, the Texas outlaw, soft-spoken with smooth manners. Allison is sort of a blowhard, and if it had been him, half the men on the train would probably have been shot or killed. Personally, I think it's Ward Cantrell."

They were interrupted by the men climbing back into the coach, stamping their feet, cursing, and breathing hard from the exertion of running around searching for their guns. Smiling at Leslie, the one named Ben stopped beside Loving and put his arm around the young man's shoulders.

"Our boy giving you all the lowdown, miss?" he asked in a jocular manner.

"Why, yes, he was telling me all about the Devil's Canyon Gang..."

"Don't nobody know much about that gang. Leastways no one outside the gang. Myself—I reckon that yaller-haired fellow with the little chili pepper wench that we saw is the leader. I always usedta think it was Clay Allison till I got a look at him today. Reckon now that there was Ward Cantrell."

A third man stopped and joined the conversation. He was tall, lanky, with a face that looked like tanned leather.

"Cantrell ain't no train robber," he said emphatically. "Cantrell is a gunfighter. I seen him once in Taos. Greased lightning. Killed three men 'cause they beat and robbed a friend of his—an old cripple man Cantrell took a likin' to. The old man had a little money. Guess to them it was like smellin' whiskey through the jailhouse window—couldn't resist it! Killed 'em 'fore the last one cleared leather."

"Cantrell went up against Dodge Merril in Holbrook five years ago," another man interjected. "Didn't see it, but Cantrell walked away from that fight without a scratch. Cut the article out and saved it. You know how those damned reporters are always swarming around. They's three of 'em in the lead Pullman coach right this minute, writing up a storm. Them slick eastern rags pay big money for stories about western bad men. I heard tell the *New York Times* has a half-dozen reporters don't do nothing 'cept roam from town to town writing fast as they can."

Ben grunted in disgust. "I happen to know there's a lot of men sidle up to them greenhorns that call themselves writers and fill them so full of bull…excuse me, ma'am, I mean hogwash."

"Well, yeah, they's a lot of exaggeratin' goes on, ain't denying that, but when it comes to letting Judge Colt settle a dispute, I put my money on Cantrell any day. He don't need to rob trains. Hell—'scuse me, ma'am—I heard they's a man up in Wyoming paying a cool five hundred dollars a head for every blasted one of his enemies turns up dead, no questions asked. Cantrell could spend a couple weeks up there and ride away a right rich man."

"Like shootin' fish in a tank for a man like him," another man agreed, nodding his shaggy head.

Breathing hard from exertion, a fourth man stopped beside Ben. "Hey, Ben," he panted, "Allison died last year! A loaded wagon ran over his neck—broke it clean as a whistle. Died in Cimarron last summer."

Ben grimaced. "Coulda been Cantrell. 'Bout the same build. This feller was a towhead—so's Cantrell."

"Naw! Didn't you fellers get a look at 'em? Rigged like a puncher, he was, for comfort, not for looks. The top cover was a good Stetson; bandana was silk for ridin' drag. I seen his saddle—it was low horn, rimfire, and there was a good rope hanging on it. I know a cowpuncher when I see his rig. Cain't fool me! A good-looking, long-backed cowpuncher sittin' on a high-forked, full-stamped Texas saddle with a live hoss between his legs is something I cain't be wrong about. If he ain't from Texas, he buys his rig there anyway," he ended flatly.

"Could be he just rigs himself real careful like so's he don't stand out in a crowd," Ben said thoughtfully. "I seen a man once, California fancy man, he was. Custom-made boots with them extra long heels, silver spurs, packing a silver-plated forty-five Colt with a pearl handle. When the sun hit that feller he blazed up like a big piece of jewelry. Could see him for miles on a sunny day. Barrin' Mexicans, he was the fanciest cow-dogger I ever did see. But he spent all his time admiring what a fine shadow he cast."

The train started to move, and the men headed toward their seats, still talking. "Yeah," one of them said, "I seen Cantrell less than a month ago in Silver City, New Mexico, with one of the purtiest little chili pepper wenches I ever did see. Course, this little tamale he had with him today weren't no slouch. If it was Cantrell, and I'd swear it was, I heard he got himself a hankering after the little *chileñas*, won't even give the white girls a tumble."

A woman up front turned horrified eyes on the speaker, her thin face looking permanently shocked, then stared at Leslie as if she had somehow caused the offending conversation, before she gathered her young daughter into her arms, covering the girl's ears with her hands. Leslie suppressed her own smile and spent the rest of the trip listening, most of the time to Annette, who was appalled by so many tales of murder and by how impressed they all sounded with an outlaw who was good at it.

They weren't yet off the train, and it was already apparent that this Wild West was all that the nickel novels and pulp magazines claimed it was—maybe more.

For days Leslie had stared out the window, watching the West unroll before her disbelieving eyes. In the settlements they had passed through, she had seen tall, gaunt scarecrows of women wearing their dingy dark-colored frocks and their slat bonnets, and she could only imagine the deprivations that had brought them to look the way they did. On the farms laid out beside the railroad tracks she had seen women walking behind teams of horses, plowing long, slightly crooked furrows, staggering over clods of dirt. When the train passed, invariably the woman would straighten her back and lean on the plow, watching the train until it was out of sight, her face impassive. Each time, Leslie felt a lump in her throat, imagining herself in the woman's place.

She glanced out the window now and saw a small, square log cabin sitting like a blemish on the desert, surrounded by cactuses. There was a woman standing beside a large, round pot that hung over a small fire. Smoke curled up in a pale wisp around her, swirling her skirts. She was stirring her laundry with a long stick, and Leslie could see her look up at the train.

Her own life in comparison had been almost leisurely. Thanks to her father's generosity, she and her mother had been able to afford domestic help, leaving them free of daily drudgery so they could pursue their interests in art. Leslie had been born in 1869 while a wounded nation muddled through its reconstruction. She was nineteen now, and not much had changed. Black males were enfranchised in name only. Women were still holding conventions trying to secure the right to vote, and politicians were still plundering the nation's resources while greedy investors made and lost fortunes.

Leslie sat easily on the hard wooden seat, her slender back straight and proud. Annette stifled a groan and picked up her fan to wave it impatiently, wishing she had as easy a disposition as her mistress. Leslie Powers, lovely and talented, from a comfortable home, seemed to her to have lived a charmed existence, until recently. She had been the only child of affectionate, indulgent parents who were both dead now. Her father had gone west fifteen years before and had been killed four months ago in an accident on the ranch he owned with his brother. Leslie's mother, an artist, well known for her vibrant landscapes, had died only three weeks before him when an abscess burst, flooding her system with poison. All this only two months before the end of the school year and her nineteenth birthday. Only Leslie's boundless energy and fortitude had enabled her to struggle through those last weeks and to endure both losses with amazing strength for one so young. She had been quite close to her mother. They had shared an intimacy more common to sisters than to mother and daughter. While it had been obvious to Annette that Leslie was shattered inside, she had functioned with admirable competence.

Just as she did now. Annette, who was an odd mixture of flat-footed common sense and hysteria, marveled at the younger woman's even temperament and wondered what thoughts flitted through her mistress's orderly mind as she gazed out the dust-coated window.

Leslie swayed with the monotonous, undulating motion of the rail car. Her slender white hand left the smoothly polished mahogany armrest to pat impatiently with her limp handkerchief at her perspiring brow. For the hundredth time since she had left Wellesley, Massachusetts, for Phoenix, Arizona, she was questioning her sanity. When she had been safely at home, amid the customary refinement and ease of civilization as it was practiced in Wellesley, she had been bored by it. Now that she had experienced a taste of the Wild West, she was miserable from the oppressive heat and fully aware of the numerous opportunities for disaster.

So far only the scenery had made this trip bearable and only then because she lived and breathed art. She saw the world not as a moving panorama but as a landscape. Riding a train through Kansas had been like floating across an ocean of tall, pale grass that stretched out endlessly.

New Mexico, with its strange, vast, contorted rock formations, had thrilled and amazed her. Expanses of sterile, unblemished sand with enormous, fantastic crags jutting up into a cloudless blue sky—her mind groped for words to describe adequately the rock imagery of New Mexico, where massive monoliths dotted the arid tracts, rising up like decaying, abandoned castles.

I must have been insane to come west, she thought. After all, she reminded herself, I didn't come when my father was alive. Why did I come now? Because Uncle Mark had written that last letter, making it sound like he wanted and needed her? Was it his insistence or her mother's memory that had started this journey?

Leslie stared out the soot-coated window at the Arizona desert. If she had had a sketch pad, she would have been tempted to try to capture the fierceness and mystery of this wild, bandit-haunted landscape that spilled away from either side of the train...She would start with the clouds that hovered at the horizon, so white they looked like colossal cotton balls hanging over the sparse mountains. Then she would...

As always happened when she was experiencing something that could be captured artistically, she wanted desperately to share the experience with her mother. But her mother, who had always seemed too fragile, was dead. In the last hour of her life, while Leslie had still denied that death could claim anyone she loved, her mother had insisted on talking instead of resting as Dr. Klein had advised.

Now, over the monotonous clank-a-tee-clunk of the wheels against the tracks, Leslie could again see her mother's dear, wan face, hear her mother's voice edged with pain: "Leslie, I've never been a proper mother to you. My selfishness and fear kept you from knowing your own father. No, don't stop me. I need to say these things. You need to hear them." Her pale hand, so translucent that Leslie could see the blueness of the veins beneath the skin, waved her daughter's protestations aside. "I was never good at self-sacrifice. I was an impatient mother. I wanted you to hurry and grow up so I would be free to paint." She sighed as if words were an effort for her, but she stopped Leslie's attempt to silence her. "I cheated you of your father's presence; I cheated him of knowing you—all because of my painting...You paid a dear price for my selfishness..."

"Mama, please, you're perfect, Mama. No one could be a better mother than you," she had whispered, meaning it. In her guilt, her mother had forgotten how much they had shared. Now Leslie rushed to remind her, only to be shushed into silence.

"Hush, child. Listen," she said urgently. "Don't spend your life alone as I did. Don't be so filled with fear that you cannot live life. You have wonderful, warm instincts. Use them. And forgive me if you can..."

"Mama, please," she said, the vacantness of her mother's expression scaring her, filling her pounding heart with pain and helplessness. "I know you love me, Mama."

"It's not enough. And now I'm dying before you even finish school," she said, her eyes closing with the effort. "Now I am abandoning you."

"No, Mama, you'll get well. I know you will."

"Leslie, go to him. Go to your father. You're like him in so many ways. He was so bursting with life and energy, as you are. I should have sent you long ago. But I was selfish." She patted her daughter's head. "Promise me you will go."

"I promise, Mama. We'll go together."

But her mother had died within the hour. Her father had answered immediately in response to her telegram, sending her money for necessary expenses and her transportation to Arizona. Part of her had wanted to go flying into his arms, but another part of her was too wrenched by her mother's death. She had moved like a sleepwalker, unable to make any definite decision. Ten days later word came to her that her father had been killed in an accident. Then he seemed little more than an image conjured from photographs, pieced together by words and phrases uttered by her mother. Now that the woman who had created him for her was gone, so was he. At times she wondered if he had ever existed at all.

Wellesley College had graduated Leslie with honors, but she had barely noticed. It had taken four months for her to come to terms with her parents' deaths. She and her mother had been unusually close, and in the end it was this closeness that had saved her. Margaret Powers' love now rested inside her without that earlier sense of abandonment and rage. At last she had made peace with her mother's legacy—she trusted life enough to risk again.

Now, glancing out the window of the train with eyes dimmed by a mist of tears, she knew that Phoenix was only miles away. Annette, who had been crocheting, sighed beside her, and Leslie reached over and absently patted the woman's hand. Annette had been her family's cook, maid, and housekeeper for three years and a source of much comfort these past months. Her simple French-peasant mentality had been a godsend. While in the throes of depression, Leslie had agonized over every decision; Annette merely decided, typified by the look on her plump, cheerful face when Leslie had asked her if she would accompany her to Arizona. *"Oui, mademoiselle*, your *maman* would wish it."

Leslie sighed. Boston, New York, Wellesley were another world entirely, in no way similar to the barren sweeps of land that stretched away forever into dreamy ghostliness on either side of this wretched train.

She picked up her reticule and used it to stir the tepid air. If the windows were open, soot and sparks flew in, filling her head with visions of burning passengers, but if the windows were closed, she could barely breathe. She cursed herself for packing her fan in one of her trunks, where it was completely useless to her. Then, irritated with herself for whimpering, she settled back and closed her eyes, determined that since she had initiated this "adventure," she would endure it as stoically as possible.

She would see her uncle, come to an agreement about the value of her father's share of their joint holdings, get her money, and leave. She would go back to Boston to continue her studies—in a civilized city where people appreciated the finer things in life and didn't glorify the questionable virtues of train robbers and murderers.

CHAPTER THREE

"Hey, Ward!" Doug Paggett said, nudging Ward in the ribs. "Whooee! Would you look at that little beauty. That is some high-tone fluff if I ever seen it!"

Ward heard his good friend but chose to ignore him. Instead he smiled down upon the petite Mexican girl clinging so worshipfully to his arm. Little Maria. Her skin was a soft golden brown that looked ripe to bursting. She wore a loose *camisa*, gathered at the sleeves and around the neck, and nothing, not even a shift, under it. Her dark brown nipples pressed like tiny buds against the soft cotton. She snuggled close against him, looking as eager as he to leave this fiesta crowd and find a quiet place where they could get to know each other better.

"Tell me you wouldn't like to get next to that little beauty." Doug persisted, jabbing him again with his sharp elbow. "I bet she smells like lilacs and rosewater, all powdery and perfumy. Makes my body ache just thinking about it." he whispered.

"Well, go get her." Ward chuckled, not taking his eyes off Maria, whose firm flesh was practically simmering against his hand.

"You're going to be so sorry…" Doug warned, shaking his head.

Ward laughed, but there was something in Doug's voice akin to awe that finally motivated him to look up and search out the "little beauty" Doug was raving about.

"There!" Doug hissed, pointing.

Ward followed his friend's finger. A woman in a white gown and hat was stepping out of a carriage about half a block away. In profile all he could see was that she was beautifully gowned, no doubt the height of fashion, with her skirt pulled tight over her hips, outlining a flawlessly slender figure. A bustle of ruffles and flounces cascaded behind her as she was lifted down by the man helping her disembark from the fancy phaeton. It was no wonder that Doug had noticed her. She was as out of place in the fiesta crowd as a pile of gold coins in a pigsty.

He'd always thought bustles ridiculous, but on this woman, offset by a tantalizing glimpse of a dainty ankle, it made for a very charming picture. Instead of standing her in the dusty street her escort changed his mind in mid-swing, gathered her into his arms, and carried her to the rough plank sidewalk, where he gallantly deposited her.

"Isn't that romantic?" a woman beside Ward whispered to her companion.

"Pure de ole foolish, if you ask me," the man grumped. "No one but a fool would tote a perfectly healthy woman around in this heat."

"Well, I think it's romantic," she said, irritated.

"A woman who cain't walk to the sidewalk by herself shouldn't be allowed to come to town," the man persisted.

"I don't know why I bother to talk to you," she said, dismissing her husband and turning to a female companion. "Aren't they a handsome couple?"

"I purely love the way he dotes on her," the friend whispered. "D'you s'pose he could still love her as much as he seems to? Don't rightly seem possible, does it?"

"I wouldn't give a flip one way or the other. He treats her like he worships the ground she walks on...That would be good enough for me."

Obviously disgusted, their male companion turned away and spat a stream of tobacco into the dust at their feet.

Ward was typically unimpressed by fancy gowns, but there was something about this woman that held his interest even though Maria was squirming impatiently against him, pressing her warm breast to his arm, demanding his attention. Absently, he found her hand and caressed it while he squinted at the other woman, trying to see beneath the rakishly angled Rembrandt-style hat that covered part of her face and most of her hair.

She lifted her skirts and started to walk toward where Ward, Maria, and Doug were standing in the shade in front of the saloon. And while she was completely circumspect, there was no way she could hide the vibrant energy that radiated from her movements. Ward smiled to himself. Only a dancer could look so graceful and so leashed at the same time, as if she were only momentarily contained—as though any second she would throw off her restraint and leap into dance.

Now he urgently wanted to pierce the anonymity of her fancy gear, but something deep inside resisted. And as if he had no control over it, he felt his attention shift. He turned away and scanned the holiday crowd.

Phoenix had changed in the six years since he had first visited the town. There had been no Paris bonnets then. In 1882 it had been a pleasant little farming town, surrounded by cotton plantations, acres of wild alfalfa, peaches, beans, and corn, all because an enterprising man by the name of Swilling had seen the ancient irrigation canals abandoned by the Indians who used to farm the Salt River Valley and had formed his own irrigation company. Swilling had cleaned out the silt and sand and made the canals functional again. His friend who had the forage contract with the army joined him, and they began raising alfalfa instead of just hacking down what they could find along the river banks. Their farms supplied hay to Fort McDowell and fruit brandies to neighboring towns. There had been cattle then too, but for the most part the ranchers respected the farmers. The cattle roamed the brakes where farming was impossible or where the irrigation canals did not reach. Few cowboys bothered the residents. Phoenix had been a sleepy little town of two thousand, half white, half Mexican, with the Mexicans living south of town in adobe huts, tents, and squalid shacks.

Now Kincaid's railroad had changed all that. Phoenix had become a magnet for cattle drovers from the north who wanted to ship their cattle back east for the big prices the Texans had been getting for years by driving up the trail to Dodge City.

The population had doubled since the arrival of the steel tracks and the soot-spewing locomotives. Now there was a fancy hotel—the Bricewood West. Thinking of the name brought a rush of bitterness. Kincaid's Bricewood West—an expensive and authentic copy of a French Second Empire palazzo set in the middle of the Arizona desert. Leave it to a bastard like Kincaid to pull a stunt like that, Ward thought bitterly.

Doug nudged him again, and he forced his angry thoughts back to the female he was supposed to be admiring—probably one of Kincaid's imported females. Kincaid was notorious for hiring any local who wanted a job and was still attracting easterners by the thousands to swell the towns along the path of the railroad—sort of like building a railroad to nowhere and bringing in the people to use it. But Ward had to admit that, as much as he hated the man, Kincaid did have a few good ideas. Women had a civilizing influence. They insisted upon all the trappings of civilization—no matter where they had to live. Put a woman down in the middle of the Sahara or the Arizona desert and pretty soon a French dress shop would spring up across the street from her. Without turning his head he could see La Roche Fashions only two doors from where the elegantly groomed couple had paused. A banner over the door announced the latest in Paris originals.

The woman in white turned toward Ward, not seeing him, searching the fiesta crowd, and he saw her face for the first time. A pale, perfect oval of creamy skin, wide dark eyes, a lush curve of wide lips...Ward felt an involuntary pang of recognition—like a fist in the stomach—and wondered why he hadn't recognized her escort...

Jenn!

Jenn...

A pulse began to pound in his temples. The part of him that had loved her was jumping up and down inside, wanting to cry out to her, "Jenn, Jenn, I'm here! I'm here!" He could imagine her joy at seeing him, but the part that remembered the way she had abandoned him in favor of Kincaid throttled his momentary joy, and he stood there with his breath turning to pain in his lungs and throat, like a solid column of ice, all the way down to his belly, a long, slow ache he could not control...

His emotions in a turmoil of confusion, he continued to watch her walking with that brisk, leashed elegance through the festive, noisy crowd. The man at her side, Chantry Kincaid III, was as solid and sturdy as Jenn was luminous and ethereal. Eight years had changed him very little—still lean, still as smooth and handsome as he had been when they'd met him. "He reminds me of a barbarian," Jenn had remarked after she saw him for the first time. "Attila the Hun in a green velvet Prince Albert coat— wicked good looks and all the assurance in the world." They had laughed about it then, until Jenn had succumbed to those wicked good looks and the challenge promised in Kincaid's deceptively warm green eyes.

No doubt Kincaid still moved in the hard, realistic world of business where he took what he wanted with diabolic ease, whether it be a railroad, a string of warehouses that just happened to belong to someone else, or a woman. Jenn had been quite a feather in Kincaid's cap. At twenty-three, when they had first met, she was already a legend—the daughter of one of New York's most respectable old families and a sensation on the stage—unheard of in polite society, but Jenn had carried it off with her customary verve and elan.

Time and the reality of Phoenix suddenly vanished in a flood of memory. Eight years of Ward's life peeled back as though it had never existed.

• • •

He was back in the house on Fifty-seventh Street, in New York City, across from the park. The moon glistened on the icy trees and streets. From his upstairs bedroom window, the pond in the middle of the park looked like a large oblong silver serving platter left outside by accident. His name was Peter then. Peter Van Vleet. If he looked north out that window, up the wide expanse of Fifth Avenue, he could see a row of houses like the one he and his sister lived in. Fifty-seventh Street was an avenue of millionaires' mansions—a long tree-shaded avenue lined by looming chateaus, cavernous castles, villas, neo-Renaissance palazzos, and in the middle of all that opulence, the Van Vleet townhouse, bought at a time when the Van Vleets had more wealth than those social upstarts, the Astors.

A woman named Bettina had shared his bed and snuggled warmly against him. He didn't know what had brought her there that night. He hadn't asked. He hadn't seen anyone associated with Kincaid since the night Kincaid's men had beaten him senseless. He hadn't wanted to see anyone. Except Bettina had come to him, after he thought Simone had betrayed him to Kincaid's men, and he couldn't think of any reason to send her away. Except that Jennie had never liked her. He was just beginning to feel like he might live, and the first thing that came back was his need for a woman. So Bettina had stayed. He reached over and slapped her smooth, white, thrusting buttocks.

"Go get us some food."

"What do you want?"

"Bring everything. I can't keep this up without food."

Bettina scampered cheerfully off the bed, grabbed his robe off the floor, and did as she was told. They ate in the center of the bed, and then in the middle of a sentence, with her mouth full of apple, she started talking about Jenn.

"Did you know your sister came back today?"

Peter refused to let Bettina know he had been agonizing in a sickbed, wondering why his sister hadn't even bothered to see if he had lived or died.

"From where?"

"Don't you know? Her honeymoon! What kind of brother are you anyway?" She giggled mischievously, took another bite of the apple, and continued. "Mr. Kincaid came back ages ago—she just showed up this morning. What a row that was!"

He could feel the blood draining out of his head to be replaced by a giant heartbeat. *Married to Kincaid? His sister?* The last time he had seen

Jenn was the night he had been beaten so brutally that he could barely breathe through the mess they had made of his nose and mouth. That night, three weeks ago, Jenn had been horrified and repulsed at what Kincaid's hired thugs had done to him. How could she now have married the man responsible for his beating and left on her honeymoon? He had the sudden urge to throttle Bettina, to choke the truth out of her.

Rage burned in him like a fever. Jenn couldn't have married Kincaid. She knew Kincaid had tricked their mother out of her proxies, then had used them to bankrupt the Van Vleet warehouses. She knew Kincaid's interference had driven their father to kill their mother and then himself. Jenn knew! That's why she had finally agreed to help him expose Kincaid for what he was. He felt like throwing back his head and howling in his pain and disbelief.

"Peter, you're not listening to me," Bettina protested.

So he arranged his face into a listening mask, trying to ignore the hard ache in his chest. He felt as if part of his insides had been ripped out. Any second his remaining blood and organs would stop working.

Bettina squirmed her round little bottom into the bed. She loved to gossip, so Peter knew he would hear every detail no matter what he did. Bettina worked for Kincaid as a chorus girl in the same theater where Jenn was the headliner—the New York Bricewood's Grand Salon. The Bricewood East was the *ne plus ultra* of the hotel and gambling circuit and Kincaid's pet project. It was the headquarters for all Kincaid's other enterprises as well.

"Your sister came back like one of the furies," Bettina said. "She fired Edgar, that tight-assed little know-it-all who used to run the lift, and…" She paused, eyeing him to see the impact of her words. "And Simone."

That jarred him only slightly. "Why?"

"That's not all she did. She threw Latitia Laurey's clothes and all her things out of Mr. Kincaid's suite. And Latitia! I didn't see it, but I would have given anything to have been there. Your sister may look like such a lady that butter wouldn't melt in her mouth, but she can sure fight for what she wants. Can you imagine that? She came home from her honeymoon, and he had already moved another woman into what was supposed to be their love-nest!"

Bettina wiggled in anticipation, watching him with her enormous baby-doll eyes as if he would be able to explain his sister's actions. He shrugged and plumped the pillow at his back, pretending that his sister was no concern of his. To distract her, he reached over and caressed the firm underswell of her breast and saw the nipple blossom and harden.

"Peter, stop that. I won't be able to concentrate." She settled herself like a chicken making a nest. "Your sister came back again in the evening, in the middle of a big, ritzy dinner party that Kincaid and Latitia were giving. This part is absolutely delicious! One of the serving girls told me about it. Well—not exactly—she heard it from one of the girls who was there, though. Anyway, your sister threw Latitia Laurey, Miss High-and-Mighty herself, out of that party bodily. Can you imagine? In front of all Latitia's hoity-toity friends! She even had enough spunk to dump a bowl of some gooey salad down the front of Latitia's dress. She ran out of there screaming like a banshee. I bet that was a real cat fight," she said with satisfaction.

Peter closed his eyes, trying not to see it. The thought of his sister lowering herself to the level of a street-fighting, hair-pulling harridan for a man like Kincaid nauseated him.

The next morning Peter rang the Bricewood East and asked for Mrs. Kincaid. When he heard his sister's voice on the line, he quietly broke the connection forever…That afternoon he joined the cavalry and gave notice at the brokerage firm where he had worked since leaving Harvard.

Three nights later, when Simone came, he was packing to leave for the Dakota badlands. He had gotten the assignment he had asked for. And the promise of a commission in six months.

Simone. She reminded him of a wounded doe, a wary forest creature, with her brown eyes full of stars. A strange mixture of goodness, need, and weakness.

When he closed the doors to the study, she rose from where she had been huddled beside the fire, looking very small and vulnerable. Was this the same woman who had spent two loving hours in his bed so he would be sure to be home when Kincaid's men came for him?

She moved toward him, but something stopped her—perhaps the look in his eyes. "Oh, Peter, *chéri,*" she whispered, biting her lush bottom lip. "I didn't know you had been hurt until tonight…I came as soon as I found out. Are you all right?"

"Yes."

"I waited for you. I hoped you would come to see me…"

She looked so defenseless that he couldn't bring himself to hurt her. Maybe she had been taken in and used by Kincaid, too. Why should he expect Simone to be any smarter than he or his sister?

"I've been busy. I'm leaving tomorrow."

"Oh! Oh, I'm sorry," she said brokenly. "You're going away for good!"

"I joined the cavalry."

"Oh, Peter, *chéri*..." She started to cry. Tears came up in her brown eyes, turning them into oceans of pain. She'd never gotten anything she wanted, she'd confided. Sometimes she got close, but someone or something always snatched it away.

Still crying, she reached up gently and touched his face where the greenish tinge of a bruise still showed. His aristocratic nose looked broader, with a hump that probably wouldn't ever go away.

"Oh, your poor face, your poor broken face...It was so beautiful," she said mournfully.

Peter grimaced. Beautiful? Maybe Kincaid had done him a favor. He liked this one better. It looked lived in.

Her lips started to tremble and tears streamed down her pale cheeks in a solid sheet. "Those men who did this came after I left, didn't they? Oh, Peter, I swear to you that I didn't know..."

He shrugged. "It's all right. It doesn't matter..."

Simone turned away, sobbing brokenly, and he moved to hold her almost by instinct.

"Oh, Peter, *chéri*, I didn't know. I didn't know..."

He stroked her slender back, sighing. "It's all right."

"No, it isn't. It never will be. I love you. More than anything. More than life...I will die if you leave me."

"Hush. People don't die of love," he said gently.

No, they died of much worse things—especially Simone. Things that left a man's gut twisted with hate. But he hadn't known that when he had decided to bring Simone with him.

An urgent whisper at his side jarred him back to the present. Maria was tugging on his arm. He glanced down at her face, at the dusty Phoenix street, the fiesta crowd that was milling and pushing and shouting, and then glanced back at his sister. Once he had gotten over his hurt and rage, he had tried to be fair to Jenn, but there was no way he could justify what she had done. Was it any wonder that the railroad that he and Doug and the rest of the gang lived off of, like it was their own private little money tree, was owned by Kincaid?

His head buzzed with a dull, puzzled anger...

Jennifer Van Vleet Kincaid. My sister the whore, he thought. Part of him rose up in anger at his blasphemous words, but the embittered part of him swelled up and silenced the protest. How he had loved her, worshipped her. The way only a little brother can love and worship an older sister.

"Hey, Ward," Doug whispered. "What'd I tell you? Ain't she somethin'?"

CHAPTER FOUR

Ward's head snapped around, and Doug recoiled at the look of fury on his friend's face.

"All right, all right. Sorry I brought it up," Doug mumbled, stepping back to disappear into the crowd.

Ward dragged in a deep breath, willing himself to relax. He was as surprised as Doug had been at that blind and heedless instinct to defend his sister's honor, that is, if a woman who married the man who had stripped her of family and fortune could still have honor.

Or perhaps, he thought bitterly, the act of marriage cancels out all the rest. Was that the way it worked? Did a man have a right to feel betrayed when another person, even a sister, chose to live life on her own terms? Even when he didn't understand or approve?

Ward's lips twisted into a wry smile. When had Jenn ever sought approval? His or anyone else's? She might look like a wisp of silver, without substance, as innocent and pure as a vestal virgin, in her fashionable white brocade, but she was as spirited as any female he had ever known. She had spent her life in training to be a ballerina. And when she wasn't dancing she was singing, because she could not decide which was her first love. Physically, she was as strong as spring steel. Mentally she was as determined as any woman on earth to have her own way. Her wide purple eyes could flash with imperious scorn, melt icebergs with their poignant appeal, or tantalize, seduce, bewitch. Now he thoroughly understood why Kincaid had carried her from the carriage to the sidewalk. The man was no doubt besotted with her.

Maria nudged him again, and he felt like a fool standing in the hot sun, eulogizing his treacherous, beautiful sister...But self-righteousness also sickened him. Wasn't it possible that Jenn's only error had been one of judgment? What gave him the right to stand aside and judge her, then to inflict his childish punishment by running away? Jenn had once loved him completely.

He was remembering a time when their nanny had jerked him up by the arm and begun to whip him across his bare thighs with a belt. He could not remember the reason for his punishment or how old he had been. He only remembered that Jenn, her face tight with rage and determination, had thrown herself between him and the stinging blows of that belt, screaming invectives at the woman. In anger, the nanny had turned on Jenn and punished her soundly. Their combined screams had attracted head cook's attention, and the nanny was fired, but Jenn had carried welts for days.

Maria stamped her foot, demanding his attention. He looked down at her, but his voice failed him.

"Ward, *mio*." Maria pouted, a note of demand in her voice.

"Come on," he said, his own voice harsh, strained. Part of him was being pulled toward his sister, irresistibly, but another part, even stubborner than the other, took Maria's arm and guided her through the crowd. If Jenn had loved him, she would have at least checked to see if he had survived the beating of Kincaid's thugs; she would have tried to find him long before now. Kincaid's finely wrought network of hired talent could find anything it set out to locate.

"Let's go find us a nice quiet place," he said abruptly, burning with the sudden desire to forget Jenn and all the memories that went with her. Forgiving those who trespassed against you was for saints and the dying; if Jenn had seen him and recognized him, he might not have been able to turn away. But she hadn't.

"But where?" Maria demanded, smiling.

That was a good point. They were in the middle of the fiesta crowd in the hottest part of the day. It wasn't going to be easy to find some privacy. He had a room at the Rancher's Hotel, but women weren't allowed in the rooms.

Maria's family had a covered wagon tied up next to the livery stable. The whole family shared it at night, but now, at midday, it was deserted. Her parents were avid Catholics and were probably attending one of the many masses at the old Spanish mission, celebrating Mexican independence, the purpose of the fiesta days.

"Come," she said, scampering up into the deep well of the wagon. Ward stepped on the small platform and leaped easily inside. He knelt on the pallet that covered the floor of the wagon, cleared it of strewn garments, and Maria slipped eagerly into his arms, lifting her lips to be kissed.

Maria was seventeen, and she didn't know how old this *caballero*

Ward was. She only knew that he was so *rubio* and so handsome that she had been unable to resist him. Now his warm mouth was on her face, burning into her lips, her cheeks, her eyes. She was breathless and weak with the unexpected trembling he had started in her helpless body. Never had she felt anything like this when the young men of her acquaintance had managed to steal a kiss. Never had her body trembled and collapsed the way it did now.

His tongue teased her lips and darted into her mouth, causing ripples the length of her body. One warm hand slipped from her back, where his fingers were pressing against her spine, leaving a burning trail to her breast. His fingers caressed the sensitive engorged nipples, and she moaned in her throat at the heat that surged into her belly. His kiss deepened, and his hand slipped down to stroke her smooth inner thigh. Heat flooded Maria, but a small voice, the voice of her dear mama, interrupted her. An internal argument ensued, and the part of her that liked the way Ward's lips and his hands made her feel argued with much eloquence against her mother's imagined voice, which was loud and insistent, even though it was losing the argument on every point.

She struggled against him. "No, Ward, *mio*, please…"

He laughed softly and forced her down onto the pallet. "Hush. You want half of Phoenix looking in this wagon, seeing us like this?"

"No, Ward, no, I can't," she panted, beginning to struggle against him.

Ward lifted his head and looked into the girl's eyes. "For Christ's sake," he grumbled. "Why not?"

"Please," she begged him. "Don't do that!"

Ward's hand was on her thigh, beneath the thin cotton skirt. Her skin was soft and pliant beneath his touch. Her eyes pleaded with him even while they told him yes. Only moments ago she had led him in here. Moments before that she had pressed her hungry little body against him as if she were as eager as any female he had ever bedded. Now she was saying no.

Ward sat up abruptly, a thought forming in his mind. "Are you… Have you done this before?"

"N-no," Maria whispered, tears beginning to slip down her cheeks.

"Damn! Have you seen my hat?" he demanded, cursing the luck that would cause him to pick a virgin out of all the available women in Phoenix.

Heartbroken, Maria threw her arms around his neck, clinging tightly to him. She was trembling all over, and the tears were wetting his neck. He held her for a moment, stroking her dark hair. "Wipe your face," he said, brushing the tears off her cheeks. "Why didn't you tell me?"

"I didn't know…I thought I could do it," she said, breaking into new sobs. He pulled her close and soothed her until her broken sobs subsided.

"You can hit me if you want to," she said, sniffing.

He laughed in spite of the warring emotions that still seethed within him. Between this little vixen and the Kincaids, he was having one helluva day. Hitting her would serve no purpose and was not something he would even consider. If he was angry at anyone, it was at himself, not the girl. While Doug Paggett and his men might think him an irrepressible cocksman, he alone knew he had thrown back more fish than he had kept, though he wasn't above letting the false attributes circulate, since they added to his image. Now he pulled away, gently but firmly.

"I'm so ashamed," she said.

He noticed a pair of trousers that had been flung almost out of the wagon in their original haste to make a place on the pallet. He tossed them back into the pile of clothes beside the pallet, then took her hands and pulled her to her feet. He wiped her tears again and teased her until she was smiling, then laughing in his arms.

"Next year at fiesta time, you be here," he said, threatening her playfully. "Then, if you don't behave yourself…" He put his fist to her jaw pretending to hit her. "Next year," he warned.

She laughed, nodding her pleasure.

"And if I don't find you, I will come looking for you, *comprende?*"

Maria nodded and hugged him as tightly as if he had just saved her life.

CHAPTER FIVE

"Magnifique, mademoiselle, you will be zee most elegant young lady in zee fiesta parade," Annette breathed, stepping back after she had buttoned the last of the long row of tiny gold buttons.

"I have carefully weighed my uncle's request, and while I agree that every impulse of feeling should be guided by reason, I cannot indulge his whim in the matter of this parade," Leslie said, turning to admire the gown in the full-length mirror. They were in an elegant suite of rooms at the Bricewood West, which was a paragon of grandeur compared to the dusty squalor of Phoenix.

Annette sighed, dazzled by her mistress's delicate language as well as the striking picture she made in the golden gown. Leslie was taller than average, elegantly slender, with a face that reflected the sweetness of a sunny disposition combined with a charming vagueness that came from preoccupation with her own thoughts. After three years in the same house with her, Annette realized that Leslie Powers lived almost entirely in her imagination. Her wide-apart lime-green eyes reflected both the innocence of her genteel upbringing and intelligence honed by fourteen years of intensive schooling. Thanks to Margaret Powers, Leslie had received a fine education from serious and demanding instructors who did not subscribe to the common view that a woman's primary responsibility was to marry, raise children, and be charming at table. Leslie had graduated from Wellesley College at the top of her class, proficient in algebra, biology, chemistry, Latin, history, French, English composition, and geography. She had also excelled in a variety of art classes where she'd mastered everything from color and light to neo-classical traditions.

Most young women her age exchanged endless visits with other young women, received young men into chaperoned parlors, and contemplated marriage. Their dainty fingers were curled around china cups at tea with friends, who whispered, giggled, and gossiped among themselves. Leslie rarely walked out with a young man more than once. She had been introduced to handsome young stockbrokers, barristers just out of law school, and even a dapper young physician. And while Leslie was polite in her responses, her manner always revealed that although she was not bored, she was certainly not eager. Few young men possessed the composure to cope with such indifference.

And like most people dedicated to their work, Leslie was never happier than when her surroundings managed to take care of themselves without her help. She had known a moment of ecstasy when she entered the Bricewood suite and saw a small sign beside the light key which said, "This room is equipped with electric light. Do not attempt to light with match. Simply turn key on wall by this sign. The use of electricity for lighting is in no way harmful to your health, nor does it affect the soundness of your sleep."

She and Annette, both accustomed to electricity in large eastern hotels, had smiled with superior glee at the time. Now she turned, surveying her slender figure in the mirror, dabbing with a slender, graceful hand at the glow of perspiration on her smooth brow. While she was too well cultivated and gently reared to speak all her thoughts, even to her maid, she personally believed there was something sinister about her uncle's request.

"*Oui*, breathtaking, *mademoiselle*," Annette exclaimed, clasping her tiny hands under her chin in admiration. She was only three years older than Leslie, and her guileless blue eyes were filled with rapture at the elegant vision of her mistress before her. "And," she said, knitting her straight tawny brows in a frown, "your uncle eez a very determined man."

Leslie Marlowe Powers lifted her firm chin and turned to look over her shoulder to see herself at another angle. The gown her uncle had practically ordered her to wear was beautiful—there was no question of that. It was the most extravagant creation Leslie had ever seen, obviously an antique, probably from the romantic era of Madame de Pompadour's court, when female fashions were distinguished by full sleeves and skirts, square, low-cut necklines, and narrow waists. The inlay in the bodice was intricately and lavishly embroidered and piped in thick gold thread; truly a dress fit for a queen. Even the gold slippers were perfect, including the way their soft, costly leather molded itself to her feet like a caress.

"That is true," she sighed. "He is singular in his desire to control my activities. Unfortunately I am equally determined not to ride in the parade."

But there was a note of regret in her voice, and looking into the mirror, she could see that her cheeks were flushed with color. The limegreenness of her eyes fairly leaped out at her from the mirror. She *was* excited by the opportunity to wear such a magnificent gown. Weeks of being deprived of suitable companionship must have undone her, else she wouldn't be considering it. She wasn't usually obstinate, but her uncle's plan to display her in this fashion had repelled her. He had made elaborate plans and preparations: outfitting his riders with fancy charo suits, silver-studded saddles, and blooded horses. The horse he had chosen for her was a pure white Arabian—so she could "gleam like a little jewel," he had said. Her reason warned her that, to her uncle and Dallas Younger, this was not just a casual, frolicsome event…

Usually she would not have had even a passing interest in wearing this gown, but she had been on the ranch for three weeks, and frankly, she missed the opportunities to wear fine gowns and be appreciated by young men she admired. There was some tension as well over Dallas Younger and his unwanted attentions. When he wasn't working away from the ranch house, he dogged her steps, making sly, insinuating remarks.

The plump Frenchwoman was about to reply when they heard a loud knock on the door. Annette whirled as if she had been caught in some mischief and rushed to the door. "Who is zere?" she demanded.

"It's us."

"It eez your uncle, *mademoiselle.*"

"Let him in."

Mark Powers and Dallas Younger shuffled into the room and stopped in the middle of the oriental rug in front of the horsehair sofa. Leslie was instantly aware of Younger's eyes on her body and felt herself flushing with a renewal of the irritation she felt when he was near her. The man had made life miserable for her since her arrival. He had apparently decided that she was going to be his woman, and he seemed perfectly capable of ignoring her feelings in the matter.

He was a rough-hewn giant, well liked and obviously respected by other rough men. He was built like a lumberjack, with slightly more refinement of feature, so that to the casual eye he appeared quite handsome, but there was such an air of careless arrogance about him that Leslie mentally recoiled. He was a man perfectly capable of ignoring her wishes, and she was too accustomed to having her opinions considered to find such thoughtlessness attractive.

Now he was devouring her with his dark eyes. Frowning, she glanced from Younger's ruddy face to her uncle, her expression demanding that he reprimand his foreman, but Uncle Mark did not appear to take notice.

Powers cleared his throat. "Well, now," he said, taking in the sight of her, "you do me proud—real proud!"

Leslie's eyes widened in surprise and frustration. She needed his protection, and all he gave her was his approval of how she looked in the gown he had provided.

Mark Powers was a stocky man with an open, usually friendly face and an infectious smile that he used to his advantage. He had a wide, short neck to match his stocky build, and a face with small features— nose, mouth—even his eyes were small. And while he might look like pictures she had seen of her father, she knew from her mother that the resemblance ended there. Her father had been an honorable man. She had only known Mark Powers for a few short weeks, but she felt no sense of security from his guardianship.

For although she had not been mistreated, Powers routinely made decisions for her that he fully expected her to abide by. She had decided that he was conservative, quiet, a little sneaky in his relations with people, not particularly intelligent, but a man who had done well because he didn't let his affairs become too complicated. He could be easily embarrassed—he was not a man who relaxed with people until he knew them quite well. He presented such a neutral image to the world that he affronted no one, except her.

In dealing with her, he had been both generous and as tight as the bark on a tree, which suggested to her that he was subject to moods. His moods seemed dictated by how her desires might conflict with the welfare of what he considered "his ranch." If spending money enhanced his or the ranch's image, he was generous; if it did not, he was deaf to her needs. He was a hard worker, rising before dawn and tending to the business of the ranch until late in the evening. He was liked by his contemporaries, but known intimately by no one. She knew he thought himself a good uncle.

"Thank you, Uncle Mark," she said, temporarily thrown off guard by the look of pride in his eyes. She would deal with Younger's rudeness later, with her uncle in private.

She had more important matters that demanded her attention now. She took a deep breath and faced him. "Uncle Mark, I know this parade is important to you, but..." The deceptively merry look in his eyes faded, but she plunged ahead; "...but I feel strongly advised against it."

"Nonsense!" he said, anger turning his small eyes the color of bright jade. "Of course you will!" His face had turned red with rising anger, and Annette's warning look cautioned her not to enrage him further, but she was loath to back down.

"I fail to see what difference my riding in a parade will make," she said reasonably.

Her uncle, who was a scant three inches taller than her five feet five inches, puffed up like an angry adder, and Leslie braced herself, but before either of them could reply, Younger stepped between them.

"Hey! Enough of this here yellin' and carryin' on." He took Leslie's hand in his and spun her around, ignoring her cry of surprise and protest. "It's about time you wore something that shows off that pretty little shape of yours, sweet thing," he said, pulling her into his arms. "This sure beats those high-necked, high-falutin schoolteacher duds you been wearin'."

"Let me go!" she hissed, struggling with all her strength against Younger's steely hands, which were around her waist. She felt his fingers groping her spine and the flare of her hips. Enraged, she kicked him. "Get your hands off me!"

"Owww!" Dallas yelped.

"Heah!" Powers scolded. "Ain't no call to get rough."

Leslie glared first at Younger, who had loosed his hold on her, and then at her uncle. "Aren't you going to do anything?" she demanded of her uncle.

"Dallas don't mean no harm," he said, "do you, boy?"

"None atall," Dallas agreed, grimacing. "I like my women feisty." His ruddy, sun-darkened face glistened above her. A lock of his crisp black hair had fallen forward, and he looked like some evil, smiling wolf, waiting for the right moment to continue the attack.

Leslie checked her temper with an effort. "You presume far too much, Mr. Younger," she said, controlling her voice as best she could.

"City women!" Younger said, winking at her uncle and feigning injury, spreading his hands as if appealing to Mark Powers for vindication.

"He…mauled me!" she protested. "He mauled me and you just watched him!"

"Now, simmer down, Leslie. Nobody mauled you. Dallas is a fine young man who just happens to like you, and you should be grateful that he does."

"Likes me!" Leslie gasped. She was too much a lady to mention aloud that Dallas Younger had panted after her like a dog in heat since the day she arrived.

"Don't reckon you understand our ways here, Leslie. Dallas means no harm. I only want what's best for you…"

"Then buy me out and send me home," she said, taking the chance that had presented itself.

A scowl knit his brows, reminding her how irritable he could become when she tried to force him into negotiating with her. "At the right time, we'll talk about that, but in the meantime, as long as you're living under my roof, you'll do as I say. And I say you *are* going to ride in that parade," he growled, his small mouth pursed into a look of such angry impatience that Leslie had to force herself not to flinch visibly.

"Or what?" she asked quietly, her heart pounding.

"Don't get uppity with me, young lady. You will do as I say. Dammit, you're just a woman! You don't know or care how hard I've worked to get this ranch to the point it's at now. You don't understand anything I try to tell you! What the hell do you know about building a ranch? You're here to tear it apart. I've worked and sweated half my life for this ranch, and by God I'm not going to sell it just so some snot-nosed city filly can trot back to her ritzy friends with a pocket full of money she didn't earn."

Leslie paled. The import of his words frightened her. Did he mean that there was absolutely no chance of his ever buying her out? Her money was almost gone. How would she get back home? And how would she live after she got there? Trying to ignore her fear, she spoke firmly. "I respect your love for what you consider to be your ranch, but my father worked just as hard as you did. He earned it for me. As his rightful heir, part of it belongs to me…"

Her uncle's salt-and-pepper brows pulled down into a heavy ledge of disapproval. Thrown off guard by the correctness of her logic, he cleared his throat. "I said we'll talk about it. In the meantime, you'll do as I say, and I say you are going to ride in that parade!"

"Do I also have to put up with Dallas Younger?" she demanded, flashing a look of scorn at the man who was grinning his enjoyment of the ruckus.

"You could do worse. He knows how to take care of a woman—not like those panty-waist do-nothings you're used to."

"I've never needed the questionable protection of a gunfighter," she said quietly, allowing her eyes to reflect a measure of her disgust as they swept down Younger's tall, sturdy form. Dallas threw back his dark head and laughed, supremely unaffected by what he considered her prissy fastidiousness. Leslie could see Annette's plump form behind him, her face pinched with concern for her mistress.

"You may be glad to have him around someday," Powers said vehemently.

"I find that difficult to imagine."

"You gonna ride in that parade?" he asked, his tone both final and threatening.

"Are we going to seriously discuss settling my father's estate?" she shot back at him.

"All right! You ride in that parade," he said more calmly, "and we'll talk about your share of the ranch when we get home tonight. Fair enough?"

Leslie nodded. "I'll ride if you promise."

"Out here a man's word is his bond," he said gruffly.

CHAPTER SIX

"Oh!" Leslie gasped when the door had closed behind her uncle and Dallas Younger. "They sorely try my patience!"

"*Oui, mademoiselle,*" Annette breathed, stepping forward to smooth the skirt of the voluminous gown where Leslie's fingers had crumpled the shiny gold cloth.

"Sorry," Leslie muttered. She covered her face with her hands for a moment and then straightened. "I will not let them turn me into a whimpering wreck," she said to herself, turning. She walked to the window, lifted it, and leaned out as far as she could. Heat enveloped her, making her realize her mistake at once, but she had felt so stifled by the exchange with her uncle and Younger that she didn't care.

The hotel faced south, and from the third floor she had a view of every rooftop in Phoenix except those lying behind the hotel. She shrugged off her anger and irritation and breathed deeply of the hot, dusty air that was rising from the street below. The sidewalks were crowded with holiday revelers. Sounds of music, tinny and exuberant, floated above the raucous laughter and the babble of voices. Horses standing in the streets occasionally whinnied and stamped. The sharp smell of their urine caused her to wrinkle her nose, but it was not enough to drive her back inside.

A cowboy and a young girl left the crowd and turned down the alley across the street from where she watched. The man was dressed in the rough garb of a seasoned cowpuncher. Leslie could see very little of his face, which was sheltered from view by a tan-colored Stetson, but somehow his overall appearance seemed familiar. He was taller than average, with narrow hips and broad shoulders, and he moved with lithe purposefulness. The young woman was small and voluptuous and wore the casual dress of the *peones* in the settlements they had passed through on the train. The girl was giggling, but the young man's actions were more urgent than frolicsome. They stopped beside a covered wagon that was tied up against the outside wall of the livery stable. The man took off his hat and wiped his forehead with his sleeve. He was strikingly handsome—darkly sun-tanned with blond hair that had no red—like pale wheat against the warm teak of his face.

They paused there only a moment and then he lifted her up into the wagon and followed her inside. Leslie smiled. She watched as they embraced and then crawled on hands and knees to the center of the wagon out of her range of vision.

"Annette, come here," she whispered excitedly.

"What?" she asked softly, responding to the urgency in her mistress's tone.

"Look at that wagon. A cowboy and a young woman crawled inside. I think they are going to...you know."

A mischievous light dawned in Annette's eyes. *"Oui?"*

"Yes," Leslie said, giggling in response to Annette's obvious delight.

Annette leaned out the window to get a better look, almost lost her balance, and squealed. Leslie grabbed her and pulled her back in. "Not so far!" Leslie gasped, breathless.

"Pardon, mademoiselle," she whispered, giggling. She righted herself, and they watched in silence for a few moments. Leslie Powers frequently surprised Annette. This time because she was not a simpering ninny the way so many of her gently reared contemporaries were. Thanks to her mother's excellent common sense and careful preparations, Leslie knew far more than most young ladies her age about what went on between grown men and their women, and far more about all of life's experiences than her sheltered peers.

According to her grandmother Eliza, Leslie's mother's liberal approach in raising Leslie constituted laxness. Letting Leslie run wild among museums and theaters and other worldly places showed "an unprecedented lack of parental vigilance." In spite of grandmother Eliza's howls of outrage, Leslie had grown into an inscrutable combination of audacity, intelligence, and innocence. Even Eliza had to admit that she appeared to be a well-conducted young lady for all her notions about 'painting' and artistic expression.

In reality, Leslie was dedicated to becoming an outstanding landscape painter. She had not chosen this goal lightly. She knew it would mean working long hours and studying for years to perfect her technique and learn the craft.

Leslie's attention drifted back to the street beneath the window. Nothing was moving in the wagon in the alley. From the window she could see the round, platelike turntable where they turned the locomotives. Down on the railroad tracks, a boxcar with its doors gaping open waited to be filled with milling, noisy cargo. The shiny black locomotive breathed heavily, sending up wads of smoke so dense that they looked like puffs of blue-gray cotton above the stack.

Immediately below she could see the parade officials working at clearing the wagons, buggies, horses, and people off the dusty boulevard so that the parade could begin. Men shouted remarks—some good-natured, some lewd—but no one seemed to take offense. She decided that the women who lived here had given up trying to civilize the ruffians who came into town. There were parts of Boston that were rough and undisciplined like this—every big city had its slum and its slum dwellers. Unfortunately, it appeared that in Phoenix there was no separation between the ruffians and the more genteel citizens or between the saloons and the churches.

To the east she could see where fences cut the land into neat squares. To the south the streets of the town fell into a scattering of rude hovels. Beyond the last sparse cluster of square boxlike shacks was the inevitable desert, reaching away into infinity, it seemed, gray and brown and covered with what her uncle called chaparral or greasewood or mesquite. Phoenix was not really a city, merely a cluster of already dilapidated frame buildings surrounding a row of stores and saloons and one real building—the hotel she was in.

Annette giggled, and Leslie's attention was drawn back to the wagon. "What did I miss?"

"See?" Annette whispered. "His *pantalon!*"

"His pants?" Leslie repeated, covering her mouth. This was the most excitement she had experienced since the train robbery. She felt like she was back in school participating in some delicious naughtiness. "He took off his pants?"

"See, zay are zere," she said, pointing to one pant leg that was carelessly thrown over the tailgate of the wagon.

Leslie searched the crowd below, but no one seemed to be paying any attention to the wagon. She peered into it, but she could see nothing. Beyond the Bricewood West and the dirty rooftops of the town's buildings there was nothing to look at that brought a sense of joy or exuberance to the eye. It was just a dirty little town in the middle of a hard, hot, flat desert with unbearably hot days and cold nights, but inside the hotel was another matter entirely. The Bricewood West was a small version of the Plaza in New York City. Its Garden Courtyard with vaulted ceiling of translucent glass was the equal of anything she had seen anywhere. Even in the short time she had been here, Leslie could tell that the hotel's Garden Courtyard had become a cultural and social center for the town's residents. People congregated beneath the large overhead fans to relax amid towering potted palms and graceful ferns. It was an oasis of civilization in the midst of filth and squalor.

There was still nothing to see in the wagon. She thought she detected a slight swaying motion and blushed to think what that might mean. Annette still leaned out the window. Sighing, Leslie straightened and scanned the horizon where she knew the river curved around Phoenix to the northeast. Younger had called it the Verde River. "Those red devils used to be thick as thieves along this stretch," he had said as they had ridden past a thick stand of alfalfa that grew along the banks. She could imagine half-naked Indians reaping the wild grasses that grew in the rich loam along the river bottoms.

If she squinted and blocked out the encroaching cluster of houses, the desert was almost pretty. It had a sort of sparse elegance about it, an immenseness of its own that was awesome, almost grand, but it could never equal for her the cool green beauty of precise landscaping and sparkling white houses, so perfect with their pitched roofs and their cavernous front porches. She loved big Gothic houses with turrets, gables, cornices, and flying buttresses. There were mysteries in houses like that, sometimes a secret cellar off the back porch with its two wooden doors opening onto damp, dark, blackness that could go down and down indefinitely.

Annette squealed, and Leslie's attention was drawn instantly back to Phoenix, only to find that Annette's excited squeak was occasioned by her almost losing her footing again.

So much for adventure, Leslie thought ruefully. The only hint of that had been the train robbery she'd witnessed. The only man in Phoenix who even looked interesting so far was in that wagon making love to someone else. She scolded herself for even thinking about such things, but with men like Dallas Younger around, who would blame her for looking? There was little opportunity for romance in a town that looked like it could have been built in three days by an inexperienced box maker. Unless, of course, you were a peasant girl who would cavort in broad daylight with strangers. Leslie smiled at herself. Was she jealous?

Annette nudged her and giggled. "Zey are coming out," she whispered, her voice breathless.

Leslie leaned out the window to see. The young man helped the girl down. She was clinging to him, her face dewy and adoring. She snuggled close against him; he kissed her on the forehead briefly, placed his hat on his head, and they walked toward the crowded street.

Leslie didn't stop to think about decorum. She leaned out the window and yelled. The man looked up, and they waved at him, then burst into giggles. The girl on the street turned bright red. The man grinned and waved back at them.

Gasping and giggling, Annette and Leslie collapsed across the bed. "Do you think he will recognize us if he sees us again?" Leslie asked when their laughter had subsided.

Annette clapped her hands over her mouth, her eyes round and mischievously questioning. She shrugged.

"Did you ever see that young man you were so interested in? What was his name, John?"

Annette sighed. *"Non."*

Leslie grinned. "Still hoping?"

Annette shrugged and wiggled her body in an unconsciously provocative way. *"Oui*...but of course."

"Well, why don't you walk down to the railroad offices and see if you can stumble onto him?"

Annette looked horrified. *"Mademoiselle!* I am a lady!"

Leslie snorted. "Ladies don't almost fall out of windows to watch things they shouldn't even be aware of. Besides, if you don't ever take matters into your own hands, you may be an old maid. He looked too shy to ever approach you…"

There was faint horror in Annette's eyes as she contemplated becoming the aggressor. "Then I shall be. But I don't think so…He will come to me…"

Leslie sighed. "I hope you're right."

CHAPTER SEVEN

The Bull Whiskey Saloon was crowded to overflowing with the gay holiday crowd. "Parade's coming!" someone yelled.

"Yahoo! Let's see them purty girls!"

The boisterous crowd surged out the double swinging doors. Ward and Doug were hanging back, taking their time. When they finally took their places at the edge of the wide street the first participants were at the north end of town.

Raucous yells greeted two pretty Mexican *señoritas* who rode in all their finery, supporting a red and white banner twelve feet in length that announced the *Fiesta Days Parade*. They were followed by a dozen colorfully dressed *señoritas:* walking, swinging their wide skirts, smiling gaily. The girls on the outside, near the crowd, were throwing flowers that must have been imported from eastern nurseries.

Next came an open carriage with four local politicians waving their hats, smiling widely; then three ornately dressed *vaqueros* looking like Spanish *conquistadores*, their heavy, silver-studded chaps and saddle skirts shimmering in the late afternoon sun.

The *vaqueros* were followed by a choir of young girls and boys dressed in long white robes, singing a song that *gringos* wouldn't recognize. Their angelic faces were lifted heavenward in shining piety, which wrenched a chuckle and a ribald comment from Doug Paggett.

"Hey, Ward, how would you like to have those three chinchillas in the front row—all at once? Wouldn't that be something?"

Ward only smiled and lifted an eyebrow. He liked the young ones but not that young. Doug Paggett, with his unruly shock of black hair and his mustache, looked older than Ward, but he was actually several years younger. He seemed a lot younger sometimes, when they were with females. He seemed to go out of control, no longer resembling the cool-headed second lieutenant who (without destroying the contents) could set a charge of dynamite to blow any safe the Texas and Pacific could devise.

45

The choir was followed by a procession of papier-mâché statuary, elaborately shaped and painted to resemble the busts of famous revolutionary Mexican leaders. The colorful busts bobbed along on thin brown legs and were followed by a long red-and-yellow paper dragon that weaved from one side of the street to the other, exactly like a sidewinder, propelled by at least a hundred legs, the humps on its colorful back undulating like waves on the ocean. Doug laughed delightedly— probably, Ward decided, having the time of his life trying to decide which of those young brown dragon legs belonged to girls.

The dragon was followed by a Mexican band playing loud, patriotic music, and then by a contingent of dark-garbed riders that brought a hush over the crowd. At least fifteen men, resplendent in silver-edged black charo suits, riding sleek-looking blooded stallions and armed to the teeth, with two guns at every waist and a rifle sheath on every saddle, rode behind a girl dressed like a Spanish queen, her beautiful gold dress gleaming in the afternoon sunlight, her carriage as proud on the stately white horse as any queen. Ward recognized her as one of the females who had laughed at him when he was leaving Maria's wagon.

One of the men beside Ward cursed. "Powers got himself a new woman?"

Another man laughed softly. "Naw! She ain't Powers's woman. B'longs to Dallas Younger. That must be the little filly from back east I heard him braggin' about last night."

Someone else spoke up, also softly, since it wouldn't be healthy to be openly contemptuous. "They got a lotta guts marching in the parade. Anyone who's done the folks around here the way they have should be in jail!"

Ward, who hadn't been in Phoenix for at least two years and wasn't aware of any changes that might have been taking place, felt an instinctive tightening of muscles in his broad back, which he made a conscious effort to relax. Politics didn't interest him—not even politics like the Powers Ranch played so openly. Ward vowed not to get involved in other people's business, but habits were strong, especially survival habits. His eyes narrowed, and he studied each face in that slow-moving group of misfits. They were the roughest he had seen since riding with the Jackson Hole Gang. They made the Clantons look like choirboys. Three of them he recognized; the rest he would remember next time he saw them.

The girl on the white horse was riding from side to side in the wide street, tossing flowers at the smiling faces in the crowd. When she zigzagged across to Ward's side of the street, she looked at the crowd and their eyes met. She recognized him as the man she'd seen climbing into and out of the wagon with the pretty Mexican girl, and he remembered her as the one Belen had almost torn into when they had robbed the Texas and Pacific. He had watched her without her knowledge on the train because she was one of those rare women who seem comfortable within themselves. She probably hadn't seen him because she didn't have searching eyes.

When he had boarded the train in Tucson, he had seen her talking in her quiet way with her lady's maid, and he had appreciated her friendliness and openness. It struck him then that she was one of those singular women without guile. She looked relaxed and composed—like a beautiful swan who would ride a choppy lake as serenely as a placid one. During the train robbery, he had been impressed again, because it had been obvious that while she might be amused by the excitement of a lifestyle wilder than her own, she was not in the least tempted by it. She could be mischievous when the mood struck her, he thought, remembering the way she had leaned out that window to taunt him...

She was prettier than he remembered. She had exquisite coloring, but it didn't take a connoisseur to appreciate coal-black hair and creamy white skin, especially when the gown she wore made it apparent that she was as graceful and comely of limb as she was of face.

"Which one is Younger?" he asked of the lantern-jawed, mustached man who had said she was Younger's woman.

"The one on that dun. Thinks he's a real ladies' man!" he snorted. "Dallas Younger is Powers' foreman. Want my opinion—it's not 'cause he's hell on cows!"

Younger had no doubt earned his reputation. There was a healthy arrogance in his lithe frame that was easy to identify. The man wasn't afraid of man or beast, and it was apparent from the look on his handsome face that he wasn't often required to prove it. One look from those steel gray eyes would discourage anyone but the most suicidal.

Ward couldn't tell, when the lady's eyes caught and held his, whether the stirring he felt was his innate competitiveness or a response to the look in her eyes: a look that fluctuated between chagrin at her own position, recognition of him, and mild interest.

He didn't have time to dwell on it beyond that one instant because a feisty little red dog pushed past them, ignoring his owner's shout, "No, Pepito! No!" and ran into the dusty street, straight at the front legs of the silky white Arabian.

The playful mutt, an alley mixture of terrier and anonymous parentage, nipped at the sleek white fetlocks, barking ferociously. The big white horse, naturally nervous and high-strung, reared, almost unseating the startled girl. Leslie, caught off guard, with her hands more occupied by the basket of flowers than the reins, screamed and dropped everything in her scramble to keep from being thrown.

Without thinking, Ward leaped forward and grabbed the reins she had dropped before they hit the ground. He dragged the horse's head down before he could bolt and then looked up, expecting to see relief on the girl's face. But Leslie was mortified and angry. Not at the man who had saved her, but at herself for agreeing to ride in this stupid parade and to throw stupid flowers at people who looked like they resented her. She had been painfully conscious of the open hostility rippling through the crowd as they passed by. Since she had gotten herself into this mess and couldn't think of any way to get out of it, she had forced herself to concentrate on the faces of the guilelessly adoring children. But when she had almost been thrown, the adults had made themselves felt, cautiously. She had seen, all in a flash, smiles of triumph and open snickers, and her anger now caused her to jerk the reins out of Ward's hands and turn the horse sharply, accidentally knocking him down. Leslie watched in mounting horror as one atrocity seemed to follow another.

Her scream had brought Dallas Younger and her uncle to her side. Before she could react, her uncle shouted an order, cursing savagely while she watched, speechless with fear and anger, as Younger pulled his rifle from its sheath and used it like a club on the man who was just coming to his feet.

"No! No!" she screamed frantically, but if they heard her outraged cries over the mounting roar of the crowd, they ignored them. Ward slumped limply into the powdery gray dust. Powers's men formed a threatening phalanx behind Younger, and the crowd that had started to surge forward stopped, quieted.

"No harm done here!" Younger yelled at the row upon row of resentful faces. "Get that bastard out of the way! This is a parade! Not a damned side show!"

Doug Paggett, who had been on the verge of drawing his gun, thought better of it in the face of the determined and concerted opposition and rushed forward to drag his friend's limp form out of the street.

The Powers contingent moved slowly forward, but Leslie felt like a statue, stiff and pale, her flowers forgotten in the dirt. She could not believe what her eyes had seen! Dallas Younger, who had seemed perfectly normal, at least for Arizona, had practically killed that man just for trying to save her from an embarrassing spill!

Dazed, she rode stiffly, until her senses began to return. With a conscious effort to still the wild pounding of her heart, she stopped her horse and started to turn it. That man might be crude and churlish, making love to Mexican girls in broad daylight, but he had tried to help her!

"Heah! What the hell you doing?"

"I'm going back there!"

"Like hell you are! You're a Powers. Sit up straight!"

Leslie's mouth dropped open. She couldn't believe her ears. Her uncle was talking to her exactly like he talked to the Mexican servants in his kitchen.

Powers grabbed the reins from her nerveless fingers and the parade moved forward again. Leslie was a captive wedged in between her uncle and Dallas Younger, whose flat gray eyes shot her a warning look.

Doug Paggett and the man who had been most vocal about the Powers outfit half carried, half dragged, Ward Cantrell into the deserted saloon.

"He hurt bad?"

"Cain't tell for sure. He's breathin' though," Doug said, frowning down at his friend. Uncharacteristically, his hands trembled at the thought that Cantrell might be badly injured.

The stranger parted the tawny hair on Ward's head and peered knowingly at his scalp. He repeated this until he satisfied himself he had uncovered the entire area.

"'Pears to be all right. Got a concussion sure, though."

"Those bastards!" Doug swore. "I saw who did it. I'm gonna kill him!"

"Better leave well enough alone," the man said kindly. "They've killed men for a lot less than accosting one of their womenfolk! They don't ride alone."

"Jesus!" Doug picked up an unfinished drink off the table above Ward and held it to Ward's lips. He spilled some of the liquid into Ward's slack mouth and was rewarded with a groan. Ward's eyes opened tentatively, focused on the worried face of his friend, then closed. The light behind Doug was a blinding ache to Ward's tortured skull. He could feel his brain throbbing with each heartbeat.

"You all right?"

Ward squinted at Doug. "What happened?" he groaned.

"You ain't hung over, that's for sure! You got hit on the head!"

Ward reached up and touched his head, wincing.

"That bitch hit me?" he asked, his memory slowly returning.

"'Twarn't her," the stranger volunteered. "She just knocked you down so's he could hit you—Younger!"

"The hell you say? Who the hell is Younger?" he asked, not remembering they had already gone over this earlier.

"Powers's strawboss. Texan. Right dangerous with a gun, from what I hear."

Ward struggled into a sitting position. He tried to stand, but his legs didn't respond. It took him two tries before he made it.

"Hey! What the hell do you think you're gonna do?" Doug demanded, not liking the look on his friend's face.

"I'm going to kill that bastard Younger," Ward said grimly.

The stranger, a long-faced New England type, shook his head. "Wouldn't try that if'n I was you, mister. Younger ain't about to meet you alone, 'cause he don't have to. Powers has fifty men in town right now, and half of them are gunfighters."

"Fifty men?" Ward asked, squinting at the man.

"At least fifty." He nodded.

"Whatcha gonna do, Ward?" Doug asked.

Ward rubbed his neck, turning it from side to side to see if it still worked. "I'm going to finish my drink and then see about dinner."

"What about Younger?"

"Someday we'll meet when I don't have a headache and he doesn't have fifty men with him," he said quietly.

CHAPTER EIGHT

Leslie rode sidesaddle beside Annette, keeping the subdued Frenchwoman between her and the others like a buffer, avoiding Younger and his attempts to placate her with cheerful conversation.

The sun set, and the desert, ever responsive, cooled. Chill night air fanned her flushed cheeks, and her agitation slowly diminished with the exertion of the ride. It was dark when they reached the ranch. A silver wedge was rising over the mountains to the east. The ranch house sat like a fortress on the hill, glistening under the stars.

They climbed the gentle slope quickly, the horses as eager as Leslie to end this ride. Once inside the protective walls, she dismounted and relinquished her reins to the young Mexican boys who ran out to greet the horsemen. Uncle Mark, apparently anticipating her, stepped up onto the wooden porch where he towered over her. "Go to my office, young lady," he said, his manner brusque.

Determined not to be cowed by him, Leslie swept past Younger, ignoring the hand he extended to help her up the stairs. She preceded her uncle into the room he used as an office and watched in silence as he settled himself into the big leather chair behind the desk. He had arranged his features into a conciliatory mask, but he fairly reeked with the self-confidence of a man who could not lose.

"Now, Leslie," he said. "You wanted to talk to me?"

Her hands tightened on the edge of the chair and she leaned forward. "I want you to buy me out so I can go back home," she said quickly.

"Uh-huh," he said. "And what do you think of the ranch?" he asked.

"What do you mean?"

"Well, you are your father's heir. It is, roughly speaking, half yours."

"I don't understand," she said softly.

"Well," he said. "You will appreciate that a half-interest in a steer cannot be divided until the steer is either slaughtered or sold to a third party for money."

"Yes, sir, I understand that," Leslie said, feeling uncomfortable, "but the ranch isn't a steer."

"Your father owned an undivided half-interest in this ranch. And frankly, Leslie, I don't think you could manage your half of the ranch," he said, smiling at the ridiculousness of her struggling with the myriad details involved.

Irritated at his obvious pleasure in what he saw as her incompetence, she leaned forward. "There is no need. If you would only purchase my half from me…"

"I have no intentions of selling or dividing any part of the ranch," he said gruffly. "This is my home! And while you may have an interest in the ranch, there is no way for you to turn that interest into money without my cooperation. Your signature on any document attempting that would be as worthless as a pile of grama grass in wheat country," he declared, slamming his fist onto his desk.

"I understand your desire to keep the ranch together, Uncle Mark," she said, controlling herself with an effort. "But I was hoping we could reach an agreement where you would purchase my interest for an amount that would be less than its actual value."

"Cash is not something we keep in great quantities. Cash is for buying cows. I can turn my money over many times by putting it into cows. And without my signature, your interest is totally without value. However," he said, holding up his hand to forestall her heated words, "you are my brother's daughter, and I have no intention of keeping you from enjoying your inheritance. You are welcome here as long as you live, Leslie."

"What? What do you mean?" she asked, incredulous.

"Your father and I spent our life's blood to build this ranch. It was always his wish that you should live here with him. I see no other way to resolve this impasse." He shrugged. "My only wish is to take care of you. I can't do that if you're gallivanting around in some city where a body can't see the sky for the haze." He leaned back in his chair, his face darkened by a look of righteous indignation. He crossed his arms over his chest, determined to get through what he saw as an unpleasant duty to an ungrateful and bothersome relative.

Recognizing that stubborn look for what it was, Leslie nearly despaired. She was not accustomed to having her wishes entirely disregarded. But time and again since arriving in Phoenix she had discussed matters with her uncle only to find either instantly or later that he hadn't taken her seriously at all, as if he were listening to a child.

Now, grim with parental purpose and righteousness, Mark Powers sat like a block of granite—impervious to reason—determined to "take care of her."

"I am not a child," Leslie said grimly.

"I never had any children of my own, Leslie, but I do know that children need guidance. I don't hold with that newfangled horse baloney your mother put such store in. You might want to read the law of the land. It'll be clear to you that I'm the one who'll be held responsible for you," he said, leaning forward. "I happen to be your legal guardian."

"I'm nineteen years old!" she protested.

"An unmarried woman needs a guardian until she reaches majority. As your only surviving relative in this territory, I am your guardian. My dear, it behooves me to care for you until you marry a fine young man who will father children my brother would be proud of."

Leslie leaned back in the chair, feeling the room closing in on her. Face pale and glowing, she sat forward. "And I suppose your being my guardian also entitles you to pick my husband for me?"

Something unrecognizable glittered in his jade green eyes, and Leslie paled. Her uncle, though his veneer of earnest regard had not worn through, frightened her suddenly. Was it possible she had skipped blithely off the train and into a trap? Had this man purposely lured her here, knowing all the time that he fully intended to toss her like a bone to his lusty foreman?

His eyes were guarded again. "I would respect your wishes insofar as that is reasonable, but I could not allow you to marry someone who would be a detriment to you."

Leslie could barely speak around the knot that had formed in her throat. "You mean you want me to marry an asset like Dallas Younger," she said bitterly.

Her uncle's brows crowded his eyes in a scowl. "Well, Dallas would make you a fine husband, no doubt about that."

"And if I refuse?"

He shrugged. "You may marry or not, as you wish. Obviously I do not expect you to manage your own financial interests. A woman needs a man to do those things for her."

A dozen angry responses trembled on her lips, but now there was triumph glittering undisguised in Powers's small green eyes. Leslie stood up and turned to leave the room, but her uncle's sanctimonious words stopped her.

"Leslie, few things are asked of you. You live a remarkably carefree existence, but keep in mind that obedience is an important virtue in a young lady."

"Have I been disobedient?" Leslie asked, her voice little more than a whisper.

He paused, and his lips tightened. "It's not safe for you to venture out alone," he said, ignoring her question. "When you want to leave the ranch you're to ask permission. Am I understood?" A sly look crept into his eyes.

"Or what?" she demanded.

"Don't get uppity with me, Leslie. You just do as you're told. When you go out I want two of Younger's men with you to protect you."

"Protect me?" she gasped. "From what?"

"From danger! From Indians! How the hell should I know from what? From whatever threatens you!" he said furiously, his face turning beet red.

Back in her room, as Leslie dressed for bed, she realized that her uncle planned to gain her half-interest in the ranch by either keeping her prisoner or forcing her to marry Dallas Younger. She feared that there was almost nothing she could do about it, unless she was willing to sign everything over to him. He would have no need of her then.

Leslie toyed with the idea, but something stubborn and intractable in her rejected that choice. She might have to fall back on that, and she would before she would allow herself to be forced into a marriage pact with that barbarian Dallas Younger.

CHAPTER NINE

Ward had been riding for three hours, and it was mid-morning with the sun already beating down when he got his first glimpse of the Mendoza farm. It was exactly as he remembered it—like a pencil drawing in a magazine he'd seen when Arizona was still a place to be read about. The small adobe house looked like a pueblo with small windows, squatting at the base of the mountain. He could see a horse in the corral, two shaggy cows in a pen, and multicolored chickens pecking at the hard ground. The house was on the east side of the mountain and would be shaded from the afternoon sun.

There was a new barbed-wire fence enclosing both the *casa* and the garden where the Mendozas grew the vegetables for their table. Food was plentiful because Mama had built her house next to a natural artesian well and taught young Pedro to dig shallow ditches to irrigate the small plot. Even the ancient one, Grandpapa, helped with the garden.

Ward stopped on a rise in the desert, amid the yellowed sand and the dark tumbleweed, in the shade of a saguaro. It had been a long time since he had been there—too long probably. It felt like homecoming in his chest. It was a good feeling.

He smiled. Mama was probably still fighting off the young *vaqueros* from her pretty daughter. If he remembered right, Isabel must be almost nineteen by now. She had been fifteen when Mama had found him delirious in the desert and packed him home to tend his bullet wound. He would have died without her help. He had taken a bullet in the back when he and the gang were fleeing from a posse. He had bled heavily and could not keep up the pace necessary to get to safety before the posse overtook them. He had veered off in another direction, lost the pursuers, who hadn't noticed his breaking away, and collapsed sometime during the night. By morning, he was watching the buzzards circling overhead. By high noon they had formed a ring around him, and occasionally one of the brave ones would waddle clumsily toward him and he would shoot it. Mama had arrived in the afternoon, when he was so weak he could barely move. She hadn't asked any questions. She had simply shoved him up onto her horse, tied him on, and hurried back to her home, where she spent many weeks nursing him back to health.

Isabel, her daughter, was young and skittish and eager to test her charms on Ward. He had been younger then, and, if possible, even more responsive to the enticing jiggle of a willing female. Isabel had followed him everywhere when he was strong enough to begin moving around. If he shoed a horse, she was underfoot. If he tried to take a nap, she would accidentally drop something to wake him. When he spoke, she hung on every word. And being male, he had known that he could have her. He had contemplated it in his mind and rejected it. Once his strength returned, and with it his desire for a woman, she brought him more than one sleepless night.

One afternoon, while Mama was in town and Pedro and his grandfather were away from the *casa*, Isabel fixed his lunch and the two of them sat at the table talking.

Isabel giggled too much and flirted in the breathless, excited way young, inexperienced girls did, and Ward was flattered, but he knew enough about girls to know that while Isabel might enjoy the thought of his making love to her, she would not be prepared for the actuality of it. She was just testing her equipment on him to see if it worked. He flirted with her and enjoyed her attention, but he did not take her seriously, even though it would have relieved him greatly if he could have ignored his own sense of responsibility to her and the woman who had saved his life.

The thought of Mama always brought a smile to his lips. She was fierce and devout, and she would not tolerate having her daughter taken lightly. The second time he had visited with them, long after the gunshot wound had healed, Mama had seen the way his blue eyes watched her Isabel, and she had sent the girl outside to work in the garden with her brother.

"Señor Ward, you are my guest. I have taken you in when you would have died. I treated your wound, fed you, prayed for you, bathed your head when you raved with the fever, but I will not let you sleep with my Isabel. She is a good girl but foolish where men are concerned. She would be easy for one as handsome as you. You have the ways and the looks to tempt young girls."

Ward started to protest his innocence, but Mama stopped him with a raised hand.

"I know what you are going to say, and it is not necessary. You see, I am not blind, and I know that you have respected my daughter in spite of her clumsy attempts to have you do otherwise."

Ward was suddenly grateful that he had nothing serious to hide from this woman. Her eyes were too direct and he would never be able to lie to her convincingly. He returned her steady look with one of his own. "It pleases me that you have seen this," he said, meaning it.

She snorted. "I am not so old or so foolish that I cannot remember the fever in young blood! You want my Isabel, and you are very fair. She is much affected. I see it in the sway of her skinny hips when you watch her. She prances like a young doe. I have also seen that while you found her attractive and available, you chose to put my interests and the girl's above your own. For that, Señor Ward, I am grateful. You are a man of honor. It would grieve me sorely if it were otherwise."

Ward flushed. He felt suddenly as if she could read his mind. "*Señora* Mendoza, I'm a hunted outlaw," he reminded her, his voice unaccountably husky. "I didn't shoot myself…"

Now her round face with the knowing eyes came alive with its intensity. "Honor is a thing of the soul, not of circumstance," she said flatly. From that day forward she called him thee and thou, and he called her Mama.

Originally, the interior of the Mendoza house had consisted of one big room used as three rooms: a kitchen and two bedrooms, separated by sheets for privacy. The kitchen was as big as both other rooms, and it was in there that Mama Mendoza had spread a pallet on the floor for him. Two years ago he and Pedro had built a wooden lean-to at the back of the house so that Pedro and Grandpapa could share a room, while Isabel and Mama shared another, returning the original house to its function as kitchen and cultural center.

They didn't speak of Isabel again, but Ward continued to protect the lovely young creature, even though she severely tested his resolve from time to time. In the last four years the Mendozas had become like family, until now they were all he wanted or needed. And they suited his lifestyle. He could drop in whenever he felt the need and always be assured of a welcome.

Although he still had family in New York City—aunts, uncles, cousins—there was no one he cared to communicate with, no one who had claim to his heart the way Jenn had. He hadn't written to or heard from anyone, not even his sister, since he had joined the cavalry. It had been, as he thought back on it, melodramatic and immature, but at the time it had seemed entirely right.

Now he could smile about such foolishness, but at the time he joined the cavalry, he had been deadly serious. He didn't get serious about things anymore. He didn't take on fifty men to prove he was a man, and he didn't fight over women who meant nothing to him. He was an outlaw and a killer of men, not a crusader.

Ward's mental wandering jolted to an end when Isabel saw him riding over the rise. She dropped the vegetables she had been gathering and ran excitedly into the house yelling to her *madre*. "Mama! Mama! Ward is coming!"

Mama Mendoza glanced up from the sock she was mending. Isabel's pretty face was flushed with excitement. Mama knew Isabel probably loved Ward Cantrell more than she loved Pedro, because to Isabel, Ward was gossip, excitement, gifts, tender interest, and an attractive man to tease and torment but who was safe and admiring. Mama sighed. What could be more perfect than that? Mama Mendoza got heavily to her feet, relief washing over her features for just a moment before she allowed her pleasure to show. "Run meet him, silly chicken. See if I care!" she said, smiling. The girl would do so anyway—no matter what. She was like a three-year-old when Ward came.

Isabel ran from the small adobe house, wiping her hands and poking at her hair, trying frantically to arrange the long straight hair into something less childish. In her haste to greet Ward it bounced and flew around her face, and she gave up.

Ward spurred his horse into a run and met her under the cottonwood trees. He dismounted, gave her a friendly bearhug, and swung her around, telling her how pretty she was while she, overcome with happiness, smothered him with kisses.

"Guess what, Ward! Guess!" she demanded, leaning back in the circle of his arms.

He grinned. "I know. You are married and you have six children and one of them, a boy, looks like me. You ran out here to warn me because your husband is going to shoot me."

"No, *idiota!* Foolish talk is not what I want to hear. Guess, really!" she said vehemently, stamping her pretty foot.

"I can't imagine what could bring such a flush to your pretty cheeks unless there is a new man in your life," he said, laughing.

"Guess, really!" she begged, pinching his arm.

Mama walked toward their nonsense, shaking her head. They were like playful bear cubs together: Ward refusing to guess to torment her and Isabel pinching and hitting him while he laughed and fended her off.

Mama came into the middle of this, and Ward set the playful Isabel aside to give Mama a hug.

"It's good to be home," Ward said, meaning it. Mama hugged him tightly and stepped back, smiling at him. She was trying to be cheerful, but it was apparent to Ward that she was troubled. He made a note to ask her later about the changes he had already sensed. But for now, he did not want to spoil Isabel's fun.

Grinning, with Isabel bouncing excitedly at his side, Ward turned to the bulging saddlebags he had on the rump of his horse. The big black stamped and pawed the ground. He had smelled the cool clear water and was eager to get to it.

"Pedro!" Mama yelled.

"*Sí*, Mama?" The answer came from the small lean-to behind the house that served as a barn for the animals and the horse that Pedro rode to town for supplies. At night it was a roost also for the chickens.

"Come at once, Pedro!" Isabel yelled. "*Señor* Ward has come!"

The young man who joined them was a surprise for Ward. Pedro had grown into a young man. Last summer he had been seventeen and a beanpole. Now he had filled out and was a handsome lad with the same friendly brown eyes that Isabel had. Mama was squat and plain, with nothing of beauty in her face, but her children were comely.

"He is almost a man, no?" Isabel asked proudly.

"Welcome, *Señor* Ward." Pedro grinned. "Mama and Isabel speak often of you. We prayed for your safe return."

"Thank you, Pedro. It is good to be back." Ward held out his hand solemnly, and the young man took it, pleased to be treated like an equal by this man he admired, loved, and worried about. Pedro had heard the stories about Ward Cantrell, and he had asked Mama about them, because he had seen outlaws who had been hanged by the neck. Their bodies had been laid out on the sidewalk in Phoenix for all to take warning. *Señor* Ward was the only adult male who had ever taken an interest in him. Ward had spent much time showing him how to care for the horse he had bought for him, how to mend the fine leather saddle that had been his last gift, even how to clean and care for himself properly. The thought of this man, with his smiling eyes and his ready humor stilled forever, lying on some sidewalk, cold and stiff, with arms folded across his chest, displayed in death as a warning to others, had filled him with anger and despair. When he had asked Mama about his fears, he had been puzzled and then pleased with her explanation: "God does not have accidents. He assigns each man to his task, and it is only important that he do it well."

And from the stories Pedro heard when he went into town, it was apparent to him that *Señor* Ward did his task very well indeed. Pedro took Ward's horse to water and care for him, and Ward followed Mama inside, with Isabel still imploring him to guess her secret.

"Tell me your secret, or I will keep all my gifts," Ward teased her.

"Give me my gift, or I will not tell you ever!" she countered happily. There was too much loneliness in her heart not to squeeze every ounce of affection and attention from this handsome *gringo* she loved.

Ward relented and dropped to his knees to beg her to share her secret. "I have a *novio,*" she rushed to tell him. "A young man from what Mama calls 'a good family,'" she said, dimpling. "And we have received permission from our parents to be married in the church at Christmas."

"Isabel, how could you?" Ward demanded, feigning injury. He clutched his heart and looked stricken, and Isabel burst into peals of wicked laughter. When she stopped laughing he took her aside, and she sobered.

"This young man, do you love him?"

Her eyes widened. "*Sí,* I love him so much I would die for him."

Ward frowned. "Does he love you?"

A smile lighted her face, and it was like the sun breaking through dense clouds unexpectedly. "*Sí.*"

"Is he good to you?"

She nodded and he could tell by the smile that she was not lying. "Does he have a job? Some way to take care of you?"

"*Sí,* his papa is a landowner. He works very hard. That is why I do not see him so very often…"

"Does he treat you with respect?"

"Unfortunately he does…" She smiled, nodding, her face flushed with pleasure at the opportunity to talk about her *novio,* and Ward relaxed, content that all was well.

Everyone loved Ward's gifts: a pretty gown with dress-up shoes for Isabel, a rifle for Pedro, wine and tobacco for Grandpapa, and a new shawl for Mama Manuela with two hundred dollars in five-dollar bills tucked inside. To her that was a year's worth of security.

After dinner Isabel proudly brought out a large basket piled high with white satin. Her eyes wide with wonder at the fine lustrous fabric, she explained to Ward that it was to be her wedding gown. It had taken her and Mama a week to cut the numerous pieces from the bolt of fabric Ward's last generous gift of money had bought for them. "We will never finish it," she wailed. "Never!"

Ward looked at Mama with alarm and fished into his pants. He dragged out a handful of bills and gave them all to Isabel. "Hire some seamstresses," he said, scowling. "I don't want you walking down the aisle in a half-finished gown."

Mama slapped his hand. "Put thy money away. That is her way of telling thee she wants thee to help with the sewing." She laughed. Pedro snorted at the thought of Ward Cantrell, a famous gunfighter, sewing with women.

"You need my help, little one?"

Isabel shrugged, appalled at what she had started.

Ward looked from Pedro's contorted face to Isabel's. "Well," he said, "don't just stand there. Get me a needle."

Isabel squealed with delight and rushed to comply. Pedro scowled his disbelief, but Ward cuffed him lightly and followed Isabel, watching intently as she threaded a needle for him. Pedro, seeing Ward's example, sighed and took the next needle from his sister's hands. Delighted, Mama got both of them started, and then settled down at the table across from Ward. She sewed and watched Ward, his big, deft hands working so carefully in the delicate fabric, and it gave her much pleasure that he set such a good example for her son. Pedro was too prone to take his sister lightly.

Laughing, giggling, saying outrageous things to one another, they sewed at the table, huddled around the brightest lamp until their backs were cramped. Mama laid her sewing aside, sighed, then patted the worn wood of the table with her chubby brown hand, causing Ward to look up from his stitching. "Is there a woman whose face thou carryest in thy heart?"

Startled, Ward scowled. The face that flashed into memory at her question was Jenn's. "No," he said grimly, knowing that she was hoping for a sweetheart, not a sister.

Mama sighed, disappointed. "That is most tragic—thou wouldst make a fine husband and father." Isabel nodded in agreement, but Pedro looked pleased that Ward had not become anything as boring as that. He wanted adventure and excitement for himself and his friend.

Ward shook his head. "I'm an outlaw, remember?"

Mama ignored his words. "What dost thou want for thyself? More than just being a fugitive…."

Ward stopped sewing and fingered the white satin. "I want a home," he said softly, meeting Mama's gaze.

At first, after Simone's death, he had rejected all symbols of commitment, but after six years his wounds had healed. He was tired of running, hungry for a piece of land...a house...a woman to meet him at the door, shading her face against the setting sun, welcoming him with quiet eyes, maybe even a child to run down the steps to fling his small body at him crying, "Daddy, Daddy..."

A hollow ache started inside him. He had surprised himself. Mama saw it and was the one to break up the group, sending Pedro and Isabel to bed. "Go, shoo, the sun comes up at the same time, no matter when you go to bed, and you are both hard to wake."

Grumbling, they kissed Ward good-night and went to their separate pallets. Mama carefully folded the sewn fabric and put the basket away. Ward poured himself a cup of coffee and sat down at the table beside her. He had noticed a new set of frown lines around Mama's mouth and that her eyes darted to the window repeatedly, even when she was pretending to be relaxed. "You look tense, Mama."

"Thou didst see the fence?"

"Problems?"

"*Sí. Señor* Powers wants my water for his cattle." Her face took on a stubborn fierceness.

Ward frowned. There was that name again. It was turning up with alarming regularity and always in a way to cause the hair on the back of his neck to bristle. "Powers? His ranch is miles from here," Ward said.

"*Sí.* That is the way it was, but he has been growing. Now there is no longer anyone left between his rangeland and ours. He has offered to buy our land, but where would we go? This is our home," she said, spreading her hands.

"What happened to your neighbors? The Randolph family?"

"Killed, along with other homesteaders."

"Powers?"

"It was made to look like Indians, but the tracks were of horses with shoes." Ward didn't like the sound of what Mama was telling him. If it was true, Powers and his riders were as dangerous as they looked. But even Powers could not run roughshod over his neighbors without someone taking exception to it. There was still law in the Arizona Territory. Maybe not as well organized as in parts east, but there was a sheriff and the United States marshal and the military up north who would serve as a deterrent, even to a man like Powers.

Ward patted Mama's hand. "Before I leave," he promised, "I will see Powers and explain to him you do not want to move. His men will not bother you again."

"He will not listen." Mama shook her head sadly. For the first time since he had known her he saw fear in Mama's eyes. Deep wrinkles creased her forehead, and the stern lines on either side of her mouth had deepened. She was showing her age. He had always assumed she was indestructible.

"He will listen, Mama," Ward said grimly, determined to take some of the burden off her already stooped shoulders. "You just have to know how to talk to a man like that."

CHAPTER TEN

Ward had been home a week. It was September tenth and the weather was growing cooler in the evenings. The nights were marked by first frost, and the leaves had begun to turn so that the evening sun, seen through a grove of aspen trees in the mountains near the Mendozas' small home, was a blazing white ball that turned sparse, dangling leaves into luminous gold. The white slender tree trunks with their black markings looked like a speckled toothpick forest. The leaves, all fiery and splendorous, seemed detached from the spindly trunks, more like golden clouds that clustered around to protect the pale rootlike trunks. The grass, wherever the sun touched it, was the color of straw.

Ward's horse, a big black one, stopped at his urging. The air was still and pungent with smells of the forest: pine, spruce, fir, rotting wood, and the smell of blood from the deer tied over the flanks of his horse. Mama Manuela would turn the buck into steaks for dinner after she had cured the meat. He kicked the black into a gallop. It would be sundown when he got back, as it was. No time to dawdle, but he did. He gathered strength from solitude. It was necessary to him.

He hadn't realized it until he joined the cavalry and discovered that military life was lived in a state of togetherness that a civilian would find incredible—there was no place inside the fort where a man could be alone. The need for privacy had been compounded by a burly drill sergeant who didn't allow any sign of emotion on a man's face, night or day. Once, shortly after he had enlisted, the pressure became so great on him that he had searched until he'd found a small corner between buildings where he could stand and be out of the sight of all eyes for ten whole minutes. The cavalry had become more bearable after he was commissioned.

The sun was slipping beneath the jagged rim of the mountain ridge that surrounded the rolling hills of the desert when he finally saw the Mendoza house, small and squat beneath the escarpment. He stopped his horse. Nothing was moving, not even the chickens who usually pecked incessantly at the earth. Unaccustomed stillness set off an alarm inside him. He held the horse firmly. He'd been a fugitive too long to ignore the warning in ominous silence. Maybe Doug had been captured and told them where to find him. He squinted his keen eyes, scanning the scene ahead of him until he saw a dark shape against the dim red earth. Kicking his horse forward, he refused to think.

The fence was down. The small garden had been trampled into dust. Not even the chickens remained. The goat lay tangled in barbed wire that had been pulled loose from its posts and lay curled into a snarl beside the lean-to barn.

He had approached from the rear, and when he rounded the corner to the front of the house, he saw what he feared most. Mama Manuela was a crumpled shape in the dust. Pedro, his hands still clutching the new rifle, was sprawled like a ragdoll only a few feet from her. Both dead. No need to kneel beside them, but he did, partly from shock and partly from the need to know that he had not overlooked helping them if anything could help. Pedro's skull had been crushed. Mama's stout form was riddled with bleeding bullet holes.

Sickened and filled with dread, he walked inside the house. Grandpapa was sprawled in a corner, sitting like a doll that had been jammed there by an angry hand. His open eyes were staring at the wall opposite, like some grim watchman. Ward turned and saw the horror that must have been his last.

Isabel lay on the pallet Mama had put there for him. Naked, her shapely legs splayed and bloody, her warm brown skin marked by bruises, her pretty face swollen and blackened where ruthless fists had smashed into it. Hands that had worked so carefully in white satin were clenched into fists, her nails red with blood. He found a blanket and covered her, then stumbled outside, away from the house, and sagged against one of the cottonwoods, gasping for breath. Without realizing it, he must have been holding his breath, not willing to breathe that smell of death, already heavy and sweet in the small cabin.

Drenched with sweat, sick to his soul, he forced himself to walk a widening circle around the cabin until he found clear prints of departing horses.

Then he knew that Mama had been right. These were not Indian ponies. They were shod, and several of the prints would be easy to recognize again. Grimly, he filed the information in memory and then took a shovel from the barn. He dug a grave—one big one. He carried each of his family in turn and laid them gently to rest, then knelt and bowed his head, but no words came to him, no tears, no comfort. Finally he stood and vowed to Mama that he would send a priest to bless the grave for her. Then he shoveled dirt onto the canvas he had covered them with.

Exhausted, Ward sat under the tree and carved their names onto a shingle, then strapped it to a stake and drove it into the soft earth at the head of the grave. Then he hacked off a portion of the deer's hind quarter and went inside to take some of Mama's salt to pack it in. As he left the small house he saw the white wedding gown lying on the floor, discarded. He remembered the way Mama, Isabel, and Pedro had looked, teasing one another and giggling over each perfect stitch. He could see Isabel's face as she told him how much she loved her *novio* and how happy they would be. He stopped and knelt beside Isabel's gown. He picked it up and walked to the table. His brown sturdy hands, sore with unaccustomed blisters from digging the first grave he had ever dug, carefully smoothed the lustrous fabric. He had meant only to put it on the table, but the feel of it under his hands released a full set of memories. He could see Isabel's pretty face, beaming with joy at the thought of the happiest day in her life, Pedro's youthful manliness as he struggled with the tiny needle and the slippery white fabric, and Mama Manuela, beaming with pride at the closeness of her family and their love for one another. The feelings he'd been numb to before, as he'd knelt at the grave, rose up in him now and his hands tightened in the soiled, torn fabric. His teeth clamped together in rage, and his blue eyes hardened, then closed, and he gathered up the white satin and began tearing it into a dozen pieces.

The next morning when the sun slipped over the eastern horizon, Ward was on a hill overlooking the Powers spread. The house and barns were inside seven-foot walls, and armed men were everywhere. Ward watched all day until he spotted his prey on the road from the enclosure. After they had moved out of sight he rode down and inspected their tracks. Markings from several of these hooves matched the unique prints he had seen in the Mendoza yard.

He straightened, not at all surprised that Powers' elite corps, the same men who had ridden in the parade, had been the ones who murdered the Mendozas. That Younger was the leader of the group only hardened his purpose. Ward knew, in that moment, looking at the fresh prints, that he was going to kill them, and he knew almost in the same breath how he was going to do it. He couldn't ride in there and take on the whole bunch single-handedly—not if he wanted to be effective. He would wait until Younger's woman came out, and he'd take her. Younger and all his men would come after them. Fifteen to one he could handle, especially since he got to lead. North into the mountains—a man could take his time, hide and strike at will. He would save Younger for last.

Ward waited the two days until she left the enclosure. He saw the big door swing open, then the woman, her hair streaming back like a black cloud, followed by two heavily armed escorts.

To get back to the ranch house, the trio had to ride through a grove of aspen trees. When they came out he was behind a boulder with a rifle trained on them. He had chosen his spot carefully and was far enough away from the fortress so that shots fired wouldn't be heard.

"Halt! Don't move!" he yelled.

"What the hell!" The man on her left clawed at the gun in his holster, and Leslie heard an explosion and saw him jerk. His horse screamed and then bolted, dropping its limp burden to the ground. Her own horse reared up, and she jerked on the reins, barely comprehending what was happening. The bullets came too close together, like a rolling explosion. Her horse reared again and lunged wildly. She clawed at the horse's mane, trying to retain her seat, but the horse moved one direction and she the other. Screaming, she tried to regain her balance as the horse caught the bit in its teeth and bolted. The man fired again; her horse ran erratically trying to change direction, and she could feel herself leave the saddle to sail through the air, right at the man who was shooting at them.

It all happened too fast for her. She saw the ground coming up at her, but nothing else.

CHAPTER ELEVEN

Younger,
    I buried the Mendoza family two days ago. I have your
woman. I'm going to sell her to the Indians after I'm done
with her.

                                                    Cantrell

Dallas Younger read the note that had been taken off the body of
one of his men and crumpled it with a curse and a snarl that contorted
his usually handsome face.

"That bastard!" Younger bellowed for the Indian tracker, Warmfoot.
When the Indian appeared before him, he explained in pidgin Apache
that he wanted him to find Cantrell. "I'll follow soon as I can. You leave
a clear trail, hear?"

Powers took the note, smoothed it against his chest, read it with his lips
pursed into anger and surprise. "Who the hell is Cantrell?" he demanded.

"He's the gunfighter that met Dodge Merril in Holbrook a few years
back. Faced the Merril gang down single-handed after that—sent 'em
crawlin', or so the story goes."

"You seen him?"

"No, but I reckon I will."

"You ain't going after him, are you?"

"Hell, yes! He's got Leslie. That's your niece."

"She ain't nothing but trouble to me," Powers said flatly.

Younger glared at him, disgust pulling the corners of his lips down.
Powers ignored him. He understood Younger and his kind. They had
some fancy code about killing that was supposed to make everything all
right, but a man was just as dead whether you shot him in a fair fight or
in his sleep. With his code, all he had to do was wait. Cantrell would take
care of his problem for him. Then the ranch would be all his.

They were standing on the long porch of the main house. The
porch overhang shaded them from the hot sun of late afternoon. Powers

mopped his forehead and gazed out across the gentle slope that fell away from the house. The yellowed grass was stiff and dry, reminding him how remorseless the desert sun was. Leslie was a rank tenderfoot; she wouldn't last long in the Arizona desert. He didn't speak. He was waiting for Younger to let the reality of his words sink in.

The house was only four years old, built after the railroad came to Phoenix, bringing with it prosperity for many. That was when rustling cattle, or burning brands on mavericks, started paying so well. This had been his home. His brother Charlie, Leslie's father, had been planning to build his a ways off, down by the cottonwoods, so he and that good-for-nothing wife he planned to bring out would have some privacy, except he hadn't lived long enough to build it. He'd found out about the rustling activities carried out by Younger and his men and had threatened to make trouble.

And while he would never condone killing his own brother, he had been secretly relieved when Charlie had died. No one knew exactly what Charlie Powers had been doing, afoot in a gully, when someone ran a large herd of steers down it, trampling him, but Mark Powers was not about to look a gift horse in the mouth. He might suspect Younger, but he'd never confront the man with it. Just as Younger should now accept what had happened to Leslie.

Younger finally expelled a heavy breath. "That would look like hell! Some bastard kidnaps your niece and you just write her off," he growled. "How the hell is that going to look to the folks in town? Like we ain't got guts enough to take back what belongs to us, that's how."

Powers frowned. "Reckon you're right about that, but you'd be doing us both a favor if you brought her back dead. Maybe you can hang that bastard Cantrell for killing her. Be damn sure he ain't alive when you bring him back."

Younger turned away in disgust. He went to the bunkhouse. The only one there of the men he fully trusted was Sam Farmer. Sam was a lanky, raw-boned, red-haired Arkansan.

"Who the hell led the raid on the Mendozas?" he demanded of the man who was stretched out on his bunk, counting flies as they buzzed overhead.

"The boss did."

"Did Powers know about it?"

"Don't know. Didn't never come up. Why you asking?"

"'Cause it was the stupidest piece of work I seen in my whole damned life!" Younger exploded. "You assholes rode in there and killed the women and kids, and now Ward Cantrell is after my ass."

"Cantrell! Jesus!" Sam came upright off the bunk.

"How the hell did Cantrell get mixed up in this?"

"How the hell should I know? Maybe he's slept with so many of them little *chileñas* he thinks he's one of 'em."

Farmer pushed the red hair off his suddenly pale face. Freckles stood out against the pasty whiteness. "How'd you find out he's after you?"

"'Cause the bastard wrote me a note," he growled. "He killed Spike and that drunk he rides with, and he took Powers's niece. Damn!" Younger's face was hard with fury. "Round up the boys and tell them to toss their bedrolls over hosses. We're riding out in ten minutes, and we won't be back until we find that bastard and the girl."

Leslie woke up slowly, painfully. After a second of frowning into inky darkness she realized she was on a horse, riding in front of someone, cradled like a babe in strong arms. Her aching head was on his shoulder, and she could smell a warm, musky man smell mingled with leather, tobacco, and sweat—a salty smell that was not altogether unpleasant. She stirred to relieve her cramped muscles and heard a husky masculine chuckle, followed by a voice that seemed vaguely familiar.

"So, you've decided to live after all."

"What happened?"

"Hit your head when you fell."

His voice did not sound like any of the men on her uncle's ranch. "Who are you?" she asked in growing alarm.

"It doesn't matter," he said grimly.

"Where are you taking me?"

Ward felt involuntary anger rising up inside him, rough and heated, and made a conscious effort to control it. She sounded as if she had just stepped out of the sacred halls of Radcliffe—the haughty insolence that only Daddy's money and Mother's handpicked tutors could buy. A lifetime of privilege followed by an Ivy League college and carefully chaperoned dates with Harvard undergraduates. What the hell was a woman like this doing with Dallas Younger? "Save your strength," he said grimly. "You're going to need it."

"You...you...kidnapped me? But why? I haven't any money. No one would pay to get me back."

"Too bad for you, then."

CHAPTER TWELVE

Leslie twisted around to look at her abductor and was aware of her breasts brushing against his arm. In the darkness all she could make out was a silhouette, a grim, dark profile against the lighter sky.

"They'll come after me, you know—Dallas Younger will follow me. He'll kill you when he finds us…" she warned him nervously.

He laughed softly, a strangely undaunted sound. "I'm counting on it."

Leslie lapsed into silence. Her head ached with a determined throb; pain laced through her temples as the flying hooves hit the ground. They were riding fast, over what looked like level ground. She had wanted to escape, but not this way. Where was he taking her? Into the desert?

Now, huddled tensely in his arms, shivering from the chill bite of cold autumn winds, memory, like an unwelcome visitor, was slowly returning. She recalled the two men who had been with her before, the strident shout, "Halt! Don't move!" the men grasping for their guns, the volley of gunshots rolling one on another, the screaming horses. She felt revulsion, nausea, and then anger and turned on him abruptly, almost unseating herself.

"You killed those two men!" she hissed.

"Somebody had to," he replied harshly.

Rage, fed by her terror, spewed up from the depths of her and blinded Leslie to everything except the urge to strike out. "Let me down!" Her fists pummeled his face and chest. "Let me go! You killer! Dirty animal killer!"

Her furious twisting and flailing almost unseated them both before Ward could get her under control. He jerked the horse to a halt and dismounted, dragging her off unceremoniously. "You damned little bitch!" He slapped her once to get her attention, then pinned her on the hard ground while she screamed in terror as the horse's hooves stamped just inches from her head. She struggled frantically against him, expecting anything, but his rough hand only held her still while he slipped a noose over her neck and adjusted the knot.

"What are you doing to me? You beast! I hate you! Do you hear me? Kill me! Go ahead! Filthy killer!" But there was a tremor of fear in her voice.

"You want to ride alone, you can ride alone," he said softly, his voice as calm and unaffected as if he were telling her it was dinnertime. "The other end of this rope is going to be tied to my saddle. You either keep up or you break your pretty little neck, you hear?" He lifted her onto the horse, astride a western saddle, handling her easily in spite of her struggles. Then he mounted a horse she didn't recall seeing or hearing before.

She learned that night what terror was. He was traveling fast, and she lived in constant fear that he would deliberately jerk her off just so she would break her neck, or that her horse or his would stumble. She had visions of dying slowly of a broken neck while those clumsy black birds Younger had called buzzards circled overhead. Or falling off her mount to be dragged to death.

She prayed that Dallas Younger would follow, and remembered her uncle's words: "You could do a lot worse than a man like Younger." And as furious as she was, she realized that Younger, with his slow Texas drawl and masculine arrogance, would come after her...

"Look out!" Cantrell yelled. "Duck!"

Leslie heard the urgent warning just in time. She ducked and her horse barely skimmed under the branch of a dead tree that had loomed up out of the blackness. Her heart leaped into her throat, pounding wildly, but the danger was past. She slowly settled back down, and, trembling, she hung on to that damned torturing horse, cursing the pain in her side and the crashing agony inside her skull. She continued to hang on until the savage pain was permanently lodged in her side, fear became commonplace, and hope had turned to resignation.

For lack of anything better to do she watched the moon rise, arc overhead, and set. Still that maniac kept up the same killing pace. If obstinance hadn't been a family trait handed down from mother to daughter for generations, she would have thrown herself to the ground and broken her own neck. Death couldn't possibly be this bad.

She had been on the very brink of death when she was fifteen, and it had been nothing compared to this! She had contracted a mysterious fever and had lain with her arms crossed over her chest, her body swaddled in warm blankets, sipping only water for days, and the only thought she had ever had was that she wouldn't mind dying—she just wanted it over with! She had no patience for whimpering, not even her own. She had been able to hear people talking about her. She had known what they said and how concerned they were, but it was as if she had watched from some lofty vantage point, not as a participant but as a not-too-concerned spectator, grateful for the distance she had managed to put between herself and that feeble alien shell.

Now she hurt all over, and there was no escape. She had never been so truly afraid before, and she resented this fact almost as much as she hated the cause of her misery.

They rode all night. When the sun was just beginning to spread warm light in the eastern sky, he finally "whoaed" his horse and raised his hand in a signal for her to stop.

They were in a canyon with sheer, soaring walls that looked gray in the first pink flush of dawn. The canyon, rough, immense, almost as broad as a valley, looked like a continuation of the high desert. The floor and halfway up the walls were covered by creosote, sage, and rocks that looked like they had been shoved up through the hard granite floor.

No one would ever find her. She was at the mercy of a madman, and she was so tired that she barely cared. He would probably kill her and leave her for the buzzards, but she didn't feel upset—she was numb.

He dismounted and came to her side to help her down. She had no strength to resist, but when he reached for her, she kicked him in the side. "Don't touch me!"

He grimaced and stepped back, his eyes cold.

"Those men didn't do anything to you! You killed them in cold blood! For nothing!"

"Not exactly for nothing," he said calmly, moving away to loosen his saddle cinch. "I needed a body to tack a note on so Younger would know where to come looking for you."

Her eyes opened wider in horror and disbelief. "You needed something to pin a note on, so you killed two men? Animal!" That one word was filled with such revulsion and hatred that Ward almost flinched under the searing contempt in her narrowed green eyes.

"Get down," he ordered curtly. There was a veiled threat in his controlled husky-quiet voice that scared her more than violence would have. She could feel her face draining of color. There was something infinitely terrifying in his cold blue eyes, as if he didn't care which way it went. He could kill her as easily as he had those men. Younger would still follow him, whether she was dead or alive.

"All right! Just don't touch me!" she said fiercely. She practically threw herself out of the saddle. She was in pain, and her anger, which was always formidable, was in full bloom. Unfortunately, her legs, which had been cramped and chilled for hours—she wasn't dressed for riding in the cold of an Arizona night—collapsed, and she fell headlong into the dirt.

"You're doing real fine," he drawled. "The cave is that direction." He started off with the other end of her rope in his hands, leading her and the horses, and she had to scramble to her feet and follow him before he dragged her or the horses stepped on her. She fell and hurt her knee and would have cried if he hadn't been there; as it was, she just glared with hatred at his damned back and stumbled ahead.

The sheer walls of the canyon were smooth, flesh-colored granite that looked like they had been carved by a glacier's passage. The cave, once she came to it, was much bigger inside than it looked from the outside. Leslie could imagine spiders, bats, and hairy black animals from the smells, but she was too weary to move, much less run. She leaned against the wall of the cave, dusty and panting from the exertion of climbing the hill from the canyon floor, her mouth dry and aching with thirst, but she wouldn't ask this madman for anything, even if she died right there.

He led them deep inside the mountain, paused, looked back, and then began to unsaddle their mounts. He spread the blankets on the floor of the cave, ignoring her, and she bored her hatred into his broad back, torn between refusing to lie on his blankets and refusing to let him intimidate her.

His tasks done for the moment, Ward poured water into a tin pan for each horse, then took a long drink out of the canteen and passed it to the girl. She looked like she might fling it back in his face, but common sense and thirst prevailed. She drank painfully and gave it back, watching him warily the whole time.

"What are you going to do with me?" she finally asked, her eyes staring stubbornly at the ground, refusing to meet his.

Ward stopped what he was doing long enough to really look at her. She was dressed in a formal riding habit that was probably all the rage in Boston for trotting sedately around the quad at the height of the social season. Now it hung in filthy tatters around her ankles where cactus and mesquite had torn the skirt in passing. Her face was coated with dust, but even dirty and disheveled, she retained a quality of ladylike refinement and beauty that both impressed and unnerved him.

He recalled what he had told Younger, but he realized that he was no longer capable of either violating her himself or allowing anyone else to do it. He didn't want to take his revenge on her personally, but he would not be turned from his purpose. He needed her as bait for Younger and those bastards who had slaughtered Mama Mendoza, Isabel, Pedro, and Grandpapa.

He couldn't name them without recalling the horror they must have endured before they died, and it was this memory that hardened his purpose and made his words harsher than they might have been.

"Nothing you can't handle," he said gruffly. He regretted his words as soon as they left his lips. It was suddenly very easy to see what was on her mind. He glanced from her terrified face to the blankets he had spread out on the floor of the cave. The thought of having to cope with a hysterical, screaming woman chilled his blood. He was too exhausted to be thinking very lucidly himself. He hadn't slept more than an hour at a time in days. He decided to ignore everything except the basics. He rummaged in his saddlebags until he found some beef jerky. "Here," he said, putting the coarse stick into her hand to distract her. "Eat this."

She took it tentatively and touched her tongue and lips to it. The smell seemed pleasant. She tried to bite into it. "Ow!" she grumped.

"Suck it. It'll last longer that way. So will your teeth."

Once she grew accustomed to it, the flavor melted into her mouth and was incredibly delicious, but the saltiness only reminded her how thirsty she was. She knelt on the hard earth to relieve her shaking legs. "Can I have some water?"

He passed her the canteen again and then lay down on the blankets, leaving a place beside him, which jarred her frazzled nerves. She watched with mounting uneasiness as her kidnapper arranged another blanket into a roll to serve as his pillow. "You'd better take advantage of this opportunity to sleep," he said, lying back.

Leslie refused to move from where she was even though she felt like an animal kneeling in the dirt with a rope around her neck. Sunlight was spreading into the cave, widening the wedge of brightness, so she knew that even though they were far back in the cave, they would be able to see clearly until after sunset. She shivered. The cave was chilled now and would probably stay cool enough throughout the day so that sleep would be possible. She desperately wanted to sleep, but she was not able to willingly lie down next to any man on a blanket with no chaperone within a hundred miles.

Ward sighed and stood up. He took her by the shoulders. She started to struggle against him, but he was far too strong for her. She heard herself moan in fear, and it was such a pitiful, wounded-creature sound that she clamped her teeth together.

"I don't have time for your foolishness. Now lie down. I don't give a damn whether you sleep or not, but if you know what's good for you, you'll lie real still so I can sleep." He measured out enough rope so she could lie down and then he tied the other end of the rope around his lean waist. His eyes closed and Leslie could see the tension slowly relaxing. In moments he was asleep. He had prudently placed his guns off to one side of the blankets so she couldn't reach them without waking him.

The cave was lit by reflected sunlight, so that its mouth, far above where they were, was bright and glaring. Down here the light was soft and muted. Too dim for painting, but she could study her captor at will. His broad chest rose and fell with his deep breathing.

She recognized him with a start. This was the cowboy who had tried to save her from falling during the parade, the same cowboy she had taunted from the hotel window. Knowing that, she was not so terrified by him, unless he was one of those mad-dog killers she had read about; but looking at him, at the lean, square-jawed handsomeness of his face and the tawny wheat-colored hair that had attracted her to him in that crowd, she could not believe he was a mad-dog killer. But why had he kidnapped her? Why had he killed those men?

He turned over onto his side, away from her, and Leslie sighed and lay down beside him. She was too exhausted to worry about all that now. She closed her eyes and huddled tiredly on her sliver of the blanket, careful not to touch him, until she slipped into a dreamless sleep that was like floating on the surface of a warm lake.

It seemed like only seconds had passed when she felt rough hands shake her awake. The cave, when she opened her eyes, was dark as a potful of black paint. She could see nothing, not even a dim outline, and she couldn't remember where she was or whom she was with.

CHAPTER THIRTEEN

"No, please, leave me alone," she groaned. "Let me sleep…"

"You'd better eat something. Last chance you'll have."

"Oh, no, please."

"Sit up. It's almost dawn. We're moving out." She struggled fitfully against his hard hands, turning to face the sound of his voice. Now he was a dark shape against the lightening cave. His strong hands lifted her into a sitting position, not unkindly, but any movement at all wrenched a groan from her. Every muscle felt torn. "All those hours in the saddle took a little of the starch out of you anyway," he said, and she thought she could hear amusement in his voice.

In the end, she ate the biscuits and jerky and sipped the water and was grateful for what she was able to choke down, because when they finished eating, they rode until the sun came up and then all that day with only a few stops to rest the horses. She felt like a squaw or a dog with the rope around her neck and a dead man's hat on her head. She was in pain, all over, and had given up hope of rescue. She had ridden the paths surrounding Wellesley. All the young ladies in her set rode, and she had imagined herself a good rider, but no more. Trying to keep up with a man who rode like an extension of his horse, effortlessly, hour after hour, never tiring, who didn't seem to need food or water, and barely noticed her, except when she slowed him down, was a nightmare…

Riding over dunes covered with blue sage, beneath sandstone cliffs that dwarfed the occasional gnarled trees, Leslie stole furtive glances at her captor when she could do so without being obvious. He was tall, with a lean, muscular form that explained why he was able to handle her so effortlessly. He had broad, tapering shoulders, narrow hips, and long legs that he used to control his horse. Awake, his lean, square jaw looked manly and resolute. He was clean-shaven in a land where every man wore either a beard or a handlebar mustache. He hadn't shaved today, but his beard stubble was so fair that it didn't darken his cheeks. He had eyes the same shade of blue as the noonday sky, a light azure that picked up the light and reflected it. He rarely spoke to her, but his eyes, which were by some miracle of birth highly expressive, telegraphed his moods. When she provoked him, his brows crowded his eyes, narrowing them into slits and cooling the vibrant color. When he was amused, she could see the merriment shimmering in the blue depths. When he lifted his hat to wipe his perspiring brow, his hair was the color of pale straw with steaks of silver that glinted in the sunlight. Its fairness contrasted handsomely with the burnt teak of his skin. Leslie gnashed her teeth, despising him all the more. If he were maimed and gnarled, his actions might have been excusable on the grounds that a lonely outcast deserved to avenge himself on a heartless, disregarding world, but this man had no such excuse for behaving as he did.

They rode interminably. Several times he dismounted to chip at the granite with a small axe. What was he doing? Certainly not marking a trail? She finally decided that whatever he was doing must have a meaning beyond her experience.

Anger and curiosity slowly turned to apathy under the relentless glare of the sun. It wasn't until they stopped for the night beside a wide shallow stream that wound its silent way through a rugged rock-strewn canyon that she found strength to speak. "I know you," she said, her voice hardly more than a hoarse whisper.

He merely glanced at her, lifting an expressive eyebrow as he tied her rope to the trunk of a slender tree. Leslie went on, "You're the one who caught my horse—during the parade."

Ward's hand instinctively moved up to rub the back of his head. "I won't do that again," he promised.

"Younger hit you," Leslie said hastily. "I tried to stop him. Is that why you're doing this?"

"No." Ward shook his head. "I have another matter to settle with Younger."

"What are you going to do with me?" she asked.

"Sell you to the Indians if you don't behave," he growled. Ignoring her gasp of outrage, he turned to his saddlebags. He took out a jar and tied the big stallion securely, then gentled him by rubbing his cheek against the horse's flank to distract the animal while his hands gently worked a gooey salve into a wound on the horse's flank. It occurred to Leslie, who knew a little about horses, that her captor was practically tying himself into a knot to accommodate his horse and spare the animal pain.

"I saw you climb in that wagon with that Mexican girl, too," she said, guardedly.

Ward turned to face her, smiling suddenly, as if the memory of that particular event pleased him. "Oh, yes, Maria," he said. "We have a date to meet each other next year."

"To do the same thing, no doubt," Leslie ventured, with her voice reflecting more than she meant it to.

"I hope not," Ward replied ruefully. Leslie lapsed into puzzled silence then, but she continued to watch her captor as he moved around their campsite. "What's your name?"

He turned and his eyes were amused and questioning, as if he were wondering at her motives. "Cantrell."

"Ward Cantrell!" she breathed.

"How did you know that?" he asked, frowning.

She smiled, enjoying his surprise. "You rob trains too, don't you?" she asked. Somehow, realizing he was the train robber brought an involuntary flush to her cheeks.

Ward turned to her again, amused. "Why is it I can't do anything without you being there?"

"I would just as soon have passed on this one," she said, shrugging a slender shoulder. Ward laughed but didn't reply. He knelt and rubbed his hands in the sand, using it like a rag to wipe off the smelly salve.

"On the train," Leslie couldn't help saying, "you had another Mexican girl at your side."

"Oh, yes." Ward nodded. "Belen."

Leslie lapsed into silence for a moment. She was remembering what someone on the train had said about his having a taste for only Mexican girls and not giving white girls a tumble. "Is it true?" she asked.

"Is what true?" Cantrell countered.

"That you love only Mexican girls?"

Ward was surprised into silence while he thought about it. "Where did you hear that?"

"Someone on the train said it," Leslie answered, waving her hand around. "Is it true?"

Ward was slow to answer. "Maybe," he said. "I never thought about it." He fed the horse and then took some cans out of his saddlebags.

By the time he handed her a tin plate with beans, bacon, and a dry biscuit on it, she took it without response, making him slant a suspicious look at her. She knelt in the dirt, eating absently, and he shook his head, marveling at what a good appetite she had for such a slender little thing.

Maybe it takes a lot of energy to feed that temper of hers, he thought. He finished eating, rinsed the utensils in the creek, packed them away, and started unbuckling his gunbelts. He laid them down, out of her reach by several feet, and then began to unbutton his shirt.

"What are you going to do?" she asked, fear clamping icy fingers around her throat in spite of the stifling heat from the setting sun. She had never been given to hysterics and despised girls who were, but her heart began to pound frightfully, and her stomach lurched in terror.

Ward didn't respond to her nervous question, suspecting coyness. He was going to take a bath, and he couldn't undress near the water, because he would be leaving his guns and clothes within her easy reach. And, he rationalized, it wasn't like Younger's woman would be seeing anything new.

He undressed as if he were alone, efficiently, matter-of-factly, unselfconsciously, until he was down to his thin cotton drawers, and even through her fear, or perhaps because of it, she was struck by the arrogant, smooth-muscled strength and masculinity in that sun-gold frame.

She had never seen a naked man, except on canvas, and only the Greeks had ever caught the lean, straight-limbed grace of line she now saw. The artist in her watched unashamed, as she would have viewed any new art form. In the light of a sinking sun, his skin was golden and rife with rippling power—more Herculean than Adonian with those muscular shoulders tapering into long, narrow sinews that were flat and smooth at his waist, lean and powerful in his long legs. Part of her rejoiced in the subjective pleasure of critical analysis, but the female in her was remembering, crazily, the face of the young Mexican girl who had come out of the wagon in Phoenix with him—that young, plaintive face, all dewy and adoring. But fear, that hard knot of heavy pain, filling her throat and chest, stifled even that wicked thought when he started to approach her.

She had been so dazed, watching him, that she was taken by surprise. He glanced at her, his eyes narrowed, and he froze for a second. Frowning, she watched him move slowly toward his gun. He scooped the revolver into his hand, crouching, and said, "Don't move."

"What?"

He pointed the gun at her, fired, and missed, but Leslie was on her feet, running, before he could aim again, completely forgetting the rope that was around her neck. She heard him yell, but she did not heed his cry. She raced away from him. At almost the same instant that the rope snapped taut he caught her arm, else she might have broken her neck.

"No!" she gasped, her voice barely more than a hoarse whisper. Her heart was pounding so hard she thought she would surely die. He turned her and shoved her back toward where she had been sitting. Leslie screamed and began to fight like a wild thing, but he forced her back to the blanket she had been kneeling on. "See that," he growled.

"Ohhh!" she gasped, recoiling from the sight of a broad, clumsy-looking lizard that was moving quickly away from the spot she had been sitting on. Its fat, stumpy tail was wagging from side to side as it hurried out of sight.

"I wasn't shooting at you," he said unnecessarily.

"Echhh!" she squealed. "What is that thing?"

"A Gila monster…"

She turned on him, furious. "Well, you could have told me! You almost scared me to death!"

"If I had politely engaged you in conversation first, he might have bitten you! Would you rather I scared hell out of you or he filled you with deadly venom?"

She jerked her arm out of his steely grip. "You're hurting me!"

"Well, dammit," he growled, "make up your mind what you want to fight about."

"Leave me alone," she whimpered.

He dragged in a furious breath, but the fury was only partly at her. He was blaming himself for almost getting her killed. When he had seen the giant lizard waddling toward her, he had realized the full extent of how he had interfered in her life. If she had died, her blood would have been on his hands. But the danger was past, and he was in no mood to let her out of his sight again. He picked her up and carried her to the water.

"What are you doing? Put me down!"

"I'm giving you a chance to cool off before you bust something." He put her on her feet in the knee-deep water.

"Ohhh!" she gasped, preparing to strike out at him or bolt again. To forestall the eventuality, he pushed her down and straddled her body. To silence her, he pushed her head under the water and brought it up. "Shut up or I'll drown you." She sputtered and he prepared to dunk her again.

"You understand?" he asked. She coughed and sputtered and slowly stopped struggling. "I'm here to take a bath," he said grimly. "Get your clothes off. They're all wet anyway. You might as well have a real bath too." Her eyes filled with terror. "You going to behave yourself?" he asked, shaking her.

His knees were on either side of her breasts, and she could feel his manhood against her belly with only the cotton drawers to contain it. She would have agreed to anything to get out of that position. She nodded and his hand left her face. "Get your clothes off," he growled.

"I…I…won't," she stammered, looking like she was going to cry. She might be a little doxie, he thought, but she looked like a frightened sea nymph with her hair still dripping around her face and shoulders. He wondered what the hell she thought he could do to her that Younger hadn't already done.

He shrugged. "Suit yourself. I can cut them off, but then you won't have anything to ride in, will you?"

Leslie bit back a groan. He left her to go back for soap, and she staggered to her feet, her skirt hanging like lead around her. She stood there uncertainly, not knowing what to do, but she felt the cold silky water on her legs, and suddenly she didn't care what he did. She wanted a real bath. Besides, he would do what he wanted anyway. She might as well resign herself to her fate. If it wasn't him, it would be Dallas Younger. She realized she was no longer in control of her life. Her control had been an illusion only. Either Younger or Cantrell would take her before the week was out. She had become some sort of prize, to be fought over and won. She shivered and was unable to tell whether it was from her thoughts or from feeling the cold water against her calves. She decided that she might as well do what she wanted.

Ward saw her begin to comply and couldn't believe it. Only a second ago she had looked like a cornered bobcat—ready to take his eyes out— now she was undressing as if she were there alone. He would never understand the female mind.

She took off the cumbersome riding habit and left it to soak in the shallow water. Now, wearing only a lacy, ruffled chemise and slip that was of fine textured material, she removed her shoes and poured the water out of them before she tossed them onto the bank with a look of disgust that told him he had probably ruined the fine leather. She refused to remove the chemise and slip, but when she turned back and began to wash herself, the water soaked through the thin fabric and it became so transparent that it conveniently disappeared. Her firm young body took his breath away—hard pink nipples darkened the tips of crazily tilted, cone-shaped breasts, pointing straight up as if begging to be kissed. The provocative underswell fairly called out to his hands to cup the tender whiteness. Her waist was firm and slim, flaring gently into sweetly curved buttocks and graceful legs. The skin he could see was like creamy white carnation petals. She was a brunette with skin like a blond—no visible body hair.

She washed herself, oblivious to his admiring appraisal. She seemed satisfied that she had maintained her modesty, and he smiled, knowing she would be mortified if she knew how useless her protective garment had become. He sighed, appreciating her rich female gracefulness while she basked in girlish self-absorption. Completely unnerved, he held out the soap.

She took it and lathered herself all over with it, reaching under her chemise and slip, glaring at him until he turned his back. The water was cold, but it felt better than anything she had ever felt. Her spirits were immediately lifted. She hated being dirty and hot; she hated having a rope around her neck; she hated him, but since she had no choice, she decided to make the best of it. Why not? She'd never been given to brooding or depression. She despised girls who cried all the time.

"What are you up to now?" Ward asked, scowling at the way she seemed to have adjusted. Leslie turned wide green eyes on him, looking over her slender white shoulder; the sweet curve of her back and buttocks tempting him.

"Whatever do you mean?"

"Why are you cooperating?"

"Because I wanted a bath. It was a good idea, even if it comes from a rotten animal like you."

He grinned then, his straight white teeth like a flash of summer lightning. He had the most soulful eyes she had ever seen. She could read volumes in them, but now she just wanted to put them in her pocket, after she had ripped them out.

"Do you just change like that?" he asked, snapping his fingers. "If it pleases you?"

"Of course. I do exactly what pleases me. Why shouldn't I?" she asked, tossing the long black mass of tangled wet curls.

Jesus! he thought. In that second, with her pretty chin up and green sparks shooting out of her eyes, she looked like a brunette version of Jenn. He could almost hear his sister's sultry, haughty voice as she explained to him eight years ago that she didn't fall in love with all her lovers. Very modern. Very independent. Just like this little white-skinned, sweet-curving female who had probably survived a lot more than most women twice her age. Younger was rough stuff. Ward could hardly recognize his own voice when he finally spoke.

CHAPTER FOURTEEN

"You're pretty cocky for such a slender little thing."

The tone of his husky voice set off a small pulse in her throat, and her voice was strangely whispery. "Look who's talking."

He grinned in spite of himself. "I'm not cocky."

"You do exactly as you please," she corrected, feeling a jolt of strange energy and visualizing herself at the front of a passenger coach, holding a gun on the startled passengers while he moved up the aisles relieving them of their guns. Her cheeks flushed with heat, and she said the meanest thing she could think of. "I'm sure all men rob trains and kidnap women."

He lifted an eyebrow in a gesture that told her she had won that round, and they both fell silent. Almost in unison they turned their backs and began to wash seriously.

She finished as quickly as she could and then began to scrub the soggy garment she had worn for two days, trying to wash the grime off it. It was torn in dozens of places.

"Think I could use the soap?" he asked.

She glanced up and was instantly sorry that she had. He was facing her, standing over her, and his wet drawers concealed nothing from her startled gaze. She turned her head away and held out her hand with the soap in it. She felt his warm hand close around the soap, brushing her skin. Without looking up again, she wrung the water out of her garment, then waded out of the stream and spread her clothes on the mesquite bushes.

By the time Cantrell came out of the creek and pulled his trousers on, she was settled in the middle of their bedroll in her wet chemise and slip, admiring the colorful sunset. Red, gold, and purple clouds swaggered like flamboyant galleons sailing above the western horizon. Off in the distance, beyond the trees that grew along the slender creek, she could see a black tableland rising up to the horizon, its outline spikey with slender, pointed trees that she guessed were either pine or spruce. The setting sun bathed the foreground in heavy gold glamour, intensifying the contrast. She longed for the tools to capture that marvelous natural display.

One of the horses snorted and stamped, and she sighed, remembering that she wasn't there to marvel at natural phenomena. She was concerned now with survival, and suddenly it pleased her that it wasn't the same dreary type of survival her friends at school had talked about. This was real life-and-death, trial-by-fire survival. "I suppose you intend to sell me to the Indians," she said, remembering his earlier remark.

His eyes widened momentarily. Then a smile flickered in the blue depths. "They aren't as uninformed as you might think. Besides, there are laws about taking advantage of them."

"What *are* you going to do with me? Why am I here?"

"Don't ask so damned many questions," he said, his forehead puckered with his displeasure. Angered, she stood up, and he noticed she had taken the rope off. It lay beside the blanket. "You little hellcat. How did you get that off?"

She shrugged. "It wasn't so hard," she said defiantly.

"Where do you think you're going?" he said to her back as she turned and strolled away. There was no urgency in his question, because he was too distracted by the sight of her firm rounded buttocks beneath the wet, clinging fabric. He was already hard from the ordeal of bathing next to her. It might not be such a bad idea to bed Younger's woman after all. Anyone who could put up with Younger would not be injured too badly by anything he could do to her.

"I'm going to the powder room," she said, the lift of her chin haughty.

"Stay close by," he growled.

"I will not!" she said, horrified by the thought of his hearing or seeing her while she was so intimately engaged.

"Might want to look where you're going," he said dryly.

She turned, and her look of defiance turned into fear. The animal in front of her, a small ground squirrel, stood up in alarm on its hind legs, and she stopped, her heart pounding frightfully. Then, before she could move, a large bird, its wings spread wide in flight, swooped down and caught the squirrel in its talons. Leslie was looking into its eyes at the instant it realized its doom, and she felt the hopelessness and dread of the small animal transmitted to her. But worse than that, the look in the bird's eyes, so matter-of-fact and efficient that it stunned her, reminded her of Cantrell. Before she could react, the bird flew away with its kill, and Leslie turned her back and began, quite unexpectedly, to cry.

She sat down in the dirt, sobbing, and she did not know whether it was from the frightening ordeal she had managed to endure or for the poor little squirrel.

Ward watched her for several moments; then he walked over and lifted her to her feet. Leslie allowed herself to be pulled up into his arms. He held her close, stroking her head while she cried, and it was strangely comforting to her. Partly because she knew it would be harder for him to mistreat her in the future if she could soften his heart toward her now, however momentarily.

Leslie pressed against Ward shamelessly, feigning complete unawareness of their intimacy. Unfortunately, he was using her collapse to his advantage as well. His warm hand caressed her spine and moved down her waist to press her hips against his. She felt the bulge of his manhood through his trousers. Remembering the way it had looked through that transparent cloth—she felt strangely unable to assert herself against him. She was suddenly recalling what one of the girls at school told her—that a man's member had a bone in it. But it hadn't looked that way at all. It had looked soft, almost touchable, she thought, flushing at the wickedness of her thoughts. But now, strangely, it felt bony against her belly. His warm hand came up to touch her face, brush her lips.

"What are you doing?" she asked nervously.

"I think I'm going to kiss you."

Startled, she searched his handsome face for some sign. She knew that she could not allow him to take even a small liberty—her position was too vulnerable—but she was incapable of resisting. Her heart leaped into a hard, fast rhythm that made her feel breathless. Before she could think of a reply, his warm fingers lifted her chin, and he lowered his head. The pulse under her chin leaped. She felt flooded with weakness. His soft lips brushed hers, and her legs went rubbery. She wanted to protest, but nothing about her seemed to be working.

After that first tentative kiss, his embrace tightened.

"Open your mouth," he whispered.

For some reason that she could not imagine, her lips parted in response. This time when his lips covered hers, his tongue darted into her mouth, causing a warm ache in her belly.

"Put your arms around my neck," he murmured against her cheek. She moaned, but her arms obeyed him. This time when he kissed her his tongue explored her mouth, and his warm hand slid again to her cheek, then down to her breast.

"No, please," she whispered, feeling new fear.

His hand moved to her back and burned into the trembling flesh there as it caressed her again, moving from the curve of her spine to her shoulder and then around to her breast. His fingers teased the hard little nipple, and she cried out, but he only pulled her closer against him and deepened his probing kiss. Now, much to her amazement, her knees buckled.

"Here, lie down," she heard him say, lifting her to carry her back to the blanket.

"No...please," she whispered.

"Hush. You don't know what you want."

Now she was lying on the blanket with the scratchy wool against her back and him welded to her front. His lips abandoned hers to explore the sweep of her neck and the rosy tips of her firm little cone-shaped breasts. His wet tongue traced imaginary circles around the swollen nipples until she shuddered and cried out. His warm hand nudged her legs open and brushed softly against the sensitive inner thigh. He pulled the cloth of her pantalets aside, and his fingers tried to slip inside. "No, please..." she moaned.

His lips stopped her protests. One hand squeezed and kneaded her breasts while the other hand strayed back between her legs. She shuddered again, but this time, her treacherous body arched against him, seeking his hands.

He sighed against her cheek. "That's right, love, hold me tight." His hand deftly undid the buttons on his trousers. Leslie knew what he was doing, but part of her seemed aloof from that knowledge. His fingers slipped inside her pantalets and brushed through the tight curls between her legs; one probing finger insinuated itself inside her, and his warm, smooth shocking member was nudging at her, ready to follow it.

Out of curiosity she had lain still under his ministrations, but now she knew she could no longer convince herself that all was well. Her kidnapper was about to do the unthinkable.

"No!" she cried, beginning to struggle in earnest. She pressed her thighs tightly closed, barring his entry.

"Easy, hellcat! Settle down," he whispered, reclaiming her mouth. He kissed her long and hard, ignoring her struggles to stop him, until they were both breathless. When he had reduced her to quivering helplessness, his head moved lower to tease the sensitive inner thighs. Even in the state she was in, burning with unaccustomed desire, she felt alarm bells ringing in her head. But part of her wanted to know. Part of her wanted to experience everything that a man like this could or would do to a woman. Part of her was sick of wondering what it was men did to women that they wouldn't talk about. But her terror was too great. Gasping with fear and the effort it took to make herself stop him, she caught him by the hair and dragged his head up.

"Ow!" he yelped. "Dammit."

"Well, don't do that!"

"Little hypocrite," he growled, taking in the glazed look of desire that she couldn't hide. "You know you want it."

Her cheeks flushed scarlet. His piercing blue eyes seared into her, confirming his words; then slowly his mouth reclaimed her own, and she felt herself relaxing. His tongue claimed her mouth while his deft hands relieved her of the wet garments.

"No! Please, no!" she moaned, feeling like a hypocrite but unable to stop the instinctive plea.

"Hush, relax," he urged, gentling her.

"No, please," she whimpered.

"You would never forgive me if I believed you, you little liar," he growled against her throat. His mouth closed around her dark rose nipple, torturing it while his hand stripped the soggy chemise and pantalets away from her body. "You're beautiful, little one," he whispered. "It's no wonder Younger is so eager to have you back."

She groaned, but even as she did her body arched into his, betraying her with its neediness. She decided in that instant that perhaps he was right. She was on fire. Why should she deprive herself of the delicious promise that shimmered in his touch? Her fate was sealed in any case. Either this man would take her and have his way with her, or Dallas Younger would. And Younger's touch truly filled her with revulsion.

Ward leaned away from her, his hands caressing her. He would have liked to spend hours caressing her soft skin, but her artless movements had stirred his own passions to the breaking point. He opened her legs and guided himself into the narrow sheath there. She cried out and her eyes flew open, and they were as startled as a doe confronted by a grizzly. He thrust into her, and a scalding pain wrenched a gasping cry from her lips.

Shocked, he closed her eyes with his lips and concentrated on kissing her lips and then her breasts until she began to relax. Then, slowly, gradually, he began to move again, his male weapon creating friction against her most intimate surfaces. Her hands clutched at his broad back, wanting him closer. She was filled with tautness and an indescribable need that was becoming intolerable, until his body, sturdy and lean against her own, stiffened suddenly, and she hung suspended for a moment on a wave of aching breathlessness. Unexpectedly, he withdrew.

She cried out and threw her head back, her body arching frantically to find him again. Groaning, he shoved three fingers into her, and the terrible tension inside her exploded into gasping heat and bonelessness.

He rolled over and pulled her on top of him, breathing as if he had run for miles. Her own breathing was as labored as his. Limp and exhausted, she closed her eyes and just floated in the warm aftermath. She had no idea how long they lay like that. When she opened her eyes it was dark overhead, bright at the horizon. The moon shimmered on the water, streaking it with brightness. A coyote howled in the distance.

CHAPTER FIFTEEN

"I thought you were Younger's woman."

"I'm nobody's woman. I belong to me."

"You're damned cynical for a girl."

"Maybe I just sound cynical because I've never been…been…"

He chuckled softly. "You'll get used to it."

How could he sound so cruel? Only moments ago he had been warmth and ecstasy; now he was turning her roughly to tie her hands behind her back. She struggled against him, but it was useless. "What are you doing?" she hissed.

"Just making sure you'll be here when I get back."

Real terror darkened her lime-green eyes, and Ward leaned down and took her face between his hands. "You'll be safe here. Just keep quiet and be still and you won't attract anything you can't handle."

Her skin under his hands was soft as silk and sheened with a fine mist of perspiration from their lovemaking. Her lips were soft and full, and he couldn't resist tasting them again. She moaned a soft protest and clamped her lips shut, to cheat him of any pleasure.

He continued kissing her, and she continued stubbornly to resist, until suddenly, without warning, his thumb moved into her mouth, forcing her lips apart. She squirmed and cried out, realizing too late that she had made a mistake. With one thumb jammed between her jaws, his hot lips reclaimed her own. Now his tongue jabbed into her mouth, dueling with hers until her anger and outrage diminished, overcome by her body's unmistakable response. A wave of heat washed into her, and she felt her mouth go slack beneath his searching lips. She wanted to keep fighting him, but there was something dizzying about being so completely helpless and open to him. So aware of his rough thumb in her mouth, so aware of his tongue and lips ravaging her mouth. Tremors shook her body. His warm hand moved down to cup her breast. His fingers played with the taut, swollen nipple and a heartbeat started in that secret place between her legs. She moaned in the back of her throat, and her body went limp.

"Oh, Jesus," he groaned. He sat up abruptly and ran his fingers through his hair. "If Younger had planned this, he couldn't have done a better job..."

"What?..." Her body was crying out for the feel of his tender-harsh hands; only her anger that he was leaving her on the desert, tied up, kept her from straining toward him.

"Go to sleep," he growled, uncoiling in one lithe movement to stand over her. With the set sun and a sky full of fiery red and gold clouds at his back she could not read his expression. She started to question him, but anticipating as much, he stuffed his handkerchief into her mouth and tied it securely. He bound her feet and she watched through wrathful, spitting green eyes as he pulled on his clothes and buckled his gunbelt around his narrow hips, his eyes already remote and engrossed with the plan she could see had replaced everything else for him. Damn him!

It wasn't until all the daylight had faded and night was reality that she realized the precariousness of her position. Maybe the next face she would see would be an Indian's! Worse yet, maybe he didn't intend to come back for her. Maybe she would be left there to die, helpless, naked, alone, with only the desert creatures to keep her company— the scorpions, snakes, Gila monsters, spiders...She shuddered. And only one thin blanket over her. She had heard her uncle and his riders talking about the deadly inhabitants. Now all those names she had forgotten were there—like nightmare creatures—all the worse because she did not know what any of them looked like. Or which was the most deadly...

Would an Arizona spider be worse than a scorpion? Or a snake? She shuddered at memory of that enormous Gila monster that had waddled off, wagging its fat, blunt tail. Did it take large bites out of a person? Or inject venom? She had visions of being eaten alive one bite at a time by monsters of such ugliness that her mind veered off into numbness.

Stop it, fool! Even if it is true, it serves no purpose. But by midnight, when the cooling ground was alive with crawly things that had eyes that seemed to glow in the inky darkness, she finally gave way to her terror, crying like a small child, and none of her bravery helped in the least.

• • • •

Dallas Younger woke up first and knew even before he opened his eyes that something was wrong. He lay there, still warm in his blankets, listening to the shriek of the birds, feeling the sun on his face, and his black brows knit into a frown in his handsome, sensual face. He sat up abruptly and looked around at the camp. The fire had died to cold ashes; men still slept in their blankets. *Why the hell hadn't the night guards woke them at sunrise?* He came to his feet, pulled on his boots, roaring for his men to get the hell up.

A piece of white caught his eye, a note torn from butcher paper and slipped around one of the buttons on his shirt. Growling, he ripped it off his shirt and read it with his mouth dropping open. It was written in the same hand as the note on Caswell two days ago:

> Younger, this is where I'm going to put a bullet. Keep a close eye on your belly. Cantrell

"Where are those goddamned sentries?" he bellowed, paling perceptibly. Cass Ewell, who had walked out a distance to relieve himself, hollered, "Over here!"

Emmet Wilson, one of the two who had been charged with first watch, was dead—his throat cut from ear to ear. They found the other guard less than fifty feet away, probably lured out by some sound, maybe even Wilson's dying.

"Stupid bastards—serves them right for being so damned careless!" Younger snarled. "Saddle up! Then spread out and find his trail. I want that bastard! When I get my hands on him he's going to be praying for death a long time before he gets his wish!"

Ward Cantrell left his horse at the stream, took off the saddle, tied the horse securely next to the girl's mount, and then moved as silently as an Indian over to the blankets. He slipped off his boots, lay back with a sigh, and heard a soft, muffled sob that caused him to look sharply at the figure huddled next to him.

"Hey, you all right?" he whispered, reaching out to smooth her hair out of her eyes. Her face was wet with tears and felt cold and clammy under his hand. Christ! Now what? He untied the gag and then her hands and feet and took the silent crying girl into his arms. He'd thought she would be sound asleep—not crying like an orphan left to die somewhere.

"Hey, what happened? Did something scare you?" Jesus. She was cold as death all over.

"Hey, are you all right? You're all right. Just scared," he whispered, brushing at her face gently. But she only shivered uncontrollably and huddled her slim body against him, trembling. In the moonlight, which now silvered the sheer walls of the canyon, her face was like wet marble and as cold. He lowered his head and pressed warm lips against her cheek, brushing tears away with his warm hands.

"Hey, don't cry. Everything is all right. You're okay Nothing bad is going to happen to you." But he could see she wasn't responding. Tears kept spilling down her cheeks, and she was shivering like she'd taken a chill.

"Did something bite you, a snake or something?" She didn't respond, just kept crying as if he weren't there. He pulled the blankets back and inspected her all over to be sure, but there were no signs of injury, no swellings or bumps anywhere. He took his clothes off and pulled her back into his arms to share his body heat. Even without the blanket he was warm. Her cold body felt good against his, and it seemed natural to slip inside her and begin moving slowly. And just as natural to kiss her wet face and then her cold lips until he felt them become warm and responsive. He continued the gentle rocking motion until he felt her beginning to relax, her cold limbs becoming warm and pliant instead of cold and stiff.

Leslie woke with a strange headache that lasted until noon and finally receded. She ate whatever he gave her that day, did what he told her to do almost like a mechanical doll. She felt strangely bemused and confused but grateful he didn't keep the rope around her neck. By the time they had stopped for the night she was exhausted but almost back to normal emotionally. She looked at him strangely then, as if she were trying to remember something. She had a vague recollection of a nightmare filled with nameless terror and then nameless, faceless comfort. Had she dreamed it or had he made love to her again—for a long time, gently, with warm kisses and soft murmurings?

She couldn't tell by his actions today. He was remote, cool, efficient—the same as before. If he had comforted her, if she had needed comfort, neither one of them seemed willing or able to talk about it. Maybe it had been merely a nightmare.

She couldn't tell anything from his reactions. His clean-shaven face was as impassive and stoic as any Indian she could ever imagine. She would like to know, but she couldn't imagine asking him about it, and they were still traveling too fast for conversation.

The land was no longer level. They rode through hills now—small hills and great rolling hills, through wild canyons, basins, and valleys, sometimes crossing narrow streams. The land was still gray and brown, still strewn with rocks and cactuses and small tufts of grass—the very same type of land as before but turned on end, receding off into ominous-looking mountains. Sometimes she saw live things, but she had no idea what they were—just small slithery things. One second they blended into their surroundings, into the rocks they sat on; the next they slithered away—disgusting!

CHAPTER SIXTEEN

They made camp this time next to a dry stream bed, and Leslie watched Ward take a shovel from his assortment of packs and begin to dig until water, murky and sluggish, bubbled up.

"How did you know there would be water there?"

"Guessed." He built a small fire, opened a can of beans, and heated water for coffee. He moved deftly and with an economy of motion that Leslie found fascinating. The artist in her saw him as one of the simple rustics used by so many painters, herself included, to enhance a landscape. She leaned back on her elbows, her legs stretched out in front of her, covered by her tattered gray riding gown, and amused herself by planning a landscape with the simple pots and pans, the brown of Cantrell's clothes, the yellowed desert sands, the orange glow of the small crackling fire, the blue sky turning fiery red and purple as the sun lit the clouds from underneath. She could use bravura brushstrokes for the sky and clouds, but she would need a finer brush to capture the unexpected refinement of feature she saw in this bandit: the thick, curling, honey-colored lashes fringing his fine blue eyes, the rich smoothness of his lips, the handsome angles of his face…In this light she would use ocher to simulate teak for the symmetrical sweep of his dark arms, where muscles swelled and tapered with masculine strength and competence. She would have to balance the fiery, evanescent sky against the dark and warm tonality of the man.

Art was her first love, and no matter how much she might personally despise Cantrell, she could not help framing him in various poses. He had a lithe, striking form. With his tawny, flaxen hair and his azure blue eyes, set in a warm, sun-bronzed face, he would tempt any painter. The artist in her did not need to judge his personal worth. He would serve as a decoration, a mannequin only.

She felt very superior thinking her fluid, lofty thoughts, denying his manhood in the bargain, but she soon tired of her diversion. After they ate he used one of the tin pans and washed from his waist up, then shaved, scraping the red-gold stubble off his lean face with a wicked-looking blade he carried in a sheath behind his gun. She had never watched a man at his toilet before and found this fascinating. She forgot that she hated him and that he was a killer and began asking questions.

"How long have you been a train robber?"

He glanced at her, his face darkened with a scowl. "Three, four years," he finally said.

"What happened to your girlfriend? The one on the train?"

He grinned, remembering that little Belen had gone back to Mexico in a fit of temper brought on by her jealousy during the train robbery. "You two didn't exactly hit it off," he said, ignoring her question.

"What did you do before? You haven't always been a train robber, have you?"

He chuckled. "Seems like I have." He sighed and put down the razor. He rinsed his face. He'd been a hunted outlaw for six years, doing whatever he had to do to survive and little else. The world was full of people who could spot a fugitive on sight. Honest work was damned hard to come by. The closest thing he'd had to a legitimate job was when he worked for the Que Ti Qua Ranch, enforcing Colonel Goodnight's Winchester Quarantine to keep fever-bearing herds of longhorns from crossing the Texas panhandle. Mostly that had involved riding from point A to point B, armed to the teeth, looking dangerous enough to discourage trespassing, and occasionally leading a herd down a designated trail to avoid contaminating the local stock. It hadn't been legal, but the law had deliberately ignored the activity because it successfully protected the ranchers in the panhandle…

"Hey, remember me?"

Ward grunted. "What the hell are you doing? Writing an article?"

"I'm here at your insistence, not my own, and I'm bored. You don't need to be ashamed of your past. There's no way you could impress me."

The look he gave her was one of bitterness. "What do you want to hear? That I'm lower than a mineshaft? Well, I am. I rode with the Jackson Hole Gang in Wyoming, fought with McSween in the Lincoln County range wars, enforced illegal quarantines. Rob the T and P at least once a month. I do whatever pays the best until it stops paying, then I move on."

"So who's paying you to kidnap me?"

"Once in a great while I do charity work," he said grimly.

"Charity work! If this is your idea of benevolence…" She was speechless. Finally recovering, she asked, "Is there nothing too low for you?"

"I don't dig post holes," he said, grinning suddenly.

"You mean you don't do anything that consists of honest toil." She shook her head and the wind picked up tendrils of her dark hair and fanned it over her face. She brushed it back with a slender hand. "I despise men who can't do anything useful. Being an outlaw is another way of avoiding responsibility, or not doing the drudgery that each one of us has to do for survival."

Ward laughed. "You look like you know a lot about drudgery. Your smooth, white hands have never pushed a plow."

Leslie flushed. There was too much truth in his words. She decided to change the subject. "Is that El Paso accent of yours real?"

"It's real enough, I guess."

"You must have attended school somewhere. Did you graduate?"

Now he picked up the rag he had been using as a towel and wiped his face. "I almost graduated from Harvard, but I was expelled three months before," he said, grinning, because he knew she wouldn't believe the truth.

"I suppose there are ways you could have heard of Harvard... Where did you really go to school?"

"Long Branch Saloon, class of '82." There was a kernel of truth in his words. His career as an outlaw had started in the street in front of the Long Branch in Dodge City six years ago...

"Ahhh," she sighed. "It suits you somehow."

"So does your outfit."

She looked down at her torn riding habit and back up at him in surprise. "What?"

"You're the kind of woman who can inspire a man to rip the clothes off her back." His eyes narrowed, and she saw muscles in his cheek bunch and writhe. "It's almost dark, little one. Come here," he said, tossing the rag away from him.

She swallowed and her frosty lime-green eyes widened. She could feel her heart thumping heavily in her chest, much faster than it should, and fought to control the fear, or whatever, that was causing her distress. She instinctively backed away from him, scooting off the blanket. She did not want a repeat of what had happened last night. She could not explain what had happened to her in his arms. It defied logic and reason as she knew it. A stranger had taken over her body, some dark demon-creature that knew nothing of traditional morality, personal pride, integrity.

Now, sitting tensely before this man she had hated, this man who had killed innocent men and forced himself on her, she felt breathless.

She swallowed and flushed and looked away from the sharp light in his piercing blue eyes. She stood up, either from nervousness or in preparation to bolt, and he took a step toward her.

"If you run I will put the rope back around your neck. If I put it on again, it stays." His voice was quiet and unemotional, but she knew he meant it.

He was too close to her. Too close. Leslie licked her lips, and for the second time since he had taken her, he saw tears sparkle in her eyes. She had eloquent eyes, and now he could read her torment plainly. She was almost too direct; it would be impossible for her to lie successfully.

"That's not fair," she whispered, turning her back.

"Kidnapping is inherently unfair," he said softly, moving to stand before her, so close she could feel the threatening warmth of his body. "It won't do you any good to run or fight," he said softly, coaxingly. "It'll just make it harder on you."

Leslie heard him with relief. At last! Something she could recognize in all that vague and fearful confusion. She turned defiantly, her eyes flashing. "I should be like you? Do whatever is easiest? Most convenient? Well, I'm dreadfully sorry, Mr. Gunfighter, Mr. Train Robber, Mr. Kidnapper, but I can't take the easy way out just because it might save me some pain or inconvenience. I have integrity, and I'm going to fight you, because not to fight would fill me with shame, and I can abide anything except that."

Ward reached out and touched her cheek, and, amazingly, she didn't draw back. Then she closed her eyes, as if from weakness, and he could feel her pulse begin beating wildly. Trembling started in her stomach, near her spine. He was so close she could feel the heat from his body.

"Please," she whispered.

Ward saw and understood—not completely or with definition, but at a more fundamental level. He felt a sudden resentment. He should teach her a lesson, all about lust and hypocrisy, but she was too vulnerable. Most females had no well-thought-out philosophy. If you took away their belief or their habit of obedience, they were adrift in a rudderless ship on a vast, bewildering sea.

He wanted her, but not enough to risk being responsible for her downfall. She reminded him of too many things he'd thought he had left behind. This girl with skin like satin represented all that he had fled eight years ago.

"Don't bother to run. I'm not in the mood for war." He caught her arms and dragged her over to the blankets. She began to fight against him, but he was incredibly strong. He tied her hands behind her, gagged her to stop her outraged cries, and then tied her feet while she glared with hate over her shoulder at him. When she was trussed up like a Christmas package, he lay down beside her and began to stroke and caress the smooth curve of her slender back. He smoothed the hair off her face and felt her become still, watchful, under his hand. He knew what she expected. Why disappoint her? He lowered his head and kissed her throat and the firm swell of her breast. There was enough cruelty in him to enjoy the shudder of fear that rippled through her.

It cost him something to leave her—to relinquish that satiny warmth—but he covered it well. "Sorry I can't stay with you, but I'll be back soon. You'll be safe. I wouldn't leave you if there was any real danger." He covered her and left, and it was full dark before her anger left her to be replaced by uncontrollable terror.

Dallas Younger posted three guards for his remaining seven men to sleep in peace. They didn't expect a visit tonight. No one would dare pull a stunt like that two nights in a row.

"Harris, Leonard, Sanders, you got first watch, and I don't want any fallin' asleep, you hear? You keep moving and keep an eye on each other. Anything out of the ordinary and you call out, you hear?"

"Gotcha, boss."

"Right!"

"Hell yes!"

"Keep in plain sight of each other so's there can't be any slip-ups!" Younger warned.

It was almost midnight, with chill winds moaning out of the hills, when a bank of slow-moving clouds obscured the almost-full moon that had arced overhead. Sanders, who had walked out the farthest from the campfire, heard the tiniest sound, whirled around, ready to cry out, and felt his nose and mouth covered by a hand with the grip of steel.

Neither Harris nor Leonard saw Sanders drop. Harris had reached down to pick up a billet of wood. He did that every time his path crossed one. It paid off. No one ever had to make a special trip looking for twigs and branches when he was around. He had mentioned what a good idea this was to the other two, but they never paid any attention to anything. He straightened and searched out his two comrades, exactly as he was supposed to do.

He saw Sanders straighten up, adjusting his rifle to carry it more comfortably, and continue the arc he had been making from the fire out to the east and then back toward the horses, then to the fire again. Sanders was too damned predictable to be a good sentry! That's the first kind a mad-dog killer like that Cantrell would go after! Himself, he just did something different every time. He wasn't taking any chances on getting his throat cut!

Harris adjusted his armload of firewood and watched with tight-mouthed disapproval as Sanders lit a cigarette and Leonard, who was always out of tobacco, walked over to join him. Harris was of half a mind to wake Younger and tell him they were messing up! Damn them! They couldn't even obey a simple directive! Harris was an old army man himself, until he had been found guilty of rape and murder. But it wasn't his fault. He hadn't known they counted those filthy squaws as people. They should warn a man—not just decide to hang him for one lousy mistake. He'd done the only thing he could have done under the circumstances, and that was to kill three guards and escape. He still couldn't figure out what all the fuss had been about. He'd been a good soldier—damned good! The girl had only been an Indian! A damned Crow, at that! Wasn't worth a damn! Certainly wasn't worth a good soldier's life!

Those damned clouds covered the moon again, and Harris couldn't decide if he should risk getting Dallas Younger awake and all hot under the collar about the way Sanders and Leonard were messing up, probably getting together to nip on the bottle Leonard always kept hidden!

They were still out there together. Probably getting drunk! He should wake Younger, but he was hell on men when he was mad, and he hated being waked up in the middle of the night. And everything did look all right. Harris saw Sanders coming toward him, and he could tell he'd been right about the bottle. Good thing he hadn't gotten Younger up—they had decided to share with him!

The man he thought was Sanders took a full swig of the whiskey and passed him the bottle. Harris tilted his head back, and let the fiery liquor burn a warm trail down to his stomach.

"That hit the spot!" he said gratefully, passing the bottle back. He adjusted his armload of billets carefully.

Sanders tucked the bottle into his hip pocket; Harris turned to resume his path back to the fire with his billets and found himself caught in a vise of steel, his mouth and his nose clamped shut. He clawed for his gun and felt a white-hot pain at his throat—the last memory he would ever have.

Man and wood crumpled to the ground, and Cantrell slipped noiselessly to the sleeping forms scattered around the campfire. He searched each sleeping face until he found Younger, bent down and pinned a note, which he had written while it was still light, onto Younger's shirt, and then slipped back into the night.

Seven down. Seven to go. Then Younger.

With difficulty Ward Cantrell found the place he had left the girl. There was no stream to follow tonight and no moonlight now to help him. It surprised him that he felt such urgency to get back to her. He knew she was safe there. He had spent years sleeping in the desert, mountains, plains, and nothing had ever threatened him, except an occasional flea or tick. She was probably crying again, and it gnawed at him, making him impatient with himself, but he had no choice.

His decision had been made for him days ago. He would abide by it even if it meant his own death. The men who could do what he had seen at that small farm, to unarmed women, an old man, and a boy, deserved to die. He would kill them without pity or mercy. He felt no guilt—no more than if he had killed a rabid skunk. The only requirement he had was that they be awake and that Younger, who had led the raid, know what was coming so he could sweat about it. It was too bad the girl got hurt, but she couldn't be allowed to change anything.

He found her and his camp when he was almost ready to give up and wait for morning. If her horse hadn't whinnied, he would have missed them altogether. She was ice cold and completely unresponsive. He quickly untied her, undressed her and himself, and held her as close as he could, kissing her face, her eyes, her mouth, until he felt her begin to respond.

Any remorse he had would be not for the men he had killed but for this slender female who trembled uncontrollably in his arms…She was sweet and curving, delicate and pure. He made love to her while she was still clinging to him like a trusting child, and that even managed to twinge the conscience he didn't think he still had.

CHAPTER SEVENTEEN

He woke her before dawn, and this time, because she was naked and she knew she'd been fully clothed when he tied her up, she knew that something had happened. The dream again, but apparently it wasn't all a dream.

Cantrell saw her sweet mouth tighten into an angry line. "You tricked me," she said, looking cross and irritable.

"Correction. I took advantage of you. That's what I'm supposed to do," he said patiently. "You're a hostage, a victim. Or had you forgotten?"

Flushing angrily, her pretty chin came up in that stubborn way she had. "I thought there was supposed to be honor among thieves, or some such code."

"You asking to join me? Or are you trying to lay down rules of conduct for relationships with hostages? A guide for all us uneducated types?" He tilted his head back and looked at her through narrowed eyes, his expression wavering between bitterness and anger. He had awakened in a strange, rancorous mood. "Might as well forget it," he said grimly. "Most of us don't read anything but our own wanted posters, else we would be into real crime—be lawyers, politicians, and railroad tycoons— where the real money is."

"I guess we're lucky you can't read. You'd be really dangerous if you could," she said caustically, beginning to jerk on the clothes he had belatedly tossed her.

The small rolling hills had turned into mountains. She was seeing real trees now—fir, spruce, pine, and oak—scattered but slowly, very slowly, becoming dense, forestlike. They were leaving the desert behind, climbing into more heavily wooded sloping terrain that looked wild and uninhabitable. They moved slowly, picking their way through the brush and rocks. The air was rich with pine and musky animal smells. Occasional pine cones littered their path. The sun was still high overhead, but mostly they rode in the shade.

Now she was seeing small furry animals—jackrabbits, the riders on her uncle's ranch had called them. And more slithery things. Cantrell didn't talk much, but as they rode he occasionally shot at a jackrabbit. She noticed with chagrin that he did not miss. Maybe he didn't try the hard shots. Soon there were four rabbits hanging from the horn of his saddle.

When the sun began to sink below the horizon, she noticed that he changed course. They were going east now.

"Where are we going?" she asked tiredly. She had been drooping in the saddle for miles.

He turned and looked at her for practically the first time. Her pretty face was streaked with dust and sweat beneath the protecting hat he had taken off one of the men he had killed. She had braided her long black hair and wrapped it around her crown. Wispy hairs framed her dirty face. She looked exhausted, and he realized for the first time that she had been subjected to a ride that would have killed most women. "You've had a pretty rough time of it, haven't you?" he asked softly. This first sign of compassion from him unnerved her. A lump formed in her throat, and she just sat there, too sore and tired to move, wondering what he was thinking.

Ward was thinking about what he had to do that night and that he didn't want to leave the girl tied up on the desert again. Her reaction to it was too damaging. He could tell she didn't understand any better than he did what happened to her, and the effect lasted into the next day. Besides, if something should go wrong and he didn't make it back... That creamy white skin was too good for buzzards. It was time to get rid of her anyway. If Younger caught up to them, there would be a hail of gunfire...Every time they had stopped to rest the horses, he had scanned the horizon, and each time Younger was nearer. He'd been a fool to save her boyfriend for last.

They rode until the sun was setting. Leslie dragged in the saddle, too weary to complain and too stubborn to beg him to stop. He grunted, and she looked up, amazed to see a small adobe house with a thatched roof squatting under a band of cottonwoods. Three days without ever seeing another person had almost convinced her they were alone in the world—that there was no other life in Arizona—if they were still in Arizona.

The adobe hut was built next to a natural artesian seep where water bubbled up and sparkled like liquid black pearl in the dusk. The family that spilled out of the rude shelter, once they saw that Cantrell came in peace, looked more Indian than Mexican. The man had a pointed head with a black thatch of hair that looked as stiff as straw. The woman had small, sullen eyes and thin, corded arms. There were four children with round, solemn eyes. They looked like chicks peering from behind the mother hen's drab feathers.

Cantrell negotiated with the man in a guttural Mexican dialect. Money and two of the rabbits changed hands. The man spoke rapidly to his wife, and she quickly gathered some things from the house. The man hitched a small burro to a cart and the family clamored into it.

"What are they doing?"

"They're leaving." He walked over to stand beside her horse. "Follow them. They'll lead you into town."

His eyes were unreadable. She could feel her heart begin a heavy, muted pounding in her chest. This should have sounded like deliverance, but it felt like rejection. "What if I don't want to be led to safety?" she asked, her voice low.

He frowned as if he didn't understand.

"Send them away," she whispered.

Ward could feel a pulse come alive in his temple. He wanted her, but he also realized that even though she had been virginal, she was still Younger's woman and, being woman, capable of more treachery than Younger could ever imagine. And even if he could trust her, he knew she wouldn't be safe if Younger caught up to them. With a dozen men shooting at him, no one would be safe. He shook his head. "No."

Leslie knew she was insane, but something was driving her. Something primitive and totally unmanageable. She leaned down quickly, before she could change her mind again, and touched her lips to his, part of her dazed by what she was doing and part of her exulted by the quiver that went through his lean, rock-hard frame.

Taken by surprise, his tawny eyebrows crowded his piercing blue eyes, but she wasn't frightened now. She turned her head slightly so their noses would not act as barriers and pressed a shy, tentative kiss on his bottom lip. He searched her eyes, frowning his lack of understanding at her and then he turned and motioned the man away. He lifted her out of the saddle, and she slid into his arms.

His lips claimed hers, and he groaned as if this were the last thing in the world he wanted, but his lips were clinging to hers, warm and demanding. His hands pulled her tight against him, and she could feel the hardness of his thighs against her own.

The Mexican family scampered into the wagon. Her arms lifted to twine around his neck, and she felt him lift her and carry her inside. The small hut smelled of beans. The bed he laid her on was a mattress of corn husks covered by ticking.

Silken lashes darkened her cheeks. Her lips were parted, expectant. He brushed his lips against them and then against the smile lines on her soft face. She tasted of alkali dust and made small mewling sounds against his ear. He kissed her awkwardly at first and then hungrily, glad her usually stormy green eyes were closed. When he could force himself to let her go, he backed away from her and began to undress himself. She unbuttoned the row of buttons on her tattered riding gown and then sat up, shrugging out of the gown, exposing the whiteness of her small breasts. She looked so tender and trusting as she looked up at him. Moving into her arms, he had the awful feeling that she was different for him. Most girls were little more to him than a flash of white skin, an open mouth...

He was right. Their lovemaking was tender-fierce, hungry, a wild mating that left them both exhausted.

She couldn't tell if she had been asleep or not. The room was dark. A coyote yipped into the night. He was stirring. His hand found hers, and she lay there quietly, content until he raised up on one elbow and brushed the hair away from her face. He lowered his head, and his lips nipped at hers, then moved on to brush against her eyes, cheeks, ears, and throat. She would have believed herself incapable of response so soon after that starburst of sensation, but she was wrong. He kissed her until she was flushed and shaking, until she was so engrossed in her own body's response that she barely noticed when his lips slipped down to her breasts and then her belly. His mouth was there, dragging a shuddering, in-drawn breath through her, burning her blood into steam to scald and plunder her before she could move to stop him. With diabolical skill he brought her all the way up, and when her body was convulsing with shock waves of ecstasy he buried himself deep inside her to bring them both soaring upward again, clinging together as if the whole world would drop away and leave them, and then, unbelievably, it did. At the moment of heart-stop, the world fell away. She would have screamed if his mouth hadn't stifled her cries.

"Oh, oh, oh, I never knew, I never knew..." she whispered, gasping.

"So now you know," he whispered, brushing black curls off the sweet oval that glowed with luster even in the almost dark room.

He was still on top of her, their limbs still meshed, warm, sweat-sheened together, his hands still tangled in the silky black mass of her hair. He groaned and buried his face in the warmth at her throat, then pushed himself away from her.

He stood up. "Where are you going?"

"You don't need to know that," he said, pulling on his pants. "I'll be back, but if something should go wrong, follow the wagon tracks into town. We're near Flagstaff. You could make yourself useful. Cook those rabbits. I'll be back in time to help you eat them."

CHAPTER EIGHTEEN

Leslie woke up slowly, disoriented, blinking at the rough adobe ceiling. She frowned, remembering that he hadn't come back to help her eat the rabbit she had cooked.

"Unnn." That sound, like a grunt of pain, had come from the room on the other side of the canvas.

"Cantrell?" she called out.

A soft curse was her only answer. She scampered off the bed and dressed herself as quickly as she could, her heart pounding with sudden fear. Running her fingers through her hopelessly tangled hair, she brushed aside the canvas over the door opening. Cantrell was seated in a chair with his back against the wall. Relief flooded her. "What are you doing?" she demanded, moving so she could see his face.

"I was hoping you would sleep awhile," he said, ignoring her question.

"Oh, my…" she gasped. He was frowning down at his left shoulder, trying to poke into torn flesh with a sharp knife. Bloody skin, bruised and burned around the edges, gaped. His shirt and pants were soaked in blood.

"What happened?" she demanded.

He hadn't looked at her yet. Now he lowered the knife and sighed as if he had finally found something he couldn't do. His eyes were momentarily desolate. He searched her face and sighed again. "Don't be scared. It's not as bad as it looks."

"How did it happen?"

"I failed," he said simply.

"Are they close?"

"Close enough, I guess."

She felt sick, but she was determined not to fall apart. "What are you trying to do?"

"Get a bullet out."

"I'll do it."

He looked at her skeptically. She took the knife from him and considered it. To her, probing inside his shoulder with something that sharp was insanity. It almost guaranteed that more damage would be done. She went to the pan on the basin, washed her hands with the stinging lye soap she found there, and then returned to his side.

"You ready?" she asked.

Her creamy white skin had paled at least two shades, but she looked game, so he nodded. She had to force herself to touch the gaping red tissue, to push her finger into the warm ooze that had been his shoulder. Her stomach lurched, turning inside out. She groped in warm flesh, fighting the faintness that threatened her. Cantrell had set his teeth against the pain, but beads of sweat popped out on his forehead, and all traces of his tan were gone. She was about ready to give up when she felt something sharp and jagged. She had to force two fingers into the wound to pry the flattened bullet out of there. At last, shaking, she withdrew; the bullet dripped blood as she dropped it on the table and collapsed into a chair.

He expelled a loud breath. "Jesus!" he groaned.

"Getting shot is dumb," she said to cover her own anxiety.

"I know," he said ruefully. He glanced at his wound and sighed. "We need to clean this thing," he said slowly, as if dreading the thought of it. "Get that bottle of whiskey out of my saddlebags."

Leslie complied. He nodded in encouragement and she uncapped the bottle. "You ready?"

His blue eyes were bleak and weary from so much pain. He dragged in a breath. "Maybe I'd better lie down."

He walked unassisted to the bed. Panting with the effort, he lay back and nodded at her, and she lowered the bottle. At the last second he turned his head away. She slowly poured the fiery liquid all over his shoulder, using her fingers to open the burnt edges of the wound. Cantrell dragged air into his suddenly convulsing lungs through tightly gritted teeth, his body stiffening, arching, and then at the very last, when the breath escaped out of him in a low, anguished moan, he fainted.

"Oh, God!" Leslie groaned. She threw her arms around him, sobbing. His skin was dry and hot. In panic, she searched his wrist for a pulse, found one, faint and thready, and sighed. At least he wasn't dead. And momentarily he was not in pain. But what would they do now?

Her mind refused to function. His head was turned away from her. His profile and the graceful column of his sturdy neck tempted her. She used her gown to wipe the beaded perspiration off his face, then lay down beside him and pressed her face against his. He looked so helpless. She reached out to smooth the hair off his forehead and ended by pressing her lips there. His skin had a salt, manly smell that was like a narcotic to her senses. She held him blindly, from some need that she couldn't name, until she felt him stir, then she slowly moved away.

He opened his eyes, tentatively, as if he feared consciousness might produce more pain. "We have to go," he said. The look in his eyes, still pain-weary but determined, told her it would do no good to argue.

CHAPTER NINETEEN

"Where are we going now?" Leslie asked, watching him carefully. He had mounted easily, but his face looked gray and he hadn't moved since he got into the saddle.

Ward barely heard her words. Black fog, swirling dizzyingly in his head, threatened to engulf him. Don't move, he cautioned himself. Take deep, even breaths. All that blood will grow back—in time. Unfortunately, he didn't have much time. Younger had gotten reinforcements from somewhere. They could not all be Powers men. Maybe a local posse? Had Powers or some local sheriff wired ahead? Be plenty of men who wouldn't mind collecting a reward, maybe two of them, if Powers was as mad as the Texas and Pacific Railroad.

The ground under his horse came slowly into focus, and he kicked the big black gently, very gently.

Leslie watched him warily. He had lost a lot of blood, and he swayed a dozen times, but he stubbornly refused to fall.

Much later, they topped a rise and saw a narrow dirt road winding around the mountainside. The air felt cool and crisp, even at midday. They must be fairly high up in the mountains. The smell was crisp and resiny.

The sky overhead was filled with roiling, tempestuous clouds, so low they were almost within reach—threatening to unleash their pent-up fury in the heat and passion of a summer thunderstorm. Mists swirled over their heads, augmenting the tension within her. She was torn between fear and anger at him for beginning something that could only end in death for him and possibly for her as well. The angry, lowering clouds, the threat of pursuit, the heavy, charged atmosphere, all combined to frazzle her usually steady nerves.

Ward swayed, fighting spiraling waves of nausea and weakness that had combined with an abominable frailty that threatened to overwhelm him. The hills and valleys before him surged sickeningly. It was an effort to speak. "Okay, this is where we part company."

"Here?" She looked around, puzzled. "I don't see any Indians."

"Flagstaff is around that bend. You'll be safe there."

She looked where he pointed, frowning, her smooth forehead rutted with worry. "But what about you?"

He had turned his horse to leave her. He had no energy to fight her, but he forced himself to sit straight in the saddle. "I'm going to cheat you out of your revenge. You can't have everything, little one," he said huskily.

"What about the Indians?"

"They'll just have to suffer."

"Where will you go?" she asked, strangely unwilling to let him ride away.

"Friends," he lied, nodding in another direction. "They'll take care of me." His face was gray, damp, set in determination. His clothes were dirty, bloodstained, torn. He kicked his horse gently, as if he didn't dare jar anything, and she felt a strange ache in her chest. Without thinking, she turned her horse, leaving the trail to follow him.

He stopped. "What are you doing?"

"I'm going with you!"

"No..." He frowned fiercely.

"You can't stop me—you're too weak. Besides, I'm not through being a hostage. You're supposed to trade me for your freedom. I read books, you know. I know how it is done..."

"Christ!"

"Cantrell, look!" she cried in sudden alarm.

A party of riders came into sight from the direction of Flagstaff, saw the two of them less than two hundred yards from the trail, and urged their mounts into a run, beginning to fire.

Cantrell spurred his horse and Leslie did likewise, following him down what looked like a natural trail around the mountain. They flew through a dark corridor of pines with the low-hanging branches slapping at them. They came out of the dense foliage and were on another trail, this one more clearly defined. Without slowing his horse, Ward searched the hollows and crests, looking for a way to evade their pursuers even though he knew it was only a matter of time. The horses, especially his, were used up.

Ward saw another knot of riders and recognized Younger at their head. Pursuit behind him and in front of him. He had one split-second to regret he hadn't traded horses with the girl, and then reached for his rifle, urging the black forward at even greater speed. He heard the girl scream his name, but his mind was already focused on what he was going to do. He wrapped the reins around the pommel, lifted the rifle into position, and began to fire into the knot of riders, scattering them.

Leslie couldn't believe her eyes. Cantrell had gone crazy! He looked like one of the wild bandits in a Salvator Rosa painting. His hat had fallen back on his shoulders, his blond hair gleamed in the sunlight, and he was riding straight into the arms of at least a dozen firing men. Bullets spanged up dirt and rocks all around him. Men were falling, horses rearing and screaming, and then a bullet caught Cantrell's big black in the chest and both horse and rider went down.

Fear that had held her stunned and immobile now sent her flying forward. She didn't see anything except that lean sprawled form. Someone shot at her and she heard someone else yell, "You fool! That's Leslie!"

She would have thrown herself on the ground beside Cantrell if someone hadn't caught her arm and jerked her aside. Horses milled everywhere and dust blinded her.

"Where the hell do you think you're going?" That was Dallas Younger's voice, snarling at her. She turned, jerking her arm out of his steely grip.

"He's hurt!" she said without thinking.

"Damn right he's hurt! If he ain't dead, he's gonna be a lot more hurt before I get through with him!"

"No!" she shouted, springing at Younger, her eyes glazed with fury, her nails curved into talons.

Like an enormous grizzly, Younger shoved Leslie aside, flinging her into the dirt with a look of rage and mistrust that reminded her finally which side she was supposed to be on.

"Get that bastard on his feet!" Younger bellowed. Two men pulled Cantrell's limp form up, holding him by the arms, and Leslie had to bite back the urge to tell them again that they were hurting him. While they were dragging Cantrell toward a furious Younger, the other group of riders who had been pursuing them joined the melee, jerking their horses to a halt just a few feet from where Leslie was struggling to her feet.

"Who's in charge here?" Their leader, a tall, barrel-chested man with a silver badge catching the light, dismounted stiffly and stepped forward. He had a rumbling, sonorous boom of a voice.

"Who the hell wants to know?" Younger demanded.

"My name is Geronimo Nieves, Sheriff of Coconino County. I have a warrant for this man's arrest."

Geronimo Nieves had the most battered-looking face Leslie had ever seen. He had two scars, one slashing diagonally across his right cheek and another dividing his chin. His face was darkly tanned except for those two white slashes flashing like lightning on a dark night. His ears were gnarled, and his nose looked permanently flattened.

"Won't be necessary, Sheriff," Younger said, ignoring the outstretched hand. "We'll be taking care of him ourselves."

Younger dismissed Nieves with a wave of his hand and walked over to where Cantrell hung limply between the two men. He jerked Cantrell's head back and watched it fall forward lifelessly.

"The bastard still alive?"

"Barely."

"Get him awake! I want him to enjoy every goddamned minute of this!" he snarled.

A third man took a canteen off a horse, and they leaned him back and poured the water on his face while Leslie struggled not to scream at them. Her heart was beating furiously.

"This bastard killed eleven of my men," she heard Younger telling Nieves.

"Maybe more," Bass Wimer, a big man with a dull simian look, said, pointing to two who lay sprawled in the dirt and two more who sat nursing their wounds and groaning.

"You know why he done it?" Nieves asked, glancing from Cantrell's slumped form to Younger's furious face.

"Crazy, that's all," Younger growled. "Kidnapped my woman, and when we followed, he sneaked back and surprised us."

Leslie was watching Cantrell with fear and foreboding. They handled him roughly, pouring water on his head and slapping him, and only despair over the reality of their situation kept her from rushing forward. He groaned finally, and his eyes blinked open, fever bright and unfocused. They stood him up, one on each side, holding him with his arms twisted back, and she groaned.

"Well, well, well, so you've decided to join us." Younger sneered. "How are y'all feeling now, Cantrell? How's it feel to know you're the one about to die, bastard?"

Younger stepped closer to his prisoner and sent his fist crashing into Cantrell's face. "You're going to be real sorry you didn't kill me back there," he said. He hit him again, causing a gash to open up along his cheekbone, and this time Leslie cried out shamefully, begging him to stop, not even realizing she had until Younger turned on her, letting his eyes rake over her like she had no clothes on. He came to her side and dragged her away from the tree she had sagged against.

"Did this man rape you?" he demanded with a snarl.

"No!"

"No?! Does that mean he didn't rape you or he didn't have to?" Younger asked, his face dark with fury.

"Get your hands off me!" she hissed. "I won't be talked to like that by you or anyone else!"

Younger glared at her angrily. "You're pretty uppity considering what you been doing with Cantrell."

Nieves stepped forward, placing himself beside Leslie. "Let her be," he said quietly.

Younger shot her a look full of venom. He dropped her arm as if it burned him and turned his attention back to Cantrell's limp form. "Wake that bastard up! I want him to know it when we hang him! Get the rope!"

Men were rushing to comply.

Leslie turned to Nieves. "You're not going to let them hang him, are you? He's a train robber. There's a reward for him—but not dead." She was improvising now, desperately. "Please, Mr. Nieves, stop them. This is all a mistake."

Younger placed the rope around Cantrell's neck, and they brought the horse forward, steadying Cantrell's slumped, lifeless form.

"Please, Mr. Nieves!"

She had a strange accent. He looked at her appraisingly. "You're not from out here are you?"

"I'm from Massachusetts, but please, stop them. They're going to hang him!"

Cantrell was sagging in the saddle they had forced him onto, still unconscious. His face was shiny with bruises; blood trickled from half a dozen cuts. She had the insane urge to take his battered head and hold it to her breast. She knew that if she lived to be a thousand years old, nothing would ever move her as strongly as that sight.

Younger's men positioned the horse and rider under a sturdy limb and threw the rope over it. Three men braced themselves, and Leslie felt her heart stop and then lurch wildly and sickeningly.

"Hold on here!" Geronimo Nieves finally stepped forward. "I'm taking this man in so he can stand trial."

"Like hell you are!" Younger roared.

Nieves held out his hand, and one of his men slapped a shotgun into it. He pointed it at the three men holding the rope. "Drop that rope or you'll die with him."

"He hangs, damn you!" Younger snarled, lunging forward to slash

114

at the horse, sending it forward. Nieves fired point-blank into the three men and the rope slid through their fingers. Leslie threw herself forward, trying to reach Cantrell, but Younger caught her, jerking her against him, peering angrily into her face before he flung her away from him with a curse. "I'll deal with you later."

The horse Cantrell had been on lurched forward, and he fell to the ground unharmed except for the fall, which must have been painful. Fortunately, he was already unconscious. Heart pounding wildly, she sagged against the tree while the sheriff and his posse loaded Cantrell across a horse and left without further incident. She watched until they were out of sight, then turned her attention to the men who had been shot.

"Get 'em on their horses," Younger snarled. "Ain't no use trying to doctor 'em here."

He grabbed Leslie's arm and put her forcibly onto her horse. His gray eyes were flat, unemotional slate. She'd never been afraid of Younger before, but now, suddenly, looking into those relentless, angry eyes, she realized that he no longer considered her a lady. She felt the steely grip of his hand on her arm, and knew soul-shaking, gut-deep fear.

CHAPTER TWENTY

The ride to Flagstaff, with four wounded men, was slow, but Leslie barely noticed. She felt immune to her surroundings, dazed, as if her mind had gone numb. Her head was filled with an angry buzzing sound, and her heart was beating far too hard. Her hands on the reins trembled as if they belonged to someone else, perhaps a fearful old woman. Surely they could not belong to Leslie Powers.

The sun was still bearing down on the trees that grew thick and green to the very edge of the rutted red clay road. It shone on the pale pink rocks that jutted out of the mountain, on the men who rode all around her but hopelessly separate from her. The air was cool; even though it was midday the weather had a crisp mountain feel to it. September? Or was it October? She would have recognized October in Wellesley…Could she ever get back there? How many thousands of miles lay between her and her past? She sagged in the saddle with the hopelessness of it, so much distance, so many miles stretching out…She could not imagine ever finding her way back there.

Occasionally Dallas Younger glanced angrily in her direction, and she felt drenched in the hate lashing out at her from his dark eyes. It was another pressure on her numb brain, but she did not ask herself what right he had to hate her. She accepted his hate. An angry buzzing sound in the distance was growing louder now, so loud she could no longer hear the sounds of their horses' hooves smacking into the hard-packed dirt road.

Flagstaff was a lumber camp. The town was much smaller than Phoenix, without the boisterous air of a cowtown. A town of workers. The shrill whine she had been hearing was the saw from the sawmill, out of sight. Flagstaff did not seem real to her. Merely a small noisy town at the base of a massive mountain whose topmost peaks were already dusted with a thin cap of snow. No railroad there. Heavy wagons loaded with trees that had been reduced to naked poles rumbled past, heading for the source of that shrill whine.

Younger dispatched his men to see to the wounded while he took Leslie to the only hotel in town, the Orlando, which was a tall, awkward rectangle of a building, two-story, with the inevitable awning. He signed the register as if he would take out his anger on it, and then took her by the arm, roughly, to lead her up the stairs to her room. He unlocked the door and then turned on her, his dark eyes narrowed with fury.

"What did you do, fall in love with that bastard? He was going to sell you to the Indians! Didn't you know that? To a bunch of filthy Indians who live on reservations like so many dogs penned up! He didn't take you because he fell for your big green eyes and your milk-white skin!" He caught her shoulder, and she cried out instinctively, angrily, twisting away from his hands.

"Get your hands off me! You either treat me as a lady or leave me alone!" she snapped.

A sneer spread across his face, curling his lips down. "Pretty high and mighty for a piece of used goods, ain't you, missy. A lady don't do what you did."

Younger was rewarded with a white-hot flaring of passion, a starburst of heat that lightened, then darkened, her eyes. Fury blinded her to everything except his sneering face. The rage, fear, and frustration that had been building for days exploded. Her arm seemed to move of its own accord. She didn't realize she had hit him until she saw the stunned look on his face and felt the pain, like a burn, on the palm of her hand.

She should have been afraid, but she wasn't. She felt a surge of joyousness at the way it felt when she hit him. Her muscles seemed to swell with strength. With unbounded energy. This was what she had been needing—someone to strike out at, someone to take out fear, anger, and frustration on.

She lunged at him as if she really believed she could kill him, as if she thought she was seven feet tall and weighed three hundred pounds, the way some of those lumberjacks had looked on the wooden boardwalks below.

He didn't seem to notice her wonderful strength. He took hold of her with rough hands, glaring into her face like he had always hated her.

"You won't be so high and mighty when I get through with you, missy," he growled viciously, jerking her around and shoving her at the door he had unlocked.

Leslie staggered into the room, finally caught her balance, and faced him again, her face pale but defiant. "Get out of my room! You have no right to be in here!"

Dallas Younger's face was a mask of hatred, his voice a sneer of condemnation. "I was willing to marry you, you little slut! I have every right! He took something that belonged to me, something I was saving. I was gonna marry you—proper—in a church! I was gonna treat you like a lady! You weren't a little whore till he got his filthy hands on you."

He slammed the door, closing them in, and it sounded to Leslie like the closing of a tomb. His eyes were filled with fury, revenge, and lust, and it was all directed at her. She stepped back, opened her mouth to scream, and he lunged at her like an enraged panther, knocking her onto the bed that dominated the small, barren room.

Her scream turned into a gasp of panic that he shut off with his hard mouth while he forced her down onto the bed. She fought like a wildcat, her eyes spitting fury, but he was just as determined as she and far stronger. His hands ripped her gown aside. Screaming, she slashed at his face, trying to take his eyes out. She missed, but clawed a bloody furrow down his cheek. He slapped her hard and she reeled away from him, barely feeling it, and came at him again, teeth bared, nails curved into claws.

"Ow! Dammit! You...damned cat!" He yelled, backing away.

"Get out of here!" she screamed hysterically.

"All right!" he shouted, backing away from the fury in her green eyes. "All right."

Geronimo Nieves paced back and forth in the outer part of the jail until the doctor came out, closing his black bag.

"Well, Ben, he gonna make it?"

"Reckon that's between him and his maker. I stopped the bleeding. He's lucky he wasn't awake for that. *If* he has a strong constitution and *if he* don't get infected and *if he* ain't already lost too much blood..."

"How soon can we move him to Phoenix?"

"Can't say—three weeks or a month, maybe. What's he charged with?"

"Eleven counts of murder, kidnap, and rape."

"Should've just let them hang him," Ben grunted.

"Now, Ben, you know I couldn't do that any more than you could let him bleed to death."

"Yeah, yeah, I know, but maybe I wonder how smart we are sometimes," he growled, waving his hand disgustedly. "See you later tonight. I'll look in on him to make sure the bleeding doesn't start up again."

"Thanks, Ben. Night."

· · ·

The ride back to Phoenix with a sullen Dallas Younger and a cadre of crippled gunfighters was far from pleasant. Leslie would have welcomed any sort of natural disaster to distract her from the outrage that still bubbled and boiled within her, but the weather was disgustingly pleasant.

They had been riding for a long time—she couldn't tell how long. The sun was high overhead, preparing to start its descent toward the horizon, which was far off and ragged with the silhouettes of majestic fir and pine. They were in a high, rough canyon, traveling south. Copses of aspen and oak, brilliant with their burnished autumn golds, yellows, and reds, were fiery against the somber green of the conifers and the smooth swirls of pink sandstone cliffs.

At last she found something she remembered. The configuration of trees that overlooked the Powers fortress. She had been riding numbly for hours...or days—she couldn't tell which—and suddenly they were on the narrow dirt road that led through the trees...

They descended the long, slow incline impatiently, as if all of them were eager to get back. Halfway down the road she saw the gates of the fortress swing open, and her heart did tiny flip-flops. Another confrontation to be gotten through before she could start that long trip back home. So many miles back...

Her uncle came out onto the long porch, shading his small, narrowed eyes from the sun. She returned his look, expecting some sort of greeting but ready to take him on as well as Younger, if need be. Mark Powers merely turned and walked into the house. She and Younger followed him to his office, and by the time she reached there it had dawned on Leslie that her uncle was not exactly overjoyed to see that she was safe. He looked from Younger's sullen face to hers.

The scene that followed was not believable. Mark Powers was stiff, formal, and deaf to anything she had to say. He cut her off by holding up his hand, and then nodded to Dallas Younger to tell him what had happened. He listened gravely and shut Leslie off angrily when she tried to interrupt.

"That true?" he asked, squinting at her suspiciously. "You talked the sheriff into saving that bastard Cantrell?"

"Yes, but..."

"Speak when you're spoken to, Leslie," he interrupted, his eyes as bright and hard as jade, his mind closed against her. "You sure he raped her?" he asked, turning to Younger.

Younger's sensual mouth curled into a sneer.

Something snapped in Leslie's head. "Why ask him?" she screamed, oblivious to ears that might be pressed against the walls of her uncle's study. "Don't you think I would know?" She pointed at Younger. "He's the one who tried to rape me!"

"What did the sheriff do with Cantrell? What did he do with that bastard?" Powers demanded, ignoring her.

"Nieves took him to Flagstaff. Said he'd bring him to stand trial when he's well enough to travel," Dallas replied, also disregarding the girl who faced them like an angry tigress.

Leslie still couldn't believe her uncle meant to ignore what she had told him. She faced him, incredulous but still determined, demanding his attention. "What are you going to do about this man? He hit me, ripped my clothes, and treated me in an abominable fashion."

Mark Powers pursed his lips into a tight little wrinkled slit. "That true?" he asked Younger, who still looked sullen and snarly.

"I reckon," he said gruffly. "She came at me like a damned wildcat."

"You still willing to marry her?"

Younger's eyes raked over her. He was furious with her. He shouldn't have anything to do with her, but like he had told Sam, even second-hand the way she was, she was still half owner of the whole Powers spread. "Yeah, I reckon so," he said finally. "I'll probably be sorry."

Leslie was speechless.

"We'll take care of it when we ride into town to watch 'em hang Cantrell. Maybe Saturday. They'll be bringing that bastard in to stand trial. She'll have to identify him."

"Won't be that soon. We roughed him up pretty damn good."

Angry words trembled on Leslie's lips, but none found voice.

CHAPTER TWENTY-ONE

The mountains were hulking gray shadows behind a brilliant display of aspen trees flaming red and orange in the early-morning air. The sun was a pale gold ball in a hazy sky. Clouds sailed overhead on a stiff wind that smelled of sand and sage and whipped her riding hat, threatening to send it sailing away. It felt good to be out of the house and on a horse again with crisp wind on her face.

October first. She couldn't believe she had been in Arizona less than two months. It felt like years. She was dressed in a very smart black and white hound's-tooth riding gown with a jaunty black hat trimmed in white ribbon and a showy white egret plume. She looked very stylish. Dallas Younger had looked at her strangely, but she noticed that he had taken great pains with his wardrobe also.

Since they were going to town, she assumed Cantrell had survived, unless this trip was for the sole purpose of marrying her to Dallas Younger. Leslie rode sidesaddle next to Annette, who had come along to act as Leslie's maid of honor. Annette rode, but it did not come naturally to her. She grumbled at every step of the horse, as if her protestations would somehow inspire the gentle mare to be more considerate of her.

The women had each packed a bag, cramming all they could into them. Leslie knew what she was going to do. Her uncle and Dallas Younger would be furious—maybe they would kill her—but they would have to do it in front of the whole town.

The majority of the population of Phoenix was lining the wide dusty street when Geronimo Nieves rode into town with his prisoner.

"He don't look like no mad-dog killer to me," a tall, lantern-jawed man in front of the saloon sneered.

"Killed twenty men in cold blood!"

"Naw! Twenty? I heard it was closer to thirty."

"Hell, he didn't kill no thirty men. Powers ain't missing no thirty men."

"He shoulda killed 'em all. Then he wouldn't be here!"

Ward Cantrell ignored the hundreds of pairs of eyes that watched him. His fierce blue eyes raked over the crowd, looking for Younger, who was nowhere in sight. He heard some of the comments, but his face gave nothing away. His muscles tightened involuntarily. He would rather have a snake like Younger out where he could see him, but since he wasn't exactly in control anymore, he forced his muscles to relax. There wasn't a hell of a lot he could do about anything, dragging chains on his hands and feet. The horse he rode was probably tired of them too.

The slow procession reached the jail, and Ward waited for the word to dismount. He was learning patience. Three weeks in jail had taught him something six years of outlawry hadn't—the value of freedom. But, he thought dryly, if Powers and Younger have their way, I won't have long to worry about freedom.

The first few weeks in the U.S. cavalry had taught him the value of keeping his thoughts to himself. His company had been blessed with a burly drill sergeant who believed that everything he said should be received with reverent respect. After watching two recruits being pounded into the turf for twitching with mirth at sheer unadulterated ignorance being verbalized, control quickly became automatic.

Now if he felt anything at being paraded through the street like a circus animal, it didn't show on his lean face or in his still military carriage as he dismounted.

The jail was bigger than the one in Flagstaff, and the cell they put him in had a window, for which he felt a rush of gratitude. Ward settled back on the lumpy mattress with relief. He was still shaky. The ride had taken the last of his reserves. Sleep came easily, like pulling down a shade.

While her uncle was at the hotel desk, arranging for a block of rooms, with hers in the middle, no doubt, she strolled to the window near the open door. She only wanted to glance out, but two of Younger's men broke away from the rest and followed her. Irritated, Leslie shot a disdainful look at Younger and walked out the door. The two watchdogs moved in closer. What would they do if she bolted into the street? She didn't find out because she was arrested in her tracks by a shrill female voice:

"Is that her? The one who was kidnapped?"

"Sure Lord looks like her!"

"That's going to be some trial! I wouldn't miss it for the world!" The woman was tall and buxom with sharply etched features and eyes that looked Leslie over as if she were one of the women of ill-repute that congregated in the saloons.

"I heard two men discussing it with my husband just last night, and one of them was a barrister. He said that trial could go on a mighty long time. They'll drag everthin' out into the open—strip her bare. You mark my words. Find out what really happened!" The second speaker was short and stocky with a sturdy, self-satisfied look about her.

"Do tell! Skinny little thing for a Powers, ain't she? Probably asked for it! She has flirty eyes—I've seen her type before!"

"Ain't that the beatingest thing you ever heard of? I wouldn't want my husband on the jury. I just hope they don't let *her* attend church with decent folks."

The other woman laughed, a prim, sanctimonious sound. "I doubt if she spends time in churches—else she wouldn't have ended up the way she did."

"Did you see Cantrell? Right pert handsome man, if I do say so myself...Bet she could tell some tales!"

"Kin tell he's a killer by the eyes. He looked my way just onct, and I felt the chill all the way to my bones. He'll hang—no doubt about that. My husband said he was withholding judgment—probably because he hates Powers!"

"Kept her long enough, didn't he?"

The heavyset woman snickered, and Leslie had the urge to walk over there and rip the woman's gown off so she would know how it felt to be stripped naked in front of a whole townful of people. Anger burned inside her. They hadn't once acknowledged her, except as an object to be talked about! She watched their backs as they walked away, feeling stunned by the force of her own reaction. If she'd had a gun, she would probably have shot them both.

As their voices faded, she heard one of them remark, "'Bout the only good thing Powers does is to get rid of some of the riffraff that drifts into town. They'll hang Cantrell. Serves him right."

Cheeks burning, Leslie turned abruptly and walked back inside the Bricewood, oblivious to the contrast of the cool, sky-lit Garden Courtyard that served as the lobby of the hotel. Palms ten feet high swayed gently. Fans hung down on slender, almost invisible cords and stirred the tepid air, swaying the graceful fronds of the ferns that were interspersed between palms and clusters of chairs.

Her room was on the second floor this time. Annette helped her bathe and slip into a cool green organdy gown, a frosty lime color that matched her eyes and had long sleeves and a high neckline with a crisp white collar. The gown was frilly and lacy with intricate pleats falling gracefully from the bustle. She chose a small straw hat with a white velvet ribbon trailing down behind her, barely damaged at all by the crush of her satchel. Annette recombed her hair and pinned it in a mass of artful curls off her slender white neck. By the time they were finished, Leslie's heart was pounding frightfully, and she barely cared what she looked like.

They dawdled so long with her toilet that Younger was banging on the door before they were ready. They let him wait. When she finally went down to the lobby, he and her uncle were with Sheriff Nieves. She recognized his scar-slashed face immediately.

"Leslie, the sheriff here wants you to identify the man who kidnapped you before he goes back to Flagstaff."

"Very well," she said docilely, turning smoothly as she deliberately ignored the arm her uncle offered her.

Younger had changed his shirt. She had to admit that he really wasn't a bad-looking man, just despicable. Leslie walked beside Sheriff Nieves at the head of the procession, ignoring the eyes, hostile, curious, or indifferent, that watched her.

The jail was a block and a half away. The men chatted desultorily, but Leslie wasn't listening. Her heart was pounding so hard she thought she was going to shake apart from it. Would the jail be a good place to make her stand? Would Nieves help her again, or would they all treat her like her uncle had? She was faint with fright and fear by the time they got there—breathless and half-terrified—but determined nonetheless.

Another lawman met them at the door. He looked like a schoolteacher who had by some accident of fate become a sheriff in a small town. He seemed confused by so much authority. He introduced himself as Sheriff Tatum, and then introduced Kincaid and Nieves and turned to her. "Miss Powers, I'd like to present Chantry Kincaid the Third. He owns most of the Texas and Pacific Railroad. He's here to pay the reward if Cantrell here is his train robber."

Kincaid took Leslie's hand and held it in a protective embrace while his clear green eyes engaged hers in mutual appraisal. She met his piercing gaze proudly, determined that she would not be cowed by anyone in Phoenix no matter who they were or what they thought of her. She nodded stiffly, and he patted her hand, taking her by surprise.

Kincaid was imposing and darkly handsome—probably in his mid-thirties, and she detected none of the condemnation she had expected to see in his eyes. They were clear and admiring. Leslie relaxed ever so slightly and noticed that while he might look like a pirate of a man, he was dressed in the height of fashion, even for the East—wearing an English "lounge suit" of blue serge with the popular wing collar and black silk scarf instead of the more cumbersome cravat. Altogether a comfortable style, and he wore it exceptionally well.

"How do you do?" she murmured, grateful she had on gloves so he couldn't feel how cold her hands were in spite of the heat.

"This must be quite distressing for you, Miss Powers. If I'd been thinking, I would have brought my wife along." He had a pleasant masculine voice. She found it surprisingly reassuring.

Leslie shot him a grateful look that Kincaid did not miss. Her response made him wonder if anyone else had bothered about her feelings. Powers had never impressed him—except as a man who was probably more accustomed to using women than taking care of them. He cursed himself for not bringing Jennie. Leslie Powers looked like she could use some female support. He hoped that this wouldn't take too long or be too unpleasant for her.

"Might as well get on with it," Sheriff Tatum said.

Kincaid stepped back, blocking Powers and Younger to allow Leslie to precede them into the jail. It took him only seconds to realize that Younger and Powers were acting as if they had forgotten Leslie Powers was a lady. Kincaid could feel his anger rising.

Nieves and Tatum took their lead from Kincaid, ignoring Powers and Younger in deference to the young lady. Kincaid was one of the most influential men in the territory. His financial holdings included a shipping line; the Texas and Pacific Railroad, with offices here and in San Diego; and a chain of hotels, including the Bricewood West, which boasted appointments unheard of in the West. He built hotels along his tracks to rival those in large eastern cities, and he was rewarded with vast profits. People paid the extra money to stay in luxurious surroundings. There was something exciting about eastern comfort on the western frontier. And it was no longer impossible. Railroads were tying the states and territories together more effectively than anything else could ever have done. The refrigerator boxcar had made it possible to transport anything that ice could preserve. The West was no longer cut off from the conveniences that made life enjoyable.

Men rarely ignored Kincaid. And now he was treating the Powers girl with every respect due a young lady of substance. Tatum could do no less. He smiled at her. This was his opportunity to show Mr. Kincaid, who was also active in town politics, that he was doing a good job. As the host sheriff, he cleared his throat and interrupted the several low-voiced conversations that had started up.

"Well, I guess you know what we're here for, but I'll say it officially. Miss Powers is here to identify the man who kidnapped and uh…"

Kincaid scowled him into silence.

"Excuse me, ma'am. Uh…" He turned toward the cell where Ward Cantrell lay stretched out on the thin mattress, his eyes closed. "Cantrell! Stand up! The lady's going to take a look at you!" Cantrell came up easily. He was thinner, and his nose had a new hump in it, but the eyes, those sky-blue, pitilessly cold eyes, jolted through her like a shock wave. He looked more like Alexander the Great than a train robber. Even in his ragged, dirty clothes, with his hair longer and wilder than she remembered it, he had the kind of bearing that was unmistakable.

Or had she read too many nickel novels? His eyes never flickered. He just looked at her in that opaque, unemotional way he had about him and she turned away, frowning.

"I'm sorry, Sheriff Tatum; that isn't the man who kidnapped me." Her voice was clear as a bell and very firm in the sudden silence.

"Wha—?" Powers turned on her. Younger grabbed her arm and jerked her back around to face Cantrell. "Take another look!" he snarled. "That *is* the man!"

"No, it *isn't!*" She jerked her arm free. "Sheriff, I would like to make a complaint of my own, though, against Dallas Younger and my uncle. They are trying to force me to marry Mr. Younger, and I have refused. I am half owner of the Lazy P Ranch, and if they can force me to marry Younger, my uncle and he will have full control. I am asking you to intervene in my behalf before they force me into marriage with a man I despise."

"You little baggage!" Younger stepped forward menacingly as if he were going to hit her, and Kincaid dragged Leslie back and placed himself between them, but not without noticing the reaction of the prisoner. There was murder in those blue eyes for Younger.

"That's enough," Kincaid said flatly, staring coldly and unflinchingly at Powers and Younger.

Leslie could feel the hate like a tangible cloak surrounding her. Thank goodness for Kincaid! He stood protectively close while the sheriff from Flagstaff who had been there at the capture questioned her.

"But Miss Powers, this is the man you were with," he insisted gently, in deference to Kincaid's protective posture.

"I know that, Mr. Nieves. Don't you remember what I told you? I said, 'That man is a train robber. There's a reward for him.'"

Nieves frowned. "That's right, by Jove, that's what she said! But—how did you get away?—How did you happen to be with him?"

"The kidnapper left me at the road and went south. I saw this man and started to ride toward him when I saw you. He fled and I panicked. I thought perhaps you were bandits...I had no idea why he ran away..."

"How did you know he was a train robber?"

"I recognized him. He robbed the train I was on."

"That right?" Nieves asked, turning to Cantrell. "You a train robber?"

Ward Cantrell's eyes gave nothing away. They flicked over her once, bringing a warm flush before he chuckled. "You'd try to steal meat from a grizzly, wouldn't you?"

"Now wait just a goddamned minute! This man's name is Cantrell! He rode right into my camp, killed my men, and threatened to cut my throat. He signed a note telling us he was going to sell her to the Indians. He signed it Cantrell," Younger ended furiously. "Cantrell!"

"D'ya have the note?"

"Hell, no! My word is good enough," Younger blustered.

"'Fraid not," Tatum said gallantly, earning him a reward when Leslie smiled at him. "'Fraid, Mr. Younger, that courts only act on evidence, either hard evidence like that note, or an eyewitness account. We have a witness who says this ain't the man," he said, enjoying Younger's rage, since there was nothing he could do to him at the moment. Everyone knew Younger always kept up the pretense of staying on the right side of the law.

"Ask him how he got shot," Younger demanded. "One of my men shot that bastard up in the mountains."

All eyes were on Cantrell then. Leslie held her breath, praying Kincaid, who was standing protectively close, couldn't hear her heart pounding in the stillness. But Kincaid was engrossed in Cantrell. Ever since he had entered the jail he had been thinking that he knew Cantrell from somewhere, but so far he hadn't been able to remember from where.

Tatum grunted. "Check 'round—we'll probably find out there was another train robbery that day."

Younger wouldn't be stopped. "He wounded four of my men in front of your eyes, Nieves! You saw him go riding at us like some fiend out of hell! Do you deny that?"

Cantrell let his eyes, still cold blue, but now with glints of amusement flickering in the depths, rake over the red-faced Younger. "Guess I'm the excitable type, Sheriff. Men in front of me, shooting at me, men behind me, shooting at me—I guess I took it personally. Didn't realize they had me mixed up with somebody else," he drawled coolly.

"You lying bastard! I'm gonna get you for this!" Younger snarled viciously.

"I may not be unconscious next time, Younger," he said quietly, his husky voice steely. Cantrell dismissed Younger and turned his attention back to the girl, wondering what had made her decide to lie for him. He had been shocked to learn that she was Powers's niece. Sounded like she had troubles of her own with both Younger and her uncle. There was real loathing in her pretty eyes whenever she glanced at either of them. He saw her sweet face, so fresh and tense, and knew that he had been worrying about her. It had been blind and hidden from him until now, but seeing her so crisp and demure and ladylike freed him from some burden he had been carrying without knowing or being able to identify it. All dressed up in cool green organdy that matched her defiant green eyes, she was a vision of rare loveliness. Her cheeks, as velvety smooth as carnation petals, were flushed with warm rose. She looked as if she had survived with little permanent damage to her fine feminine spirit, and he felt a surge of relief in that knowledge.

The thought of her at Dallas Younger's mercy did unaccountable things in his chest.

Younger wasn't about to give up, but it was Powers who stepped forward. "Sheriff, my niece lied about that man not being the one," he said stoutly.

Tatum sighed heavily. "Cantrell ain't going no place. Even if he ain't the one, she identified him as a train robber. I'll be checking through all the warrants. Mr. Kincaid here's been looking for Cantrell for some time himself. From what I hear about Cantrell we'll get enough to hang him anyway."

"You'd better see to it! My niece may have been taken in, but I damn sure ain't! I mean to see justice done!"

Powers and Younger turned and stalked out the door.

Tatum faced Leslie, clearly flustered. "Now—uh—Miss Powers, ma'am—about that—uh—complaint of yours, ma'am."

"I'm willing to drop it if you can guarantee that Mr. Younger will not be allowed to molest me while I am in Phoenix. I intend to leave town as soon as I can get a train out of here," she said firmly.

Kincaid smiled admiringly and offered her his arm. "Miss Powers, my wife and I would like to invite you to be our guest for the duration of your stay in Phoenix. I can assure you that no one will molest you again. If you would be so kind, we can go directly to the bank and arrange for a transfer of the reward money to your account. I'm in your debt, Miss Powers."

Leslie glanced at Cantrell, saw the flush of anger come into his face, and then looked quickly away, wondering why the thought of her going with Kincaid should evoke a reaction in his stubborn eyes where very little else did.

"You're very kind, Mr. Kincaid, but I couldn't accept a reward. But I do accept your hospitality. I must confess that I feel the need of your protection."

CHAPTER TWENTY-TWO

"Mr. Kincaid, I want to apologize for airing the family laundry and putting you in an awkward position…"

Kincaid shook his head. "Please, Miss Powers, don't be embarrassed. I know something of your uncle. People don't choose their relations. I only hope that you weren't too badly treated."

They were on the sidewalk now, and Leslie squinted against the brightness of the sun as she looked up into Kincaid's face. "I didn't tell the sheriff everything, Mr. Kincaid. My uncle will not be satisfied until Mr. Cantrell is dead…What will happen to him now?"

Kincaid noted the quiver in her voice and the sudden paling of her cheeks. Gossip that she had fallen in love with her kidnapper had reached him. Everyone in town had heard about Younger's anger at her for trying to save the outlaw from being hanged on the spot in Flagstaff. Kincaid instinctively felt pity for her. Not just because she was so young and so lovely; the West needed young women with the fire and spirit Leslie Powers had exhibited. Unfortunately, the West was so raw and in such a hurry that its justice was oftentimes as crude as it was abrupt. He felt sorry for her, but he didn't want to give her false hope.

"I'm convinced in my own mind that Cantrell is the leader of the gang that has been robbing the Texas and Pacific. I'll have some of my men who've seen him come in to take a look at him. I, uh, expect, with all the other things he's wanted for, he'll spend a good many years behind bars." He stopped short of telling her that Cantrell would probably hang. No sense upsetting her at this point. He took her arm and steered her toward his carriage. "Do you need to pick up anything before we ride out to the house?"

"I have some bags and my lady's maid, if you're sure your wife won't be upset…" She was remembering the women who had talked about her that morning in front of the Bricewood West. What if Mrs. Kincaid were one of those?

"Nonsense," he said, helping her into the buggy. "Jennie will love it. I'll drop you at the house and come back for your things." Leslie Powers was obviously determined to do whatever had to be done—she was spunky as hell—but he wanted to spare her another confrontation with her uncle so soon.

"Thank you. I'd appreciate that," she said gratefully, settling back against the upholstered seat.

He slapped the reins on the horse's flank, and Leslie steadied herself as the carriage moved away from the jail. She ignored the eyes that followed their departure. The warm sun felt good to her. It seemed to ease her trembling. She sat back, relieved that the confrontation with her uncle and Younger was over.

They were passing through a part of town that Leslie had not seen from the windows of the Bricewood West. Here streets were laid out in the familiar New England grid that she was so used to, lined with row upon neat row of sturdy homes. She could hardly believe her eyes. She had thought the town consisted of the hotel, the livery stable where her uncle had left the horses, and the wide street lined with saloons and stores that she had ridden down in the parade.

"Oh," she sighed, "this is like a real city!"

Kincaid chuckled. "You sound homesick."

"I guess I am," she admitted. "What are those?" she asked, pointing at trees with blue-green, spiny branches that reached twenty-five or thirty feet into the air, lining the dirt road on either side of them, providing filtered shade.

"Paloverde trees," he chuckled. "I wanted tree-lined roads for Jennie. We transplanted them from the desert."

"You certainly went to a lot of trouble. You must love your wife very much."

"When you meet her, you'll understand," he said simply.

Leslie fell silent, glancing at the houses, which appeared to be smaller versions of the spacious rectangular structures of New England, half-timber, half-clapboard, with steep roofs and tiny casement windows, except they had exterior chimneys instead of the central chimneys of New England. The eaves projected more, and the houses looked stark and uncomfortable perching on flat grassless lots, sometimes separated by fences, sometimes not. Most of them were two- and three-story—ungainly, top-heavy, and boxy. They were the kind of houses she was accustomed to, but they looked so forlorn here, surrounded by sand, rocks, and Paloverde trees. One was a perfect copy of the cozy, white-washed Dutch houses with their stone gables and projecting eaves. One was modeled after the rural Jacobean English houses. She recognized the grandiose baroque style, the geometrical gables, exterior chimneys, and stair towers. Inside she could almost see the elaborate moldings, carved balustrades, massive wooden doors, and arched doorways crowned with delicate fan windows. No doubt there would be four rooms to each story. Next door was an elegant, boxlike brick structure of classical Georgian style.

If she closed her eyes so she could not see the strange trees, and the stark lots, if she nestled these houses in imaginary spruce, willow, and ash trees, she could be back in Massachusetts. But even without that assistance she had to admit that this was a real neighborhood. It lacked the classic precision of planned eastern communities, the roads were not paved or even cobbled, but it was apparent that this had not been a random happening. She could hardly believe it.

"Is this…I mean, how long have these houses been here?"

Kincaid laughed. "Not very long. This happens to be my first humble attempt at subdividing land. What do you think of it?"

"Why, it's marvelous, but where did you find so many people who could afford nice houses? I mean, it is not exactly Boston, but it's not Phoenix either."

"When I came here the first time in 1882—that's when the railroad reached here—there were two thousand people. It was a pleasant little community that had just been incorporated into a city. For miles all you could see was sand and rocks, relieved occasionally by clumps of ocotillo shrub, cactus, and a few Paloverde trees. Now there are almost four thousand people. I imported many of them myself, to run the hotel, the railroad, the bank, my ranch. In 1864 this was nothing more than a site where a man by the name of John Smith pitched his tents for a hay camp to fulfill a forage contract for the army outpost at Fort McDowell. They named it Phoenix because this town was built on the ruins of an Old Indian pueblo.

"Actually it was a more pleasant town before the railroad, because now we get the cattle drovers who are a wild bunch. In 1882 we already had a school house, two churches, and the first ice factory in the Arizona territory. I remember when old Abe delivered ice in a wheelbarrow for seven cents a pound."

A wagon with children in the back, staring at them with solemn eyes, rattled past, raising a dust cloud.

"We lived at the hotel then, and Jennie was anxiously awaiting the birth of our son," he said over the noise of the wagon. "The Phoenix

Hotel had a swimming pool behind it with a canvas roof. She spent half her time sitting in the water and the other half sipping iced tea. I really shouldn't have let her stay here. I should have sent her north where she would have been comfortable, but she wouldn't hear of it. I had to be here, so she felt like she had to be here. We've never been very good at separations."

"How many children do you have?"

"Two."

"Which one of these houses is yours?"

"We're almost there. Jennie wanted to get as far from the stockyards as possible. We have corrals that hold two thousand head, and sometimes the wind shifts."

They passed a row of houses, these more elegant than the rest. Then he slowed the horse and nodded at the house on the corner, facing south. It was like nothing she had seen before: it looked like the Spanish missions she had seen, except there was a simple elegance in the lines that marked it as a home.

"That brick is called adobe. It's made from the clay of this region. We fired it in a kiln we transported from Minnesota."

"It reminds me of a monastery."

He laughed. "That's because I stole a lot of my ideas from the Jesuits. It gets very hot here. I used foot-thick adobe walls to keep the heat out and recessed the doors and windows under a generous roof overhang so that the sun doesn't shine on them. It helps."

The front of the house had a series of curved arches opening onto a deep porch. Inside, there were two massive mahogany doors that looked as if this pirate of a man had stolen them from some feudal castle. The roof was red tile and gleamed in the sunlight. Kincaid chuckled at her silence. "Total freedom encourages eccentricity. I must admit that I was tempted to do something modern, but Jennie prefers either Classic Greek Revival or Gothic, so we compromised."

"What do you call it? I've never seen anything even remotely like it."

"I stole my ideas from the Indian pueblos, the Jesuits, and our neighbors to the south—the Mexicans."

"It is magnificent! You designed this yourself?"

"You are very kind. I am an engineer…with aspirations. I don't believe architects create. I think they compile. The first job of any good designer is to discover what works well in the area where he intends to build. The second is to organize those things into a design. Heat calls for thick walls and that generous overhang."

"Oh! That's very good. You know…when I was on the train, coming here, I talked to a young man named John Loving. He called you a visionary. I can see that he was right."

"John is very kind. I have imagination. I don't know if that qualifies me as a visionary, but I can't help remembering something I learned in school about Major Stephen Harriman Long, a man who explored far more territory than Lewis and Clark, and gained almost no fame for it, because he was consistently unimpressed. He toured the richest farming region of the eastern seaboard, around Lancaster, Pennsylvania, and found it depressing. I believe the words he used were 'sinks of dissipation and debauchery.' When he reached the site of what would be Chicago he wrote in his journal that it was unfit for either commerce or agriculture. He was later given credit for convincing Americans that the Great Plains was a desert. He saw mountain ranges merely as obstacles. A man totally without imagination. I look at a desert and imagine any number of possibilities. All it takes is a little water, a road, maybe a railroad, and cities sprout like mushrooms. I think in quarter-acre lots. It is an occupational hazard. Leave it to me and the entire continent past the Mississippi River will be subdivided."

"I prefer your vision to many others I've heard. I am tired of fat, fashionable frame houses. I think I like your western architecture."

"That's partly why I'm here instead of in New York. The East has become exhausted, sluggish, and inhibited. Here we have space to be innovative and the opportunity to build whole cities in a decade. We are not tied to a uniform ceremonious style or any other style. I prefer western barbarism to eastern philistinism."

"You have real plants! A real garden!" she cried, noticing the shrubs for the first time.

"My wife is from New York. She insists on the civilizing influence of a thoroughly irrigated garden around any house she lives in."

"It's so beautiful!"

"Then why the tears?" he asked gently.

"You're very observant," she smiled, dabbing quickly at her eyes. "It just made me homesick, that's all."

"Where are you from?"

"Massachusetts, Wellesley," she sniffed.

"Beautiful country."

She sniffed again. "Yes." Oh, God! She missed it so much! Now that she was letting down she felt tears crowding up and struggled to control them.

Kincaid opened the door and a white-haired woman with deep dimples and smiling eyes was standing in the entry hall as if she had been waiting for them. There was an almost cavelike feeling of coolness the moment Leslie stepped inside.

"Good afternoon, Mr. K."

"Afternoon, Mrs. Lillian. Is Mrs. Kincaid home?"

"In the library, sir."

"I want you to meet Leslie Powers. Leslie, Mrs. Lillian has been with the Kincaid family since I was born. She raised me, my brothers and sisters, and ran the family practically single-handed. She is also the repository for the Kincaid family history. Though I admit that there are parts of it she's been ordered not to discuss, for reasons known only to a few," he said, chuckling.

Mrs. Lillian smiled and Leslie was completely enchanted with the woman. She looked the perfect grandmother, from her silver-gray hair to the frilly pinafore over her blue silk gown.

"Don't listen to him, my dear. I have never been good at remembering what I'm not supposed to discuss."

Mr. Kincaid threw his head back and laughed. "Well, at least you are honest," he said.

"Welcome to the family, my dear. If you need anything at all, please let me know. I'm always around. The children do not take all my time by any means." She patted Leslie's hand and turned. "I'll go tell the missus you're home."

Leslie turned her attention back to the interior of the house and had to control the urge to gape. It was a dream. In the front part the ceilings were at least thirty feet over her head, open to the roof, but the back half of the house had two stories. Sweetly curved stairs seemed to float on the air, so gracefully were they designed. Somehow the long roof-overhang had given the impression that the very house was hugging the ground, almost blending into it.

It was light, airy, open—not anything like she had expected from the massive, heavy look of the outside. There were tall narrow windows that reached all the way up to the ceiling, and while she could tell that sunlight did not fall directly on the windows, except in early morning and late evening, the rooms were not dreary, even at midday.

"This is the *sala grande*," he said with a sweeping movement of his right arm to indicate the spacious area to her right that looked like a ballroom. Crystal chandeliers hung on long chains from the high ceiling. Simple wicker furniture and potted palms similar to the ones she had seen in the lobby of the Bricewood West were scattered around the enormous room.

"What does that mean, *sala?*"

"Spanish for parlor or large room," he said, smiling. He liked her direct questions. Too many girls either would not have been curious or would have pretended they knew. "Straight ahead is the library, and the room to your extreme left is Jennie's music room."

Leslie turned, following the sweep of his hand. From inside the music room, the ceiling looked like it had been made in a waffle iron: recessed squares separated by raised dividers. One enormous window dominated the far wall. It was shaped like a tall, narrow cupola, coming to a point at the top like a triumphal arch. It was at least twelve feet wide and twenty feet tall. Clear leaded glass, with diagonally cut panes, was set flush with the outside wall of the house. Since the walls were so thick, it was deeply recessed into the wall and framed by a wood cornice. Sheer cream-colored lace curtains were pulled back by velvet ribbons, softening the harsh sunlight. Except for a few chairs, an elegant white Steinway grand piano was practically the only piece of furniture in the room. A mirror twelve feet high and as wide as the north wall, probably thirty feet long, brought a gasp to Leslie's lips.

"Oh," Kincaid said, "the mirror. My wife was a ballerina before we married. She still goes through her routines every day. Says she feels better…"

"How marvelous!"

"That's why there's no rug in here. She needs good solid hardwood."

"The floor is beautiful. The whole house is beautiful." She did not exaggerate. It was a house designed to lift spirits as high as the ceilings.

They walked slowly toward the back of the house, and she caught sight of paintings on the staircase enclosure. It was an art lover's paradise. She felt dizzy with so much to look at. Dozens of paintings, hung on blind cords, were artfully arranged by someone who had an eye for proportion.

"How cleverly you hang them! Oh! That has to be a William Prior! My mother had one. Isn't his modeling exquisite? Did you know he is one of the most skillful portraitists in New England? He was a Bostonian, and he could paint flat-featured portraits or excellent rounded features— whichever the client could afford. He is the only artist I've ever heard of who put style on a class basis—only his wealthiest customers would pay for the refinement of modeling the features, or I guess people who were acquainted with the more academic proficiencies of European artists. Oh!" She stopped, suddenly self-conscious.

Kincaid chuckled. "I take it you enjoy art." He seemed relaxed, and not the least put out with her. The nicest smile!

"My mother was an artist and an art teacher. I paint, but not well enough to earn a living at it. She was listed in *Who's Who of American Painters,*" she said proudly. "I want to be one of the best landscape artists in America. I studied art at Wellesley, but I want to study in Europe."

"My wife is the collector. Get her started and she will talk your leg off."

The library was decorated in celery green with none of the weird grandeur that was so prevalent in the homes of the rich. The walls were papered with soft green silk, and the draperies were of the finest green brocade. The room had a light, fresh look about it that was unlike the heavy, overripe opulence of the period. There was none of the heavy velvets, in deep, rich colors made from the new aniline dyes that were so violent and so popular. Nor did the room have the appearance of being overcrowded, as was the fashion. There was a feeling of sparse elegance in the Kincaid home.

CHAPTER TWENTY-THREE

They found Mrs. Kincaid seated at a small writing desk beside a tall, narrow, elegantly draped window. She glanced up, smiling. "Just a moment, please. If I don't write this down, I will forget it." She wrote quickly and then stood up. "That's done! Thank goodness," she said, walking quickly toward them.

"Jennie, love, I'd like you to meet Leslie Powers."

"Oh, Leslie! I'm so happy to finally meet you," she said, smiling warmly, directly, into Leslie's eyes so there could be no mistake about how she felt. Relief flooded Leslie, and she smiled.

"How do you do, Mrs. Kincaid?"

"Please, Leslie, call me Jennifer or Jennie."

"Oh, no, I couldn't presume..." Leslie demurred.

"I insist. Unless, of course, you want to insult me," Jennifer said, smiling.

"Oh, no, I would never want that..."

"Good, then it's settled."

Jennifer was a head shorter than her handsome husband. Her waist was slim and her body supple. She went up on tiptoe and kissed his cheek, then smiled at him.

"Well, I was delighted to receive your message about our houseguest. Do they have your train robber in jail now?" she asked, her voice a delight to the ear, pleasing, well modulated.

Kincaid grinned. "Sure looks like it."

"Thank goodness, Chane," she said, turning to Leslie. "He has fretted about that for years. It will be a relief to worry about something else." She paused suddenly. "I can be informal to a fault," she said, shaking her head. "You would probably like nothing better than an opportunity to rest and collect your thoughts, and we stand here making small talk. Come, Leslie, I'll show you the way to your room."

Leslie followed obediently, noticing that while Jennifer was striking as a still portrait, she was even more striking in motion. There was tremendous energy in her—it was apparent in the way she carried herself. She had hair the color of pale summer wheat, highlighted with streaks of silver, a glory of shiny, shimmering tresses drawn back from her dainty ears in cascading curls. She was blessed with radiant skin the color of old Brussels lace, and her cheeks were warmed by a hint of plum that echoed the deep purple of her eyes. Jennifer Kincaid was most assuredly not the type who would make cutting remarks on the street about a total stranger. Mr. Kincaid had not had to explain Leslie's predicament. Jennifer was naturally compassionate.

"Jennie, love," Chane said to his departing wife. "Leslie is an artist. She was admiring your collection."

"Oh, how wonderful!" Jennifer flashed Leslie an excited smile. "Tell me what you think of these," she asked, taking Leslie's hand and leading her to the east wall.

The room they called the library was a combination art gallery and reading room. One wall was devoted to books, one to a fireplace, and the other two to paintings hung all the way to the ceiling, which was twelve feet high. The variety and quality of paintings took Leslie's breath away. There were two Rembrandts, three Claude Monets, two Van Goghs, several Orozcos. Enthralled, she walked the length of each wall, her eyes wide with wonder, like a small girl on a holiday.

Jennifer smiled and took Leslie's hand again. She led her to a collection that was very special to her and waited while Leslie absorbed what she was seeing. The look on the younger woman's face was all that Jennie needed to know that the two of them would get on famously.

"Oh! I've always wanted to own one of these! They are original Patroons! The old Dutch families of New York hoard these like the very devil. How did you ever?"

Jennifer laughed. "I happen to belong to one of those old Dutch families. I am the one who is currently hoarding them," she said gaily. "My maiden name is Van Vleet. This painting here is of my great-great-great-grandfather Jonathan Van Vleet. It was done in 1710. That is Peter Van Vleet, my brother. He was seven. It was painted in the Patroon style, but as I'm sure you know, the Patroon painters existed only until about 1730, more or less. A friend of the family, Christopher Chambard, could mimic the style. Isn't it adorable?"

"Yes. And what a manly-looking seven-year-old! Did your brother live up to the promise?"

Pain flickered in Jennifer's eloquent violet eyes, and Leslie groaned.

"Oh! I'm sorry! Please forgive me. I'm so forward. My mother spent years trying to keep me from asking inappropriate questions, to no avail…"

"No, please. It's just that I haven't seen my brother for eight years. I don't know if he is alive or dead…"

"I'm so sorry."

"Don't be. Please." She quickly changed the subject. "This one is by De Peyster Manner. See the ships in the background. They belonged to dear old Moses. He was a very successful merchant. Moses Van Vleet, my great-great-grandfather. What a pompous dullard he looked!"

Leslie was entranced by the primitive beauty and the vivid colors. "Have you ever seen so much innocence and contentment? You would feel, looking at that painting, that that man could not possibly give short weights in his store!"

"You're right!" Jennifer agreed, laughing. "Maybe that is why the Dutch, who were shrewd businessmen, liked the Patroon painters! Maybe at one time this hung in the window of his establishment right next to the Bible!"

They both laughed.

"Let me show you to your room. You must be tired."

They climbed lush carpeted steps, elegantly curved, to a spacious hallway and a large comfortable bedroom with a small balcony that overlooked a surprisingly green lawn and garden in back of the house. Leslie shook her head in disbelief. The trees and flowers could have come directly from Wellesley. Under the noonday sky, the lawn was apple green, partitioned with English hedges, neat rows of local flowers she didn't recognize, and all carefully manicured. A high stone fence enclosed the garden. A spacious barn, carriage house, and stables in the same style and adobe as the house were ringed at the northern perimeter by a row of tall trees that afforded privacy.

"Oh! It's so lovely!"

"Thank you. Arizona's concessions to a New York girl!"

"I had no idea Arizona made concessions! I thought this was a hopeless desert."

"You have no idea how deep Chane's engineers had to go to find year-round water!"

"China?"

"Almost!"

They laughed again and Leslie squeezed her hostess's hand. "Jennifer, I want to thank you for being so nice and for taking me in. I truly appreciate it! I can't tell you how much," she said shyly.

"It is our pleasure. We love having a guest. Just relax and don't worry about a thing. Let us take care of you. Chane didn't say…Are you Mark Powers's daughter?" Leslie could tell by Jennie's face that she was not impressed with Mark Powers.

"He is my uncle. I came here to try to settle my father's estate. But Uncle Mark…" Her throat tightened, and she felt tears stinging behind her lashes.

"Charles Powers was your father?"

Leslie waited in silence. If Jennifer had disliked him as well, she wouldn't be able to bear it. There was a lump in her throat and a sense of rampant dread in her chest.

"Yes," she said tremulously.

"I didn't know him personally, but Chane said he was a fine, decent man."

"Thank you," Leslie whispered gratefully. She realized in that moment that while she hadn't known her father, she had created a wonderful, warm fantasy about him that she was still emotionally attached to. She really wouldn't have been able to bear it if Jennifer had smashed it with a careless word.

"Leslie, do you need anything? I'll be going to Bauer's later to do some shopping. If you don't feel like venturing out, make a list. I'll pick everything up."

"Thank you, but if your husband sends my bags and Annette, I'll be fine."

"Do you have any plans?"

Leslie shook her head. "I don't know what I'll do. I used most of my money to come here to try to settle my father's estate, but I don't think my uncle intends to give me a cent."

"Well, my husband is pretty good at business matters. Something will turn up." Jennifer smiled reassuringly. "Would you like to meet the children?"

They were beautiful and extremely polite, treating Leslie like a princess. The boy was dark-skinned and black-haired, with green eyes—a miniature pirate like his father—and the girl was a delicate, creamy blond with striking blue eyes, elegantly fringed with thick lashes.

"Oh, she didn't get your eyes," Leslie said, without thinking.

"Nor Chane's," Jennie laughed. "Actually, she has my brother's eyes." Pain darkened her eyes momentarily and then she brightened. "Blue is better anyway. No one trusts a woman with purple eyes."

Leslie admired the toys that they wanted to show her and then allowed Jennifer to rescue her and take her back to her room. "They liked you. I think they would keep you all day, talking your leg off," Jennifer laughed.

"Thank you. They are adorable. I don't usually like children," she admitted.

Jennie laughed, "I admire your honesty. Few people like children, except their own, and not always then. I told Chane I would have his children on one condition—that the boys looked like him and the girls like me. I had nightmare visions of great, hulking females and delicate, fragile boys…"

They laughed, and Jennifer left to let her relax. Leslie tried the bed. Two bounces told her it was as comfortable as it looked. A painting caught her eye, and she went to stand before it. She stood there a long time, studying the dark, warm, tonal style, the directness of the presentation, with a growing sense of excitement. She knew the artist! She was sure of it!

Trembling in her eagerness, she turned the canvas and searched for an inscription—finally found it in the top right corner. "Girl at the Piano to Jennifer with love, Theodore Robinson." It was he! In her excitement, she reacted by habit, looking for her mother to share it with.

Art had always been the center of their life together. Meals were rarely on time; household chores, laundry, even shopping, were done haphazardly, or to accommodate their schedule, which revolved around lighting.

"The house is here to serve us, not vice-versa!" Margaret would say emphatically when her friends who did not paint would look askance at the cozy clutter of paint pots, brushes, and drying canvases.

Leslie grew up with the resinous smell of oil paints and turpentine, eating cold meals, and loving it. She despised clocks and schedules and felt truly sorry for friends whose lives were meticulously regulated.

There had been many times when she'd been summoned from classes for a "family emergency" that turned out to be a chance for the two of them to rush across town to chat with some visiting artist, and at least as many times when she'd skipped school altogether to see a show or a collection. When there was money enough, which was very seldom in the early days, they would purchase tickets to Boston, pack a big basket of chicken, wine, cheese, and fruit and stay overnight in the city, visiting the art museums from the time they opened in the morning until closing time at night. They would ride back on the Pullman coach and arrive in Wellesley late at night. Leslie remembered walking in the very middle of the wide, dark streets, hurrying through shadowy, scary aisles, her small hand tucked warmly inside her mother's.

Now her mother was dead and Wellesley, Massachusetts, was thousands of miles away, shrouded in shadowy mists, unreachable. Even the memory of those green and pleasant hills seemed like a dream. She was filled with a vague sense of anxiety. By publicly denouncing her uncle, she had broken her last family tie, as bad as it was. She felt the way she had after the funeral, when she had walked back in the house and seen the canvas her mother had been preparing for her next painting...

She didn't realize she was crying until Jennifer, who had come up to bring her a tray, pulled her into her arms and began to stroke her back. "You've had a rough time of it, Leslie," she crooned softly. "Let the tears fall; let them come. Don't fight it. There, that's better. A good cry will do wonders, there, there..."

Jennifer held her closely while great, gasping sobs shook her slender body. It seemed much later when Jennifer moved to dry Leslie's tears, after the worst had passed.

"Feel better now?"

"I feel drained," she said, shuddering. "I never cried before, not until after my mother died. Now I seem to be crying all the time. It isn't like me. I just don't cry," she said, shaking her head, still sniffling.

Jennifer sat down on the bed and pulled Leslie down beside her. "You lost both your parents in a short time; you were betrayed by your uncle and kidnapped. You have tremendous strength, or you wouldn't have survived all that. You must be reeling emotionally." She paused and patted the slender hand that was lying limp in Leslie's lap. "I remember when my parents were both killed. At the time I seemed to be coping with everything, doing what had to be done, going about my life the way I thought I had to do, until one day I realized that I had just been keeping myself busy so I wouldn't have to realize they were really gone. It was very difficult," she sighed. "You loved your mother very much, didn't you?"

Leslie nodded, feeling her bottom lip tremble.

"Your mother loved you very much as well. And being a mother myself now, I realize that if I should die suddenly, I would want my children to have a good cry—one time only—and then do whatever they had to do so they could remember me with happiness. A mother loves her children as long as *they* live, not just as long as she lives. When I die I want my children to be happy, not sad, as soon as possible. Your mother would want the same for you. Love wants only love for payment, not unhappiness nor tears." She hugged Leslie and changed the subject. "Maybe you've been holding too much inside. I remember when I was about your age, I began tearing up at the slightest provocation. I discovered that I was in love."

"With Mr. Kincaid?" she asked, sniffing.

"Yes."

"But he is so perfect for you..."

Jennie laughed. "It didn't seem so at the time. Falling in love with him was equivalent to the worst disaster imaginable. You see, I thought he had been responsible for my parents' deaths. It was far more complicated than that even, but suffice to say, he appeared to be entirely unsuitable."

Leslie felt new tears welling up into her eyes. She felt sure suddenly that everyone in the world knew that she had tried to protect Cantrell. She would never live it down.

"I'm sorry, Leslie," Jennie said softly. "I'm so dense sometimes. I didn't realize..."

"It's all right," she said quickly.

"Do you love him?"

Leslie shrugged, feeling desolate. "No. I don't know. At first I hated him. Then I felt confused. I didn't want them to hurt him. I don't want him to hang."

She looked up, blinking back tears. Jennie smiled and pulled her into her arms again. "You are a very honest young woman. Sometimes people don't understand such honesty. That was the case when I fell in love with Chane. Even my brother didn't understand. He..." Jennie stopped, unable to continue.

"What happened?" Leslie asked, pulling away to search Jennie's wide purple eyes, now clouded with pain.

"I don't know. He disappeared eight years ago, only days after my marriage. I haven't seen him since. I don't know whether to grieve for him or to be furious with him...And so I have done both—for eight years."

"You love him very much..."

Jennie nodded. "I love him the same way I love my children, with the same unreasoning passionate possessiveness..."

She sighed heavily. "As a child, he had the most expressive face. When he smiled he could light up a room. When he glowered, he could dim the sun. I always knew what he was thinking—we thought alike. I blame myself. Because I knew he suspected I was in love with Chane—and I didn't try to explain to him." Tears welled in her dark eyes, and she tried to blink them back, continuing as if she couldn't help herself.

"I was angry. I said stupid, stupid things to Peter, forgetting how much he loved me. I forced him to leave. It was all my fault."

Jennie's voice was choked with pain. Leslie wanted to stop her, but she felt helpless to intervene. "I was so self-centered," she said bitterly. "I didn't take into account that he hadn't recovered from our parents' deaths, that he was in pain and struggling with his own survival. You see, Peter was so stoical that he fooled me. He could turn to stone, become unreachable. And sometimes he used that to trick me into thinking all was well." She paused, covering her face with her hands. "He must have been in such pain, thinking I had fallen in love with the man who had caused our parents' deaths...Peter loved them and it was obvious he worshipped me. I could see it in his eyes even when he didn't want me to. I should have known that I couldn't keep hurting him the way I was. There is no justification for me, because you see," she said, wiping the tears off her cheeks, "if I had talked to him, everything would have been fine between us, but when I first fell in love with Chane, I refused to explain my actions, because I couldn't—I didn't understand them myself."

Leslie sighed and Jennie dragged in a ragged breath and patted Leslie's hand. "I'm sorry. I didn't mean to tell you all that."

"Please don't apologize. I feel honored that you did."

"So!" Jennie said, standing up and becoming brisk and cheerful. "You must be hungry. Eat something," she said, waving at the tray, "then you can take a nap. That will help you to acclimate yourself. If you're like me, nothing ever looks quite so bad after a meal or a nap. Mrs. Lillian prepared this special tray for you so you can spend some time by yourself...if that suits your mood. If not, come downstairs for dinner. I'll leave it up to you."

Leslie smiled in gratitude.

Jennie found Chane in the kitchen fending for himself while Mrs. Lillian fussed at him for stealing food.

"I need to talk to you."

Chane sobered instantly. He took her arm and led her into his study. When the door closed, Jennie faced him. "I want you to save that train robber."

Chane looked at her as if he didn't quite believe his ears. "You want me to save the man who has been robbing my trains?"

Jennie shrugged. "Yes."

"But why?" he said, incredulous and frowning. A muscle bunched in his cheek, and Jennie reached out to touch it.

"Because Leslie is in love with him. She's a bright, sensitive, warm-hearted young woman. If she loves him, he can't be so bad."

Chane threw back his head and laughed. Jennie waited patiently while he sobered. "You're serious, aren't you?"

"Yes," she said, the light in her eyes steady and determined.

He shook his head. "The paper gets wind of this, they're going to think I've lost my mind."

Jennie smiled. "You'll do it?"

He grinned and held out his hands in helplessness. "For you, love, I would give up my entire fortune, but," he said, sobering, "don't expect a miracle. At this moment the prosecutor is deciding whether he has enough evidence to try Cantrell on eight counts of murder, mayhem, kidnapping, and train robbery or on just a hundred or so counts of train robbery."

He sighed. "God knows what else he's done." He shook his head. It was typical of Jennie to allow her ready compassion to rule her in these matters, but it could only cause her more pain if he wasn't able to save the young man. "I'll do what I can," he said. "But I'm not able to perform miracles."

"Of course you are. I can't wait to tell Leslie exactly how you did it."

"Dammit, Jennie." He laughed. "This is serious."

"I know, but you'll think of something."

"Well, don't say anything to Leslie. It will only hurt her more if I fail."

CHAPTER TWENTY-FOUR

Chane arranged for Leslie Powers' luggage and her lady's maid to be delivered to the house, and then headed back to the jail.

"Sheriff, I'd like to talk to your prisoner."

"Cantrell?"

"Please."

"Help yourself."

Kincaid walked over to the cell where Cantrell's lean form was sprawled on a cot.

"Cantrell, I'd like to talk to you," he said quietly.

Ward shoved his hat up off his nose. "So talk."

"Leslie Powers said Younger intends to kill you. I would like to know why."

Ward considered telling Kincaid the truth, but his stubbornness refused to let him do that. Kincaid was not his friend. He was still the same man who had caused the deaths of both his parents. Nothing could change that, not even the fact that he had married Jenn. But he would keep him in mind, because he did want Younger and Powers punished for what they did to the Mendozas. If he found that he would not be able to deliver that vengeance, he would tell him later. For now he only shrugged. "Maybe I know too much about Powers's activities—or—" He shrugged. "Maybe she's wrong."

"What is Powers afraid of?"

"That's between me, Powers, and Younger," Ward said flatly.

"I think I could help you if you would trust me."

Ward Cantrell came to his feet then and walked over to the center of the cell. His cold blue eyes locked with Kincaid's. "I don't want anything from you, Kincaid—ever."

Chane frowned, his straight black brows crowding his piercing hazel eyes. There it was again—that feeling that he should know this man. They stood eye to eye, Cantrell insolent and dangerous, from his warlike stance of a gunfighter to the curl of his lips and the steely glint in his narrowed blue eyes. He was a warrior, body and soul—there was no doubt about that—but that didn't explain Chane's feeling that he should know this man. But where? When? If he knew, would it explain why the man had concentrated so intensely on the Texas and Pacific?

Chane cursed the inadequacy of his recall, wondering how he could face Jennie if he failed. He groped for some way to motivate this young hellion.

Recognizing Kincaid's frowning thoughtfulness as a warning, Ward turned away.

"I wasn't," Kincaid said succinctly to Cantrell's broad back, "planning to *give* you anything, except a chance to earn your freedom." He was more than a little irritated. "Somehow I had thought a man facing the gallows would be a little more reasonable."

"Save your breath, Kincaid," he drawled, his husky voice freighted with contempt. "I don't want your help."

"I did some checking around, Cantrell," Kincaid said slowly, ignoring the man's obvious dislike. "You have the kind of experience I'm looking for. You know men, and you know how to lead them. Before you came along, that bunch you put together never did anything right. You turned them into one of the most effective outlaw gangs in history—never got caught—except that time they tried that bank job without you."

He didn't mention Cantrell's reputation with a gun. His own experience along those lines kept him quiet. Cantrell had worked his way right up the line—he was a target now for every would-be gunfighter who wanted to make a name for himself. But he was something more because he chose his fights. He turned down men he didn't want to kill and even managed to make friends of some of them. He had charm and apparently intelligence as well. That was what had been bothering him about this thing with Powers. Why would a young firebrand like Cantrell suddenly turn into a vigilante? He wasn't the type. Wilcox's report was filled with incidents that would seem to prove he didn't get serious about anything—not guns, horses, or women—he took what was easy and what fell his way. He did not go looking for trouble.

"You know a hell of a lot about me, don't you?"

"I get monthly reports…That's why I think it would be a waste of time and money to let you rot in jail for ten to twelve years."

Cantrell scowled. Anybody but him; anybody but Kincaid, he'd snap at the chance. He'd been everything there was to be, done everything. He didn't mind the idea of wearing a badge and taking his chances against rustlers or bad men, but he wouldn't work for the man who had caused the deaths of both his parents and dishonored his sister, even if he did marry her later.

"No deals with you, Kincaid," he said flatly, turning back to his cot.

"Think it over," Chane said, feeling a mixture of anger and frustration.

Kincaid left the jail and found his attorney, Winslow Breakenridge, in his office. He spent ten minutes with him and then went directly to the governor's office in the back room of Bauer and Stanton, General Merchandisers. Governor Ed Stanton was in a meeting with three men seated casually around a large mahogany desk that was Ed's only concession to his high office. He had been appointed governor of the Arizona Territory by the president, had been elected for one term, and was already worrying about being reelected. Chane waited only a few seconds before Stanton looked up, saw him, and excused himself to come out of the small room.

They shook hands, smiling like old friends who enjoyed each other's company.

"You pretty busy?"

Stanton grinned. "Talking bullshit—just between me and you," he said in a low voice. "These gentlemen are trying to persuade me that we should move the capital to Tucson."

Chane chuckled. This tug-of-war between the residents of Tucson and Phoenix over the site of the capital had been going on for years. Endless behind-the-scenes haggling, such as this visit by Tucson's finest, was only part of the politicking that went on.

"Don't they know they don't stand a chance as long as you live here?"

Stanton grinned. "They figured that angle already—offering me a governor's mansion."

"Seriously?"

"Sounds serious."

"Guess we'd better up the ante," Chane said, only half joking. There were many benefits that befell Phoenix because it was a state capital, primarily economic. The Arizona Territory now had two colleges, one at Flagstaff and one at Tempe. With the capital here, it was almost guaranteed that the next one would be in Phoenix. Young people would no longer have to go back east to get educated. The ones who could afford it still would, because of the status it bestowed on Phoenix's wealthier residents. That wouldn't change. Men still liked to demonstrate their superiority to their surroundings.

"When can you get away? I need to talk to you," Chane said.

"Saratoga Club in ten minutes be all right?"

The Saratoga Club was a private saloon in the Bricewood West, frequented by card-carrying members only. The memberships had been Kincaid's gifts to the men who owned businesses and ranches around Phoenix. It encouraged their patronage, and the exclusivity was strictly maintained. The atmosphere was deliberately circumspect, even dull, but it was restful. There were no women allowed. No rowdies allowed either. Peers met there and were assured they were special. It was a bastion of old-boy politics on a raw frontier. And it was good business. It did not pay its way financially, but it more than paid for itself in other ways, when Kincaid could find the time to visit there. The gossip was always revealing, the more so because the men who frequented the staid bar felt like compatriots.

Men waved and nodded as Chane made his way to a table. The walls were paneled in ornately carved mahogany. The bar occupied a place of prominence in the center of the big room for gentlemen who liked to stand while they drank. Clouds of blue smoke swirled gently, stirred by the large hanging overhead fans. Small round mahogany tables, each with two or three leather captain's chairs, clustered in front of the bar. Glasses were raised, gold coins clinked on the hard marble surface of the bar, and the men nonchalantly flicked cigar ashes into the deep maroon pile of the carpet.

Stanton was only ten minutes late, a record for him. He was always late because people stopped him anywhere and everywhere to tell him their problems. He was totally approachable by stranger and friend alike, and he loved to talk.

He dropped into the chair opposite Chane, and a waiter was there magically with his usual drink—whiskey and milk.

He took a sip of his drink. "My ulcer needed that," he sighed, leaning back. "What brings you out this time of day? Hotter'n hell out there, isn't it?" he asked, appreciating the relative coolness of the staid, dimly lit Saratoga Club. He reached into his pocket for his nail clipper.

"There was a meeting of the Cattlemen's Association here last night," Chane began slowly, careful not to point out that Stanton hadn't been there. Chane knew Stanton always spent Monday nights with his mistress, Kate Fletcher, at her place, to reward himself for being an attentive son-in-law, father, husband, and uncle all weekend. Wednesday nights he rewarded himself for working so hard and Friday nights to fortify himself for the long weekend ahead with family and ritual.

"Ahh, I see. Anything important?"

"They appointed me as a committee of one to let you know how unhappy they are that nothing has been done about the cattle rustling, which has been getting worse every week," he said, exaggerating only a little. He knew Stanton would believe every word because the morning's paper had carried a story along those lines. The *Gazette* hadn't mentioned his committee assignment, because he had just invented that.

"Damn!" Stanton growled, letting his displeasure show in the angry darkening of his already florid face. "You're the third man today to tell me that," he growled. "If I weren't sitting in this cool room, enjoying this life-saving concoction, I would kick your ass," he said gruffly. "Now how the hell am I going to get out of this?"

"Why don't you appoint a special ranger unit to concentrate on the rustling hereabouts?"

Stanton scowled at his friend. "Terrific idea—except where the hell do I get the money to pay for it?"

Chane quickly calculated the cost. At forty dollars a month, a half-dozen men only cost two hundred forty dollars. Even for six months it was under fifteen hundred dollars. A small price to pay if it made Jennie happy. "I'll donate the money, if you keep quiet about where it came from."

"Why the hell you doing this?" Stanton asked suspiciously.

"Because, they are stealing my cattle, remember?"

"Oh, yeah," he sighed. "But who the hell do I hire?"

"Gotta be someone with real leadership ability. A man who can take charge," Chane said, as if he were mulling it over. "You really can't let this rustling continue. They're getting too blatant. They cleaned out Frank Jones—didn't leave him a steer. The ranchers want every last one of them caught and hanged."

"Go on," Stanton said.

"I think I've found the man who can find out for us."

"Who?"

"Ward Cantrell."

"That gunfighter that kidnapped the Powers girl?"

"She came into town today with her uncle. Said he wasn't the one."

"Humph!" he snorted. "Have my doubts about that. What do you know about Cantrell?"

Chane grinned. If he told him everything, Stanton's ulcers would go into convulsions. "Lawmen possessing the ideal mixture of fearlessness, expertise with firearms and lily-white morality are damned hard to come by. Two out of three is the most we could hope for," he said dryly.

"So I'll be careful not to ask embarrassing questions," Stanton said, grinning before he settled down to business. "Cattle is big business," he mused, frowning, his florid, heavy-jowled face intent with thought. "All right," he said slowly. "Suppose I agree. We've got too many problems. Cantrell's wanted for killing a passel of Powers's men. If what I've heard is true, he's wanted in Wyoming. He's wanted for robbing your trains. He's probably wanted in other places for no telling what else. Even if I gave him a full pardon, that might just be for the little stuff. How would we handle that?"

Chane sighed. "I don't know. I talked to Winslow Breakenridge. He says we have to let him stand trial. But he thinks that no one is actively looking for Cantrell on those old charges. He thinks that after the trial, you could, in the interests of the territory, commute his sentence if he agrees to provide certain services to the territory."

Stanton snorted. "Great! The judge sentences him to twenty years breaking up boulders in the hot sun or to hang, depending on the mood old fire-and-brimstone Cadwallader is in, and there's no doubt what Cantrell will decide. That's no choice! You offer a man a deal like that, and he'll choose life over death any day. But as soon as he's out of sight, he'll run like hell! We'll never see him again," he said flatly.

Chane frowned. "In theory, you're right. But Cantrell is a man of honor. I feel it. I don't know why, but I'm willing to guarantee it. If he says he'll do it, he will."

Stanton shook his head, grimacing before he took another sip of his drink, set it down, and began pushing at his cuticles again, fairly caressing the shiny nail clipper he always carried.

"You aren't going to like this," he said heavily, "but I think it's too damned risky."

Chane nodded. "I agree that there's some risk, but we're just about pushed up against the wall. If you don't do something about the rustlers, you'll never get elected again—not even as a dogcatcher."

Stanton groaned. He dearly loved being governor. It was a position that provided unlimited opportunities and prestige. Even his wife never questioned him about his many absences. She knew and accepted that the governorship made extreme demands upon his time and energies.

"I can't just pardon the man who has been robbing and killing my people," he snorted.

Chane leaned forward. "So they hang him, everyone cheers, and five minutes later he's forgotten. But you, my friend, still have a problem. Men like me keep complaining to you about losing cattle. Men might even start saying rude things about your leadership abilities."

Stanton frowned. "Is that a threat?"

Chane shook his head in denial. It had been close, he thought, amazed at himself. Was he so besotted with Jennie that he would even stoop to blackmailing his friend to please her in a whim? He didn't even like Cantrell. He was suddenly remembering a casual remark he had overheard once about his being henpecked. Anger flushed through him. It wasn't justified. He loved Jennie and wanted her happy. That did not make him henpecked. But something hardened in him. Cantrell was a grown man. He had damned well known the penalties when he began his career as an outlaw. He could damned well take what was coming to him.

Angry at himself, he stood up. "I'll see you later, Ed."

"Whoa! Wait a second," Stanton ordered. "This is pretty important to you, isn't it?"

Chane sighed. "I don't know."

Stanton nodded. "Let me think about it. That reminds me. I've always wondered why this Devil's Canyon Gang only seemed to rob you. Have you given that any thought? Maybe he knows you?"

"What are you implying, friend?" Kincaid asked dryly.

Stanton chuckled. "Sounds pretty bad, doesn't it? But you have to admit—most outlaw gangs hit banks, stagecoaches, anything they can."

Chane sat back down. He sighed and picked up his drink. "I've thought about it. I had Wilcox working on it from that angle. He checked out everyone who resembled the description we had for the leader of the gang. That's how we picked up Cantrell's name, but we couldn't trace him back more than five years."

Stanton laughed. "He looks older than that!"

Kincaid grinned, and they both fell silent.

"You sure he could do the job?" Stanton asked.

"I'd stake a lot on it. I had Wilcox give me a full report. Cantrell is a born leader. He prefers to go it alone, won't follow man or beast unless they were already going where he wanted to go. He doesn't do anything he doesn't want to do. He's no good-time-Charlie who goes along for the ride. Like I said, his history only goes back five years. There's no telling what he did before that."

"Please," Stanton said, reading Chane's mind, "my ulcers are bleeding already."

"You have sort of a strange relationship with your nail clipper, too," Kincaid grinned, nodding toward Stanton's hands, where he was absently pushing at his cuticles with the blunt edge of the clipper.

"This may seem strange to you, but it never gets headaches."

"You should have married it."

"No. I should have stayed single. I was never this horny when I was single."

Ward Cantrell had several opportunities to regret turning down Kincaid's offer of help. The sheriff increased the number of deputies who were always on guard, and he was given a court date—two days away. An attorney by the name of Winslow Breakenridge, placid and smooth as a frozen lake, appeared out of the blue to announce that he had volunteered to be his counsel during the trial. He asked a lot of questions Ward either couldn't or wouldn't answer and left the jail, shaking his head sadly. "I'm *your* attorney, Mr. Cantrell. If you won't trust me—I can't help you."

The trial, since it was only for train robbery, was poorly attended. Leslie Powers was not called upon to testify. Apparently Kincaid had seen to it that her presence would not be needed. Ward was grateful to Kincaid for that. Leslie had been through enough already.

The trial was held in the Garden Courtyard of the Bricewood West, which seemed ironic to Ward. The room was packed with Kincaid's special agents. Ward recognized Ben, Three Fingers, and a couple of others from the last train robbery. Breakenridge sat beside him at the table facing the judge's makeshift bench. Kincaid stood in the back of the room and watched him with cool, unreadable eyes. The whole thing was totally predictable. It took four hours. The jury was out of the room for only twenty minutes, but there was no doubt in Ward's mind what their verdict would be.

Guilty. The foreman looked right at him when he said it. The judge nodded, asked the defendant to stand, then read him the sentence: hanging, to be carried out at sunrise tomorrow. Ward didn't even flinch; he just stood there listening to the drone of that sanctimonious voice with a fresh wave of bitterness choking him into silence. They led him past Kincaid and a heavyset man with silver-streaked gray hair and a heavy florid face he didn't recognize, and he stopped.

Kincaid nodded. "Nasty break."

"You got tobacco on you?"

Kincaid passed him the makings; Cantrell rolled a smoke with deft brown fingers and passed the makings back.

"Got a light?"

Kincaid handed him a small box of matches. Cantrell ignited one match with his thumbnail, held it to the cigarette with a steady hand, and then looked up, bringing the full force of his cold blue eyes into play.

Cantrell held out the matches, dropped them into Kincaid's hand. Chane held out matches and tobacco, offering them back to him.

"No thanks, Kincaid. If I want anything from you, I'll ask," he said quietly, coldly.

Kincaid watched him walk away before he turned to Stanton. "Well, what do you think of him now?"

"He's got guts. There's some fire in that boy. His hand didn't even quiver."

"He'd kill me right now if he had even half a chance."

"You saw that, too, huh?" Stanton grinned.

Chane nodded. There was still something about Cantrell that bothered him, aside from his impending death and Stanton's unwillingness to commit himself to pardon him. There was a quality he saw in Cantrell that he saw in his son—an unwillingness to bend. Unfortunately, not bending could mean breaking instead. That was why the trait bothered him in young Chantry. Such stubbornness was rarely rewarded by society.

Stanton must have read his mind. "Looks pretty cocky now, but that young man has just been ushered to the gates of hell. It'll take him a little time to realize it, but when he does he could crack under the pressure."

Kincaid shrugged. "I've been wrong about men so many times. I've seen what looked like brave men who had to be carried to the gallows, kicking, screaming, and crying like babies. I've also seen little wimps who walked up the steps and put the noose around their own necks. So don't ask me to tell you which way he will do it," he said gruffly.

Stanton grunted. "Did you decide yet?" Chane asked, wondering how he was going to stall Jennie again.

Stanton shook his head. "I'm still thinking about it. I gotta see which way the wind is blowing."

Chane cursed his friend's political bent, but he knew there was nothing more he could do. Jennie and Leslie would just have to live with it, whichever way it came out.

• • •

Ward Cantrell had never been given to soul-searching, but with the promise of death at sunrise, he knew he would not sleep. "Anybody you want to see?" the sheriff asked after dinner.

Ward thought about his sister, but that was out of the question now. He couldn't make peace with Jenn without crawling to Kincaid, and there was absolutely nothing in it for Jenn. All he would be giving her would be a chance to grieve. She didn't need that. He knew, at least on one level, that Jenn would rather see him than not, no matter what the outcome, but he was too practical to indulge himself at so great a cost to her. There was nothing anyone could do to save him now, and no reason to open old wounds. Jenn had no doubt made peace with his disappearance. She had earned her right not to be disturbed again.

The first hours of the night were spent in denial—he could not believe that tomorrow morning he would die. He prepared for bed in the usual manner, ignoring the small table the sheriff had moved into his cell, ignoring the paper, inkwell, and quill. He laughed to think that he was supposed to want to write letters at a time like this.

About nine o'clock, a wagon rattled to a stop outside, and he moved to stand so he could watch. Two men leaped down and unloaded a long pine box. They carried it inside and put it down on the floor beside the door. The sheriff and his deputies were noncommittal, but the two delivery men looked significantly at him. He felt the first faint stirring in his chest. He walked to the window and looked out. The incessant hammering had stopped hours ago. Now, in the dim light of the street lamps, he could see the gallows where they intended to hang him. He glanced back at the long pine box. All the preparations for his death had been made. Everyone except him had accepted it. He sat there for a long time, looking at the box, and finally the realization sank in that even though he was alive now, and even though it felt like it was permanent and unconditional, these men had the power to end his life. He had never felt uncontrollable fear before, but now he felt himself quaking inside. He really was going to die. This was not a bad dream.

Once he accepted that fact and measured his own helplessness, those emotions gave way to more anger and bitterness. Rage swelled up inside him. If he could have, he would have torn that small cell apart, but he suddenly realized the futility of it.

It was not until the guards had gone to sleep and the moon had arced overhead, that he settled into acceptance of his death and his sister's importance to him. Then he desperately wanted to see her. He was grateful that he didn't have the option to send for her, because he would be forever ashamed of himself for subjecting her to that. Besides, he remembered, she was a Kincaid now. There was still bitterness there, but he did not blame Kincaid for what had happened to him. Kincaid may have speeded up the time schedule so that he would hang tomorrow instead of next year, but there would be no real difference. He was still a nobody, going nowhere. One more year wouldn't have changed anything.

Once he faced that, he knew what had been bothering him for the last year. Now that it was too late, he could admit that he wanted to do something with his life—something to look back on with pride. Maybe that was why he had been hoarding half of the money from his share of every job. He decided he would give his sister the key to his safe deposit box. That way, in case she was staying with Kincaid out of necessity, she would have a way out of the marriage. There was enough money there to give her a new start.

Thinking about Jenn and his family always reminded him what a failure he was. At least there was no one there to verbalize that fact, or tell him what was expected of a Van Vleet. They would hang him in a few hours, and it wouldn't even be noticed in Phoenix, much less make the news in New York. If it did, he could see the *New York Times* headlines now: "Scion Of Once Wealthy Van Vleet Family Hanged For Train Robbery." There were people in New York who would enjoy that tremendously. Dying in anonymity had some advantages. At least Jenn would be spared that final indignity. He hadn't spared her much else, he thought bitterly, suddenly despising himself for his stubbornness.

CHAPTER TWENTY-FIVE

Ward sprawled on his bunk, staring up at the plastered ceiling and wondering if there was anything he could have done differently so that he wouldn't have ended up here, waiting to die.

Could he have stayed in New York? Instead of joining the cavalry? It hadn't seemed so at the time. Too many things had happened that last year in New York. His parents had died, both shot with the same gun. It had been touted as murder and suicide, but he and Jenn had known that their father had been driven by Chantry Kincaid III to that final act of desperation. Then Jenn had by some inconceivable process fallen in love with Kincaid. And he had incurred Kincaid's ire by proxy and had been beaten so brutally that he still carried the scars. And even before he had recovered, Jenn had married Kincaid, without even bothering to tell him.

He had joined the cavalry. Simone had begged him to take her, and he had. Could he have changed his fate by not leaving the service? Would that have changed the outcome of that fateful day in June of 1882? He searched for a beginning, and his mind always came back to that night when he came home to find Simone sobbing into a pillow, sprawled across the bed in the small house they shared…

"Hey, what's wrong?" he asked, moving to her side.

"Nothing, everything," she said tremulously, sniffing noisily.

"You want to tell me about it?"

"No…yes…I don't know," she wailed.

He lay down beside her and took her into his arms. Her lips were salty, trembling, and cold beneath his. He kissed her for a long, slow time, until her breathing changed, settling down into rhythmic looseness that indicated a mood he could handle. When he finally lifted his head, she smiled shakily.

"You're going to hate me," she whispered.

He looked at the luminous delicacy of her face, seeing the tears glisten on her cheeks and the flicker of pain in her wide brown eyes, and felt that same sense of wonder he always felt when he looked at her. "I love you," he whispered, leaning down to brush the tears off her cheeks.

"Hold me." She sighed. "Please hold me."

He held her close to him. "Tell me what's wrong."

"I'm...I'm...pregnant," she blurted.

"And?" he prompted.

"You don't want a baby," she said. New tears brimmed in her dark eyes and spilled over, cascading into the dark hair that fanned out on the pillow. He brushed gently at the tears, letting the relief he felt ease some of the tension that had been building up inside him when he thought there was something serious wrong.

"Of course I do," he whispered. He held her close, feeling the trembling in her slender form. He had no family left of his own, except Simone. Simone was all he had, all he wanted. She was good and loving and loyal, and she had no one except him.

When they had come west two years before, they had brought her mother with them because she had tuberculosis. She had seemed to get better, but she had died eight months ago. And while it was true that he had never actively wanted a baby, and also true that this might not be the best time in the world, since he was scheduled to be officially mustered out of the army in ten days, he was also sure that he could find some way to provide for them.

"We'll manage just fine with a baby," he said firmly. "Why wouldn't we?"

She cupped his face in her hands and they were cold and trembling against his warm skin. "You aren't angry, *chéri?*"

He searched inside himself to see how he did feel about it. His father had always been too busy for him. His mother thought boys belonged in school—the farther away the better, probably. Only Jenn had really seemed to love him. If he had any feelings about the matter, it was probably just that his son would not grow up like that. He would have two parents who cared about him, and he would go to school only if it was within walking distance from home. His son would not learn riding and hunting from strangers and teachers. There were some things a boy should learn from his father.

He must have scowled, because Simone's face registered alarm. "Peter, *chéri*, what are you thinking about?" she asked.

"I was just thinking that I don't want our son to be a bastard."

Tears sprang into her eyes. "But what can we do about that?" she said, the last words dissolving into a wail of sheer anguish.

"We can get married," he said firmly.

Now Simone covered her face with her hands and burrowed into the pillow as if she would hide herself there. "No, no, you don't know..." she moaned, turning away from him.

"Know what?" he demanded.

"I-I don't know enough to be a mother," she wailed.

He chuckled softly. "How do you know that?"

She reached under the pillow and pulled out a tiny blue sock that was dirty from so much handling and strangely misshapen. It had an extra bulge on one side, and the soft, thick yarn still hung from it. Deformed and tiny, with strings hanging from the toe, it seemed so pathetic that he couldn't help himself, the laughter bubbled out of him, surprising him.

"See?" she wailed, covering her head.

"Well," he said, stifling the laughter as best he could, "that's not so bad for a first try. You'll get better. You have months to practice." He kissed her until she forgot her misery, and they made love. Life seemed full and rich.

The next day was his day off. He bought two tickets on the stagecoach, and they went to Dodge City and got married there so no one in Fort Dodge would have to know that they weren't already married. He didn't want anyone throwing that up to her.

Two weeks later, when he was standing in line in the bank in Dodge, waiting to cash his last check from the army, he noticed two white men outside hazing a big, black soldier named John Trayner, while at least a dozen laughing men egged them on.

"Hey, nigger! Come outta that store! Your skin may be black as the ace o' spades, but your liver is lily white! Come out here this minute 'fore we come in there and drag you out!"

The big Negro, an aide to one of the officers at Fort Dodge, was justifiably reluctant to tangle with drunken white men, especially in Dodge City, which was one of the wildest towns in the West. Dodge was the end of the line for all the crews that drove cattle up the trail from Texas, and those southern boys didn't cotton to smart-alecky blacks.

"Yassah, I's coming out, suh!"

"Yassah, yassah!" a tall, lanky, raw-boned man in a large black Stetson mocked him. "You make me sick, nigger! Ain't no wonder they use manure like you for fertilizer back home."

160

"Reckon he wouldn't even make good fertilizer!" the other one laughed. He was a pale, red-haired Georgian who had gained notoriety because of his habit of refighting the Civil War every time he got drunk. "Hey, nigger! This your wagon?"

Sergeant John Trayner, whom Peter knew as an industrious, hardworking man, with a wife and two small children at home, peered out of the doorway of the general store, his eyes round with fear. He hadn't worn a sidearm, probably because he was only coming into town for supplies. There was undoubtedly a rifle in the wagon, but with those ruffians where they were, the rifle might as well have been a hundred miles away.

"Nawsuh! Belongs to the army," Trayner said, still holding a fifty-pound sack of flour he had been in the process of carrying to the wagon the man was pointing at.

"You hear that, boys? This here is a nigger wagon! Hey! Y'all come on! Let's take us a ride in a nigger wagon!"

Men up and down the wide dusty street lounged about in chairs tilted back against the storefronts. Other men stood in small clusters. They could have been talking about the heat, or the lack of rain, or the news they had read in the *Dodge City Expositor*. Now they stopped talking and turned to watch.

Six of the men who had been shouting encouragement now left the shade of the sidewalk and scampered aboard Trayner's wagon. The one who had started the hazing stood in the back of the deep wagon bed. He leaned down and picked up a bag, held it up for Trayner to see, then pulled his knife and slashed the bag, laughing as the contents spilled out. The other men yelled lustily and laughed as the black man dropped the sack he had been carrying and plunged off the sidewalk to save the rest of his supplies.

"Yuh can't do that. That's gov'ment property!" he shouted, his rage overcoming his desire not to cause trouble. Before he could reach the man, the wagon started to move, whipped by one of the rowdies who had taken up the ribbons.

"Who's gonna stop us, nigger?" the one with the knife shouted, laughing at the helpless look of rage that had transformed the black man's face. "Who's gonna stop us?"

Trayner no longer realized that they were all armed and he wasn't. He ran as fast as he could after the wagon and the jeering men. "Stop! Yuh can't take that wagon!"

"Come and get it, nigger!"

The driver whipped the team as the men in the back all laughed and mimicked the black man. One of the men began throwing the sacks and boxes of tins out of the wagon, trying to trip the man who ran after them. Another man grabbed tin cans and began pelting the Negro with them.

"Them's gov'ment property! Stop that! Come back here with that wagon!" he yelled, jumping deftly over the sacks of flour and sugar they threw in his path, fighting his way through the shower of cans.

Peter was just coming out of the bank when the wagon came even with him, the men howling and laughing with insane boisterousness. Peter was shoving his money into his trousers pocket when he saw one of the men draw his gun and fire. Trayner stumbled and dropped, and Peter didn't think beyond the moment. He drew his own gun, fired, and hit the one who had shot the unarmed soldier. The man flipped out of the wagon and lay motionless on the ground.

A yell of outrage rose up from the men in the wagon. The driver *whoaed* the racing horses to a halt, and the men in the wagon bed dropped down, clawing for their revolvers. Peter dived behind a water trough and returned their fire. He saw one man hit—he was flung backward, screaming.

Someone in the wagon called out to the driver to get that damned wagon moving. Peter saw Trayner begin to inch his way out of the wide, dusty street. A man in the wagon lifted his head and pumped another bullet into Trayner. Peter fired almost simultaneously and the man stood up, pivoted, and fell headlong out of the wagon as it began to move forward again.

Peter ignored the receding wagon and rushed to the fallen man's side. Trayner was breathing slowly with an audible rattle. Blood had already soaked through his clothing and was spilling into the dirt, turning dark brown.

"My wagon," he groaned. "They got my wagon."

"The army can get your wagon back. Here, let me help you."

"Aaahhh…no, please, Cap'n. Hurts too bad to move."

"Jesus! I didn't think. I'll go for the doctor," Peter said, cursing himself.

"No." Trayner gripped his arm with desperate strength. "No, won't do no good, Cap'n Van Vleet. I'm a goner, me. Gotta say something to you, though," he panted raggedly, gasping as the pain hit him in waves now. The rattle became more pronounced, and his face was the color of clay, gray and damp.

"My wife," he gasped, "she's a fine, proud woman. It would hurt her to know how they shamed me. She comes from a proud family, wif

THE LADY AND THE OUTLAW

brave menfolks. It would hurt her too bad. Tell her…Would you…tell her I died like a man, please, Cap'n?"

Peter's chest felt clamped by a vise. He was remembering the pretty brown-skinned woman who would have to receive that message. He remembered her as a hardworking woman and a good mother. He felt a weariness inside him. She didn't deserve this, but neither did John Trayner. Peter nodded, gripping the cooling black hand. "I'll tell her," he said, his voice thick.

"Cap'n Van Vleet…"

Peter didn't bother to remind him that he wasn't a captain anymore. He was officially out of the cavalry now.

"Yes, Sergeant Trayner."

Trayner smiled at the title of respect. He opened his eyes, and they were unfocused and glazed with pain. "Tell her, Cap'n," he panted around the deep rattle in his chest, "tell her that I love her."

Peter nodded. He didn't have to ask if he should send for her. John Trayner was too proud to be subjected to that final indignity—having the woman he loved see him lying in the street like a stray dog that had been shot for stealing scraps.

"I'll tell her, Sergeant," he said gently.

One of the spectators shouted that the wagon was gone, and men merged into the street, silent and curious. Snake Edwards, an army scout and a good friend of Peter's, helped move Trayner to the shade of the sidewalk. Someone went for the doctor, but Trayner died before the doctor arrived.

Peter closed Trayner's eyes, covered his face with his vest, and then stood up. There was an unnatural stillness inside him, as if he had not fully realized what had happened.

Snake spat a stream of tobacco into the dirt and shook his head. "Sure wish you had'na butted in the way you did."

Peter frowned his lack of understanding. "What?"

"Didn't change nothing. He's dead just like he woulda been if you'd minded your own business, and now you got yourself a peck of trouble. Those men are on the vigilance committee. They'll either come back here and get you themselves or put a price on your head—won't be nothing you can do about it."

Peter shook his head. "The vigilance committee? I thought that was just storekeepers and property owners."

"Used to be—at the beginning. But the crews coming up the trail got rougher and wilder until the honest men, even in a pack, couldn't

163

handle 'em. So's they let in some of the wild ones and then some more until now the wild ones control."

"So what now?" Peter demanded.

"Depends on how mad they are..." Snake shrugged, his lean face noncommittal. "But I wouldn't stay around waiting if I was you. I'd get my woman and head out of town, far as I could get."

"Run? From a bunch of drunk cowpunchers? There wasn't a man in the bunch. They were a pack of snot-nosed kids," Peter said, incredulous.

"Those *kids* would as soon kill you as look at you," Snake growled. "You've been holed up too long with your pretty little wife. You're out of touch, Captain."

CHAPTER TWENTY-SIX

They borrowed a wagon and took John Trayner home. Peter broke the news to his wife as gently as he could, and then he and Snake carried Trayner in and laid him on the floor of the small, well-scrubbed parlor.

"How did it happen, Captain Van Vleet?" she asked, holding herself stiffly as if her dignity were the only thing left between her and utter and final hopelessness.

"Your husband was attacked by a pack of sneak thieves, Mrs. Trayner. They killed him and stole the wagon and supplies."

Her dark eyes searched his face to see if he was lying to her. Then she looked away. "Was he...did he suffer?" she asked softly.

"No, ma'am. He died quickly," he said.

She stooped down and touched her husband's hand, lying cool and limp across his chest. "Did these thieves...did they shame John?" She looked up at him, and he could see something hardening and coiling within her at the thought of strange men shaming her husband. She knelt on the floor beside his body protectively, and Peter could see her convulsing with fury and violation, speechless with the welter of emotions that were threatening to overwhelm her.

"He had no reason for shame. He did all that he could have done, Mrs. Trayner," he said, his voice strangely thick.

She swallowed and closed her eyes, fighting for control. "You see, John was a good man, a gentle man. That's why I loved him so much. My brother and my father are brutal, hating men, Captain. I never understood them before."

Dragging in a deep breath, she stood up. "Thank you, Captain. I'd best get busy and tend to John."

"Mrs. Trayner, if there is anything either I or my wife can do..."

She nodded as if she understood, but he could tell by the look in her eyes that she would never ask. "Thank you, Captain. I think it fitting that he be dressed in his best uniform, don't you? I'd best get him cleaned up before the children come home from school. You'll excuse me, please, Captain. They'll be here soon, and I don't want them to see him such a mess."

When Peter had turned the wagon and snapped the ribbons, sending the horses leaping forward, Snake, who was doing his best to hold on to his seat, asked, "Where we going now?"

"I'm going to ask Simone if she will come stay with Mrs. Trayner, then I'm going back to town to settle this thing."

Snake rolled his eyes and shook his head. "You're hauling about one brick short of a load, boy."

"I don't give a damn. You tell me who else will stay with her. She needs some female companionship, dammit."

"I ain't questioning that. I'm questioning how smart it is for you and Simone. Those boys weren't play-actin' this afternoon. They're meaner'n poison."

The house was neat and orderly and smelled of the strong lye soap Simone used to clean, but Peter could tell immediately that the place was deserted. He also knew that it would do no good to go looking for her. She had many friends in Fort Dodge. She could be anywhere. He searched his memory to see if he could remember what she had said that morning. She usually told him what she was planning to do, but, husbandlike, he usually didn't listen too closely.

They returned the wagon to its owner and spent the afternoon going from saloon to saloon looking for the men who had killed Trayner. It was nine o'clock, almost full dark when Peter decided they might as well give up their vigil and return home. Snake insisted on riding with him. "You were lucky, boy. Those men could have made a lot of trouble for you."

"Wonder what happened to them."

"Maybe somewhere sleeping off their drunk. Don't rightly understand it myself. Any other time they woulda been right back, raring to finish what they started," Snake grunted.

There was a light burning in the cabin, lighting the windows with a warm, cheery, luminous glow that shone out at him and quickened that little leap of gladness he always felt when he saw the house he and Simone shared together. It was an automatic but welcome response. He smiled into the darkness.

As they drew closer, Peter became aware that something did not feel the same. It was elusive and oppressive. On the surface everything looked like it always did, but the smile faded and he slowed his horse, tightening his legs around the animal's heaving sides. His eyes narrowed as he tried to penetrate the darkness. They drew closer, and the same nerve-end tingle that had made him such an effective Indian fighter now sent an alarm racing along his nerves. He reached out to signal his friend.

"Get down!" he hissed, throwing himself sideways off his own horse just as bullets whined over his head, puncturing the air where his body had been only a split-second before.

The night was torn apart by gunfire. Peter dashed for the cabin. His hand was on the door when he heard Snake drop. He spun around and threw himself in the direction of the sound. Bullets were spewing up a cloud of dirt and dust that blinded him. Gropingly, he located his friend, and with bullets spanging and whining all around them, he dragged him into the cabin. He kicked the door shut and crawled over to the table to put out the light and froze in mid-breath. Simone's arm, clearly visible through the doorway into the bedroom, dangled from the bed onto the floor, white and limp.

Ignoring the crash of gunfire that filled the small cabin with frightful, strident concussions, he crawled into the bedroom. Simone was naked, sprawled across the bed. Her pale skin was blotched with bruises. Her throat gaped where a knife had opened it. The bedclothes were drenched in her blood. The smell of it was sweet, intimate, and cloying in his nostrils.

Peter curled over, unable or unwilling to breathe, his lungs filled with heaviness and clamped by icy bands. Forgetting the men outside, he stood up and pulled the coverlet over Simone, as if that simple act would somehow comfort her. He huddled there on the floor, holding her cold hand, overwhelmed by a welter of emotions, blaming himself. If he had been here…If he hadn't left her alone…If he hadn't gotten involved in something that wasn't his problem…If he had listened to Snake, found her, and left town instead of trying to play the hero…

"Come out, you nigger-loving bastard!" a loud voice called out to him. "Light those torches! He'll come out then."

Snake groaned, and Peter roused a little. He forced himself to crawl back to Snake's side. He didn't bother to put out the lamp. The shooting had stopped momentarily. Snake's eyes were glazed and unfocused. He had taken one bullet in the stomach and one in the chest, high up. Blood mixed with a frothy spittle dribbled from his mouth, creeping toward his ear.

"Simone…okay?" Snake whispered.

"Yeah," he lied, moving to wad his vest up and put it under Snake's head.

"I need a...drink."

Peter crawled to the cupboard where Simone kept their lone bottle of whiskey, tucked it under his arm, and scooted back to Snake's side. He uncapped the bottle and held Snake's head so he could take a swallow. Snake groaned, then coughed. The ragged, tearing sound in Snake's lungs grated through him the way chalk grated on a blackboard, setting every nerve in his body on edge.

"That's better," Snake whispered. "Now, boy, you get the hell outta here. They're gonna burn this place."

"I'm not leaving you," Peter said firmly.

"I'm a goner, boy. You git. Before it's too late."

Peter shook his head. His eyes fell on something small and blue. It was the baby bootie. Without thinking, he put it into his pants pocket. Snake groaned, and Peter clamped his teeth together, praying for an end to his friend's pain. He felt numb and insulated against his own feelings.

"Gimme another drink."

Peter held his friend's head, let the whiskey trickle into his mouth. Snake started to cough—a ragged, tearing ugliness that twisted inside Peter like some crazed reptile, coiling and lashing. Snake's hand groped for his, and Peter held it tight. Snake returned the pressure for a second, and then his eyes rolled back in his head. The rattle of his breathing stopped. Peter sat on the floor of the lighted cabin, holding his friend's hand. He didn't know how long he sat there. The firing had stopped, and he could hear the sound of a few crickets chirping off in the distance as if this were any normal evening.

A hoarse yell rent the stillness. There was the crash of glass breaking, and a torch arced into the room, sailed over his head and struck the lamp, to send kerosene spraying over the other half of the room.

"Come on out, nigger lover!"

Another voice joined the first. "Get a rope! Bring a rope with yuh! We're gonna hang this lily-livered bastard." Others joined in, until a dozen men were yelling obscenities.

The flames caught and leaped up, illuminating the inside of the cabin and filling the small room with a wild roaring sound like a waterfall, close up. Heat slammed into him like a wall that could not be walked through. Peter stood up slowly and walked to the mantel, where his shotgun hung. He scooped up a handful of shells and loaded quickly. He knew he couldn't get all of them, but he was sure he could get some of them before they got him. Flames were licking at his legs; he walked toward the door, the shotgun hanging alongside his right thigh.

"Here he comes! Wing him! We're gonna hang that nigger lover! Teach him a lesson!"

The men were either drunk or overeager. Three of them rushed forward, ignoring or not seeing the shotgun. Peter waited until they were close together, melded into one tight target, and then he swung the gun up and pulled both triggers. The men flew backward as if they had been jerked by hidden wires. The night was shattered by the crash of answering gunfire. Peter reloaded and kept walking. Two men to the left of Peter stood up and yelled. Peter swung around and they caught the twin blasts in chest and belly. A man to the right of Peter panicked and stood up to run. Peter dropped the empty shotgun, drew his revolver, and shot the man in the back. At that point, it turned into a rout, with Peter clearly outlined against the burning house, his gun blazing. When the hammer landed on an empty cartridge, he was the only one standing.

They weren't all dead. He could hear someone groaning, but the fine white fury had drained out of him. He could hear the roar of the fire and smell the acrid, heated smoke, but he could not feel the warmth. He holstered his gun, walked slowly to his horse, mounted stiffly, and kicked the horse into a trot.

He didn't have a single scratch on his body. He rode most of that night, only stopping when the moon set and it was too dark to continue without endangering his horse. He had no food or water. He unsaddled the mare, tied her close to a lush patch of tall grass, and gathered twigs to build a small fire to take the chill out of his bones.

Blind to the threat of pursuit, he kicked a small depression in the earth, arranged the dried limbs and bark, and reached into his pocket for a small tin of matches. The fire caught, and he sat down, shivering with a mixture of shock, exhaustion, and cold. Damp wood popped and crackled in the flames. A coyote yipped in the distance, and the mare snorted in response. Stars blinked overhead. The fire leaped, spreading warmth and light. Something on the ground caught his eye. Puzzled, he picked it up and recognized the small misshapen bootie that Simone had struggled over. He had touched it without recognizing it, but now a whole passel of memories rushed into the void of his numb mind as if they had been somehow attached to the yarn. He was seeing Trayner and Snake dying, Simone and his unborn child dead, and Mrs. Trayner's grief, with sights and sounds and smells and the helplessness and anger all mixed up together so that he felt paralyzed. The memory cut like a razor into soft flesh until it grated against the bone, and he groaned softly and doubled over, unable to free himself from the pain of it, rocking with helplessness.

Two days later, when he stopped at an isolated ranch house to buy supplies off a settler, he heard that ex-army Captain Peter Van Vleet was wanted for the murder of his wife, her lover Snake Edwards, and eight members of the posse who had tried to capture him.

He couldn't get honest work because someone always recognized him. The blaze of silver-streaked flaxen hair made him an easy target. Easy to describe. Easy to recognize. And once he had started running, there wasn't any way to stop.

Now Ward Cantrell, the former Peter Van Vleet, stood by the barred window, looking out at the dark, quiet shapes of the buildings outside the jail, smelling the sage from the desert, letting the soft night winds cool his face, feeling that perhaps there hadn't been anything he could have done, except be someone else entirely. Someone smarter and wiser and more cautious…

He could hear a dog yipping off in the distance and the faint sounds of dance hall music. The sky was beginning to lighten on the eastern horizon—dark purple instead of black. Purple, a few shades darker than Jennifer's eyes.

At twenty he hadn't been able to forgive Jenn for falling in love with Kincaid, but in the last eight years he had learned a lot about women. Too many of them didn't seem to have any control over whom they fell in love with. Sometimes a man's just standing in the right place at the right time seemed reason enough. Too bad he hadn't bothered to recognize this fact about women earlier so that he could have forgiven Jenn before he died…

That thought brought a sardonic gleam into his eyes and a smile to his lean face. They couldn't help themselves any more than Leslie Powers could stifle the passion and fire in her wild little body. She was all woman, definitely unique in the best sense of the word, and every inch a lady.

Leslie Powers. Her name conjured up a well of turbulent emotions, not the least of which was guilt. He had wronged her in every possible way. He had taken her virginity, destroyed her reputation, and left her vulnerable to Younger and others like him. And amazingly, after all that, she had faced them in the jail with courage that bespoke an indomitable spirit. She had shown herself as a woman who would not be cowed. There was something very rare in that one. It was unfortunate that he had met her too late and under the worst possible circumstances.

He sighed. Had he fallen in love with her? Was that why his heart leaped when she walked into the jail?

He closed his eyes, unwilling to answer either question. There was nothing he could do about it now. He glanced at the eastern sky. The horizon had lightened to violet. It was almost time.

His heart constricted. Realization was like a net closing around him. Fear was like a wild thing inside him. *He did not want to die. He wanted to live!* He gripped the bars, pressing his face against the cold metal, eyes closed, fighting for control.

He had faced death many times before, but this, locked up and waiting to be executed by men he hated, was the worst. Much worse than when Mama Mendoza had taken him in. He'd lain on her lumpy pallet for days in a near coma, wracked with fever and pain. Then death would have been a relief. On the field of combat it would have been at least quick. It was a very different thing to contemplate your own death by hanging. It was a simple thing to die after a lengthy illness and quite another to die when you were young and healthy and the blood in your veins could still sing at the mere thought of a pretty girl.

He watched the sky turn from violet to gray; then he sat down at the small table and took up the quill.

> Dear Jenn,
>
> There is far too much to say and too little time to say it in, but I feel compelled to tell you that I left New York in a childish fury when you married Kincaid, and I realize now that it is I who should have begged your forgiveness. Forgiveness for judging you harshly and for waiting until it was too late to come to my senses and to realize that no matter what has gone before, we are still brother and sister. I hope when you think of me it will be without bitterness. I love you more than anything or anyone. Please forgive me. I was and still am a stubborn fool. By the time you read this letter I will be dead. There is no way I can explain all that brought me to this moment, except to say that I did the best I knew how to do. It just didn't work out. Please take care of yourself. It gives me comfort to know that you are happy, so please endeavor to stay that way. The key is to my safe deposit box at the First National in Phoenix. Use the money in any way that will increase your happiness. I love you.
>
> Your brother,
> Peter

He reread the letter, put the key inside, and sealed the envelope. Then he fished a small leather pouch out of his trousers pocket. He painstakingly opened the drawstrings and pulled out a tiny blue sock that was soiled and misshapen. His fingers smoothed it out so that the extra bulge almost didn't show. The yarn was gritty with age and wear. Beneath that, in the bottom of the pouch, there was a delicate gold locket. He opened the locket and Jenn's smiling image stared out at him. Clasping the two objects, the small sock that Simone had struggled and despaired over so long ago and the locket he had taken without Jenn's knowledge, he slowly walked to the bunk, and lay down to wait for Arizona's justice.

When the two deputies, neither of whom he had seen before, came for him, he carefully concealed the locket and the tiny sock in the pouch and gave it and the letter to Tatum's night guard. He asked the man to deliver them to Mrs. Kincaid.

"I'm going that direction about ten this morning. That be soon enough?" the man asked.

"Sure. Ten is fine."

CHAPTER TWENTY-SEVEN

Malcomb stopped before Mrs. Kincaid and bowed slightly, proffering his tray. His expression clearly said, "Who could be sending anything as disreputable as this?" Jennifer looked from his haughty eyes to the cheap envelope and stained leather pouch, then raised her eyebrows in acknowledgment of his unspoken question.

Though he considered it a dreadful imposition, Malcomb was accustomed to delivering pleas for help from women less fortunate than his mistress. Many times she ordered him to saddle a horse so she could ride to some adobe hut and console a woman who had lost a child or a husband. As much as he disliked it, he dared not refuse to bring her anything that was sent to her, for fear of incurring her quick wrath. Her husband's employees and their families were her family.

She lifted the envelope off the tray. "Where did this come from?"

"I know not, madame. The deputy said nothing except that it was for you."

"Deputy?" Her four young guests were talking freely. Jennie walked to her desk, picked up a letter opener, slit the long edge of the envelope, and a key dropped out. She stooped to pick it up, then sat down at the desk, her skirts flowing out around her in graceful sweeps of shimmering silk.

She unfolded the letter and her heart leaped with excitement and joy as she recognized the bold script—it was Peter's handwriting. She would know it anywhere. She read the letter quickly, and the glad light faded to be replaced by disbelief and then anguish.

Sensing something out of the ordinary, the young women fell silent, watching her. They saw Jennifer's cheeks pale, saw the letter crumple in her fingers, and heard Jennie's low moan. Leslie rushed forward and knelt in front of the stricken woman, her eyes beseeching her.

"He's dead," she whispered. "My brother is dead." She clutched the letter, her wide, purple eyes filling with such pain that Leslie could feel tears welling in her own eyes.

There was pandemonium as the others rushed to Jennie's side, two of them bursting into sympathetic tears. Details were forgotten as they helped Jennifer up to her bedroom.

Chane came in at eleven o'clock, content with the way things had gone with Cantrell. The young man wasn't going to forgive him soon, but he had accepted the governor's alternative and agreed to recruit and lead a special force of rangers to catch the rustlers who were preying on the ranchers' stock. They had leveled with him about the dangers involved, and Chane had recognized the same traits in Cantrell that he knew so well in his brother, Lance. Tell him it was a job that couldn't be done, that good men had died trying it, and his blue eyes filled with dancing lights. His husky drawl had been like hearing Lance. "I'm sure you're right, Kincaid, but since my choices seem to be temporarily limited, I guess I'll try it."

Ed Stanton had been tickled. "I should have known you could pull it off. You gave him a challenge he couldn't resist."

"I may have also signed that young man's death warrant."

"God! I feel a hundred years old when you say 'young man' like that. I'm going to have to see Kate to find out if I'm still young enough."

"Do that."

Chane was still smiling when he handed Malcomb a stack of mail. "Where is Mrs. Kincaid?"

"Upstairs, sir. She is being seen by the doctor."

"Matt is seeing Jennie? For what?" he demanded, alarm flooding into him. Jennie was not prone to sudden illnesses. "Has she been hurt?"

"Her brother died. She became quite upset. We thought Dr. Wright could help…"

Chane could see the question in Malcomb's eyes. "That's fine," he said. "You did well." Chane took the stairs three at a time. Leslie and three young women he knew only casually were clustered in a sympathetic knot, whispering in front of Jennie's door. Dr. Matt came out, spotted Chane, and came forward, meeting him at the top of the stairs.

"She'll be all right. She's in shock. She wanted you, and now that you're here, she'll be fine."

Chane brushed past him. Jennifer was on the bed, tears slipping silently down her cheeks into the silvery blond tresses at her temples. He knelt beside her.

"Jennie, love, I'm so sorry," he whispered, gathering her gently into his arms. She pressed close to him, new sobs racking her body. He moved onto the bed, and she huddled against him, crying silently, her body jerking with the force of her convulsions. He stroked her hair, kissing her face and aching with the need to take this burden of pain off her slender shoulders. He barely remembered Peter; the young man had avoided him because of their misunderstanding, but he knew Jennie had loved him far out of proportion to his apparent worth.

She cried and it was a terrible thing to watch—there was such fierceness and rage in her crying—as if Peter had betrayed her by dying while they were still estranged. She was convulsed with fury and violation, crying raggedly, like a stricken wounded creature, unable to speak, like a mother who had lost a dear child, wailing her pain. He held her as best he could until the worst of it had passed, and she collapsed in his arms, silent tears still slipping down her cheeks. He kissed them away and brushed the soft damp hair off her swollen, reddened face.

"How did he die?"

Jennie sighed, exhausted. "I don't know. It said that by the time I received the letter he would be dead. Oh, Chane, you don't suppose he... committed suicide, do you?"

"When did the letter come?" he asked, puzzled, since he had personally picked up their mail.

"One of the deputies brought it."

"Oh." He subsided, accepting that explanation.

"Hold me, Chane," she whispered, her silky voice husky and trembling.

He moved to comply, pulling her closer against him, as responsive to her now as he had been eight years ago when she had walked into his well-ordered life, captured his heart, married him, and then smashed his life down around his shoulders. Only days after they had married, her brother had been beaten, and she was carried off by one of Chane's enemies. He had searched madly for her, and found her only when Commodore Laurey, who hated him, was ready for him to find her. Only after photographs of Jennie, naked and flawlessly beautiful in the arms of another man, were delivered to the Bricewood East in New York City. Heartbroken and betrayed, he went to the address given to retrieve his wife. But once there, he found she was not the same woman he had loved and married. She was holding a gun, which she fully intended to use to end his life.

"Do you remember the day I found you, after you were kidnapped by Laurey?" he asked, his lips against her ear.

Jennie shuddered. She remembered opening the door eight years before and finding Chane there, unshaven and disheveled, his dark eyes filled with a mixture of pain and the lingering hunger he wasn't altogether able to hide. She had still been so thoroughly under Laurey's spell, so filled with his lies and his drugs, that she had almost killed Chane. As if it were only yesterday, she could see his narrowed hazel eyes, hear his strained voice.

"How many ways can you kill a man, princess?" Then his voice hardened. "Either shoot that thing or put it down."

As she thought of what she believed he had done to Peter, how his hired thugs had almost killed her brother, her finger trembled on the trigger, aching for the strength to do what needed to be done. Chane reached up and tapped the center of his chest, where she could remember laying her head, listening to the reassuring thud of his heart. His husky voice was deliberately cold and taunting. "Too low, Jennie. Raise the barrel and point it a little more to the left. The large arteries are here."

He was giving her information as unemotionally as any physician. If she pulled the trigger the way his forest-dark eyes were daring her to, he would never use that tall, lean, clean-muscled body to lure another girl to her death. One tug of her trembling finger, and she would avenge her mother, her father, and Peter with one swift bullet.

She and Peter truly believed that Chane had been the cause of their parents' deaths. Peter had come home from Harvard before the end of the school year, expelled for cheating, the president's letter said. And only weeks after his homecoming, Reginald Van Vleet had killed his wife and then himself, leaving a note that said he had lost everything because of proxies Vivian Van Vleet had signed over to Chantry Kincaid III. She had found their bodies in the study, read the note, and hidden it from the police. Then she and Peter had set out to avenge their parents by bringing Kincaid to his knees. It might have worked, except that she had fallen in love with him, become pregnant, and allowed herself to be married to him. She had been so ashamed of her weakness for Chane that she hadn't been able to tell Peter. Then, before she could correct that terrible omission, Peter had been beaten by men who purported to be working for Chane, she had been kidnapped, and Laurey had spent days drugging her and telling her lies so she would kill Chane when he came for her. She hadn't known until later that they had taken photographs of her with another man and given them to Chane so he would hate her as much as she seemed to hate him.

She didn't know Peter had found out about her marriage to Kincaid until after he had disappeared. By then it was too late. They searched for him, but they did not find him.

It was no wonder she almost killed Chane that day. Facing him, believing all those lies, she knew she had to pull that trigger…His bronze chest, warm and sturdy, swam before her eyes, and she imagined his blood pumping out of torn arteries and felt a wave of nausea sweep over her. She flung the gun away from her and turned away, covering her face with her hands.

"What's the matter, Jennie? No guts? You can't do anything in a straightforward manner? Would it help if I turned my back?"

She turned on him then, her eyes flashing purple fire, all hint of velvet smoothness gone—she was a tigress, poised for attack. "You dare mock me! The man who never, ever takes care of his own dirty work!"

"I'm not going to ask what you mean by that. Your actions defy my understanding. But I don't want to understand what makes you tick. I only want to be insulated from your treachery. You'll understand if I have Steve take care of you, won't you?"

"Oh, yes!" she screamed. "That's your way! The Kincaid way. You certainly wouldn't handle these nasty little details yourself." For just a second she was tempted to give him the gun and make him do it himself, but not even anger could carry her further against the scorn she could clearly read in his eyes. She actually believed he had come there to kill her.

What a twisted, painful time that had been! Only their love had kept them coming back together, searching for the kernel of truth they both knew existed in their emotions for each other. Her love for Peter should have saved him as well…Fresh tears streamed down her cheeks. Peter had never had a chance, not really. Everything he believed in, his whole world, had been ripped away from him. Even she had abandoned him…

"Jennie, love, please don't cry. I didn't mean to bring up painful memories," he whispered, tightening his embrace. He felt her pain keenly, but he could not forget that he had a great deal to be thankful for.

Jennie was one of a kind. There could not be another woman anywhere who could inspire as much love as she did despair. Now she was in pain, and there was nothing he could do except hold her and encourage her to remember her brother with love and let him go.

"You were so close to Peter…" he whispered.

Jennie nodded against his chest. "He was much more than a brother. He was my best friend. I could tell just by the look in his eyes that he was so proud of me—of everything I did. I loved him so much. He had beautiful eyes—very expressive. I always knew exactly what he was thinking. When he smiled he could light up a room. When he glowered, as he often did, he could blot out the sun. He was like a young princeling—girls were crazy for him—but he was cautious. He had a good mind, a good sense of humor." She sighed. "I always compared him to Alexander the Great because he was wonderfully competent. He could do anything: sailing, fencing, languages, dancing, riding, shooting. Everywhere men needed to be good, he excelled. He could have been anything he wanted to be." New tears welled up, and he kissed them away.

"Oh, Chane, darling," she said, faltering, "I would give anything if I could have seen him, talked to him…"

Chane nodded. "I know, darling."

They were silent for several moments. "Did you know he graduated from St. Cyr with honors?" she asked.

"St. Cyr in France?"

"Yes…It was the West Point of France, attended by some of the most brilliant young men on the Continent. He was outstanding in the classroom and on the field. He quickly became a champion with a broadsword, an épée, even a pistol."

"How long was he there?"

"Two years. Then he joined the French cavalry. They sent him to Saumur."

Chane whistled. "I'm impressed," he said softly. "That is *the* finest cavalry school in the world. I rode two hundred miles fourteen years ago to watch a demonstration of their drill practice."

"They are very impressive on horseback. They start with the best horsemen and make them into something really special to watch. They turn away ten men for every one they accept. They only bother with the *crème de la crème.*"

"Why did he come back to the States?"

"We were still doing things as a family. I had a chance to star in *Aida*, so Father talked him into hiring a replacement to complete his commitment to the French cavalry so he could graduate from Harvard. That was highly unusual, but Harvard accepted the transfer conditionally, to be based on their testing of his academic skills. Of course, they wanted to do it for Father because he was one of their most generous supporters, but even stuffy old Harvard was impressed after they tested him." The smile faded and Chane could tell that another dark memory had encroached.

"What's wrong?"

"That was strange, that last six months he spent in New York. Something was wrong, but he wouldn't talk about it. Then our parents died, and neither of us seemed to be able to cope with all that was happening to us. By the time I met you we had grown so far apart we almost never talked. He was like a stranger." She sighed. "And I guess my tumbling into your bed didn't help matters—"

"That reminds me," Chane interrupted. "I know this won't help a lot, but Cantrell accepted Stanton's offer of a pardon in exchange for catching the rustlers…"

"Ohhh." Jennie sighed. "I'm so glad. Leslie will be so pleased."

"She knows. She was up this morning. I would have told you as well, but you were sound asleep…" A knock at the door brought Chane's head up. He kissed Jennie and strode to the door. Malcomb's stern face was puckered into a frown.

"There's a young man downstairs who says he needs to see Madame. He was quite insistent."

"Did you get his name?"

"No, sir. He asked if Madame had received a letter earlier. When I told him she had and was very upset he said he had to see her."

Chane glanced at Jennie, who had curled into a tight shivering ball without him to hold her. She has been through far too much already, he thought grimly. "I'll come down."

The young women had departed. The house was quiet. Ward Cantrell was standing in the entry hall, his tan Stetson in his hand. When he saw Kincaid his blue eyes narrowed into flinty chips.

Chane stopped in front of the younger man. "What can I do for you?"

"I need to talk to Jenn."

"Jenn?" Chane could feel his eyebrows crowding his narrowed eyes. He didn't like this familiarity.

"Mrs. Kincaid, then," Cantrell said, flushing but stubbornly determined that he would not be sent away.

"She's not able to see anyone. She just lost someone who was very dear to her."

"I know," Cantrell said grimly. "I wrote that letter."

CHAPTER TWENTY-EIGHT

Leslie Powers succumbed to the many entreaties of her new friends and decided not to run like a scared rabbit back to Massachusetts. Mr. Kincaid hired attorney Winslow Breakenridge to represent her, and he convinced her that with a little time they could force a settlement of her father's estate. So Leslie accepted the Kincaids' offer of hospitality and prayed for a speedy resolution to her difficulties.

Jennifer seemed to recover rapidly from the loss of her brother, saying they hadn't been close in a long time—it was just such a terrible shock. Life went on as usual. The Kincaids moved in the diamond glitter of a Phoenix Leslie had never seen before.

The fifth night she was there the Kincaids had a dinner party to launch Leslie into the mainstream.

Mr. Kincaid had insisted on paying Leslie the reward for Cantrell's capture. They had ignored her protests, refusing to listen to her disclaimers. Jennifer finally prevailed by telling her that Ward Cantrell was an old friend of hers and that the reward was actually for saving his life when Younger tried to hang him.

"Please accept it, Leslie. Ward is a very dear friend," Jennifer pleaded, her purple eyes filled with warmth. "It is important to me. Really, it is."

Leslie finally shrugged helplessly. "How could anyone refuse you?"

Jennifer laughed and pressed the money into her reluctant hand. "Now, let's go shopping. You're feeling much better, and I've planned a small dinner party for tonight. Let's buy ourselves new outfits—top to bottom!"

Jennifer's enthusiasm was infectious. They shopped all morning. Leslie found a lime-green satin gown, cut quite low in front with gathered sleeves that fell in smooth fullness toward the elbow. The skirt started just under her breasts and fell in graceful gathers all the way to the floor in front and trailed after her in back. Very Grecian in its long clean lines. The skirt was decorated with gold embroidery, very delicate and intricate. No need for corset or bustle under this creation!

Annette put her hair up in a Grecian style, like a beehive, with heavy ringlets falling down the back, tiny ringlets around her face.

Leslie found herself seated next to Chane's business associate, Tim Summers, and wondered if Jennifer had taken up matchmaking also.

"You are absolutely ravishing, Miss Powers," he whispered, his black eyes warm with admiration.

A week of Jennifer's support and Dr. Wright's medicines and salves had restored much of Leslie's confidence and vitality. She had managed to retain her dazzling smile, but the weeks of uncertainty had left their mark, at least inside, and she regarded Tim Summers speculatively. She had seen him on two other occasions, deeply engrossed in conversations with Chane, and now the thought came to her: Was he, since he was Chane's valued friend, privy to all the details of her story? Did he perhaps think, as her uncle had, that once the loaf is sliced, anyone can have a piece?

Everyone in Phoenix knew Leslie had been kidnapped by a man who had held her captive almost a week. Only Jennifer's subtle but nonetheless powerful influence over the female population had stopped overt displays like the one in front of the hotel, but she still, even in recall, smarted from the sting of that deliberate affront, and kept her voice cool as she answered him...

"Thank you, Mr. Summers."

His smile was magnetic. He was an attractive man with lustrous black hair, fair skin, and black eyes that reflected perfect self-confidence. A man serene in the sure knowledge of his own worth, from the excellent cut of his custom-tailored suit to the deep cleft in his firm chin.

Leslie noticed that she was receiving covert but envious attention from at least two of the young female guests, and her natural female competitiveness asserted itself. The next time he leaned close to whisper a compliment, she giggled and was rewarded by more begrudging smiles. Tim Summers was, apparently, a desirable catch. She could understand why—his coloring was striking, and he *did* have good strong features and beautiful manners. Jennifer had said only the day before how hard he labored and how much Chane depended on him. In five years he had worked his way to the top of the Texas and Pacific Railroad Company.

Tim was attentive throughout dinner, barely taking his eyes off Leslie, keeping her wineglass full, and with very little prompting, telling her interesting tidbits about life in the Wild West. He was a transplant also, having been born in Newark, New Jersey.

Jennifer watched her guests with growing relief. She had taken great pains with this party to introduce Leslie to Phoenix. She had imported a ten-piece orchestra from Chicago, ordered cases of French champagne, and stolen Chane's head chef and three of his assistants from the Bricewood West. They spent the day preparing trays of delicacies from the shipment of special foods. This party was proof that the railroad was more than a minor convenience to her. Chane's wonderful refrigerated boxcars carried shrimp from New Orleans, oysters from Boston, caviar from New York.

The Texas and Pacific had changed the face of the American continent. Phoenix was a burgeoning metropolis compared to what it was before the railroad. Now citizens who could afford it had all the necessities and many of the luxuries that were available in the most sophisticated eastern cities.

Before her guests arrived, Jennifer had appraised the accommodations with the critical eye of a woman raised in Paris, London, Vienna, and New York City, and she was pleased. As a Van Vleet, she had moved in the highest circles of society with the Astors, the Belmonts, the Vanderbilts, the Waldorfs, and hundreds of minor luminaries who revolved around them. Now, as the wife of one of the most powerful men in the Arizona Territory, she had deliberately forced the matrons of Phoenix into a corner where they either had to snub the Kincaid family or accept Leslie. If attendance at the dinner party was any indication, Leslie would not suffer at the hands of narrow-minded hypocrites any longer.

This party pleased Jennifer tremendously. In New York City there were any number of arenas for launching a debutante and carrying on the usual mating rituals: the Academy of Music, Delmonico's, or the Patriarch's Balls held at various mansions, but here in Phoenix the most useful tool was still either a dinner party, a dance, or a combination of both.

Caroline Astor might bank a room the size of the Coliseum in roses and orchids and invite the famous "Eight Hundred" to introduce one of her daughters to society. The first families of New York City did not scrimp on their own. Jennifer could remember when her friend Carrie Astor married Orme Wilson. That had been a wedding celebration to remember. The gifts had been valued at over one million dollars at a time when factory workers earned twelve dollars a week. It should have dismayed her, but she had always been part of that world. She took their extravagances and their social rivalries in stride.

In Phoenix, Jennifer had raised a few eyebrows herself. Her own attempts to create a civilized home for herself and Chane had caused a minor uproar in the town—not on a scale like the first families of

New York—but it had been controversial. There were at least two dozen families in town who were wealthy, and five of the women were extremely competitive. They had screamed the loudest of all. When Chane built their home, new homes had sprouted overnight. If Jennie gave a party, she could count on at least five other women trying to outdo her.

Now, with Leslie's future at stake, she was looking forward to some lively competition, because if the rumor mill ground accurately, her predictable peers had already launched into their rivalry.

Five parties were scheduled for the coming two weeks.

Jennifer watched impatiently for her brother. She saw Tim's determined interest in Leslie Powers and enjoyed it on one level. Partly because it would point out to Peter—oops, she corrected herself, to Ward—that Leslie was a very desirable young lady.

Tim Summers leaned close to Leslie, whispered in her ear, and Leslie smiled. What were they talking about? Jennie sighed, wondering if she had made a mistake inviting Summers. What if Leslie fell in love with him instead of Ward? Where was Ward anyway?

"Grew up around railroads," Tim was saying. "Newark lies in the path of most direct routes to New York City. Nearly all the trunk lines have terminals in Jersey City, which is only a few miles from Newark, so it was natural that I would become interested in railroads. There are fortunes to be made in railroads, and a smart man who knows how can beat out the competition. You have to get in first, get a stranglehold on the territory, then keep out competition."

"Sounds very dog-eat-dog," Leslie said.

"It is. You have to get them before they get you," he said, his black eyes shining with missionary zeal.

"Are you good at getting them?" she asked politely.

"Good enough," he said with satisfaction.

When the gaily chattering group moved into the library for after-dinner liqueur and coffee, Tim stopped her abruptly.

"May I call you Leslie?"

She nodded, transfixed by his eyes. He had the most opaque eyes she had ever seen—like black sponges—light and images obviously went in, but nothing came out. The pupils were not distinguishable from the dark irises. Somehow that made her uncomfortable.

"I would like to ask Mr. Kincaid for the privilege of calling on you, if you do not object."

How formal he was! Leslie had the wild urge to laugh. She had been kidnapped, held prisoner for days, maligned on the streets by hateful women, and because of the Kincaids' influence, he was treating her as if nothing had changed, as if she were the same lady with the same impeccable reputation she had enjoyed before.

"Mr. Summers, I am not exactly…" She stopped, struggling for words.

"Please call me Tim."

I am no longer a child, she thought angrily. *As a woman who has lost the magical power of her virginity, I am not someone you could be seriously interested in, and since I am not in the mood for an amorous affair at this time and may never be again, I advise you to look elsewhere for your entertainment.*

But aloud she said, "I'm sure there are many women in Phoenix for you to choose from, Mr. Summers. You have been more than kind. I am truly honored at your interest. And I sorely regret misleading you, if I did, but I am not prepared…"

For the first time she saw a reaction in the midnight pools. His black eyes flared with a starburst of crystallized heat. He turned abruptly and left her standing there while he made his excuses to Jennifer, then retrieved his greatcoat from Malcomb.

Furious, Tim closed the door behind him. One of the cats that hung around the Kincaids' stable meowed plaintively and he looked down. It brushed against his ankle. In a rage, he kicked it in the ribs as hard as he could. Howling in pain, the cat limped into the bushes.

He was on the lawn, heading for his horse, when Leslie opened the front door.

"Mr. Summers. Tim!" He stopped and waited for her in grim silence. Apparently his intensity extended into his personal life as well as his professional life. She stopped about three feet from him, feeling the chill night air, feeling slightly ridiculous. "Why are you leaving?"

"Because you have prejudged me," he said softly, vehemently. "Because I haven't a chance with you. Maybe no one does—I don't know—but I resent being placed among that group of people who have hurt you by their callous disregard for your feelings. I resent the fact that you assumed because of your unfortunate experience that I could only be interested in you either as a casual light of love or a charity case. I see no reason to stay under those circumstances." There was anger and tension in every line and angle of his handsome face and lean form. He was furious, and somehow the intensity of his emotion finally stirred a response in her. He turned on his heel to leave.

"Please don't go," she said to his back.

He turned slowly and she could see him relax slightly.

"I'm sorry," she said softly. "Please feel free to call on me if that is your wish."

He came back every night she allowed him to. Within a week he admitted that he was in love with her. There was no doubt about her recovery after that. She was still female, still effective. She bubbled with life and new happiness. She had survived a terrible ordeal and come out whole. She felt older but more capable. She was grateful to Tim for bringing her back.

She let him kiss her a week later, then he proposed to her, and she refused, gently.

"Leslie, darling, think about it."

"No. I don't want to be married. I'm only nineteen, and I would be a dreadful wife. I would rather paint or manage an art gallery than run a house."

"We'll have a housekeeper. I can afford it. I'm a rich man, darling. You won't *be* a housekeeper. You'll be my little jewel. My princess."

He was easy to manage, but she could feel the pressure building. He wanted her, and she was stalling him. She didn't want to get that deeply involved, to risk pregnancy—or worse yet—marriage!

Kincaid entered the comparative dimness of the Texas and Pacific offices with relief. It was hot as hell outside, especially for November. He had just left his brother-in-law. It had been three weeks since Ward Cantrell had admitted to being Peter Van Vleet. They had done a great deal of talking. Hearing Peter's version of the events eight years before had amazed and vaguely horrified him. It was a miracle they had all survived. His mission today was a result of their talks. He was going to begin the process of helping Ward sort out all of his legal problems.

"Good morning, Mr. Kincaid."

Chane's eyes searched the large room, darting from desk to desk. The large office was well lit and seated four young men who worked under Summers, handling all of the administrative detail it took to operate a railroad. Kincaid did not involve himself with the daily operations. His interests were in creation, not maintenance; that was why Summers was such a godsend to him. He seemed to thrive on all that trivia. The men smiled and nodded.

"Sorry, sir. Over here."

The sound must have reverberated. Chane turned, frowning. When he saw the young man who had stood up, a smile lighted his dark face.

"Is that you, John?"

"Yes, sir!" John Loving came forward with a broad smile making deep dimples in his chipmunk cheeks.

Chane held out his hand. "Good to see you. I sure don't get over here very often, do I? Are you liking your job?"

"Oh, yes, sir," he said with as much enthusiasm as he could muster.

"How do you like Arizona?"

"Oh, well, it's certainly not New York, but I'm learning to adjust."

"Did you come alone? No family?"

"Yes, sir. My folks are still there. I really miss them."

"Come out to the house for dinner. I'll have Jennie fix your favorite dishes. She'd love to see you again."

"Thank you, sir. Any time you say."

"Good. I'll have her set a date."

Kincaid passed on through, and Loving followed him with his eyes. It was plain to see that Loving held him in the highest regard.

Tim Summers was in his shirt sleeves, up to his elbows in paperwork, when Kincaid leaned in the doorway.

"Good morning. Got a second?"

Tim looked up and smiled, coming to his feet. "Always. Have a seat. What can I do for you?"

"I need a complete list of all losses we've suffered that could be tied back to the Devil's Canyon Gang."

Tim frowned. "Okay. I'll put someone on it immediately. May I ask what's up?"

Chane hesitated only a second. Tim Summers had been with him for five years. He was a hard worker, competent, and bright. He decided to trust him.

"The gang's leader is making restitution."

"Cantrell? Where would he get that kind of money?"

"He inherited it."

"So he pays us back. Does that end it? I mean—isn't there still the problem of some broken laws?"

"Yes, but Governor Stanton commuted his sentence and made a deal with him. I agreed, on behalf of the railroad, to drop all charges. Cantrell agreed to make restitution, and Stanton decided, based on all that, to take him back into the fold. In addition to that, Cantrell's inheritance was quite substantial. He's a millionaire now. That looks like a pretty solid guarantee that he won't be robbing any more trains."

Tim frowned. "Maybe my Calvinist forefathers are still haunting me, but wrong is wrong—no matter how much money a man has. Some of the biggest crooks ever had millions."

Chane grinned. "You're absolutely right, but Stanton isn't going to give Cantrell something for nothing. Cantrell has agreed to clean out the rustlers that have been giving us so much trouble. It's a fairly common practice."

"Hire a thief to catch a thief?"

"Something like that."

"But—he has been an outlaw for a long time. He must be wanted other places."

"He's not being actively hunted anymore. He dropped out of sight, as far as they are concerned, years ago. If nothing stirs them up, they aren't going to push it. Later—when he's squared away here—he can see about settling with them."

"What's he wanted for?" Tim asked casually.

"He's wanted in Dodge City for ten counts of murder."

Tim whistled.

"No definite charge. He's wanted for questioning. He fought on the winning side in one of their range wars. About a month after he rode away the other side got reinforcements and regained control. They owned the sheriff, and they had a grudge against Cantrell so they issued the warrant. If he got picked up and turned over to that faction, he'd never make it to the jail alive."

Tim grinned boyishly and shook his head, sighing. "Hard work does have its rewards. At least I don't have a lynch mob dogging my heels."

"True."

"We'll get that figure for you right away," Tim said crisply.

"Good." Chane stood up. "Oh, and send notices to all our offices to cancel any rewards we posted for any members of the gang. And, Tim, this isn't common knowledge."

"Yes, sir. You can count on me. I'll take care of everything."

"Thanks."

His next stop was to see his wife.

"Jennie…"

"In here," she called, loudly enough for Chane to hear her.

"What are you doing in here?" he asked, his frown changing to a smile at the sight of her on the floor of the unused guest bedroom, her voluminous skirts fanned out around her, surrounded by boxes of family portraits, tintypes, and small souvenirs.

She glanced up and her eyes were unusually dark and solemn. "I don't know exactly. Trying to validate a memory...or perhaps dispel a perception..."

"About what or whom?"

"Peter..."

Chane closed the door to assure privacy. "What about him?"

Jennie sighed. "He's changed so much...I hardly know him...He's so...so...aloof, so filled with resolute masculine purpose. He's one of them...the way you were...Oh, how I hated that...when you wore a gun...Do you remember the first time I saw you in your western clothes...how horrified I was. You had the same look of competent masculine arrogance he has. The same spirit of lawlessness. He appears so uncompromising...so unreadable...with such deadly skill..."

"Did he say anything to hurt you?" he demanded, anger rising in him instantly and hotly.

"No, no," she sighed. "I almost wish he had..."

"Why?"

"I was a stranger to him...He was polite. He tried to do everything exactly right so as not to hurt my feelings. But he felt nothing for me except perhaps guilt. If he loved me, it was in the abstract."

Scowling, Chane dropped down beside her and picked up one of the tintypes. It had mellowed into pinkish brown tones. A younger Jennie stood beside a handsome young man—blond, dapper, open of visage, with good humor smiling out of his bland eyes. She was right. There was little of Peter Van Vleet left in Ward Cantrell, a man who projected pure animal power and prescience. A man whose narrowed blue eyes could bristle the hair on a man's neck at twenty paces. A man who could lead an outlaw band, kidnap a woman, and kill ten men in cold blood.

"It's no wonder I didn't recognize him," he muttered.

"Nor I..." Jennie whispered.

Chane was stunned. He searched her face. Under his scrutiny the beautiful, coolly composed face he carried in his heart began to quiver in anguish. Pierced to the quick, he pulled her into his arms. "Jennie, love," he whispered, breathing in the sweet feminine fragrance of her silky hair. He had mistakenly thought her the happiest of women since Peter's—Ward's—return.

"Is there anything I can do?"

She shook her head. "Not unless you can turn back the clock. Trade a cynical man, purposely brash and aloof, for a warmhearted, playful young man who isn't afraid to love..."

Chane frowned his puzzlement. To his eye, Cantrell had done what any man confronted with a startled, stunned, and then weeping woman would have done. He had held her tenderly and with obvious consideration. He started to say as much, but Jennie stopped him with a frown.

"I know...I know. It meant nothing! Because he felt nothing more for me than he feels for any woman in distress. I wasn't real to him!"

Chane chuckled, his green eyes filled with a mixture of sardonic amusement, love, and desire to understand. "There's nothing particularly unusual about that among men of Cantrell's ilk..."

"That is exactly my point. Peter *is* Ward Cantrell. He has become *a man of that ilk*. I admire him tremendously, but I also hate it. I admire the strength that allowed him to survive, but I hate the barriers he has erected, the cold calculation I can see in his eyes on occasion. He weighs everything, risks, rewards...It is too easy to see the roots of his military experience—his easy military carriage, his ability to *take a necessary action*, as they say. At some point a man like that stops being a man and becomes something else. I don't want Peter to be that way. In one sense, though, it was as if we had never been apart, but in the most important sense he was accommodating me..."

"So?" he asked, frowning. That seemed acceptable to him. Why shouldn't Cantrell accommodate his sister? It was the least he could do after all these years.

Anger flared in her violet eyes. "So how would you like to be accommodated? What if we made love and you were fully involved and I was being *accommodating?*..." she said, making the word sound like an insult.

Chane chuckled. "I've always been able to find ways to get your full attention," he said, his eyes darkening.

"But what if you couldn't?"

He frowned. "I guess I'd be concerned. So what do we do now? What do you want?"

"I don't know! I...I guess. I want him to feel his own joy or pain, his own homecoming."

Chane took her hand and kissed it, groping for words to comfort her. He was remembering the way Ward Cantrell's husky voice had thickened, finally failed, when he related the events leading up to Simone's death, how his eyes had hardened into arctic chips as he told the story of the Mendoza family. There was no doubt in Chane's mind that Ward had been through holy hell since he had last seen his sister. While Jennie had grown in her ability to love, nurturing two bright children, Ward was struggling to survive, had been forced to put love aside. Maybe he should explain those incidents to Jennie, but he wanted to spare her...

He kissed her palm and then her lips. "He'll come around...It'll take time...Unfortunately, I don't want him any different yet—he's got a job ahead of him that will require all his nerve and skill."

"I don't mind his toughness. But he's so unreachable. I don't think he expects to survive this..."

Chane laughed. "There, my love, you are wrong. There is a finely honed survival instinct beneath that nonchalant, devil-may-care facade. What you see is Ward's bone-deep belief in his own ability. Some call that arrogance. I call it self-confidence. All he lacks now is the strength he lost when he was wounded. I've ordered him to rest for a minimum of two weeks. By the time he leaves Phoenix, he'll be in top form. Even now he's like a cat—lean, wiry, and indestructible—but there's no depth to it yet. He needs a little more time. I know men. I'll know when he's ready..."

"Do you think he still loves me?" she asked, her bottom lip quivering.

"I know he does. If he hasn't shown it to your satisfaction, I can only assume he can't peel back eight years of reserve in a day or two. Give him time. If it came easily, you wouldn't give a damn for it anyway, if I know you..."

Jennie sniffed, but a smile broke through the forlorn look. "Humph. A lot you know..."

Relieved, he kissed her. Jennie hadn't changed much in the almost nine years he had known and loved her. If anything, she had become more exacting, but in the direction of personal relationships, not in material matters. She was still blithely unconcerned in that regard. Possessions were not essential to her, but the happiness of her close circle of loved ones was singularly important. He gave daily thanks that so far their life together had not been marred by any significant loss.

Fortunately, Chane had always been able to give Jennie everything she needed. Now he frowned. In the future he could give her almost everything...except her brother's safety...and her brother's love...

Annette and Jennifer clustered around the mirror in Leslie's bedroom, admiring Leslie as she posed.

The new red satin gown was far more sophisticated than anything she had worn before. It had a plunging Parisian-style neckline, a chiffon vestee that hugged her breasts, tiny cap sleeves, and saucy flounces over a pert tournure that nipped the waistline. The fabric, which was a very fine silk, fell into a short train in back, emphasizing the slenderness of Leslie's waist and hips. What would Tim think, Leslie wondered, seeing me in such a provocative style?

Annette had created a confection of a hairstyle to complement the cosmopolitan gown—masses of curls twisted into a smooth, high-crowned coiffure that exposed her slender swanlike neck. With the elbow-length gloves that were *de rigueur* for evening wear, Jennie knew there was not a man alive who would not yearn to press his lips at the base of that graceful alabaster column. Leslie looked totally self-confident, as if she could face anything, whether it be the matrons of Phoenix or Ward Cantrell...

Jennie, a hopeless romantic, believed with or without provocation that Leslie was meant for her brother. She did not spend hours plotting ways to get the two of them together, but her creative mind, so keenly focused on Peter's welfare, gave bonuses. This second event was for the express though covert purpose of introducing Ward to "society," in effect bestowing upon him any protection and benefit that her and Chane's considerable influence could afford him.

Ward, upon hearing about it, was skeptical. Chane shrugged. "It can't hurt anything, and it *might* help." With Chane's endorsement and backing, Ward reluctantly agreed to attend. Should she tell Leslie that Ward would be there? Or should she allow her house guest to discover him for herself?

"Do you think it is wise, with my tattered reputation, to wear such a flamboyant color among strangers?"

The gown in question was Jennie's. Her laughter was a typically throaty, well-modulated, sultry release of notes that routinely caused women's mouths to tighten with disapproval and envy. "Why not nail our colors to the mast? If people don't like it, we don't need them. As a *danseuse* and later as an opera *diva*, I found that people respect you more if you are not wishy-washy. That dress is smashing on you! It would be a crime if you *didn't* wear it!"

Even Leslie's dainty kid slippers, low-heeled for dancing, were bright carmine red. Black hair, black gloves, and that shamelessly red gown... Even if she were not vain, the look in Jennie's and Annette's eyes would have satisfied her completely.

"No one else could wear that particular shade of red so well, *mademoiselle!*" Annette said frankly; then, upon realizing her faux pas, she blushed and stammered an apology to Jennie, who brushed it off with a forgiving smile.

"She's right, you know. I ordered the gown and never wore it for that reason." Jennie smoothed the skirt over Leslie's hip. "This gown does marvelous things for your complexion. With your green eyes…" Jennie sighed. "I hope the other young ladies will not be too badly injured by your presence tonight."

"I, for one, hope they are devastated!" Leslie said, her eyes lighted with mischief.

The unexpected reply delighted them. "Bravo!" Jennie cried as the three women burst into peals of wicked laughter.

When they were alone, Leslie turned to Jennifer.

"I'm really grateful to you and Chane for all you've done for me. I…I'm not good at saying things, but I just wanted to let you know that if you ever need me, it will give me great pleasure to assist you in any way I can…"

Pleased and flattered by the genuine sincerity she saw in Leslie's lovely green eyes, Jennie smiled and took her hand. "We've loved having you. I…we both…hope you will consider staying here…making our home yours on a permanent basis. Both Chane and I want you to know that we consider you family. If you have any needs at all, we will be hurt if you do not let us know. If we can help you in any way…it is our wish to do so."

Leslie flushed with a sudden urge to cry. "I can't tell you how much your support means to me…"

Jennie squeezed her hand. "It's not necessary that you do so. To us it is only necessary that you are happy."

Something hard stirred in her chest. "Thank you so much."

To change the subject Jennie said what had been on her mind for a long time. "I'm amazed daily by your resilience and strength. I say this because I have been through a similar experience and know some of its consequences. You've been through so much these last weeks and months. Perhaps when you are ready I will share some of it with you. Remember that I, too, have been through a great deal.

"But now I will give you the advice my agent gave me on my first professional appearance. When you face the harridans of Phoenix in your red gown, there is only one thing you must remember—don't let them hear your knees knocking."

Leslie laughed. "This reminds me of my mother's adage for preparing me for my modest debut into society: 'Social courage is a contradiction in terms: it means a strong desire to be accepted taking the form of elegant indifference.'"

"What a singular analysis! Had I champagne at hand, I would toast your mother's wit *and* her beautiful daughter!" She lifted an imaginary glass. "To Leslie Powers, who is living proof that a woman is exactly as happy as she decides to be."

"Hear, hear!" Leslie cried, getting into the spirit, even as she wished, contrarily, that she were either a better actress or truly happy.

CHAPTER TWENTY-NINE

Debbie Denning had an unruly mass of reddish brown hair that curled like a short, woolly cap around her pert face. Her skin was a healthy, tawny color, made vibrant with rosy cheeks and large, lively brown eyes that sparkled with intelligence and vitality. Jennifer had invited Debbie to meet Leslie the day before the ball, so the young women were no longer strangers to each other.

Jennie's orchestra played rousing waltzes and brisk polkas. So much so that no woman could dance every dance. Leslie and Debbie were temporarily alone, Tim and Winslow having gone to the heavily laden banquet tables along the south wall of the *sala grande*.

"Are you beginning to like Arizona now?" Debbie asked, pausing to cast a critical eye at the enthusiastic couples dancing past.

"Not Arizona, no. But perhaps this house, these people. I love this house. It's a house that a person can feel safe in…"

"There is something so special about this house," Leslie said, "It's exactly like they are. Don't you feel it?"

"You like the Kincaids, don't you?"

"Yes, I do. Mrs. Kincaid, Jennifer," she corrected herself, "is like my mother. Independent, interested in a great many things, and very energetic. She glows with an inner delight, as if she understands everything around her and likes it anyway."

Debbie nodded appreciatively. "That's very good! You've caught the essence of her. And Mr. Kincaid?"

"The rock of Gibraltar, solid, warm, protective, and endlessly reliable."

Debbie was silent, awed by the picture Leslie painted with her words. Then—

"You *are* an artist. You see with an instinctive, undistorted clarity and passion…Is it always this easy for you to reach to the heart of people?"

Leslie laughed. "No, sometimes I can't see beyond the first layer of skin." She was thinking now of Cantrell—for the first time—wondering suddenly what was beneath that iron reserve he hid behind. Man or only a clever imitation? But she stopped herself. This was no time to think about Ward Cantrell…

The Kincaids' ballroom glowed with the timeless elegance of classic design. It was awash with party colors, alive with talk and music, ablaze with candle glow, illuminating the vibrant energy of a hundred young women flirting with two hundred young men.

The dance followed only days after the dinner party. Leslie was astonished by the amount of work the staff had accomplished in such short order. People began arriving on foot and in carriages, women in their carriage bonnets and wraps, the men in their claw-hammer tailcoats, frockcoats, and Stetsons. They filled the house by eight o'clock and threatened to overflow into the garden. The Kincaids greeted each guest by name, warmly, and made it plain to Leslie and probably them as well, that they were keeping track of who was treating Leslie Powers with the respect they had decided she deserved, and who was not.

It was their intention to introduce Ward Cantrell with the same careful attention to detail. Unfortunately, Ward was either late or had decided to forgo society. Jennie fretted inside. Fortunately, her stage training assured that it was her secret. Not even Leslie suspected. There were times when Jennie felt terrible keeping their young house guest in the dark about Ward and his significance in their lives, but Chane assured her of the absolute necessity for secrecy. "The fewer people who know, the better. We cannot afford to have the name Peter Van Vleet bandied about. The authorities in Kansas would be only too happy to reissue those murder warrants."

The men were all in black, but the women burst forth like the colors of the rainbow. Champagne flowed, diamonds glittered, and Jennifer felt unaccountably proud of her small victory. No one dared snub Leslie! She had been accepted!

Jennie searched for Chane in the festive crowd. She found him near the outer fringes of the dance floor, heading toward Tom Wilcox. Tom had worked for Chane for many years. He was the head of the security division of Chane's various enterprises. A totally nondescript man who was loyal, hardworking and seemingly able to blend into any background without effort.

"Good evening, Jennie," said a familiar voice.

"Ed! How nice you could come." She gave him a chaste, ceremonial kiss befitting the governor of the territory, and he smiled. He was robust and jovial. A diamond ring sparkled on his hand, drawing attention to a glass of strangely tinted milk.

"You couldn't keep me away. Jennie, you've outdone yourself this time."

"Oh, isn't it lovely? I'm so proud of this town, these people."

"You did it."

"But they came!" They chatted amiably until the governor saw Kincaid and Wilcox part. He excused himself and caught Chane before he could disappear into the melee of dancers and revelers. They came together at the entry hall of the *sala grande*.

"You treating your ulcer again?" Chane grinned, his green eyes twinkling.

"Milk looks like hell at a party doesn't it? Folks are going to lose confidence in me. What's happening with our boy?"

"He has a lead. He thinks there's a definite possibility that the line we built to the new silver lode is being used at night to move stolen cattle."

"I'll be damned! Now why didn't we think of that?"

"Too old-fashioned, I guess. I'm not used to the idea yet. I can't adjust to the thought that my cattle are being rustled and moved in my trains."

Stanton shook his head. "Jesus, God! What will they think of next? Does he have a line on who's behind it?"

"No. That's why he's back in town. He wants to spend some time at night going through the railroad records to see if he can unravel it."

Stanton nodded, but at that moment was pulled away by a town matron eager to gossip with the governor.

Chane expelled an angry breath. He didn't like Cantrell's latest report. This new possibility meant that someone he trusted, someone in a position of authority in his company, was stealing him and all the other cattlemen in the area blind. But the first report of Cantrell's activities had pleased him. The young firebrand was running true to form. He had assembled the toughest cadre of rangers the Arizona Territory had ever seen and had managed to turn them into a team. Five men, all ex-bandits and outlaws themselves, two of them sworn enemies of Cantrell's, and he had taken charge. Wilcox was still shaking his head over that.

Chane could hear him telling it:

"He gives an order to them to follow him and then he just takes off. Doesn't look back to see if anyone is following him or not—he rode right into a bunch of suspected rustlers. Well, let me tell you, I was worried. Here he is taking on five men all by himself. The others sat their horses awhile, looking at each other like they couldn't believe it, then one of them kicked his horse forward and they all followed him into the fray! They been following him ever since. They could have just let him get killed, but I think they were

afraid he'd take them by himself and they'd look like cowering sissies. He has that kind of blind confidence. After two weeks, when he tells them they are going to do something, they know they will. They don't know how, but they don't question him. He has picked a second lieutenant already and is bringing him along, a young Wes Hardin type named Dusty Denton. They hit it off right away. Denton is smarter than the average bad man, spent some time with the Jackson Hole gang in Wyoming. I think Cantrell rode with them for a while too—maybe at the same time, but I can't prove it."

"*See that you don't,*" Kincaid had told Wilcox with a wry smile. Ed Stanton's ulcers would have grandchildren.

Chane saw Cantrell with Sandra McCormick on his arm. He would have given a great deal to know how he had managed that one. Sandra was one of the prettiest girls in town. A slender golden-haired girl with big smoky gray eyes. He had seen her around town with different young men, usually Winslow Breakenridge. Winslow was a good attorney, but he didn't appear ready to settle down. He walked out with Sandra and Marybelle Lewis, sometimes Elizabeth Cartright. The rest of the local girls were unremarkable, except Debbie Denning, who was new to Phoenix. Debbie was something special, almost like a member of the family the way she fit right in and made herself at home. But then Jennie had a way of doing that—making everyone feel comfortable. He had been married eight years, and it still amazed him how his thoughts always came back to Jennie...

"Hi, Mr. Kincaid," Cantrell said, almost grudgingly. They were still uncomfortable with each other.

"Evening." He nodded. He had deliberately put himself in their way because he wanted to talk to Cantrell. He had thought of more questions he wanted to ask since their talk this morning.

"Trinket, you know Mr. Kincaid..."

"Hello, Sandra."

"Evening, Mr. Kincaid. Nice party," she said, smiling.

She was clinging to Cantrell's arm in a possessive way, certainly not conducive to giving him up so he could talk business with one of the old fogeys.

"Enjoy yourselves," Kincaid said. He knew when he wasn't wanted. He watched them disappear into the throng on the dance floor and turned to seek out Ed Stanton again.

"How long has Powers been ranching in this area?" Chane asked when he and Stanton were alone.

Ed frowned, pulling bushy salt-and-pepper brows down in a heavy ledge of concentration over his narrowed gray eyes. "Oh, ten years, maybe more."

Chane scowled. The T & P reached Phoenix in 1882, six years ago. About four years ago we built the spur line to my brother's silver mine. There doesn't necessarily *have* to be a connection...

"How long has Powers been doing so well? He's running close to ten thousand head of cattle, if Wilcox is right about his estimate. Ten thousand head and better than fifty men."

"Four years, more or less."

"About the time we started losing cattle, wasn't it?" he asked dryly.

The orchestra played the stilted, mincing music for a quadrille and then a minuet, but only a few brave dancers participated, so Jennifer reminded the orchestra leader to play lively tunes—mostly waltzes. This was not New York City!

Leslie danced with Chane, Tim, then Winslow Breakenridge, her new attorney, and was just being returned to Tim's side when she saw a tall, tawny-haired man in an elegant black frockcoat who looked like Cantrell. Her heart didn't cease its mad thumping and she didn't realize she was staring until Tim caught her look and turned to Winslow Breakenridge, who was there with Marybelle Lewis.

"Who's that with Sandra McCormick?"

Winslow searched the crowded dance floor until he found the pretty blonde. "An ex-client of mine—Ward Cantrell."

Leslie felt the blood drain from her face. It was him.

"Are you all right, Leslie?"

"Dance with me, Tim." She sounded tinkly and brittle as she talked, and she had the wild irrational impulse to run upstairs, lock her door, and cry. But why should the sight of him with a girl in his arms have that effect on her? He was nothing to her.

The dance ended and Tim steered her toward Jennifer. He was due to dance with his lovely hostess.

Too late Leslie recognized the man standing beside Jennifer. "Leslie, Tim"—Jennifer caught Leslie's hand and pulled her close—"I would like you to meet someone. Leslie Powers, Timothy Summers, this is an old friend of mine, Ward Cantrell. You both know Sandra, I'm sure."

Leslie heard herself murmuring the proper "how-do-you-do's," even making small talk, but she could feel nothing except the clamor in her body. In a black silk frockcoat with white silk waistcoat and white linen shirt, Ward Cantrell was cool and handsome in a way she had never dreamed. He had been attractive before, but now, set against a sumptuous background, dressed in the right clothes and looking negligently at ease with both, he was like a young prince. Everything about him bespoke a noble lineage. Even the tint and texture of his clean-shaven face looked as if it had been chosen for him with infinite care.

The lean and dangerous look was still there, especially in his eyes—they moved over her like a warm caress—and she saw tiny glints of mischief in the azure depths.

Sandra McCormick didn't once take her eyes off Ward's face. He accepted her adoration as if it caused him not even the mildest surprise. Apparently he was used to quick conquests. That shouldn't surprise Leslie. He looked like a young Apollo descended from Olympus, not a train robber and kidnapper. Her heart was shaking her entire body.

She hadn't missed the affectionate look Jennifer gave Ward. Jennifer was so obvious when she liked someone—she probably wasn't even aware she had taken his left hand and held it all during the introductions.

Leslie didn't know why or how it happened, but when the music started up again they were alone.

"May I?" he asked.

Why not? Neither one of them seemed to be good at small talk. It surprised her that he danced well, though.

He grinned down at her. "You're a real little beauty with your face washed, Leslie."

Leslie flushed. Was he deliberately reminding her of that time they bathed in the stream?

"Thanks," she said dryly. "I thought you spent all your time murdering and pillaging."

"I've stopped."

"You've stopped?"

He chuckled softly. "I'm not murdering anybody now, am I?"

"Can we hope this trend will continue?"

"I can be bribed."

"Is that how you got out of jail?"

"Blackmail," he whispered, brushing her cheek with his lips.

"Stop that!" she hissed.

"Jealous boyfriend? Tell him we're old friends."

"I don't consider you a friend..."

"Too bad."

"Why aren't you in jail?"

"I forgot how much you nagged. Jail was too dull." He shrugged negligently. "I complained and Mr. Railroad gave me a job."

"A job? What do you do?"

"Guard the trains."

"Does he know about you?"

"Everything."

His hand on her bare back was causing a muted ache down the entire length of her body. She lowered her lashes and pretended to be engrossed in watching the dancers all around them while she tried to analyze it. She had danced with a dozen men in the last two hours, and not once had she been aware of a man's hand on her back unless it seemed to move threateningly close to something he shouldn't be touching. Now, as if she didn't have enough problems, she was tingling all over because this outlaw put his warm hand on her bare back.

As if he had read her thoughts, Ward moved his hand slowly up her back to firmly cup her shoulder, sending a sharp hungry pain through her belly. *Damn him!*

"You have the silkiest skin, Leslie," he whispered, pulling her closer. "Let's get out of here," he said, his warm breath tingling on her cheek.

Leslie groaned inwardly. She couldn't believe she was actually considering it! Damn him! What did he think? That he could kidnap her and then drop in and seduce her whenever he felt like it?

"I happen to be with Tim Summers. He's a very nice man. And you happen to be with Sandra," she said waspishly, feeling her cheeks stain with color.

"I don't consider that a condition. You sound like it has an incubation period or something. Is it contagious?"

He was laughing at her now. She could feel the fury bubbling in her veins. "I'm not going to play games with you, Ward Cantrell, and I didn't tell the sheriff you weren't the one just to help you. I was..."

"I know why you did it," he said evenly, his eyes holding hers. He had added that to the list of reasons why he was going to kill Younger.

Leslie forced her lips into a smile and pretended to be distracted by the gaiety and laughter all around them. Damn him! Why did he have to look like he cared?

They danced in silence for a while.

"I'd still like to show you the stars, Leslie."

"No thank you," she said evenly.

The dance ended, Cantrell concentrated his charms on Sandra the rest of the evening, and Leslie couldn't help noticing how effective he was. By midnight Sandra allowed Ward to take her out into the moonlight on the long veranda, and they left shortly after that. There was no doubt in Leslie's mind where they were going or for what. The only questions were why should she notice, and why hadn't she warned Sandra what an unscrupulous bastard he was? But would she have cared? Sandra looked blinded to everything except Cantrell.

Anger and frustration made her reckless. When Tim asked if she'd like to step outside for a breath of fresh air she let him take her out onto that same veranda and returned his kiss with an ardor that pleased him and awakened his hopes and desires.

"Leslie, darling, you take my breath away," he groaned.

"Do I?" she asked, nipping at his earlobe.

"Oh, Leslie, I need you so…"

Leslie returned his kiss and asked him to take her back inside. She danced with a dozen men and feigned gaiety, but underneath she felt a frustration that she could not escape.

Ward's intention was to leave the pretty blonde at her front door and go to one of the saloons to pick up a willing *señorita* for the night. He helped Sandra out of the carriage, and escorted her to the front door of the gingerbread mansion, but she stopped him with a pressure on his arm.

"Ward?" she asked softly.

"What is it, Trinket?"

She searched his face in the moonlight. "I'm not like what you think I am."

What the hell? Ward could feel himself frowning. He hadn't been thinking about her at all. As far as he was concerned there were only two kinds of girls: available and unavailable. Sandra was the latter.

"Oh, I know what you're going to do," she challenged. "You'll leave me here and go find a girl to sleep with…"

Christ! Girls have changed. Maybe Jenn was right. First that hellcat Leslie and now a passionate little female who reads minds.

Blond Trinket tossed her hair with a touch of shy defiance and continued. "I don't want it to be that way."

"How do you want it to be?"

She was trembling with urgency. She wanted him…He had been like an ache in her blood since she'd seen him with a young Mexican girl, a pretty *señorita* with flashing eyes and an insouciant smile. He had looked like he was trying to leave her, and she was trying to keep him there. He had allowed her to tease him for a while, apparently even enjoying it, but when he was finished, he was finished. Sandra McCormick, Daddy's golden girl, who looked shy and virginal, had watched the way Ward Cantrell had handled that girl when he was through playing with her, the way his lean brown hands had looked biting into the creamy white flesh of her arms before he kissed her and put her aside, and she had been sick with anticipation ever since. His hands had been inexorable, handling her easily—as if the girl had been a toy or an object to be used any way he wanted to use her.

Sandra moistened her lips nervously.

"I want to be the girl you bed," she said softly, her voice almost breaking up.

Ward helped Sandra back into the carriage and took her to the house on Barton Street that belonged to Lance and Angie Kincaid. He had the use of it for as long as he needed because they were in Austin visiting the elder Kincaids, and Yoshio, their houseboy, liked having a guest. He hadn't met them yet, but Jenn had raved about her handsome brother-in-law and his pretty young wife. Apparently the brothers were very close. Lance and Angie were supposed to be away for a month or more.

There was a master suite upstairs that he was using. He stopped at the credenza that served as a bar along the wall next to his bedroom door. The house was well built. Each bedchamber had a sitting room with comfortable chairs, a desk, shelves for books and bric-a-brac. On one side the room was crowded with engravings in bronze: horses' heads and fine-looking horses. There was an elegant Wilton carpet on the floor, its chief color a rich blue, and the curtains and hangings were a delicate amber. A chromo of Whittier's *Barefoot Boy* hung on one wall. The double doors to the sleeping chamber were open. The light from the sitting room spilled into it in a widening wedge.

"Would you like a drink?"

Sandra flushed. She wanted this, but it irked her that he had come directly upstairs to his bedchamber. Didn't he realize that she was a nice girl? A well-brought-up young woman of substance?

"Is it going to hurt?" she asked shyly.

His eyes narrowed in suspicion or irritation; she couldn't tell which. "Haven't you done this before?" he asked, watching her closely.

"Not exactly," she lied. What did he expect? That she would admit it?

Ward's lean brown fingers closed like steel bands around her arm, above the elbow. He dragged her forward abruptly, almost savagely, the look on his face changing from irritation to anger that darkened his eyes almost to violet and roughened his husky voice.

"Rich little girls who want to play around should stay in their own crowd." He turned her loose contemptuously. "I'm sure someone will accommodate you."

Damn! She had guessed wrong. She couldn't believe it. He was furious. She had thought he would be excited—the others had been. The thought of deflowering a cringing virgin excited lots of men. Some of them were so aroused they couldn't do anything; they went out of control. Well, she wasn't about to give up. She would try a different approach. She let the tears spill out of her eyes, let her lips begin to tremble.

"I want it to be you," she said softly, tremulously.

"Is that why you tracked me down and asked me to that damned dance, so you could get your ticket punched, have a little fun, and still keep your lily-white reputation among your fine friends?"

She started to cry in earnest. He was harder than she'd thought. She was going to have to use her hidden weapon. Still crying like a heartbroken child, she began to unbutton her gown. This always worked.

"No," she said softly, shaking her head, "No, I—I—saw you in town yesterday and I wanted you ever since." That part was true—too true.

Suddenly the trembling was real. There was something about this man…watching her with a strangely impassive, knowing look in his eyes that frightened her. He wasn't like any of the others. He couldn't be tricked or manipulated.

He reached out slowly, his steely fingers closed around her arm, above the elbow, and she could feel the heat in her belly spreading out like rivers of fire. Her breathing was shallow and painful. Her mouth felt like cotton suddenly, and the pain in her arm, where his warm fingers were biting into it, was sending a sweet savage ache all the way down to her toes. If he sent her away now, she would be sick—violently sick. She wouldn't be able to bear it. If he wanted her to beg…

She opened her mouth to say whatever she had to say, but it wasn't necessary. She saw it in his eyes. He knew she had lied and why.

Trembling, she moved close enough to feel the dry tingling heat of his lean, hard-muscled body. Her eyes holding his, she placed his hand over her breast and pressed forward so she could feel the hard pulsing warmth of him against her belly. His hand closed around her breast, its heat wrenching a low moan that strangled in her throat. She reached up to pull his mouth down to hers, but he stiffened, realizing for the first time in his life that while his body was raging with its usual response to a beautiful, willing female, his mind was strangely unresponsive, holding him there, immobile.

He started to ignore the reluctance. She was very desirable, and he hated pain, especially his own—he would have a miserable night if he took her home now—and there was no need to. He owed allegiance to no one. Leslie Powers had made it clear to him that she was not harboring a lingering desire for him. Trinket's flesh against his was warm and insistent, but he disentangled himself.

"What's wrong?" she asked, a small frown puckering the perfect smoothness of her lovely face.

"Nothing." He took her arm and led her toward the door.

She resisted. "What are you doing?"

"Taking you home where you belong…"

Desire blurred into the pain of rejection in her wide gray eyes, and he felt a corresponding wrenching within himself. He hated it almost as much as she, but he recognized his mental reluctance as an unwillingness to engage in another relationship with another lost female. He had six years of that behind him. It would be too easy to take advantage of her neediness and too hard to get rid of her after he had…

Sandra peered into his face, saw the stubborn light in his blue eyes, and lashed out at him furiously. Her hand struck him across the cheek once, but before she could repeat the blow, he grabbed her arm and held it.

"Let me go! You bastard! Don't hold me! I hate you! I hate you!" But he didn't relent, and she couldn't. She glared at him with hatred until tears blurred her vision and she collapsed against him, sobbing. She cried bitterly.

Strangely, he could have made love to her then; she had become real. His mind would have found the energy for him to cope with her needs afterward…He pulled her close and let her sob out her frustration on his shoulder. When the storm had passed he wrapped her in one of Kincaid's long coats and led her outside. In the buggy she would not speak to him—she huddled as far away from him as possible—hating him.

"Take me back to the dance," she said grimly, blotting Ward Cantrell out of her mind. When the buggy stopped, she flung off the coat, leaped down, and ran across the lawn, her cheeks burning with the shame and desperation she felt.

A man stepped off the front porch and headed across the lawn toward her. In the dancing light and shadow from the play of the electric porch light against the trees she recognized Tim Summers. He stopped. "Sandra?"

"What?" she asked sullenly.

"Are you all right?"

He was glancing at the buggy that still waited at the curb, wondering if the dark shape was Cantrell and what had transpired between them that she was fleeing from him so, and if he could somehow use that knowledge to his advantage. He watched her in the shifting light, noting the simmering anger in her eyes, and decided he could.

"Would you care if I wasn't?" she demanded, her voice strangely taut, choked with pain.

He hesitated the way he did when someone asked an unexpected question of him. "Of course I would."

Of course I would, she mimicked bitterly to herself. Like hell he would. She wanted to hit him the way she had Cantrell, but she didn't know Tim Summers. There was something intimidating about him. Something about the way he watched her that told her he might not send her away… She dragged in a ragged breath, letting some of her anger subside.

"Are you leaving?" she asked.

"Yes," he said. Leslie Powers would not miss him. She had begged to be excused and gone upstairs. She did not seem to crave society the way most young women her age did. She had been polite, proper, but not impressed. Her lack of concern over his attentions had irritated him to the point of fury, but he had managed to contain it. Now he saw Sandra, who looked as if she had been rejected by Cantrell, as a possible means to an end. "Would you like to go back inside, or would you rather go for a ride?" he asked, watching her closely.

"A ride," she said without hesitation.

They rode out to the river, which flowed about half full this time of year. The moon streaked the quietly flowing water with a wide silver band that twinkled and shimmered. Sandra moved close to him, and he put his arm around her and lifted her face to kiss her.

Normally he would not have considered Sandra McCormick a woman to spend time with. He had a natural contempt for her type. They reminded him too much of his mother, who had been the bane of his life until her death four years ago. He had lived in fear that she would track him down and visit, showing the world that he was not what he appeared, that he was only the son of a woman who couldn't seem to keep her gown down around her ankles, where it belonged. His father had abandoned them when he was six; the reasons were not clear in his mind, but he believed it was because of her. She'd had the same look of vague self-interest bordering on madness that reminded him of Sandra and most young girls. He had hated his mother, but Sandra excited him in some strange way. The excitement was a heady overwhelming experience, but when he was not under the influence of the moment he preferred the sort of class that was apparent in Leslie Powers. He had been irresistibly drawn to her level gaze and her well-developed sense of self. She was not impetuous and experimental. Sandra, if not for her father's wealth and position, would be a common strumpet like his mother, like most women. But he had Leslie now. If he were going to woo and win Leslie, it would take patience and the ability to weather a long sexual dry spell. Leslie had made it clear to him, however demurely, that she was not interested in a casual romantic liaison. Sandra could give him the edge he needed, the ability to endure a prolonged courtship.

To Sandra, his kiss was nothing in itself, but the contact of a man she considered powerful had the ability to draw out the dark poison that had welled up in her at Cantrell's rejection. Now she shuddered and relaxed, allowing the warmth and nearness of this man to cleanse her. She didn't care about the consequences of her actions. She was numb to everything except the compulsion that was driving her blindly forward, toward the satisfaction that she needed.

Sandra touched Tim intimately as if she knew him well, and felt him shudder. His kisses grew wetter and more hurtful, but it didn't matter; the only thing that mattered was that he not abandon her, and she knew how to assure that...

Without warning his hand tangled in her hair, hurting her. "Oww!" she cried out, arching backward.

"Promise me something," he growled.

"What?" she whimpered, squirming awkwardly.

"Promise me that you will not tell anyone that you have been with me, ever." His voice was taut, angry, as if she had already betrayed him. Shame flushed through her. His hand was still tight in her hair, but she forgot the physical pain in light of this new demand. She should leave him, refuse to let him touch her, but strangely, her body was responding to the pain. An ache started in her loins, and she groaned in dismay. Mistaking the pitiful sound for protest, he tightened his hand in her silky blond tresses.

"I promise," she whispered, shamed to the core.

"I mean never, never tell anyone. Do you understand?"

"I understand..."

"You'd better. If you know what is good for you..." His voice was hard, frighteningly hard and cutting. In spite of everything, the secret place between her legs throbbed insistently. Tears of shame, fueled by a dark pool of ugliness swelling inside her, spilled down her cheeks.

She made one pitiful move to get out of the buggy, to prove to herself, if no one else, that she still had pride. His hand dropped to her breast and clamped around it like a vise, causing her to cry out in anguish.

"Shut your mouth, slut. Unless I tell you to open it." There was no further opportunity to assert herself.

CHAPTER THIRTY

Ward Cantrell was at every party Leslie went to for the next week, but he didn't ask her to dance again. She watched him with Sandra, Elizabeth Cartright, Marybelle Lewis, and her anger seemed to grow each time she saw him. After almost a week of his presence in Phoenix society, the women were talking of nothing else. He had become an item.

"My father said he made an extremely large deposit at the bank."

"Heavens! All that and money too? I can't believe it!"

"Where did he come from? I mean, I would like to know where they cultivate such devilishly attractive young men."

"Don't laugh! Elizabeth is still in shock. I don't think the poor girl knows what hit her, and he's already moved on to the next girl."

"Where do you go to queue up? I don't care if it is for a short engagement."

They were being deliberately blasé, but Leslie felt her temper rising. Damn him! He had seduced Sandra that first night. They left the dance early, and anyone who saw her could tell just by looking at her now that she wasn't the same girl. Shy Sandra had been replaced by a girl who was very much aware of her body, as a source of pleasure and as a weapon. Ward had taken her out twice and then showed up with Elizabeth Cartright while Sandra was becoming a Venus's fly-trap. Men were buzzing around her like flies around a honeypot. She was a woman now—you could see it in the swing of her hips and the look in her eyes.

Elizabeth and Marybelle, and then Ward had flitted back to Sandra like a stallion with a herd of mares to service.

Leslie was furious. He would go his merry way, but those girls were ruined! He had destroyed their reputations, and he obviously didn't even care for them.

Sandra was at the refreshment table with Phoenix's most exciting young bachelor. She was clinging, laughing, and teasing—almost as engrossed in him as he was in his drink!

The dance tonight was at the Lewis house. Amboy Carlton Lewis was the manager of Kincaid's Bricewood West. Lewis had been in hotel management for twenty-five years—an assistant manager of the Bricewood in New York City. He probably would have remained an assistant manager the rest of his life—good jobs did not open up very often—if Kincaid hadn't offered him this job.

The Lewis house was typical for the period if not for the location. The formal parlor, reading room, and dining room were laid out in tandem along the back edge of the house. The rooms did not have walls separating them from one another. As was the custom the year before when the house had been built, the rooms were separated by decorative doric columns, and the furniture was arranged as if the walls were there. Now the furnishings had been pushed back along the walls opposite the veranda. It was chilly outside, so the several sets of double French doors that opened to let in cooling night breezes were closed. Only one set of doors at each end of the long row of rooms was open to provide ventilation for dancers.

Thank goodness Charles Frederick Worth had dethroned the hooped cage and the crinoline. Leslie Powers's gown was a vision of restraint. She had no desire to look like a walking version of someone's overdecorated drawing room. She was wearing a peacock-blue silk faille gown by Worth. It had been forced on her by Jennie who had never worn it, claiming it did terrible things to her complexion. Leslie did not believe it for a minute, but who would refuse Jennie when she wanted to do something? And it was perfect for Leslie. The peacock blue brought out a smoky blue-green look in her eyes that she liked. The décolletage was a little extreme, the waist wonderfully tiny and belted with a wide velvet ribbon, but the bustle was smaller than most and had a saucy pert look to it that was marvelously flattering. The skirt was pulled tight over her slender hips, hugging her figure and then bursting forth in back into a waterfall of flounces and ruffles, falling into a short train. She loved it!

Leslie and Tim made their way to the punch bowl, and Leslie heard Sandra's irritating voice.

"Ward, darling, please say you'll come tomorrow night. It's so important to me," she pleaded prettily.

"Don't push so hard, Trinket. I'll make it if I can," he said absently, his cool blue eyes scanning the crowd.

Marybelle Lewis and Winslow Breakenridge joined Ward and Sandra, and Winslow dutifully asked Sandra to dance. Marybelle had him well trained apparently. As soon as Sandra was gone, Marybelle moved in on Ward, wanting him to dance with her, and Leslie heard herself almost with shock.

"Well, well, Ward Cantrell. Fancy seeing you here." She smiled sweetly and insincerely as she practically dragged Tim toward them.

"Leslie. Summers." Cantrell nodded curtly at Tim, then dismissed him and let his eyes go back to Leslie.

What female could resist warm blue eyes that so openly told her how beautiful she looked? She might hate him but...he did look handsome— even in a somber black frockcoat that looked like all the others around them, counterpoint to the brilliant colors of the females.

Since mass production had begun with such a passion in the 1860s, fashion was accessible to all. The frockcoat Ward wore was of the finest, softest wool, and the fit across his broad shoulders and around his narrow waist was impeccable. The cut of the lapel was slightly different, though, suggesting that perhaps his suit was a French cut. But where would a lout like Cantrell get a French-cut frockcoat? Unless it belonged to Mr. Kincaid's brother. But if it did, would it fit so perfectly? The trousers were custom fitted too, from the same soft wool. Even the shoes looked like the softest, shiniest leather. If she hadn't seen him the other way, dressed in rough clothes, with guns around his waist, she would almost believe he *was* a gentleman.

The music started again, a waltz, and Tim, always the gentleman, held out his hand to Marybelle, who had no choice but to take it. Leslie suddenly felt too nervous and keyed up to stand there inventing small talk. She looked at Ward almost angrily, and he held out his hand, his azure blue eyes narrowed speculatively. Leslie lifted an eyebrow at his damned arrogance, and his lips almost lifted in a real smile as he swung her out onto the dance floor.

"You dance exceptionally well, Mr. Cantrell. I thought you were only a train robber..."

"Liar. Everyone in Phoenix knows I am an *old friend* of the Kincaids..."

"Was that bitterness? But why should you be? The Kincaids are exceptionally well received everywhere."

Ward's eyes flicked over her, taking in the elegant blue gown she wore. He rarely looked at women in detail. He saw that they were attractive or not. His eye did not notice geegaws and ribbons—only whether or not they enhanced or detracted from the vision. And it was apparent to him that Leslie, with her eye for color and detail, did not fall into the trap that caught so many women.

She looked fresh, small, and delicately made, but with a curious richness and spirit in the way she held herself that caused a tiny spark to leap instantly alive in him. In contrast, he was remembering the way she looked that last morning. There'd been something completely defenseless about her then.

"Did you sleep well?"

"How I sleep is no concern of yours, Mr. Cantrell."

"Sorry," he said, retreating with a grimace.

She was instantly contrite. If they had to engage in this charade to convince Phoenix society that they were both respectable, upstanding citizens, it would be better if they could at least enjoy the conversation, wouldn't it? In repose, Cantrell seemed calm and formidable—as calm as a ray of cold sunshine and as formidable as a typical military officer— manly and up to his duty.

"So you made quite a splash in Phoenix society," she said. "You charmed poor Sandra quite out of her head. The town is teeming with gossip about your being a friend of the Kincaids...You haven't tripped over your spurs once. That is quite an accomplishment. You must be proud," she said, not mentioning he had also seduced the willing Sandra. "I thought you were only a simple train robber."

"A good train robber is a jack of all trades," he said. "Besides, I only worked at that a few hours every few months. The rest of the time..." He shrugged, letting it drop.

"You were in pursuit of ladies fair and pastures green," she said, finishing his sentence.

"No more than you are," he replied, leaning his head back and looking at her through eyes that were mere slits.

She ignored his remark. "Now that you are no longer devoting all your energies to seducing the lucky *señoritas*, word gets around. It is very fashionable to be pursued by you."

A smile tugged at those perfectly etched, insolently sensuous lips. "I thought young executives were all the rage now," he drawled.

Leslie blushed, and Cantrell lifted an eyebrow, while tiny glints of amusement danced and flickered in his eyes like starbursts of summer lightning. Something wild and hungry, like an invisible current, passed between them. A pang of hopelessness stabbed into Leslie, and she articulated what had enraged her.

"Young executives have a future. No woman in her right mind would deliberately get involved with a man who could be hanged by the neck at any moment."

His eyes stabbed at her, and she quailed before their intensity, before the power and maleness of him. He did not believe himself vulnerable to man or beast, but she could not forget that he had been within minutes of being hanged when Governor Stanton finally commuted his sentence.

His arm relaxed its hold around her waist, and that careless, handsome smile came over his face, transforming it again. "You're right," he conceded.

Leslie didn't know what had passed between them, but she felt dazed by it. They seemed to lose the ability to enjoy jabbing at each other after that exchange. She danced in silence.

"I'm glad to see you didn't suffer any permanent damage," he said softly.

Why did Cantrell always remind her they had been intimate? Didn't he ever forget? "No thanks to you," she said sourly. She was tempted to tell him that Tim Summers had called on her every evening since she met him. Would Ward Cantrell care that they sat in the music room after dinner and carried on pleasant, civilized conversations? She with the still life she was painting, Jennie at the piano, and Mr. Kincaid chatting desultorily with Tim, who kept stealing unobtrusive glances at her.

"You're the most beautiful woman in the room," he whispered, his hand tightening around her waist.

"I'm surprised you had time to notice," she said, hating herself the moment the words were uttered. Stop admitting you watch, dammit!

"I don't usually waste time admiring women who are out of my league," he admitted. "Train robbers don't work as steady as young executives."

"By design, I'm sure."

"So," Cantrell said, changing the subject again, "you're walking out with Mr. Dull."

"He is not dull," she defended.

"Sorry," he said, his eyes filled with that sharp light that jolted through her like the electric current she had felt at the state fair in Boston. "You're walking out with your dashing young executive," he corrected.

"He is not dull!" Leslie repeated, instantly angry at him for being so damned observant.

Ward quirked his eyebrows and grinned. "God forbid anyone should even suggest such a thing," he said, his eyes filled with superior knowledge.

He had known the moment he had seen her tonight that any contact with her would be a mistake. The sight of her, cool and lovely in a peacock-blue gown, with her hair pulled back off her ears, but otherwise loose on her shoulders, had caused a hungry ache to race through the entire length of his body. He had hoped he could be as impervious to her as she was to him, but seeing her in her proper setting, armored with all the artillery a lady of impeccable upbringing has, he realized the insanity of his position. Leslie Powers, indignant, with her face set in that imperious, untouchable mien, like some snow goddess cloaked in lacy, crisp fabrics, reminding him of all the untouchable females he had ever known, completely overwhelmed him. In the light of a thousand candles, with her skin so incredibly soft and dewy, she glowed with the purity of an arctic thing. Her gleaming beauty, her extreme femininity, like a young, virginal school girl except for the décolleté gown, her very imperviousness, made him ache to remind her how flawlessly her body could respond to his.

She was so different from Sandra, who pursued him publicly, acting as if they were lovers, as if she didn't remember she was furious with him for refusing her offer.

Seeing the angry set of Cantrell's jaw, Leslie sighed. Now it appeared he did not want to be drawn into conversation, and somehow, knowing that made her absolutely determined that he should be. "So how long have you known the Kincaids?"

He shrugged. "I guess I've known Mrs. Kincaid quite some time. I don't really know Mr. Kincaid all that well."

"They're very nice, aren't they?"

"She is."

Leslie looked at him curiously. "Don't you like him?"

"I don't feel like I know him well enough to decide if I like him or not." A muscle bunched in his cheek, above the lean, square-cut jaw. "He seems to be what she wants," he said, shrugging. He pulled her closer, and she bristled, bringing a look of sardonic amusement into his blue eyes.

"Were you in love with her?"

Surprised, Ward looked down at the flying feet of strangers skimming over the smooth marble dance floor. "She married him. I can't change that."

"You didn't answer my question."

"Maybe I don't see that it's any of your business."

Leslie flushed. "I still can't believe they just let you out like that. Do you suppose they can be that irresponsible?"

"Thanks," he said dryly.

"Well, it just seems like you should be in jail somewhere," she said, realizing perversely that she was beginning to enjoy herself.

"Probably should be," he said grimly.

"I'm serious," she said. "Why aren't you in jail?"

"What did the Kincaids tell you?"

"I didn't ask. They mentioned something about a conditional pardon…But I don't really know what that entails."

"Then you know as much as I do about it. Conditional pardon means they have the right to keep me on a short leash while I do their dirty work, then jerk it back when I'm done. If I please them, they might—*might*— lengthen my leash."

"And if you don't?"

"Maybe they'll hang me. I don't know…"

"Please them at what?"

"Guarding the railroad," he lied.

"Set a thief to catch a thief?" She laughed. "How fitting. How have you done so far?"

He shrugged. "My heart's not in it, but they seem to be patient, probably hoping I don't get a better offer."

"They're right to worry…"

Strangely stung by her words, he kept his tone light, teasing. "Maybe I could go straight."

"Why would you?"

"Why not? Kincaid's paying me almost as much as I used to make robbing his trains."

"You just do whatever is easy?" she demanded, contempt obvious in every carefully measured word.

"Don't you?" he asked, glancing at Tim Summers, his husky voice caustic.

"Tim wants to marry me," she said defiantly.

Blue eyes fairly danced with devilment; his low, well-modulated voice was freighted with awe. "A real catch. Think how respectable you will be."

"You, you…"

"Bastard?" he asked courteously.

"If the shoe fits…"

"There's a lot of bitterness under that satiny little veneer you show the world, isn't there?" he asked softly.

Leslie was strangely breathless. She had danced too many waltzes. "Why should I be bitter?"

"I don't know, but maybe I'll find out," he drawled. They were beside the raised portico where the orchestra played. The french doors opening onto the veranda were only steps away. It was apparent he didn't care who saw him whirl her forcefully out the doors. If she weren't so bemused by the ordeal of dancing with him and trying to carry on a decent conversation, she would have protested, but he gave her neither time nor opportunity.

Once outside, away from the prying eyes of Phoenix's cadre of humorless matrons who watched the young people with envy and suspicion, she turned on him, her eyes glittering like a cat's in the moonlight. "What are you trying to do? Ruin the lives of half the girls in Phoenix?"

"You mean Trinket? What about her?" he asked, frowning.

"Marybelle was Trinket," she corrected him.

He shrugged. "What about her?"

"You've got the whole town talking about her."

"Correction. *She's* got the whole town talking about her. I didn't touch her…"

"I hope your happiness is not dependent upon my believing that."

"No more than yours is."

"Ohhh!" She turned away. "It's a beautiful night, isn't it?" she gritted, her voice painfully brittle.

He didn't answer. He turned her, pulled her firmly into his arms, and set his mouth over hers. Leslie couldn't tell if she cried out or only wanted to. Darkness closed down, shutting her off from reality. Moon, stars, even the strains of music and activity on the other side of the wall, faded out of consciousness. Her fisted hands, white fluttering butterflies against his black coat, made one futile attempt at resistance before they slid up to twine and cling around his neck.

His lips were ruthless and plundering. His hands slid down to caress her back, pulling her against him, crushing her breasts into his warm sturdy chest. This was trial by fire, and Leslie felt herself losing control. He kissed her until her body was aflame and trembling with a recurrence of the hunger she hadn't felt since the last time he held her.

When the kiss ended, he stepped away from her to lean against the banister and roll a cigarette. Trembling, she watched bitterly as his deft fingers quickly and efficiently completed the task. His lean brown hands cupped the blue flare of the match and he shook it out and dropped it. Was there some symbolism there for her? He could light them and he could put them out. What was she to him? Just a girl he had kidnapped once? He wanted her now, though, at least momentarily. But how long did his passions last? A week? Two days?

"Why did you kiss me?" she asked.

"Because I wanted to."

"Why?"

"You keep turning up in my arms, Leslie. I want to know why."

"So, did you find out?"

"Maybe—maybe not." He was holding back now and not sure why. He wanted her, and the kiss told him he could have her, but suddenly he needed more—maybe to punish her for giving herself too easily to Summers.

"Well"—she turned away, hiding the sudden bitterness that welled up within her—"let me know if you come up with anything useful."

She was almost to the door when he stopped her and shoved her against the wall, letting his control drop away, leaning his warm, hard-muscled body into hers, trapping her there while he flicked away the cigarette he had used as a diversion and let his hands cup her face.

"I just thought of something," he said, his voice gruff with some unidentifiable emotion. His warm mouth, only a hair's breadth from hers, brushed lightly over her parted lips, and Leslie had to stifle a groan. Damn him! He was toying with her now, enjoying the effect he had on her! Could those hateful blue eyes see every weakness? Could they see her blood turning to steam because his body was molded into hers, or did his hand, caressing the curve of her cheek, feel the tumult in her traitorous arteries?

"Come home with me, Leslie," he whispered huskily.

"I didn't know train robbers had homes." She was stalling now, praying for strength.

"Will you come or would you like to be kidnapped—for old times' sake?"

"Would what I want make a difference?"

"Try me. It might."

Then so quietly that she almost didn't hear it or didn't believe she heard it: "Give me a *chance.*"

She was suddenly quiet, the frustration and confusion of the past days and weeks strangely stilled in her, everything fading except his presence. Even the urge to issue a witty, cutting remark subsided.

His eyes held hers; a rich current of energy moved through him to her similar to the dark flood of passion he normally aroused in her, and yet richer, more peaceful, awakening a hunger for pure, nonsexual closeness with him she hadn't felt before.

A door edged open and a couple slipped out onto the veranda. The girl was giggling nervously, soft and breathlessly, but the young man's voice was low-pitched, urgent. They moved as far away as possible, partly shaded from view by an encroaching tree, and their negotiating continued.

Leslie looked back at Ward. His eyes had not strayed from her face. Behind him, the moon cast a silvery glow on the roof of the stable at the back of the Lewises' property. Small electric lights encased in festive Chinese lanterns lit the garden pathways with colored light. Laughter and music mingled with the sounds of soft wind and an occasional horse neighing. A dog barked. The other couple was silent now, engrossed in each other, unaware of anything else. The smell of flowers from the garden mingled with the dry night smells of sage from the unseen desert.

"Wait here," he said on impulse.

Bemused, Leslie watched as he leaped over the wooden railing and dropped catlike into the soft earth beneath them. He sprinted to a bush, broke off a flower, walked quickly up the steps, and bowed low before her.

"A flower for a beautiful lady," he said softly.

Leslie had seen a hundred expressions on his handsome face— its mobility of expression was part of his attraction—but never this one. He looked like a little boy, his eyes filled with something so sweet, innocent, and youthful that she felt a melting sensation that started low in her spine and swept upward, bringing a flush of heat and moisture so overpowering that she couldn't speak. She blinked back the heated rush of tears, unwilling to let him see how touched she was. She took the flower, a small, delicate native ornament from his warm hand.

"Thank you," she whispered.

CHAPTER THIRTY-ONE

What would have happened if Marybelle Lewis hadn't chosen that moment to fling open the double doors nearest them and step outside, sending a wide arc of light onto the balcony beside Leslie and Ward?

"Ward, darling," she drawled. "Are you out here?"

Ward stepped away from Leslie, shielding her from Marybelle's sight. "Here, Trinket."

"Oh, sorry to interrupt. Mr. Kincaid was looking for you. I thought you would want to know."

"Thanks. Tell him I'll look him up in a few minutes."

She didn't look like she wanted to leave, so he walked over, pointed her in the right direction, opened the door, and guided her skillfully inside with a firm hand on her small waist that reminded Leslie of too many unpleasant things about him.

"Sorry about that," he said as he returned to her side.

"How many Trinkets do you have?" Then without waiting for him to reply, "They have names. Why don't you use them?"

"I have a lousy memory for names."

She laughed, and it was a soft, bitter sound that probably told him far too clearly that she resented his having so many women that he couldn't remember their names. "Maybe *you* have a terrible memory, but I don't." Furious, flooded with a sudden consuming anger that had kindled when he touched Marybelle's waist in that casual, proprietary way, she stepped away and moved to brush past him, but he caught her arm, pulling her against his warmth and hardness again, his mood as transformed as her own.

His lean fingers biting into her arm were like a narcotic on her senses. She could feel her heart pounding wildly; she wanted him, but she refused to be another one of his Trinkets.

"Let me go!" she hissed.

He leaned down and found her mouth, kissed her lightly, his warm lips searing into her like a shock wave, but she refused to respond. Then, just as abruptly, he relinquished her lips and stepped away from her.

"All right," he said softly, grimly. He opened the door for her, and Leslie stifled the urge to throw herself against him to tear his hateful eyes out. She forced a smile and stepped back into the pandemonium.

Ward singled out Debra Denning, and she didn't stand a chance.

Debra was her closest friend in Phoenix and too sweet and unsuspecting to deserve what was happening to her. Leslie tried not to watch, but her eyes found Ward Cantrell in spite of her attempts to the contrary, cutting a lithe and graceful figure on the dance floor. The waltz was all the rage, and Ward looked handsome gliding and whirling his rapt partner over the floor.

When the music paused, Ward slipped something into the hand of one of the musicians, they broke into the strains of Beethoven's *Moonlight Sonata*, and Ward bowed low and formally to Mrs. Kincaid. Jennie's face glowed with happiness as he twirled her out onto the floor.

They danced beautifully together, seeming to float in time with the rhythm, swept along by the melody. Couples stopped dancing to watch them. Leslie glanced past Tim's shoulder and found Mr. Kincaid. He was standing alone, watching them with a look of rapt pride and happiness that jangled her nerves. If a man like Cantrell, with his reputation as a womanizer, were dancing with someone Kincaid cared about…

Elizabeth Cartright moved to stand beside a heavyset matron Leslie knew only casually. They exchanged pleasantries and then Elizabeth dropped her tone to one that was obviously conspiratorial.

"Mrs. Kincaid and Mr. Cantrell certainly dance beautifully together, don't they?"

The matron lifted her chin and sniffed. "They should. I heard from a very reliable source that they were lovers in New York. Of course, that was years ago."

"No!" Elizabeth gasped, feigning shock.

"Yes. I heard there was a terrible scandal surrounding it, too. Mary Freake, the McCormicks' cook, used to work for the Astors. She told Sarah, my downstairs maid, that the Kincaids separated for quite a spell, and it wasn't that long after they were married. Sounded to me like Jennie may have married on the rebound, regretted it, and just took off. I've heard of that happening before. Of course, I don't know that Ward Cantrell was the reason for that split-up, but she certainly seems quite taken with him for a married woman."

"Mary said the separation was caused by another man?" Elizabeth prompted.

"That she did. Mr. Kincaid took it right hard too, from what she told my Sarah." The matron lifted her lorgnette and expanded her lungs. "Heavens! Well, Mr. Cantrell is a fine specimen of a man. I daresay if he put his mind to it, there aren't many women who could resist him."

Elizabeth sighed. "But one would think a *married* woman would be a *little* more discreet."

Debra Denning and her escort joined Leslie and Tim. The two women listened as Tim and Winslow exchanged greetings, then Debbie winked at Leslie. "I imagine the mothers of all the single females in town are giving thanks this night that Mr. Kincaid had the foresight to marry Jennie."

"What do you mean?" Leslie asked, frowning.

"Well, she looks like the stiffest competition around, doesn't she? I'm sure they're all grateful she's already taken."

Leslie frowned Debbie into silence.

"Sorry, I meant no disrespect. The Kincaids are dear friends of mine. I don't believe that dreadful gossip. I know Jennie is totally devoted to her husband. I was being facetious."

"Sorry," Leslie murmured. "Oh…well…they are attractive together, aren't they?"

"You have truly mastered the art of understatement, Leslie Powers," Debra said, sighing. "Truly mastered it."

"I personally think all that washed-out beauty is overrated," Tim said, reaching to take Leslie's glass from her fingers. "Let's give them something to watch besides blonds." He set her glass on the buffet and swung her out onto the dance floor, and Leslie gratefully lost herself in the music. The sonata ended, another waltz began, and Chane Kincaid cut in on Ward to reclaim his wife. Ward rescued Debbie from Winslow Breakenridge, who was a graceless dancer at best.

When the next dance started Leslie saw Cantrell making his way toward her through the crowd. Tim saw him also.

"Looks like you're about to be singled out for the high honor of the evening," he said, his eyes watching her closely.

"What do you mean?" she asked.

"Cantrell is headed this way to do his duty by you again."

"He has no duty to me," Leslie said, flushing with anger.

Tim laughed. "Easy, darling. No insult intended. I was merely remembering something I overheard to the effect that perhaps Cantrell has eyes for only one, but as a pseudogentleman, he is being careful to dance with a number of young ladies…to disguise his real interest."

"Dance with me, Tim."

Ward danced two more dances with Debbie, concentrating all his considerable charm and attention on her while Leslie danced intermittently, sipping at the champagne Tim brought her.

Debbie smiled a lot, obviously enjoying whatever she and Ward were discussing. He had made another conquest—that was apparent—especially to Sandra McCormick, who watched him with barely concealed petulance.

There was tension everywhere. Leslie felt hot and jangled. Tim was watching her with what seemed like cool speculation in his black eyes. He didn't say anything more, but the tension between them was intolerable.

Before Ward Cantrell could leave with Debra, Leslie allowed Tim to take her out into the moonlight. He kissed her and she clung to him, returning his kiss with ardor.

"Leslie, my treasure, you take my breath away! I love you so...I want you so," he groaned, holding her as if he couldn't possibly let her go.

"Do you really love me, Tim?"

"I love you so much, my dearest jewel, that I am convinced I invented the emotion. I'm wild with despair one moment, elated the next. Awake or asleep I dream of you. Say you'll marry me and end this tumult. Please, darling. Say that you love me..."

It was nice to have a man who didn't chase every female in town. Loyalty deserved to be rewarded. She wasn't willing to marry him, though.

"Where could we go?" she whispered.

"Oh, my darling treasure. Do you mean it?"

"Yes, but where?" she breathed, not daring to examine her impulse.

"My house?"

"Fine," she said, elated that this time Ward Cantrell, womanizer extraordinaire, would watch her leave early, snuggled in a man's protective embrace! She giggled her most sultry champagne giggle when they passed Ward and Debra; she waved fuzzily at her new friend and was rewarded with a flash of narrowed blue eyes from Mr. No Comment before Tim wrapped her shawl around her shoulders, brushed a kiss on her upturned lips, and led her out into the night. Let him look! He might have been the one to awaken her to the pleasures of sex, but she got to decide whom she shared them with!

Leslie shivered at the crisp feel of the chilly night air. It smelled of sage. Night sounds were not audible over the trotting of the horse and the creak of Tim's buggy. The moon had gone down, leaving the road dark except for what light the stars gave blazing down on them. The buggy rocked and swayed, jerked around by the deep ruts in the road.

She didn't have to guess—Tim lived on one of the lots Chane had made available. Two blocks from the Kincaid house and only one block from the house on Barton Street that Jennifer had pointed out as the current residence of Ward Cantrell.

Tim's house was one of those fashionable frame houses she had told Chane she had grown tired of—the clean white rectangular boxes with simple pitched roofs, crisp, painted, and made pompous with engraved cornices and curlicues around the porch and on the support posts. She was reminded of a story she had read in a Chicago newspaper about a firm, in business since 1867, that "is happy to furnish cottages and villas, schoolhouses, stores, taverns, churches, courthouses or towns—wholesale or retail—and to forward them, securely packed, to any part of the country." Was that what Chane had done? Laid out his lots in a typical New England grid and then ordered himself a village? She would have laughed if she hadn't already begun to regret her impulsiveness. Her hands felt cold and clammy, even when she pulled her shawl around her as tightly as she could.

The interior was stark, sparsely furnished, and warm from the heat trapped in the wood. It smelled new, as if no one lived here really. The sound of their shoes on the hardwood floor echoed and bounced around the walls.

"Needs a woman's influence. I'm not here enough to make the place look lived in," he apologized.

"It's no wonder. Mr. Kincaid relies on you for everything."

Tim glowed. "Isn't he amazing? I can't believe my good fortune. I would work twenty hours a day if it was needed."

"What do you do exactly?"

"I'm in charge of the line all the way from San Diego to El Paso. Phoenix is the main office. This is where all the major problems get solved—right here. You need to ship anything at all, see me. I can fix it for you."

"I'm impressed."

He was busy while they chatted. He uncorked a bottle and poured wine into two glasses and led her to the couch in front of the fire.

"You're very efficient, Mr. Summers," she said, feeling embarrassed now. "You must have done this before."

"None of the 'befores' ever mattered, though, Leslie. You feel like the first. There are so many things I want to say to you, so many things I want to do with you. I feel like a schoolboy." He put his glass down and lifted her chin.

Tim kissed her long and skillfully, whispering love words. Once, groaning at the effort it cost him to be gentle with her, he held her tightly, shuddering. His powerful reaction stirred something in her. Even if she didn't like him, she would have responded emotionally to such ardor and extravagant praise; but in spite of both their efforts, her body remained wooden and unresponsive. The face that surfaced out of that welter of confusion in her head was the color of teak: an irresistible swell of smooth lower lip, and narrowed blue eyes that picked up the light and sent it stabbing into her heart. So singularly appealing...

"Leslie, my darling, I'm going to make you forget everyone except me," he whispered, his voice rough with feeling.

What did he mean by that? Everyone? There hadn't been that many! And besides, she didn't need him to make her forget. She was going to forget Ward Cantrell because he was a hopeless womanizer who couldn't be trusted any farther than a beaver in heat!

Tim was kissing her again, this time insistently. She cursed the part of her that was always leaping into situations without any idea how she would get out. Had she needed so desperately to make a statement to Cantrell that she hadn't thought once about the consequences of coming here with Tim?

Now he was urging her up, no doubt to lead her into the bedroom. "Leslie, my treasure, you are so breathtaking."

Was that her voice, sounding so whiny? "Tim...I'm sorry...but my head hurts so...I think I drank too much champagne. I'm sorry," she said miserably. "Please take me home...I don't want the Kincaids to worry about me."

Tim, the eternal gentleman, stifled whatever response he felt. "Of course, Leslie. I forget how fragile you are, my sweet. It has been such a short time, really, since your ordeal. And...I'm a patient man," he said ruefully, "as much as I hate it." His voice, so urbane, took on a note of forced jocularity. "Take all the time you need. Argh!" He yelled like a man being tortured, startling her. "I can't believe I said that!" He half groaned, half laughed, dropping his head in his hands in mock tragic despair that wrenched a nervous, grateful laugh from Leslie.

The house was dark when she slipped in the front door with the key Jennifer had given her days before—the one she hadn't needed until tonight. Her bed was cold and haunted. She shivered between the cold sheets, staring at the star-silvered balcony, watching the intricate, spidery leaves of the trees being whipped about by the chilling night winds. Tim was forgotten.

In memory, she was back on the veranda, fighting for her very life. His mouth was set in grim purpose. He could have been facing Younger…except for the look in his eyes…That one fleeting moment…

"Why did you kiss me?"

"Because I wanted to. You keep turning up in my arms, Leslie. I want to know why."

Did he know now? Had he spent the night making love to one of his Trinkets and feeling empty?

Damn! She should not let Ward kiss her. Just the memory of it, and she was throbbing with that strange weakness and lethargy his kisses and his presence awakened. That wild, impetuous feeling his touch caused was only an ache now—a long, sweet ache that didn't stop. Suddenly she was remembering another time and she could hear her own words, half-strangled with the remnants of passion, half-dazed: *"I never knew…I never knew…"*

In memory, he was a flash of blue eyes, warm teak skin, a certain musky male smell, his hands tangled in her hair. She could not forget the way he groaned and buried his face in the warmth of her throat, then pushed himself away from her.

He was always pushing himself away from her. He might not be interested in her, but at least someone was. Tim wanted to marry her. Tim loved her.

"Leslie, darling," he had counseled, "it takes time and practice to learn to respond." If only he were right about that. Her instinctive angry response was stifled by the gratitude she felt to Tim for graciously allowing her to renege on an implied consent. Thank goodness for Tim and his wonderful sense of humor, his consideration, his support. She would work harder in the future to deserve him.

Without warning, a heavy thrill ran down her nerves—half pleasure, half pain, obliterating thoughts of Tim. Was the flower still in her quickly discarded gown, tucked between deep ruffles?

It was there—small, wilted, and fragile—almost as fragile as the moment when she imagined that unbelievable look on Ward's face—indescribable yet so reminiscent of sweet, innocent youth that she felt the melting sensation again. He had looked so open, so vibrant with feeling…like a young boy with his first crush.

Was it that expression that had started in her this heavy, mindless will to connect with him, to be close to him? Was it the memory of that expression, once gone, erased as if it had never existed, that had wrought such a fury in her when he touched Marybelle Lewis in that smooth, suave, careless, entirely characteristic way?

She wanted to toss the flower in the waste paper basket, but it was so delicate, so sweetly formed, so fragrant, that in the end, even though she chided herself for it, she pressed it between the pages of a book.

I will not become one of those horrid spinsters who hoard books with pressed flowers, she thought savagely. Ohhh! That would be *intolerable!* She closed her eyes and gritted her teeth. Damn you, Ward Cantrell. I hate you. *I hate you!*

Kincaid watched his chance and finally caught Cantrell without one of the girls clinging to his arm.

"I would ask you to step out on the veranda, but I'm afraid you wouldn't respect me in the morning," Chane said softly to Ward while they both gazed out across the sea of swaying bodies on the dance floor.

"What the hell am I supposed to call you?"

"Call me Chane."

"That seems a bit familiar for an outlaw and a railroad tycoon, don't you think?"

"Did Jennie tell you that your parents left each of you over a million dollars?"

"She mentioned it but I still don't understand."

"The letter about the bankruptcy was the fake—not the letter from me. I did write your mother a note thanking her for her proxies—standard courtesy letter—didn't even remember it. The letter advising your father that loss of those proxies had resulted in financial disaster for them was written by Latitia Laurey after she killed them. It was supposed to provide the incentive for your father to have killed your mother and then himself."

"Christ! Twisted but cunning. We fell for it—especially me."

"Unfortunately, by the time the assets could be inventoried and their solidity verified, you were gone. Jennie placed ads in newspapers, wrote letters to every contact she could think of. She always expected to hear from you."

"I transferred money to the bank here. As soon as you give me the amount, I'll make reimbursement for the money I stole."

Chane nodded and they fell silent, each lost in his own thoughts.

Ward was remembering seeing Latitia Laurey that one time at the Palace Theater, through the one-way mirror. Recalling the way she had behaved in that room with Kincaid when she didn't know she was being observed, it was easy to believe she was a woman driven by a powerful, twisted sexuality. After she had been arrested, Latitia had confessed that she had had an affair with Vivian Van Vleet. Ward cringed at the knowledge that his and Jennie's mother had…

He cut off those thoughts. Vivian had tried to break off the affair, Latitia fought with her, and Reginald Van Vleet had overheard enough to scare Latitia into thinking he would expose her. Unwilling to live with the fear of exposure, Latitia killed him and then Vivian. Commodore Laurey's hatred—inspired by his fury at Kincaid for costing him millions of dollars in a business transaction, and fed by Latitia's pain when Kincaid rejected her for Jennie—had grown into an obsession. When the truth came out, Laurey and Latitia had both been sentenced to life in prison.

"I'll call you Mr. Kincaid in public."

"How long do I have to stay in town to satisfy…Mrs. Kincaid?"

"That depends on how you're feeling. If I allow you to begin riding hard before you have fully recovered and something happens to you, my life won't be worth a plugged nickel. Are you getting impatient to be on with it?"

Ward expelled an angry breath. "Yeah."

"Sounds like you've already begun," Chane said, slanting a look at the younger man, and not missing the simmering hostility evident in every line and angle of his lean frame. Not even fine clothes could hide the leashed tension he was controlling with an effort.

Could Leslie's leaving early with Summers be the cause of this? Chane wondered to himself. Had Cantrell fallen in love with the girl in the time they spent together? He didn't probe, because it was apparent that Cantrell was not in a mood to answer personal questions.

"Wilcox tells me you may have a lead on how our cattle are being rustled, and who is doing it," Kincaid ventured.

Ward sighed. "Not who. Though I suspect Dallas Younger and Powers. I've scouted a little. I'm convinced they're using your spur line to move stolen cattle, and then shipping them like any other herd. I mentioned that I've sent telegrams to some friends and acquaintances of mine. The last one should be riding in any day now. Did you ask Stanton if his offer of amnesty could be stretched to include them if they're willing to work?"

"I think so. What are your plans?"

"Nothing fancy. We'll catch Younger with some stolen cattle if we can. If that doesn't work, I'll round up a herd and try to make contact with the person in your office who is being so accommodating."

Chane quirked his eyebrows in approval. "Sounds simple enough to work all right," he mused, his mind tracing the steps and then projecting the various outcomes.

"Dallas Younger and three of his 'special force' are mine," Ward said, his voice hard, as if this point were not negotiable. "I have a score to settle with them. The rest of them—I'll leave their fate to you. If you want them alive, we can scare billy hell out of them and let 'em run or bring 'em in. I don't care either way."

"Doesn't sound like that oath you took soaked in very deep," Chane said, chuckling, then he sobered under Cantrell's glowering look. "Use your instincts. There are some men who'll run like a coyote until dark and then come back to kill you as soon as you go to sleep."

They watched the dancers in silence. Then Chane glanced at his young companion. "Be careful of Younger. He's no four flush. He's a real gunfighter—fast, fearless, and cool as the north side of a January gravestone. I saw him draw once in Tombstone. He can't be rattled by talk or threats."

Ward stiffened, and the anger that had been seething under the surface since Leslie had left with Summers boiled up now, seeking release. "If I need my diaper changed, I'll let you know," he said furiously.

The look and tone jarred Kincaid. Frowning, he sorted their conversation in his mind. Then realization hit him. This man who stood beside him as sturdy and solid as a young oak was the same kid who had hated him eight years ago. Peter hadn't forgotten their old animosity and resented being treated like a child. Peter—Ward, he corrected himself— was a man now, with a man's competence, strength, and scars. And he didn't want anyone, especially his sister's husband, to forget that. Pride surged in him. Peter was a man—one he grudgingly admired; but in his eagerness to protect Jennie from worry or pain he'd almost forgotten that.

He cleared his throat. "I didn't see the gunfight between you and Dodge Merril, but I heard about it," he said, glancing at Cantrell's fierce profile. "Dodge was rated with the best. I heard you gave him draw advantage and still put two slugs in him." He paused for a second. "Younger's probably not as fast as Dodge, but I can't help worrying about you." Chane moved so that Cantrell had to look at him. "I know you don't want my advice, but I need you to understand my position. My wife has been mourning your loss for eight years. Oh, it's true we had a good life, because your sister has tremendous energy and heart, but there was always that cloud that I could see behind her eyes, that eternal waiting and hoping that would surface in little things, and then as time drew on and you didn't show up, in bigger and bigger things. The only comfort I could offer her was that you were obviously alive because my people would have known if you weren't. Now I won't have that to help me. If something happens to you now, she will know it, and knowing it will kill something in your sister that won't ever come alive again."

Chane expelled an angry breath. "And, dammit, I got you into this. It's me Jennie will blame if something happens to you. It could destroy Jennie or our marriage or both if you are killed. You can get mad if you want to, dammit. But I have too much to lose. You *will* be careful of Younger, or by God I will assign a half-dozen men to your tail, and *they* will take care of you," Kincaid threatened.

Ward met that furious green gaze, and it was apparent his brother-in-law meant every word. There was fury and strength in those hazel green eyes and an equal amount of angry stubbornness. But that was not the deciding factor. Ward was moved by Kincaid's description of his sister's plight. Somehow he had thought that she grieved him for a week or two and then went about her life. Learning that she had carried his loss for the full eight years sobered him to the realization of what he had done to her.

"Thanks for the tip about Younger," Ward said.

Chane dragged in a ragged breath and relaxed a little, knowing he was at least partially forgiven. "I only mentioned it because I'm not sure I could beat Younger, and I was considered pretty good in my prime."

"You were a ranger—Texas Rangers are noted for their short primes. If you lasted at all, you had to be damned good."

Chane grinned. "What is this, respect for the elderly or admiration for law and order?"

It was Ward's turn to get serious. "Maybe both. I've, uh, been meaning to tell you that I'm grateful for the way you've taken care of Jenn. I was a fool. I've always been too stubborn for my own good. If there were any way I could make it up to her, I would do it," he said, meaning it.

Chane nodded and they were silent for a while, watching the dancers. "Use your judgment with the rest of Powers's hired hands. If they're following Powers's and Younger's orders, scare hell out of them and let 'em run. If they're likely to hang around making trouble..." His words trailed off. He was remembering how hard life was for a range-riding cowpuncher. Sometimes a man got tired of moving from range to range looking for an honest man to work for. He'd personally known some good men who put up with a crooked spread for a while. A man could do that as long as they didn't ask too much from him personally. He should have known that Cantrell, of all men, would think of that angle.

"Consider it done," Ward said quietly.

Ward found his hostess and thanked her. He located Blueberry in the welter of horses and carriages in the front yard. Mounted, he turned the horse toward the house on Barton Street, sorry he had gone to the social.

The wind was cool and dry against his skin. Seeing Leslie with a man who could offer her all the things she needed and deserved had forced him to face some hard truths about himself and her. She was strong, fiercely loyal to the man of her choice, and accustomed to life's better offerings. She was not a woman who would settle for a man living under a cloud, even if she were physically attracted to him. Bright, vibrant, passionate, she could and would walk in the sunshine.

The horse snorted. The lighter outline of the Kincaids' stable loomed before him. He stabled the animal, unsaddled him, and did the chores he hated doing in the rotten mood he was in. After he changed clothes he would walk to the offices of the Texas and Pacific and continue the task of going through the books, in hopes of finding some clue.

There was a light in the library—a bright yellow line beneath the door, shining into the hallway. He opened the door slowly. Trinket and the blue-eyed girl whose interruption had infuriated Leslie were sitting on the sofa, smiling at him as if he should have been expecting them.

Scowling, he pulled his coat off and tossed it over a chair. Blond Trinket was standing in front of the fire that Yoshio, the Kincaids' houseboy, had laid. Ward walked to the buffet along the wall and poured himself a drink. He tossed it down, felt the hot jolt of the whiskey, but beyond that—nothing. The mood that had started when Leslie turned him down for Summers was still in him. "Ladies." He inclined his head. "What's going on here?"

"We wanted to see you," Sandra said.

Ward had visions of a posse breaking down the door to rescue the two of them and shook his head. "See me in the daytime. Are you crazy?"

Sandra stood up and walked toward him. "We wanted to be with you."

Normally he would have appreciated all the trouble they had probably gone to so they could come here to surprise him. "Does your father know where you are?" he demanded.

"We sneaked out. Please, Ward, don't be angry. I need you tonight," she said, stepping against him. "I was miserable at the dance. You didn't pay any attention to me." She slipped her arms around his neck and buried her face against his chest. "Ward, darling, I belong to you. Please let me stay."

Ward glanced at the other girl, and she shrugged and looked embarrassed, not sure what part she was supposed to play. He disengaged himself and walked back to the sideboard, smelled the decanters, and then poured himself another drink, stalling for time. He tossed down half of it, enjoying the heat that spread out inside him. "Do either of you want a drink?"

"No." There was something in the way she said it that brought his head around. Sandra had wiggled out of her gown and stepped away from it, leaving it in a heap behind her. She looked like a sleepwalker, and the other girl, instead of looking shocked because her friend was naked except for her jewelry, looked equally dazed. She was barely breathing. He had the wild impulse to walk out of that house and never return. How had she managed to undress so fast? What happened to the usual accouterments that women wore?

She slipped into his arms, and his impulse to flee vanished. Warm body with the feel and smell of female always worked. His body knew what to do—even when his head was completely confused. She lifted her lips and dragged his head down to meet them, and the dark knowledge of the body took over.

That's the way Denton found them: Ward still in his black suit, Sandra McCormick naked and breathless in his arms. A beautiful dark-haired girl on the sofa watching them. Denton stopped in the doorway, his mouth gaping like a catfish.

Dusty Denton, born Robert Buckmeister Denton, had been on this wild frontier for seven years, almost as long as Ward. He knew that in the Territories the standards of morality had relaxed to a remarkable degree, but there were limits, and these looked like daughters of respectable residents. He had seen the females who weren't. He also knew that in any group of people, females included, there would be a certain percentage who did not obey the rules—even when they were from good families and knew them all by heart. He'd met his share of women like that. It had never mattered whether they were from rich families or poor. Morals didn't seem to understand class boundaries.

In large eastern cities the netherworld of the criminal elements who lived off the scraps of society were tucked away in distant parts of the city. Nice women were not exposed to that sort of thing. Here, saloons, dance halls, churches, and brothels existed side by side—each influencing the other. Sharp lines of demarcation between good and bad got blurred. Cattlemen branded mavericks, gunmen shot men in the streets, prostitutes got married and went to church regularly.

Frontier natives did not have time for lengthy courtships. Men lived and died with surprising suddenness. Alive one second, dead the next. Frontier towns did not breed gentility—in its men or in its women.

He had no guarantees either. He could be dead tomorrow. Or the next day. Kincaid and the governor had carefully explained the risks and rewards. He decided to follow Cantrell's example, whatever the risk.

There was a moment of stunned silence before Ward spoke, his husky voice smooth as velvet in the stillness. "Which one do you want?"

Nobody breathed. The muted ache that had begun when Ward had kissed her spread downward, turning her knees to rubber.

Dusty Denton almost strangled in his attempt to remain as calm as Ward looked. A beautiful naked girl, in a room with two fully clothed men, turned his blood into steam. His voice sounded hoarse. "The blonde."

Sandra turned back to Ward. "Are you serious?" she whispered, her eyes enormous in her face. She was tingling in spite of the sudden fear that turned her heartbeat into a heavy thumping in her chest. She was on fire—all over. She knew by the quiet knowledge in his blue eyes that Ward could tell. Something relaxed in her, secure in the knowledge that she didn't have to pretend with him.

Ward shrugged. "Do you want me to be?"

Something was born in Sandra's eyes, something primitive and vibrantly alive. "Yes," she said softly. "I belong to you. You can give me away if you want to."

Ward leaned down and kissed her, but he could tell she had already transferred her passion to the other man. She turned obediently and walked into the young man's arms.

Denton looked like he might double over with the sudden ache her solemn, wide-eyed compliance caused in him. He shot a look at Ward, who picked up his glass and was draining it. A cry for help, but the girl took his hand. He followed her out of the room.

Ward turned to Blue-Eyed Trinket. Excitement and fear mingled in her eyes. He could see the pulse in her throat. He took her hand. "Come on, I'll take you home."

"No," she said, the sound small and frightened, but defiant as well.

He hesitated. Leslie was in Tim Summers's bed. He had known by the defiant look in her angry green eyes. He might as well enjoy himself. He damned sure wasn't going to become a monk because she rejected him, but even as he said it, a part of him recoiled. He definitely would not become a monk, but he also could not make love to another woman tonight. Not with the pain of Leslie's rejection so fresh.

His grip tightened on the girl's arm.

"Yeah," he said, forcing a grin. "I knew you were teasing."

Frowning, she allowed herself to be led away.

"Where's your coat?" he asked.

"I didn't remember it. We left in sort of a hurry."

Ward took one of Lance Kincaid's out of the closet and put it around her shoulders. "This should keep you warm till I get you safely home."

CHAPTER THIRTY-TWO

Just before noon on Saturday Tim Summers stopped beside John Loving's desk. Loving stood up quickly.

"Yes, sir?"

Summer's cold black eyes raked over him, making John squirm inside. This last month on the job was the most precarious in his career. His confidence in himself was badly shaken.

"Come into my office," Summers said curtly.

He knew by the tone of Summers's voice that he was in trouble. Loving followed quickly. Summers poured himself a cup of coffee and sat down. John remained standing uncertainly. Summers didn't usually allow him to sit.

"Sit down," Summers said crossly. "I hate having to crane my neck to look at you."

Flushing, John took the seat across from Summers's desk. He resisted the urge to loosen his collar, forced himself to endure the cold stare of his boss, but he couldn't control the reddening of his face.

"I saw that memo you wrote to Jack Frazier telling him to buy from Smith Mercantile instead of Bauer's." There was barely controlled fury in Summers's black eyes. The angry set of his features stunned John Loving.

"But that's what you told me to do," he blurted.

"I don't give a damn! When I tell you to do something, I want you to do it—not write memos about it covering your ass!"

Summers picked up a letter. "Mr. Summers has directed that in the future we purchase all uniforms from..." he quoted sarcastically from the memo; then he threw it savagely at Loving. "What the hell are you trying to do—set me up?"

"No, sir," John said miserably.

Summers slammed his fist on his desk. "From now on, I want to see any correspondence you write before anyone else sees it—do you understand that?"

"Yes, sir." John's face was dusky red all the way down to his collar.

"Wenton came to see me this morning. Apparently you are trying to mishandle the feedlot as well."

"I am?" John asked, frowning.

"You are! We make a good part of our income there, but we won't if you keep operating it the way you seem to want to."

"What should I be doing?"

"You should be shipping the big herds first—the herds that are too big to hold in the pens."

"But, sir." John paused, frowning. "I mean, why?"

"Because, dammit," Summers gritted, "we can hold the smaller herds in our feedlot and charge them twenty cents a day for feed per steer. The big herds always stay outside of town anyway until time to ship. We don't have the capacity to handle them, except on a pass-through basis."

"But in Dodge City, when I worked there, we made it a practice to hold all herds four or five days, regardless of size, to prepare them for the trip. It increases their chances of survival, improves their weight for sale, and it was fairer. We shipped them on a 'first-in first-out' basis..." His voice trailed off.

Summers's black eyes were boring into him. "Mr. Loving, we are not here to play Santa Claus. We're supposed to be making money," he said flatly.

"Yes, sir."

"Do I need to repeat these instructions again?"

"No, sir."

"Do you think you can handle this without writing a memo?"

"Yes, sir."

"Good. Do you know Simon Beasley?"

Loving flushed. Summers knew he did. Everyone knew Beasley. "Yes, sir. He's the buyer for Consolidated Can Company."

Summers nodded. "That's right. Any herd he owns can be shipped immediately—no waiting."

John swallowed. He knew better than to ask why. If Summers wanted to tell him, he would, but apparently his eyes gave him away.

"Why?" Summers asked for him. "Because Mr. Kincaid relies on me to see that the right people are taken care of. I don't expect you to understand local politics, Mr. Loving. Just to do as you are told. Is that clear?"

"Yes, sir. Is that all, sir?"

Summers stood up, giving the signal for Loving to do likewise. "If you have any trouble, you come to me and no one else. Is that understood?"

"Yes, sir."

After taking Sandra home, Ward didn't sleep until almost dawn. The combination of pain over Leslie's rejection and frustration triggered by Sandra's deliberate attempt to arouse him kept him tossing and turning until the sky paled into luminous gray. He slept an hour or so and went for a ride.

The fierce running of the powerful horse, its hooves skimming the levels, skirting the scrub and creosote, leaping narrow gullies, plunging headlong across the desert, brought Ward's muscles into play and helped cool the fires that raged in him. He let the stallion run until a semblance of sanity returned and the sun was growing hot. Then, slowing the heaving bay, he wiped the perspiration off his forehead and turned the big horse back toward Phoenix.

He found Jenn in the music room, singing as she played the elegant Steinway, her voice sultry and golden with a hint of thrush that was as pure as a bell, a mixture of perfect tone and vulnerability that was appealing and provocative. She was alone in the room. He leaned down and kissed her cheek while she smiled serenely and continued to sing to him. In a soft navy-blue morning gown she was so lovely, so shiningly cool, clean, and feminine, that he felt five years old again.

She ended the sonata and stood up. Ward didn't think. He pulled her into his arms and buried his face in her soft hair. For the first time since they were reunited he felt the warm glow of love at full surge. It had worked in him like a tide, slowly and remorselessly building, only now to crest. It was as if he had not really seen her before. Had not connected this woman with the one he'd rejected. He hugged her as if he dared not let her go for fear of losing all that he lost before, losing it again, irrevocably.

His need was like a balm, drawing a barb out of her heart. A dam burst within her as well, releasing the tears she hadn't cried when she could have, tears of joy, love, and long years of heartache streaming down her cheeks, tears held back because to shed them might increase her sense of loss, might somehow cement that loss or precipitate it. "Peter, Peter, Peter, I'm so glad you came back," she whispered, trembling, holding him as tightly as her arms could hold him.

"So am I, Jenn. So am I." His husky whisper was filled with pain as deep and wide as her own. She clung fiercely to him, soaking up the comfort, letting his nearness heal her wounds. She drifted in a daze of happiness. The two people she loved most in the world were becoming friends, and Peter was truly back—the way he had been before all the trouble.

Her voice was strained and husky with emotion. "When you left New York I blamed myself the way you are blaming yourself now. I know how awful it is to lose people you love…and to blame yourself for it. Please try to see that you…you can't." Muscles in his lean brown jaw bunched, and she reached out to touch his warm cheek, groping for the words to ease his pain. "If you had died instead of Simone, would you want her to blame herself? Or would you want her to make a new life? Find a new love?"

He turned his head away, but she had her answer. "Why are you so forgiving with the ones you love and so hard on yourself?" she whispered. "I love you," she said fiercely. "I know you far better than anyone else does—even you—and I know that you always did the best you could… You're strong, and you love deeply…but you're not God. You can't save everyone you love. Someone deliberately killed each of them. If they hadn't accomplished it then, they would have picked another time. You can't stand guard over the ones you love."

His eyes looked bleak, ravaged, before he closed them, clamping his jaws together the way she had seen him do from childhood on up, refusing to cry, trying to reject the comfort she offered him. Jennie put her arms around his waist and hugged him hard, burrowing her cheek into the crook of his neck. He was rigid. She felt the heavy pounding of his heart beneath the firm, warm muscles. "I would give anything to make you realize how special you are," she murmured.

He laughed and it was a bitter sound. "Some men are blessed. Everything they touch turns to gold. Everything I touch dies…I've failed at everything it's possible to fail at. Face it, Jenn. I'm not what you think. I walked in the house one afternoon only minutes after Mother and Father were killed. I led my friend into a trap and got him killed. Simone died because I was in town acting like a goddamned hero. Mama Mendoza, Isabel, Pedro, Grandpapa…I almost got Leslie killed…Everything I touch." He sighed, as if too exhausted to continue.

"That's the most outrageous piece of rationalization I've ever heard!" she said, suddenly angry at him. "Did you ever stop to think that in the last eight years thousands of people died without your help? How on earth do you suppose they managed it?"

Ward shrugged, looking sheepish. "Are you implying I could be less than perfect?" he asked, a touch of his usual humor returning.

"You are so stubborn," she whispered, hugging him again. "And so powerful. I'm feeling sorry for those poor misguided souls who think God arranges these things. What should I tell them?"

She felt a shudder ripple through his lean body. He had changed in so many ways. He was broader of shoulder, harder, and more capable... and stubborn as ever. His eyes hid more from her. "Well, whatever you do, don't fall in love with Elizabeth Cartright. We can't afford to lose her—no one in Phoenix would ever know what anyone else was doing."

Ward laughed and it was the sound of pain overflowing into mirth. "Maybe I could make a living hiring myself out to fall in love with people's enemies. I could get rid of women, children..."

He could joke about it now, but she knew he was protective of women and children. As a child he was willing to give his most treasured toy to comfort a friend, then stoically take a tongue-lashing from their nanny or their mother for "losing" it. His generosity knew no boundaries. A beggar's pain was as real to him as his own. Others could look through such unpleasantness. Ward could not. Wherever he went he usually arrived home with empty pockets. Now if she was interpreting his morose mood correctly, he was determined to spare Leslie Powers. Jennie decided to appeal to his generosity. "Are you saying that you don't care for Leslie?"

"What? How the hell did she come up?"

"I just want to know. Would you break her heart? What if she loves you?"

"She doesn't, and she won't if left to her own resources." Ward sighed. "I have nothing to offer Leslie Powers. She's a lady, accustomed to a different life. She is horrified by me and my past—and rightly so. I'm horrified by it, but I have to live with it; she doesn't."

"Could you be wrong about that?"

"No."

"How wonderfully omniscient you've become," she said dryly, lifting her eyebrows. She leaned back against the circle of his arms, unwilling to let him go just yet. "Will you have lunch with me?"

Ward chuckled. "You haven't changed a bit, have you? Tears in your eyes and you're still hungry. How much ballet practice do you put in, anyway?"

"Three hours"—Jennie shrugged—"more or less."

"You are incorrigible."

Her laughter was a golden tinkle of notes that warmed him, putting all his devils at rest. Jennie came up on tiptoe to kiss him, and that is the way Leslie found them: Jennifer so soft and lovely, a perfect cameo in profile; Ward so lithe, sturdy, and handsome—and both of them so engrossed in each other that they didn't notice her, frozen and mute in the doorway. She turned to leave, and Jennie saw a movement out of the corner of her eye.

"Leslie, dear, were you looking for me or Ward?" she asked, pleased with herself for remembering not to call him Peter.

Leslie didn't look at them directly; she pretended to be gazing toward the kitchen, looking for something, but Jennie didn't move out of Ward's embrace. They seemed unaware of the picture they presented. Thank goodness Chane hadn't caught them this way, she thought, turning. Aloud she said, "No, I was going out. I just wanted to let you know."

The laughter had gone out of his eyes. Now they were impassive, watchful, cool, where before they had been filled with warmth and probably love. He was wearing a blue linen shirt, open at the throat, and tight-fitting black corduroy pants with a gun strapped to his right thigh. His thick wheat-colored hair was windblown, but the medallion-sharp features were disgustingly pleasing to look at.

"Won't you have lunch with us?" Jennie asked.

"No, thank you, Mrs. Kincaid." She gave them her brightest smile, tossing her heavy black mane of curling tresses, and demurred. She didn't consider the polite invitation. She knew instinctively she did not want to come between him and one of his women. "I'm going riding with Debbie. She's probably waiting for me now."

"Have fun. Be careful, dear."

Leslie threw them an insouciant wave. She did not expect to have fun. Her hope was that she was not thoroughly miserable. If she hadn't agreed days ago to go riding with Debbie, she certainly wouldn't consider it today. She had tossed and turned half the night, only to have her sleep, when it finally came, tortured by dreams of Cantrell making love to her. After what she had just seen, she was grateful she hadn't confided in Jennifer about Cantrell.

Debra was in a good mood, lighthearted and gay. They rode to the foothills on the east.

"Are there Indians around here?" Leslie asked.

"Probably a few strays, but they're harmless. The majority of them are on reservations. I suppose there could be danger if a band of renegades left the reservation and decided to make trouble. My father says that doesn't happen anymore."

The air was crisp, clean, and redolent with the odor of sage. It was a particularly pungent smell that Leslie was slowly learning to love. At first it had been unpleasant.

On top of a hill, with gentle breezes blowing and the warm sun on their shoulders, they ate the lunch Debbie's mother had prepared for them. White clouds sailed overhead like Spanish galleons. The panoramic view Leslie sketched from the mountaintop was breathtaking. The desert sparseness was rugged and wild, stretched out endlessly under a stormy sky without being intimidating, because she could not believe it was real. It was as dreamlike as her response to the knowledge that Cantrell was in love with Jennifer.

"I hate to mention this, Leslie, but I think we'd better start back. I need to be home by three."

Leslie sighed. "As I do."

Back in town, they stopped at the corner of Main and Front streets to say good-bye. Buggies rattled past; horses snorted and stamped along the streets in front of the stores, which were doing a brisk business. Children let out of school loitered in front of shops and played in the dusty road.

"Will you be at the McCormicks' dinner party and dance tonight?" Debbie asked, stroking her horse's damp neck with a gloved hand.

Leslie nodded, fighting the urge to say she was sick of parties. It was disloyal and ungrateful of her. Jennie had gone to a great deal of trouble to arrange for her friends to give these parties in her honor.

A small surrey, white-fringed and sparkling in the sun, pulled up next to them and stopped. Elizabeth Cartright was cool and lovely in white organdy.

"Hi! You two plotting what you're going to wear?"

"Not exactly," Debbie said, squinting into the sun.

"Everybody will be there. Personally, I wouldn't miss it for the world! I'm dying, absolutely dying, to see who Ward Cantrell brings. I heard the most delicious rumor, and, darlings, if it is true, *if* it is true—" She stressed "if" significantly, leaning forward and looking both ways as if she feared being overheard. "And mind you," she continued, "I'm not saying it is, because *frankly*, it would be insanity for a certain young matron we all know, absolute insanity!" She ended breathlessly.

Debbie looked at Leslie, her brown eyes exaggeratedly wide and amused. "Heavens!" she said innocently. "Who could he *possibly* bring?..."

"It will rock this little desert dump back on its heels," Elizabeth said knowingly.

Leslie stifled a sarcastic remark. Elizabeth smiled archly and condescendingly, savoring her scandalous secret, her brown eyes fairly dancing with mischief. "You don't know?" she asked. "You really haven't guessed?"

"We haven't the foggiest, for heaven's sake—not the foggiest! So why don't you just tell us. Because I have to go. I promised to be home by three," Debbie said irritably.

"You're both blind! I mean really, actually, totally blind. He's going to bring Jennifer Kincaid."

"I don't believe it!" Debbie said vehemently. "Jennifer Kincaid is a lady, and she is in love with her husband! She would never..."

"My, are you naive! Married women cheat all the time. I could give you names and dates," Elizabeth said smugly.

"Some do. She wouldn't," Debbie insisted. She turned to Leslie. "You live with them. Have you seen anything that would make you think she would do that?"

"Absolutely not," Leslie lied with matching vehemence.

Elizabeth shrugged and *giddahupped* her horse. Leslie said good-bye to Debbie and watched her leave. She waited several seconds before she turned her horse toward Barton Street. She knew which house, because Jennifer had pointed it out to her. Bathed in sunlight, with a cluster of soaring, showy aspens dropping their fiery autumn leaves, the two-story white frame house was homey and charming. A shiny-leafed vine crept and twined its way along the roof line of the porch that ran across the front and around the side of the house.

This house was immaculately maintained, though not of recent origin. It had an air of permanence about it. There was real grass beneath the leaves that scattered in the wind. The vine had grown the length of the long, deep porch.

Seeing this house, so charmingly New England, with its clapboard siding and its steep roof and neatly framed casement windows, she could imagine a crystal epergne with sweets nestling in its dangling cups, a pair of dumbwaiters hoisting vintage wines from a well-stocked cellar, a tearoom awash with sunlight, or sparkling china set ablaze with candleglow. Its solidity bespoke gracious living.

A hundred yards away, a house, framed but not roofed, was surrounded by chaos—the lot strewn with mounds of dirt, stacks of bricks, and racks of lumber.

It was apparent that this was not one of Mr. Kincaid's instant houses. From here the mountains on the east rose with high craggy peaks and wooded slopes.

Maybe Ward wouldn't be there. Her heart was making a terrible racket in her chest. She tied the horse at the hitching post, determined to brazen it out. She owed the Kincaids too much to let her own revulsion stand in her way. But even so, the walk up to the door was a heart-stopping experience.

Her knock was answered by a wiry little Oriental with black-rimmed, tortoiseshell spectacles and sleek black hair parted in the middle.

"Yes, prease?"

"Is...Mr. Cantrell in?"

"Yes, miss. Come in, prease." He stepped back, bowing from the waist, then led her into another room to wait.

She was in a library with an enormous seascape on one wall, so realistic she could almost smell the ocean. It drew her irresistibly. It was surprisingly good! The plasticity and atmospheric color were the creation of a supremely gifted artist. It had radiance of light, resonance of tone, dramatic mood, and tremendous imaginative meaning.

She was transfixed, gazing in rapture. She could almost feel the spray on her cheeks. She prayed she really could—maybe the burning would stop. It was foolish to feel flushed and scared just because of a man she despised.

"Good afternoon."

Where had he come from so silently and quickly? She turned abruptly, swallowing, trying to arm herself.

"Hello."

A small pulse started in his temple. She was wearing the black and white riding habit she'd had on when she stopped at the door to bid Jenn good-bye before her ride. The smooth velvet was almost as black as the wind-blown tresses that fell to her waist. She was lovelier than ever. Her cheeks were flushed with warm color, and her hair was a fog of wispy curls framing her forehead and ears. Her skin glowed with the exertion of her ride.

"Can I get you something to drink? Tea? Anything?"

"No, thank you," she said, stalling. "Do you know the title or the painter of this?"

"That's very good, isn't it? It's by Washington Allston. According to Yoshio, he painted it for the Kincaids when Chantry the First was a sea captain. The story is that dear departed Chantry saved Allston's life. It's called *The Rising of a Thunderstorm at Sea*. You paint, don't you?"

"My mother acquired a rather formidable reputation. I hope to follow in her footsteps."

"What genre?" He didn't realize he had said something very untrain-robberish until he saw her eyebrows quirk up.

"What genre!" she repeated, realizing she had not adjusted to all the information she had about him. Yesterday Jennie had mentioned that before he left New York he had been a stockbroker. Somehow, thinking of him as growing up in New York, going to school with Jennie's brother, and working on Wall Street was unsettling, but she answered him. "She taught naturalism, a little luminism, but I'm starting to lean toward impressionism. It's all the rage in Europe. Unfortunately, America is still so colonial. It will be ages before the schools here teach it."

An awkward silence ensued. Since she didn't know how to begin, she glanced around nervously, saw they were alone, and blurted it out.

"I came here to ask you to…because I…I want you to give up your relationship with Mrs. Kincaid."

Ward frowned, not sure he had heard her correctly. "What?"

"Because it's hurting her. People are talking about her and you. This is a small town. It could ruin her. She has a good marriage. She loves her husband. You don't need her. You have more girls than you can keep track of now." She stopped. Blood was staining her cheeks. She was breathing hard, completely unstrung, and he just stood there, looking at her with his blue eyes strangely impassive.

"Why do you care?" he asked, hiding his surprise.

"Because they've been good to me. They're good people. They don't deserve to be gossiped about."

Ward flinched at the earnestness in her green eyes, the vibrant emerald color of sea foam on a sunny day. He ran his hands through his rumpled hair, smoothing the tawny thatch into some kind of order. He had been sleeping—to make up for working at the T & P office most of the night.

"Your trust is a wonderful thing to have, your ladyship. It makes me yearn to deserve it."

"Oh! Don't try to act as if you only do despicable things because I suspect you of them. You were doing despicable things long before I met you."

Anger kindled in his eyes, crackling like tiny white flames in the depths, but Leslie didn't care. "If you care about her, you'll give her up."

Everything was forgotten now—his desire to spare her, his guilt at the way he had wronged her, everything except the implied insult in her earnest request. He stepped toward her, and part of him knew better than to give in to the sudden fierce urge to hurt her the way she had hurt him, waving her saucy good-bye as she clung to her lover's arm, but another part of him didn't care.

"Why should I give her up? She's a beautiful woman. You saw us together. Did she look like she was trying to escape my clutches?"

Leslie's cheeks paled, and her breath caught in her throat.

"How can you be so callous? She's married...with a family. How can another conquest be as important as that? Besides, she's older than you. Don't you care about anything?"

"She's only three years older, in the prime of life actually...Jenn is a very beautiful woman," he growled, enjoying the tension in every line of Leslie Powers's flushed face and slender body. "And in answer to your question, no, I don't care billy hell about anything."

Trembling, she started past him.

His arm shot out and stopped her in mid-stride. "What's your rush? I thought you wanted to help your friends."

Her green eyes looked him up and down, flaring with scorn and fury. "No one can talk to you. You are an animal. All you ever think about are your own needs."

That strange light flared in his eyes, darkening then lightening the blue, from violet to sky-frost, turning them as cold and flat as his husky voice. "Then let's talk about something that interests me," he said grimly. On one level he knew he was about to send his life spiraling out of control again, but he didn't care. He would have continued even if he knew that in the next second he would be killed for it.

"Like what?" she demanded, glaring at the hand around her wrist, impeding her escape and increasing the rapidity of her heartbeat. A small, tingling current moving from his warm flesh to her own made it impossible for her to think or move away.

"Like a trade."

"What kind of...trade?" she asked, her voice breaking.

"How much of a sacrifice are you willing to make to save your friends from disgrace?" he asked, his eyes darting from her furious eyes to her heaving breasts. The riding gown was demure and ladylike, but he remembered only too well the provocative tilt and swell of her small, firm white breasts. The memory caused an ache he could not control. He wanted to hurt her, to see the same sort of pain in her wide green eyes he had felt last night. Nothing short of that would satisfy him. She tried to pull away from him, and his fingers tightened around the soft flesh of her upper arm. "Or am I the only one who is supposed to suffer?" he asked softly, hatefully.

"What do you want?"

"I want you."

CHAPTER THIRTY-THREE

"Is this some sort of joke?" she asked, her lips stiff, her heart pounding like a rail setter in her breast.

His lips quirked up at one corner, his tawny eyebrows lifted, and she knew even without the look in his eyes that it was no joke. She couldn't breathe, couldn't think. She felt flushed with heat and fever.

"You want to save your friends, don't you? You already know what a bastard I am. I do whatever is easy, remember?" She thought she saw a flash of bitterness in the cool blue depths before he smiled hatefully, mockingly. "You're as beautiful as Jenn is, in your own way. I'll accept a substitute, if you cooperate"—he paused, watching her intently—"fully."

Leslie swallowed, moistened her dry lips, her eyes darting around the room as if searching for an avenue of escape.

Ward Cantrell watched her intently, coolly, hiding the bitterness he felt.

"What...?" She couldn't bring herself to finish the question. She was too agitated: struck mute by his presence, his incredible demand, and her own surprising response.

"What do I want?" he asked tauntingly, finishing her question for her.

She nodded, unable to do more.

"I want you to be my mistress," he said softly. "My willing mistress."

Oh, God! She was collapsing inside, and it took all the courage, pride, and stubbornness she had to keep him from seeing it. She never should have come here! Ever! Let Jennifer make her own mistakes! Maybe Chane didn't care if she took lovers! Chane had seen Jennifer and Ward dancing together, too. Maybe the Kincaids had a modern marriage. Leslie wanted to flee, to run as far and as fast as she could, but she felt rooted to the spot.

Apparently he wasn't going to give her a chance to flee or respond. His hand came up, lifted her chin, traced the curve of her jaw, her cheek, her temple, scalding her with warmth and that indefinable ache that his touch caused. His fingers slid through her hair, twisting into it, holding her head still, as if he actually believed she was capable of resistance; he leaned forward slowly, his eyes never leaving hers, until his mouth closed over hers and she couldn't tell whether her eyes closed or blindness had been added to insanity.

She felt swept away, free floating, on fire, responding in spite of herself to his terrible, punishing kiss. But why should he want to hurt her? It didn't matter, though. His mouth couldn't hurt her the way his actions did. At least when she was in his arms she could forget his other women, give herself up to weakness and wanting.

Leslie couldn't remember how she got back to the Kincaid residence, up to her room. She fell across the bed and buried her burning face in the pillow.

Ward Cantrell was the worst kind of fiend—murderer, train robber, wrecker of reputations and marriages—and she had agreed to become his mistress to save Jennifer! Shame flushed through her like a stain. She would never be clean again, and the worst part was not that he had demanded that price or even that she had agreed to it. The worst part was that she wanted it. In spite of everything she knew about him—she wanted it!

She couldn't cry. Maybe people who sell their souls to Satan don't cry. That would be too simple. Oh, God! What had she done? One kiss and she had agreed. She could still feel the way his lips burned into her. It was diabolical. All he would have had to do was ask. She would have consummated their bargain on the spot if he had wanted it. Fortunately he didn't have the same lack of control she suffered from. He had kissed her and sent her away. If he behaved himself at the party tonight, she would be expected to receive him graciously. He would tell her where...

"I'll expect complete cooperation, Leslie. Otherwise no deal."

"Do you love Jennifer?" She had seen the shame in him then, and somehow his knowing how wrong his love for Jennie was softened her. There was conflict in his narrowed blue eyes as well before he finally said, "I've loved her for a long time. I'll need your help."

Leslie leaped off her bed and ran to the window, too agitated to lie quietly. The garden and stable area were deserted. Unseen starlings, flickers, and wrens argued in noisy exchange, the bold, dominant cactus wren, with its raucous cries, sounding like the winner. Nothing moved in that precise, neatly cultivated oasis. A cat sprawled in a sunny nook, daring the birds to believe his act of indifference. Sounds of young Chane and Amy playing in some part of the house mingled with the bark of a dog in the distance. Youngsters played in the vacant field behind the stable, squealing in glee and outrage. The sun was moving toward the western horizon. Leslie held on to the railing with hands that were white with tension, dreading the party that night. She couldn't possibly keep seeing Tim while she was, even secretly, Ward Cantrell's mistress. She would have to tell Tim that she didn't want to see him again.

She cursed the fates that had brought her there, only to let her fall under the spell of a man with no sense of responsibility, no future, no compassion, no morals, only a diabolical touch that left her too weak to resist him.

Ward had watched Leslie Powers depart, slim, proud, defiant, and turned away. He had gotten his revenge—she was terrified and repelled, but she had agreed to be his mistress. If it didn't hurt so bad, it would be funny.

He poured himself a double and drank it. Not even the burn and jolt of good whiskey could dispel his bitterness. The one girl he wanted, he had to blackmail into his bed; the others he could have just by forgetting to lock a window or a door.

He would tell her after the dinner party that he had no intention of accepting her noble sacrifice, but she deserved to sweat a little. He hadn't forgiven her for Summers.

That brought a sardonic smile to his lips. Unfortunately she didn't need or want his forgiveness. She would love whoever she wanted to love and do one damn fine job of it, without any blessing from him.

The McCormicks' invitation was for a formal dinner party. Leslie knew Sandra McCormick only as one of the girls Ward called Trinket. Seeing the house, like a gingerbread mansion, with turrets, verandas, gables, and loggias, she thought she had been transported to the Black Forest. "You would expect to find a house like this tucked away in some Alpine Village," she murmured to Tim, taking his hands as he helped her disembark from the phaeton he had rented for the occasion.

They walked quickly up the first concrete walk Leslie had seen in Arizona. The house and grounds were ablaze with light. Uniformed footmen helped occupants from the line of carriages that slowly crunched forward on the gravel concourse leading up to the house. A virtual army of stiff-collared waiters were on hand to assist. Leslie couldn't believe she was still in Arizona. This was like a night at the opera.

Six lavishly set tables were strategically placed amid potted palms and crystal chandeliers. Leslie and Tim were escorted to a table where Elizabeth Cartright chatted with her escort, Winslow Breakenridge. Sandra introduced her gentleman friend as Dusty Denton. They sat next to an empty chair that Sandra was trying desperately to ignore.

No one inquired as to whom it was for—Sandra was as transparent as the diaphanous chiffon wrapper she wore around her slim shoulders. But even agitated, Sandra was lovely, Leslie had to admit. She wore a fashionable, dark brown satin gown that brought out the healthy golden tones of her skin and hair and emphasized her gray eyes, making them look smoky and mysterious.

Leslie wore an elegant black velvet gown that hugged her slender curves and made her feel older. "Leslie, darling," Tim had said as she descended the Kincaids' staircase. "You take my breath away! I can't find words to pay tribute to the way you look tonight—older surely, sophisticated undoubtedly, mysterious, provocative. I could go on and on."

He had taken her hands and smiled down at her. "But what happened to the Leslie of the teasing smile and the sunshine?" She had forced a sunny smile to stop the outpouring of compliments.

"I'm in disguise, Tim! Can't you tell?"

The Kincaids made their entry together, without Cantrell, and Elizabeth looked haughty but undaunted. Cantrell arrived late, and Elizabeth leaned forward and whispered to Marybelle that Jennifer had apparently decided to play it safe. Leslie burned with the urge to tell her off, but she couldn't bring herself to say anything. She felt strangely subdued.

Cantrell looked subdued as well. He accepted Sandra's gush of gratitude silently, nodded to everyone around the table, and sat down. Leslie looked up into his eyes and was not prepared for the jolt of reaction they caused in her. The blood began to pound in her chest and throat, and she felt weak with the tension and fear that had consumed her since her visit to his house. That singular look that he flashed her—a mere quirking of eyebrows and flexing of certain face or eye muscles—communicated volumes. His eyes were filled with tiny glints of recognition that seemed to demand and evoke a response from her. Tonight, for whatever reason, his power and her response were painfully intensified.

Little was expected of her conversationally; the men at the table were engrossed in a discussion precipitated by Winslow, who had said that Prescott, up north, was the most sophisticated town in Arizona.

"What makes you say that?" Tim demanded. "We have a sizeable colony of easterners here in Phoenix. I doubt that you'll find a more sophisticated group than what is seated around this table." He eyed the others with obvious satisfaction. "Denton, where are you from originally?"

"Massachusetts."

"Cantrell, where do you call home?"

"Upstate New York."

"You see," Tim said, "even *they* were exposed to civilization at one point. We are all *émigrés*, so to speak, living on a rude frontier, but doing it in style. For the most part," he said, looking pointedly at Cantrell and Denton.

Winslow chuckled, a superior, condescending sound. "Almost fifty percent of the people in Prescott are hard-core easterners, and wealthy."

"Are you sure about those figures?" Tim demanded.

Winslow nodded, his smile smug. "Are you ready for this? Prescott does not have a single church."

Tim was undaunted. "So they are pagans. That does not necessarily make them sophisticated. If you want to talk blatant paganism, let's talk San Francisco, where houses of ill-repute are considered necessary by the city fathers to insure the safety of their daughters."

Leslie barely listened. She was too painfully aware of Ward's presence across the table from her. She had felt vulnerable and exposed ever since he had kissed her. Now, seeing him, she feared that he had reconsidered and realized that he couldn't give up Jennifer, that maybe he had decided to compromise by being more discreet in public. What was he thinking? Did he find her at all attractive? Or only a nuisance to be dealt with?

Ward was trying not to think. Leslie Powers was by far the loveliest girl there. Even with a cloud hanging over her head she managed to look composed and totally feminine. He had contemplated numerous ways to torture her for her lack of trust, but now he couldn't bring himself to use any of them. A woman willing to sacrifice her own honor to save his sister's was not someone he could torment. Funny he hadn't realized that ahead of time.

He tried to concentrate on Blond Trinket, but that was too much like reading the labels on a row of identical tin cans; there were no surprises.

He vowed that as soon as he could get Leslie alone he would tell her he had no intention of taking advantage of her, then leave Phoenix. He was tired of resting and recuperating. He longed for a return to the rougher, simpler life of the open range: canned beans and uncomplicated *señoritas* who did not linger in a man's mind, making him feel dissatisfied and irritable.

Dusty Denton had brought word that Doug Paggett and the rest of the men he had summoned were assembled in Buckeye, and that their scouting the mountains to the north had paid off. They had located pens that could be used to load stolen cattle onto Kincaid's trains. Unfortunately, the books had revealed nothing out of the ordinary. Either the man kept a separate set of T & P's books, or the entire operation was handled without the knowledge of anyone in the main office. That seemed a remote possibility, but no more remote than that Kincaid, who was a good judge of men, could be that wrong about someone working for him.

The party bubbled like champagne all around her, but Leslie felt locked away by her own feelings. She knew Ward had been raised in the East, but she had still expected him to embarrass himself with the complicated array of dishes, glasses, and silver, but he didn't seem aware of the opportunities he missed to humiliate himself. Maybe some people are just born knowing everything they need to survive, she thought.

"What school did you attend, Cantrell?" Tim asked, causing Leslie to jerk alert, completely attentive.

Ward glanced at Dusty, then Leslie and Tim. He smiled, and his eyes came alive with mischief. "Radcliffe," he said.

Dusty Denton, who should have been expecting it, because he alone at the table knew how close that was to the truth, choked on his wine. Dusty and Peter Van Vleet, now passing as Ward Cantrell, had known each other when they were young, dumb, and unable to conceal things from each other. Peter had helped him through biology, and he had stood guard in the cold while Peter stole his first kiss from Dusty's cousin behind the boathouse at Dusty's parents' house. He and Peter were senior students at Harvard University until Peter was caught by a surprise bed check with two naked Radcliffe College students fighting in his bedroom at three o'clock in the morning because they had both climbed in his window on the same night. The two girls were taking turns, and Peter was half-dead from lack of sleep. He had been, until the previous month, a serious student, studying until lights out, falling like a rock into his bed, and sleeping until reveille. Until little Kim, and later her friend, started climbing in his window. If he hadn't been so bursting with the exuberance and sexual energy of youth, he would have known better. He'd been a fool to let it continue, but Dusty, flushing with the memory of his own reaction to Sandra McCormick, knew only too well that a man's automatic defenses didn't work against warm-skinned naked girls who slipped into a man's arms.

Old Elliott, who had just happened to be Harvard's president and the father of one of the girls, got his revenge by expelling Peter four months before graduation. The reason that he gave in the letter to Peter's father, who was a Harvard alumnus and a heavy contributor, was cheating, the most dishonorable type of expulsion any family could suffer. But Peter didn't find out about the trumped-up charge until he was back in New York, and the events of his homecoming rendered it unimportant.

Sandra, who had been thumping Dusty on the back, grabbed the wine bottle from a hovering waiter and offered to fill anyone's glass.

Tim frowned. He couldn't tell if Cantrell was making fun of him for asking or if the man didn't know Radcliffe was a girls' college and was merely trying to impress them by using the name of a prestigious eastern school or if he was subtly reminding them what a ladies' man he was. Tim's expression wavered between delight at such ignorance and incredulity. He could barely control himself. "Ahhh, a serious student!"

Cantrell endeavored to look humble while accepting Tim's sardonic praise.

"Many of us," Tim said, tongue in cheek, "who attended less prestigious schools had some difficulty qualifying. I'm curious. With its being one of the most elite universities in the country, was being accepted at Radcliffe difficult in any way?"

Ward shrugged. "Well...yes and no."

Tim waited, controlling the sense of expectant delight.

"Well, you know how thoroughly they examine and scrutinize everything from your bloodline to your family's bank account," Ward drawled.

"Yes, yes..." Tim said, egging him on.

"Well, scholastically I was acceptable, financially my family was acceptable, my mother was a Radcliffe alumna. Unfortunately they approved everything except my...uh...excuse me, ladies...gender."

A flush darkened Tim's cheeks as he realized Cantrell had led him on a fool's errand, and he had blithely followed.

Before Tim could reply, Marybelle giggled. "I'll bet if you *were* accepted, you would have been the most sought-after roommate in the dormitory."

"What did you major in?" Sandra asked, joining in.

"Public service," he said, grinning. Eight years before, when he was expelled from Harvard for what he considered bad judgment bordering on stupidity, it hadn't seemed so funny.

Summers refused to be put off. "What kind of work do you plan to do, Cantrell?"

"Whatever comes easy," he said, wondering what Summers was getting at. Everyone in town knew he was working for Kincaid. No one outside of Chane and Jennie knew he was sworn as an Arizona ranger. His cover story had been in the newspaper as well as on half the lips in town.

"Are you still nursing that grudge against Mark Powers and Dallas Younger?" Tim asked, taking a sip of his wine and eyeing Cantrell from beneath hooded eyes.

"Did I have a grudge against them?" Ward asked, alert now that the questioning was showing purpose.

"Didn't you?" Tim paused, looking significantly at Winslow Breakenridge. "I heard Younger knocked you down during the fiesta days' parade. Didn't you try to save Leslie when her horse reared? I was sure someone told me you were talking about killing them both. And with your reputation as a gunfighter I don't imagine you make idle threats, do you?"

Ward chuckled, his eyes going to Leslie. "I have made threats ranging all the way from idle to outrageous—and that just covers today."

The girls laughed their appreciation, and Leslie flushed, remembering the implied threat in their bargain.

"Seriously, though, Cantrell, I did hear that Younger is making threats about meeting you—what do you gunfighters call it?—in a showdown," Tim persisted. "What will you do if he challenges you?"

Ward shrugged. "I'll decide that if it happens. I haven't noticed him looking for me in broad daylight."

"You mean he might try to bushwhack you? Kill you from ambush?"

Sandra frowned at Tim. "Don't be so morbid. This is a party—not a wake. Anyone like another glass of wine? Ward?"

Small talk resumed, and Leslie noticed that Ward neither drank nor ate much.

When they all moved into the grand ballroom to dance to the imported orchestra, she avoided Cantrell. He seemed fully recovered from his gunshot wound, perfectly capable of supporting not only his own weight but also that of the girls who seemed to cling much too tightly and closely when he danced with them. She stood as much as she could and then excused herself.

Unexpectedly, Leslie found herself alone in the elaborately mirrored powder room with Sandra McCormick. The blonde shrugged, as if she too could not imagine how this had happened. They made small talk for a moment, politely, then Sandra faced her purposefully.

"Do you love Tim Summers?" she asked abruptly.

Leslie frowned her displeasure. "I..." she began uncomfortably, aware that Sandra was her hostess, and she did not want to be rude to one of the Kincaids' friends.

"Sorry," Sandra said quickly. "You don't have to answer." The look on Leslie's face was ample reply.

Leslie read Sandra's face as well and tried to correct the impression she knew Sandra had gotten. "I like him a lot. I'm not a person who falls hastily into love," she lied.

Sandra laughed. "And Ward Cantrell?" she asked, flushing with pleasure because for a change she had the upper hand in a conversation. Leslie Powers was far more affected than her ladylike exterior seemed to indicate. In sudden sympathy Sandra reached over and patted Leslie's hand.

"You don't have to answer that either. You don't lie well at all. I thought you would." She paused. "You know, I decided days ago that I hated you, but I guess I don't."

"What made you change your mind?"

"I don't know exactly. I guess because you're as confused as I am in some ways. Oh, I didn't mean to insult you or anything."

Sandra meant it. There was something so pitiful about her apology; she truly believed that no one could possibly be as confused as she was. Leslie's heart went out to the other woman. She shrugged. "It's okay. I'm sure I'm just as confused as you, maybe more so," she admitted.

Sandra smiled and it was a real smile, full of warmth. "No one could be that confused."

"Except me," Leslie said, feeling strangely touched.

Sandra swallowed, as if struggling with tears. Her eyes were strangely bright. "We can't both win, can we?"

Leslie sighed. She didn't know if winning would mean being loved by Ward or learning to live free of him, but neither seemed possible at the moment.

"You don't have to answer. I know he doesn't care for me. I just make a fool of myself because I can't help it."

"You've not made a fool of yourself," Leslie protested.

"You haven't seen everything," Sandra said, pain clouding her gray eyes. She lifted her chin as if that would somehow rearm her, then she shrugged. "I didn't mean to say so many…revealing things. I hope you will forgive me."

"Of course," Leslie said, meaning it. "That's a lovely locket you're wearing," she said to change the subject. The intricate Chinese dragon design in the center of the unusual gold and enamel locket had caught her eye.

"It was a gift from my aunt. Would you like it?"

"Oh, no!" Leslie said, slightly horrified. "I wouldn't dream of taking it."

Sandra shrugged. "Suit yourself. It means nothing to me. Well, shall we go face the old biddies for a while longer?"

Leslie laughed. "Might as well."

When she told Jennifer about the singular conversation Jennifer smiled her slightly ironic smile. "What did you make of it?"

"I knew not what to make of it."

"That is just as well. With your genial nature you are much too prone to give generous interpretations to everyone's actions. A line from a Henry James play I did once has stuck indelibly in my memory. 'My dearest Emma, do not pretend, with your sweet temper, to understand a bad one, or to lay down rules for it: you must let it go its own way…' And I fear that is what we should do with this. Leave the interpretation to time. Then and only then will we be able to guess at its meaning, if there is one."

Leslie frowned. "Surely you don't think that aimless encounter had some deeper meaning?"

"My dearest Leslie, do not pretend, with your sweet temper, to understand a bad one."

CHAPTER THIRTY-FOUR

Through the sprawling leaves of a potted palm, Leslie saw Dallas Younger in the spacious entryway, hat in hand, speaking to the McCormicks' butler. He was presentable in a dark frockcoat, but he looked out of place among the elegance and sophistication of the gingerbread mausoleum. She stopped dancing abruptly.

"What's the matter, darling?" Tim asked, his pale, handsome face reflecting his concern for her.

"Dallas Younger. What's he doing here?" she demanded.

Tim craned his neck, peering through the palm leaves.

"Looks like he has business with Mr. McCormick."

Leslie would not be led back into the strains of the music. She watched as Younger talked to McCormick. Soon Sandra joined them, took Younger's hand, teased and cajoled for a few moments, and led him onto the dance floor. Ignoring the looks of the curious, Younger danced as if he purely enjoyed the opportunity. Cantrell, standing beside one of the double doors that led outside, watched, his handsome face impassive.

During dinner he had looked strangely vulnerable, reminding her of the Ward who brought her that one fragile flower. She'd had the feeling, vibrating to his nearness, that she could search him out and find him instantly—even in a dark cave packed wall to wall with men—the way mother bats return unerringly to their young. Maybe his damned arrogant body sent out signals to her.

Now, with his thumbs hooked in his pants pockets, even the slim horizontal shadow under his smooth bottom lip added to the impression of barely contained rebelliousness and cold passion. He was a hellion, a maverick, and he definitely looked the part tonight; even in very correct evening attire he exuded an aura of controlled recklessness that was as much a part of him as his silver-streaked, tawny hair and those insolently sensuous lips.

For all that he did not appear agitated, there was a definite threat in his stance that caused her to shudder. She cast a questioning glance at Tim, wondering if he had somehow known ahead of time that Younger might be dropping in, but, preoccupied by his conversation with Winslow Breakenridge, his face reflected no guile.

Ward searched the room for Leslie, wondering how she was taking Younger's arrival. The urge to confront the man was strong in him, but this was not the place. He was an officer of the law, sworn to maintain order, not destroy it.

Patiently, Ward waited until Younger had relinquished Sandra to a young man he didn't know. Younger made his way back to McCormick's side; Ward walked onto the dance floor and took Sandra out of her partner's arms.

"Ward, well, sir…it's about time you deigned to dance with me." Her cheeks were unnaturally flushed, and her eyes were sparkling with excitement.

"Did you invite Younger here?" he asked, swinging her into the rhythm of the waltz.

"He had business with my father. I only invited him to stay. He's very handsome, isn't he? Are you jealous?"

"I realize you're all grown-up now, and you probably don't want any advice from me, but if you're smart, you'll stay away from Younger."

"You are jealous!" she said triumphantly.

"I'm trying to warn you," he said quietly. "I've had some experience with Younger. He plays rough." Her eyes sought out Younger's villainously handsome face, took on that strange glazed look, and he cursed himself for a fool. He had probably only succeeded in making the bastard irresistible to her.

"Look, Trinket, would you trust me in this? Younger will hurt you, possibly kill you. Do you understand what I'm trying to tell you?"

"What?" She frowned at him, her lovely gray eyes clouded with confusion.

"The man is dangerous. He could *kill* you."

A sudden understanding and shame filled her eyes. She seemed to sag in his arms. They were near the open doors to the veranda. He danced her outside.

"Are you all right?" he demanded, setting her down.

In the dim light from the party she began to cry. He sat down beside her and put his arms around her. When her sobs had subsided, she stood up and burrowed into his arms. "I'm sorry," she sniffed. "I didn't mean to cry all over your jacket."

"That's all right."

"Why do I do things like that? And like Dusty? And like what I wanted to do with you?" she demanded, furious at herself and shamed to the core.

Ward shrugged. "You're looking for love."

She sighed. "That sounds so simple when you say it."

"Finding love is never simple," he said, reaching into his pocket for his handkerchief.

"I'm going to die," she said suddenly. "I know it. I'm going to die in some horrible way and I'll never find anyone to love me."

"That's hogwash."

She shuddered. "No, it's true. I know it in here," she said, touching her stomach. "I'll die and be completely forgotten, as if I never existed…" New tears welled up in her eyes, and Ward sighed, feeling helpless.

"You aren't going to die," he said, groping for some way to handle this. He looked around, wishing there was someone he could turn her over to.

"You'll forget me. Everyone will. They'll go to my funeral and say phony things about what a nice girl I was, because no one ever knew anything about me. You're the only one in the world who even knows me." Sobs bubbled up and shook her slender body. "You'll forget me too. I've always known that I would never live to be twenty."

Ward shook his head. "That's nonsense. You're going to live to be a hundred. This is a hard time for you. But you'll find someone to love."

"Do you have a cigarette?" she demanded.

"Not with me."

She was deeper than he had thought. Of course, she would have to be, since his original impression was that she had all the depth of butcher paper. He felt closer to her suddenly. He had the urge to tell her that Younger had killed a nineteen-year-old girl, but he was no longer completely sure it had been Younger. There could have been another man involved. Some shadowy figure behind both the killings and the rustling. And anything he told Trinket would be all over town. There would be hell to pay, and no way to prove it to anyone's satisfaction.

He felt frustration and a growing sense of his own helplessness. Nothing he could do or say would make a difference to her. She was so hungry for a man of her very own that she would settle for anything, as long as it was exciting and would horrify her father. For a moment, when she was crying, he had felt hope, but he knew by the look in her eyes that neither shame nor tears mattered to her. Only her need mattered. She was a female first, a person second.

"Would you like to dance?" he asked.

She sighed. "I would like a cigarette, but since you don't have that, would you do me a favor?"

"If I can."

"Promise me that you won't forget me."

Jolted by the intensity of her need, he nodded. "I promise." He held out his arms to her, she moved into them, and he swung her into the rhythm of the music. They danced for a moment on the veranda, and then Ward edged them back into the main ballroom. When the dance ended, he left her to search for Leslie.

"Tim took her home. I think Younger's turning up here had something to do with her sudden headache," Winslow said, quirking his heavy black brows.

Tim drove Leslie home and offered to stay with her, but she convinced him that she needed to be alone. He kissed her and left reluctantly. She asked Annette, who was still up, to prepare a bath, and forced herself to try to enjoy it in spite of her jangled nerves.

"Not feeling well, *mademoiselle?*"

"My head hurts frightfully," she lied, sighing.

The bath helped a little. She put on a gown, brushed out her hair, pinned it up because the night had stayed unaccountably warm, and lay like a board on the bed, holding herself half off the mattress with her elbows. Sleep did not come, so she paced in the moonlit room, cursing herself for leaving the social because now she would have to wait until tomorrow to find out if he had started a fight with Younger or gone home with one of his Trinkets or, worse yet, embarrassed Jennifer in some way. He was capable of anything.

She walked to the balcony. The moon was up, silvering the treetops and casting shadows beneath them. A dog or a coyote howled in the distance, and a breeze whipped her gown around her legs. The smell of sage mingled with the fresh garden scents. Cantrell would not come here. She was safe now from any threat he might have posed her if she had stayed at the party. On an impulse, she shrugged out of the nightgown, let it drop, and walked to the full-length mirror next to the french doors that led into her private bathroom. The pale silvery moonlight slanting into the room lighted her breasts and cast shadows beneath them that accentuated the slenderness of her waist. Liking the fragrance of jasmine her bath had imparted, she lifted her arms, posing, wondering how her body compared to the bodies of the women Ward Cantrell had known… Her in-curving waist was taut, flaring into slender hips and long, slim, well-shaped thighs. Perhaps her breasts were too small and her body too skinny…

She heard a sound on the balcony and turned in time to see a shadowy form loom suddenly, filling the doorway. Leslie drew back, gasping, her heart lurching.

"Christ!" Ward whispered, his husky quiet voice rich with consternation.

She faced him—a sweet, curving ivory wand in the moonlight that slanted into the room—and he leaned against the door frame, groaning. "Leslie…" He knew he had to tell her he was leaving town, that he had only come here to release her from their bargain, but the rapid rise and fall of her small tip-tilted breasts struck to the core of him.

"I should have known you would make this as difficult as possible," he said grimly, stalking past her to rip the coverlet off the bed. He wrapped it around her but did not step away. His strong hands used the fabric like a net to pull her close.

"Difficult?…" she repeated dumbly, frowning down at her naked breasts, left exposed to her view, her mind so befuddled that even the revealing hardness of her nipples did not faze her. The heat of his body so near, the warm masculine scent of him, added to her confusion. He groaned huskily and pulled her close against him. Without his hands to hold the coverlet between them it fell away, covering only her back. The rough feel of his clothes against her sensitive flesh sent a shudder through her slender form. She was breathing far too fast. Light-headed, she leaned weakly against him.

"Leslie, dammit." Arms tightened around her trembling body; one warm hand slid up her arm to tangle in the raven tresses, scattering the pins, fanning the fragrant mass around her shoulders. The urge to bury her face against the warm, manly crook of his neck and shoulder was irresistible.

All he had to do was touch her and that hard knot of heavy pain, coiling like a snake in her belly, brought her hands up of their own volition to pull his head down. His fingers tightened in her hair, pulling her head back, and slowly, as if he were trying to stop himself but losing, his mouth closed over hers, and she was lost, drowning, oblivious to everything except her primitive, undeniable need to couple with this man.

"No..." he groaned softly, his breath a feather against her cheek. His fingers encircled her wrist so tightly she cried out.

"Owww! What?"

"Don't do that," he growled, moving her arm back so he could capture both her hands. He dragged in a heavy breath and expelled it. "You have to listen to me," he panted, "because if you don't, all my good intentions are going to dissolve."

"I'm listening," she breathed, taking a fiendish delight in the sure knowledge that having her naked in his arms was more painful for him. Unable to resist the urge to torment him, she squirmed against him, wriggling around so that her hands were behind her, his arms around her again. He groaned, like a man lost. His mouth found hers, at first tentatively, as if he really didn't want to kiss her again, and then hungrily, his hands sliding up her arms to close over her shoulders, as if he didn't dare touch her anywhere else.

Forgetting her desire to torture him, she arched into the lean, hard warmth of him, pressing her body shamelessly against his, aware only of his touch, which satisfied a hunger that had lain dormant in her for too long, but satisfied it only a little. The tasting seemed to feed the hunger, so that it swelled and grew in her, becoming uncontrollable. Trembling, clinging to him, she pulled his head down, wanting his kisses with a fierceness and hunger that seemed bottomless.

"Leslie, love," he groaned. "Please look at me."

Why was he pulling away from her? Why was he talking when he could be kissing her? She buried her face against the hardness of his chest and felt the heavy hammer of his heart, matching her own. She sought his mouth, but he caught her face between his hands.

"You have to listen to me," he panted. His voice was husky and harsh, and his hands, holding her face, were harshly possessive.

"What?" she murmured sulkily.

"I want you, Leslie," he whispered against her face, his breath warm. "I want you more than I've ever wanted any woman, but I can't take you by trickery or deception. I just came here to tell you that I am not romantically interested in Jennifer Kincaid. I never was. I only said that because you made me so damned mad. And to punish you for choosing Summers over me." He paused, panting as if he had run a mile. "I have to go. I'm leaving Phoenix."

"Go?"

He buried his face in her hair. Air escaped from his lungs, making a sound low and filled with pain. His arms tightened around her as if he couldn't bear to let her go. "I just came to tell you so you would understand."

"So go," she crooned insincerely, pulling his head down to continue the kiss he had interrupted.

"Did you understand a word I said?" he demanded, resisting her, holding her arms in a fierce, viselike grip.

"You want to go. So go." She shrugged with perfect feminine wile, her chin lifted, her lovely eyes hooded, mysterious, not willing to let him see the joy that had flooded her that he was not involved with Jennie, that he never had been.

"I *have* to go," he whispered. "I forced you once. I can't do that again, dammit. You have to come to me of your own free will. Do you understand that? I have to know that I didn't trick you into anything."

Flushed with her own power, she laughed softly and reached up on tiptoe to kiss his neck. His hand tightened on her arm, biting into the soft white flesh, and even that pain felt wonderful to her, because she understood the reason for it.

"I'm trying to do something that you will think honorable, dammit," he growled, furious with her.

"I'm not interested in your honor. Just be yourself, Cantrell," she whispered.

"That's what I'm trying to do," he said grimly. "I'll be back in one week. You know where the other Kincaids live? If you want to see me, come to me there...or send a message and I will come to you."

"And what if I don't come?" she whispered. "What if I asked you to take me for a ride instead?"

"When?" he scowled.

"Tomorrow..."

Saturday. Could he wait one more day to join the men in Buckeye? She held her breath, waiting, until he sighed and said, "Where?"

"I don't know...I just thought that if you wanted to be honorable...a ride is a very honorable thing to do."

Tim Summers went back to the dance after he left Leslie at the Kincaids' front door.

"Where's Cantrell?" he asked of Winslow Breakenridge, who was refilling his glass from the enormous silver punchbowl.

"He was with Sandra for a while—renewing their little love affair.

Then he disappeared. Where's Leslie?"

"She wasn't feeling well. I took her home. I think Dallas Younger's showing up here upset her."

Winslow laughed. "Or Cantrell's jealousy over Sandra's obvious infatuation with Younger."

"Leslie and I are practically engaged. She has no interest in Cantrell, except as a curio. He's a little different—that's all."

"Bully for you. I personally would worry about any girl he showed an interest in."

"What makes you think he's showing an interest in Leslie?" Tim demanded.

"Love is blind!" he laughed. "Haven't you noticed? He calls all the women Trinket except Jennifer Kincaid and Leslie."

"So?"

Winslow laughed. "A trinket is a pretty bauble of little value…"

Tim searched the dance until he determined that Ward Cantrell was no longer there. He tried to ignore Winslow's taunting remarks, but there were too many things he couldn't forget—like the brooding look in Leslie's eyes whenever she saw the blond outlaw.

He signaled Dallas Younger, and they drifted into a deserted corner where they could speak privately.

"Was Ward Cantrell the man who kidnapped Leslie?"

"Hell yes! You didn't believe that story of hers, did you?" Younger's face turned dark with fury.

"As a matter of fact, I did," Tim said, his face grim. It had never occurred to him that she would lie about that. Knowing that she had changed everything—especially his evaluation of her reaction to Cantrell's presence. It explained why Cantrell had gone to the Kincaids' as soon as he got out of jail, and Leslie's reticence about making a commitment to marry him. She was either stringing him along, hoping to snag Cantrell, or trying to make one of them jealous. Or perhaps she knew that Ward Cantrell was a rich man. Maybe little Leslie was a golddigger.

He pulled Sandra aside and whispered instructions to her, then left the party, barely stopping to thank his host, and drove back to the Kincaid mansion. There was no carriage or horse around, and the house was dark. He stationed himself in a heavy grove of trees where he could watch both entrances, concealed by the shadows of the tall trees that shaded the house from the desert sun. He didn't have long to wait.

Cantrell let himself out the front door and headed, at a brisk walk, back toward Barton Street. Tim didn't bother to follow. He went directly to his own house, took paper and pen in hand and composed two letters, both basically the same, describing Cantrell in detail and telling the sheriffs of Dodge City, Kansas, and Cheyenne, Wyoming, where they could find Ward Cantrell.

He sealed the envelopes and prepared them for posting first thing in the morning. Then he headed toward town, secure in the knowledge that the letters would go out on the seven o'clock train and would reach their destinations within the week. He only had one more small chore…

CHAPTER THIRTY-FIVE

It was as if the whole of Arizona conspired to produce a perfect day. The sky was a dazzling blue. Large white mountains of clouds scudded quickly overhead without blotting out the crisp sunshine. The wind on Leslie's face was cool, pleasant. Even the horse she rode seemed to have developed a perfect gait. The heavy smell of sage hung in the air like incense. Leslie rode astride her horse in a carefully chosen white blouse and a navy blue riding skirt and bolero, with a fashionable hat to protect her face and arms from the sun. She had long ago shed the coat she was wearing when he called for her, so early that only Mrs. Lillian was there to wave good-bye to them. Was there an undertone of approval in Mrs. Lillian's eagerness to provide them with such a lavish lunch?

Leslie felt freer than she had since coming to this awesome place, no longer intimidated by the mind-boggling size of its deserts and mountains, and strangely accepting of herself and her reasons, still hidden from her, for suggesting this excursion.

Cantrell, riding beside her on Blueberry, was wearing a blue shirt that echoed the blueness of his eyes and complemented the warm teak tones of his skin. He made a lithe, striking figure on the big bay horse, and when he smiled at her, his eyes narrowed with appreciation; it was as if they had become two different people, existing for just this one day.

Ward looked younger, more open. She could almost believe, looking at him, that she'd never known him before. Maybe because he really talked to her. There was no holding back, no falseness between them. Unless this was another kind of falseness. But Leslie didn't want to think about that possibility.

They stopped in a marvelous tree-shrouded canyon with a wide, shallow river running through it. They were surrounded by bright pink volcanic canyon walls soaring a thousand feet over their heads.

Head propped on her right hand, she lay on a blanket spread over soft grass while he unsaddled the horses so they could graze. Upstream, where the river was divided by a sand bar, a white-tailed deer walked tentatively to the bank and lowered its head to drink from the cold, sweet water.

"What is this called?" she asked when he returned to drop down beside her.

"Aravaipa Canyon. In Apache it means 'Little Running Water' because even in August the river doesn't go dry, like everything else."

High above, yellow-blossomed century plants dotted the scrub-covered mountainside. On the edge of a pink cliff streaked with black, a rock formation loomed up, looking like a man with pack ready to step up into the sky.

"The Hohokam used to till this as far as you can see."

"How?"

"Stone hand tools."

"What did they grow? Rocks?"

"Grain, vegetables…"

"What happened to them?"

"A number of things. I guess what finally drove them away was a massacre not far from here. Chief Eskiminzin surrendered to the soldiers at Camp Grant, asking that his people be allowed to live peacefully in their old home in the canyon under the soldiers' protection. They agreed; the Indians settled, and they began to cultivate the lands, until the people of Tucson became upset by reports of wildcat Apache raids on defenseless white settlers. Folks from Tucson got up a big party of men, almost a hundred and fifty whites, Mexicans, and Papago Indians, and rode into Aravaipa and wiped out the entire village—men, women, children, old people—all except for a few children they sold as slaves."

Leslie shuddered. "Were they punished?"

"No. It raised a storm back east, but the guilty were tried and acquitted by local juries. Guess it showed, more than anything else, that folks were tired of worrying about the Apache."

"Are we safe here?"

He nodded, smiling at the look of unease that had clouded her lovely face. "That was sixteen, seventeen years ago. The Indians haven't been much of a threat since the war."

"You weren't here then, were you?"

"In April of 1870, I was twelve years old. We lived in New York, on Fifth Avenue at Fifty-seventh Street."

"Tell me about your family."

"My mother was beautiful, vivacious, ambitious, and infamous by the time she was twenty-two. She was the second generation of American women of society to make the stage a profession. From what I hear she was damned good at it too, though I have to admit I wasn't too wrapped up in her accomplishments. I was—don't be shocked—a little self-centered at that time," he confessed, a sardonic smile lighting his lean face. "I preferred polo, horse-breeding, and horse-racing—anything at all to do with horses."

Leslie laughed, "Well, your interest in that area has served you well."

"Early job training, with prescience."

They laughed and it was easy, unstrained camaraderie, as if they had called a truce.

"Are you hungry?" she asked.

"I'm always hungry." He grinned. "Suit yourself."

But he didn't eat much, while she was famished and showed it by eating two chicken sandwiches, some cheese, a piece of pie, and topping it off with a glass of warm milk that hadn't quite survived the trip. It had been cold when Mrs. Lillian sealed the quart jar that morning.

"Ohhh, that was wonderful," she said, sighing.

He leaned against the trunk of a tree and closed his eyes. "Wake me anytime," he said, chuckling.

Leslie rummaged in a bag she brought with her. "What are you up to now?" he asked drowsily.

"I'm going to draw you…if I can find my charcoal."

"Sort of a busman's holiday, huh?"

"Something like that…You don't mind, do you?"

"Not unless it can be used as evidence against me."

She laughed, a golden tinkle of notes; he smiled, and for just a second he was the same man who had picked the flower in the garden and handed it to her with a bold flourish. The breath caught in her throat, and she wondered crazily if she would ever forget that one moment when he revealed himself to her. Was she doomed to spend the rest of her life waiting breathlessly for another glimpse? Part of her was irritated that she could so easily be hooked. In the scheme of things, what possible significance could a fleeting glimpse have when measured against all that she knew about him? But today, with her lying on a soft blanket beneath a spread of gnarled oak limbs, under a crisp cloud-filled sky, with a warm breeze on her face, and a full stomach, with the smell of a picnic hovering around them, it was as if the scales had tipped. Leslie could not fully remember anything beyond this moment.

She sketched quickly, doing a caricature that came out quite well actually. She portrayed him with wickedly narrowed eyes, a wide jaw, an exaggerated pout on his lips, and two guns in his hands. They laughed about it, and she lay back to relax. His hand found hers, and her eyes closed. She floated in her own shade of darkness while his lean fingers played over the palm of her hand, explored her fingers, her thumb, then intertwined fully and became still, so that only the tingle of a small pulse, moving like a current from his skin to hers, was noticeable to her. She was moving into uncharted territory now, a small voice warned her, but it was ignored, drowned out by the more insistent hunger in her body. If only he wouldn't be so tender with her. She could withstand his gruffness and his insolence.

"Tell me about your childhood, Leslie. I have a hard time visualizing you as a child," he said, his voice husky and low, as he surrounded her hand in his two warm ones.

"I was very boring as a child. I was bossy, generous, and I held grudges. Every mother has a favorite story…My mother said that when I was about two years old she told me not to touch any of the things on the low table in the parlor. She said I looked her in the eye and touched each one. She slapped my hand after each defiant touch, and when I was all done, every single item thoroughly touched and me just as thoroughly punished for it, I lost interest in that table and never bothered it again. What would you call that? Principles? Or the lack thereof? I'm not sure."

Ward laughed. "I'd call that a well-defined sense of justice. If I ever have another baby…" He stopped with a slight grimace.

Leslie looked at him with a question in her eyes, and he shook his head, a scowl darkening his brow. "You might just as well tell me…If you don't, I'll imagine something ten times as bad. I promise you that," she said softly, reclaiming his hand, since he had let hers go.

He sighed. "I was married about seven years ago. My wife was expecting a baby." Haltingly at first, and then more easily, he told her about the events in Dodge City, everything. She held his hand, using it to prompt him when he faltered, unaware that she did. She had doubted his honesty before, but not this time. She listened, and a layer of resistance peeled away, like bark off a tree.

"So, you were a captain in the army one day and a hunted fugitive the next? That must have been quite an adjustment." She was fighting back the urge to fall sobbing into his arms. Part of her needed it. She had listened with much pain and not a little remorse. Her generous nature insisted now that she confess.

"Yeah."

"I've wronged you, Cantrell. If not publicly, then at least in my own mind. I conjured up all sorts of images of you living a life of sloth, irresponsibility."

"Perhaps I have."

"Maybe, but it wasn't your choosing. It's almost like a fairy tale."

"Fairy tales have happy endings."

"How did you know that?"

He laughed. "I went to Harvard, remember. They cover things pretty well. I think they called it English Literature."

She blushed. "I never really believed you." She paused. "Tell me. Harvard educations do not come inexpensively. How could you give up a world of privilege and live like a Mexican sheep herder?"

"No choice. You would be surprised what you can do under those circumstances."

She was remembering her own immersion into his life, the days after he kidnapped her. She nodded. "So you were swooped up in the daily struggle to survive. What did you do at first?"

"Bled a lot," he said ruefully.

"Were you injured?"

"I was feeling sorry for myself."

"How did you decide to become an outlaw, I mean, to rob trains, that sort of thing?"

"I got hungry," he shrugged. "Let's walk," he said, coming to his feet with that lithe grace that characterized all his movements, pulling her up with him.

Above what Cantrell called Aravaipa Canyon there was a bend in the creek. Squat, scrubby trees hugged the far shoreline. In the shadow of the canyon wall, the shallow water glistened royal blue in the afternoon shade, silver in the sunlight. Soft grass grew up to the gravel that lined the creek. The Pinaleno Mountains loomed on the north. She remembered the name from their ride around them earlier.

"Look," he said softly.

She followed his pointing finger and saw a small gray cat padding out to the water about a hundred yards away.

"That's a bobcat. The mother is not far away." He watched it until he saw it rejoin the rest of the litter and then, taking her hand, he led her directly to what he wanted her to see. Things his sharp eyes uncovered while she was otherwise occupied.

He showed her a fox's lair, an eagle's nest, then led her up a steep hill so they could watch the litter of bobkittens at play. When they were back down the hill, she laughed. "That was wonderful. You've had a good life, in spite of everything, haven't you?"

"I won't permit it to be otherwise, Leslie. I'm too selfish to waste my life anymore. I'm not willing to spend it being miserable."

"Me either."

"So what do you see in Summers?"

She shrugged. "Tim's intelligent, very handsome, entertaining, and not very demanding."

"And doesn't turn up on any wanted posters. That's important to you, isn't it? Someone predictable…someone you can take charge of, be in control of…"

"I guess so. I lived with my uncle for a couple of months and experienced what it was like not to be in charge, to be out of control of my life. It was intolerable! But why did you say that? You don't know me that well."

"I've seen you take charge too many times not to have noticed."

"Take charge," she cried. "Like when?"

"You don't remember?" he chided. "When I tried to send you off to Flagstaff."

Leslie flushed. "I still don't see how that…"

"Sure it does. As soon as you got your bearings, within two days of my scooping you off that road, you were calling the shots."

She grinned, unaccountably proud, but still seeking proof. "Well, you *could* have misunderstood."

"My foot! I got the distinct impression that you engineered everything, even when I thought I was seducing you, it turned out to be for your benefit."

He was more perceptive than she had thought. Pleased far more than she wanted him to know, she shrugged, unable and strangely unwilling to deny his accusations.

"Younger was closing in on you then, wasn't he?" he asked, his eyes narrowed.

"My uncle wanted me to marry him. Perhaps it did cross my mind that if I were no longer virginal, he might not think me marriage material."

Raucous birds cried overhead, and Ward hooted with delight. "You're one in a thousand…Can't fault your logic. Though I have to admit it piques my vanity a little."

She laughed. "Good!"

"Good? You're a heartless little wench."

"Healthy."

"True. I never cared for any woman who wasn't at least as selfish as I."

"Selfish?"

"Sure. Selfishness is healthy. You've got that well-developed sense of your own worth that's most becoming in a woman."

"How did you reach this conclusion?"

"I can see it all over you. You're too busy with your own interests to prostrate yourself at any man's feet. You paint, you read about painting, you study technique, you tote that little sketch pad with you everywhere you go. You don't really need people all that much, though you are perfectly charming when you're with them."

"You are far more observant than you appear."

He laughed. "But then I would have to be, wouldn't I?" he said, mimicking the time she used that same line to insult his intelligence.

"Touché." She laughed. "I'm curious. What makes my selfishness so attractive to you?"

"Few men have time to be a woman's whole life."

"You certainly think of everything, don't you?"

"Not usually."

"Is this different for you?"

"Did your mother teach you to be so direct?"

"I don't think so. Does it bother you?"

"I've answered questions today no one has dared ask me before." He paused. "I've told you things I didn't tell my attorney."

"Winslow? I can understand that." She laughed and mimicked Winslow's stilted speech and mannerisms.

When they stopped laughing, Leslie leaned against the tree they were standing under and looked up at him. Cantrell's eyes darkened.

"So when are you going to take charge and kiss me?" he challenged.

"What happens if I don't?"

"Then I might risk life and limb to kiss you."

"I'm not that fierce," she whispered.

"That sounds like something Sitting Bull might have said to Custer."

"Do you feel like Sitting Bull?"

"Custer."

"Ohhh! Poor thing." She sighed. "Forgive me if I don't fully believe you.

"What was the happiest time in your life?" she asked to change the subject.

"You ask more damn questions…"

"Do I?" she teased. In that second, with his eyes narrowed against the sun and his jaw clenched in mock consternation, he looked every inch the sturdy, capable army captain. Why hadn't she guessed? Perhaps because she knew so little about *real* outlaws? Had she supposed they were all so clean-shaven, so articulate and capable?

Listening to him as he told her about one of the early settlements he'd been to, she could detect the hint of his almost vanished eastern accent. Or had he perfected that El Paso drawl so thoroughly that only the most suspicious listener would catch the almost imperceptible New England twang?

"There was no law there," he said slowly. "No occupation but labor, no government, no taxes, no public debt, no politics, only an old man who kept records in a ledger of births and deaths, performed the marriage ceremonies, baptized the children, and granted the divorces on request."

"Why did you like it so much?"

"It seemed like heaven to me. By the time I got there I had been running so long...They were so innocent, so cut off from civilization that they hadn't even heard of me."

"Why didn't you stay there?"

"Nothing lasts forever."

His voice was quiet and deliberately expressionless, just as it had been when he had told her about Simone and his friend Snake. She had a heavy, smothering pain around her heart. Was it for the pain he had suffered? Or only because the sun striking the smooth, healthy teak of his skin made her want to put her lips against the sensuous smooth swell of his insolent bottom lip?

Of a sudden she took off her wide-brimmed straw hat and threw it into the air with all her strength. It sailed smoothly upward, caught a draft from the mountainside, and flipped over and over, bouncing wildly on an air current, causing her to cry out. "Oh, my hat! My hat!"

He laughed and strained upward with his arms in a futile, enthusiastic way, shaking his head.

She began to run after it, and he followed, laughing at the playful shrieks she uttered unconsciously, bobbing and darting under the diving, soaring hat, talking to the hat as if it were deliberately defying her. Unexpectedly, it came slicing downward, right at her. She dodged and squealed. By the time he reached her side she was kneeling, bending forward to retrieve the battered straw. Her neck, exposed by the hair falling to one side, gave him a sharp pang. Her breasts swung slightly in her blouse, the slender arching curve of her back was beautiful and strong. She wore no stays.

She looked up into the dark, warm look in his eyes, and her excitement stilled. She stayed on her hands and knees, looking at him, her eyes going tender before her usual defiance reasserted itself. She tossed the hat at him, and he caught it, going down on one knee. She grabbed for it, but seeing her intent, he darted away, keeping it from her. She darted around him in a mad, playful fashion, laughing. She was small and agile, quick as lightning. He pushed her aside, but she came leaping back at him, making up in energy what she lacked in height and weight. She almost fell, then shrieking with delight, she stumbled away from him only to surge back, floundering tumultuously, wild with joy. They dodged and darted, laughing until they were both breathless, then collapsed on the grass.

The hat lay beside them on the matted, tussocky grass, forgotten. "Oh, that was wonderful!" she sighed.

"You half killed me," he groaned.

"Poor thing…"

"Look who's gasping for breath."

"Is this a case of the pot calling the kettle black?"

Panting, he rolled over and pinned her loosely, his hands on either side of her breasts. "Dallas Younger couldn't have caught you."

"No," she said, becoming still, knowing what he meant, surprised that he had worried about her situation with Younger at all. He didn't move, but her hands, sliding around his lean waist, felt the slight tremor inside him. His body, usually so like a weapon, hard and implacable against her, relaxed. The heavy feeling in her heart melted. Her blood, roused from the romp and the long walk in the warm sun, surged deep inside her, making her aware of herself as a woman, aware of her power and his.

"I'm glad," he said softly. "I hated the thought of you at his mercy."

His sincerity touched her. Her heart felt crushed in a burning grip, so that she was speechless.

"I should have known you would whip him."

"I didn't humiliate him too badly."

He grinned broadly, his eyes lighted with mischief. "He was lucky to get away with his life."

She laughed, enjoying his obvious pride in her accomplishment, arching backward, her small breasts touching his chest, burning into him like fire-tips.

His lips on her throat, soft and warm, did not surprise her. His words were tortured, almost inaudible: "Leslie...love..."

The river rushed noisily beside them. The air was clean and fresh, smelling of pine and resin and river smells. The sun was warm on her skin.

Kissing her softly, shakily, he undressed her as if she were not the same woman he had been intimate with in the past. He was gentle, filled with a queer, blind clumsiness. She too was changed. Naked and with open eyes, she received him solemnly, with a sort of blind submissiveness. Their coupling was like submersion in warm water. She was lost, drowned, then caught up in a tornado and whirled around until her senses reeled. She clung to his sweat-sheened back, as if her life depended upon maintaining some connection with him, his warm skin, his hungry mouth.

They lay locked in fierce possession, clinging together as if unwilling to intrude on the mysterious stillness in their bodies. Did she sleep?

"Did you sleep?" His words sounded like an echo of hers.

"I don't know. Did you?" she whispered.

"No." He rolled off her, bringing her with him so that she lay atop him. "I would have crushed you."

They lay quietly, not talking, not wanting to. She fully understood the pain he could inflict now that she knew she cared for him. She didn't say love, even in her mind, but a small warning, like some muted bell, sounded deep inside her, back near her spine, in darkness, like the chill of a foghorn along the frozen eastern coastline.

As if he sensed the change in her, he kissed her, then disentangled himself and pulled on his pants and boots.

"Wait here." He was back in moments, his hands filled with tiny, yellow flowers that he scattered over her half-dressed body. "You deserve roses, long-stemmed red roses, but this is the best I could do."

"It's wonderful; it couldn't be better." She smiled, gathering the tiny flowers in her hands to breathe their fragrance, her strange mood completely dispelled.

The ride back to Phoenix ended much too soon. Was that because she didn't know if she would ever see him again? Or because riding back was like returning to confusion after experiencing a glimpse of clarity?

Was it the look on Jennie's face when Ward nodded his curt good-bye to her? The sudden flicker of controlled anguish in her lovely violet eyes before she lowered them and took her husband's protective hand? Had Jennie deliberately waited up for them? Did Mrs. Lillian perhaps say something she shouldn't have? But Jennie didn't look envious or resentful. She seemed genuinely happy to see them.

Watching him ride away from the Kincaid house, into the enveloping darkness of midnight, so tall and lean and straight, so manly and up to his duty, she felt that dim, muted bell in the depths of her sounding again, and she shivered.

CHAPTER THIRTY-SIX

Yoshio met Ward at the door, his typically Japanese face clouded with worry. "I tly to stop her. I tell her you be gone a rong time, maybe not come back at all, but she insist she have to see you."

"Who?"

"Brond Tlinket," he said, smiling at his own savvy.

Ward grinned at the mispronunciation. "It's okay. I'll see her."

"That for sure," he said firmly, bobbing his head. "You see prenty of her. No choice. That's what I'm dying to tell you. She in your bed."

"In my bed?"

Yoshio nodded, the tortoiseshell glasses hiding the expression in his dark eyes. "You want Yoshio to wake you in the morning?"

"I'm not staying. As soon as I pack I'll be gone until next Saturday, if all goes well. You get to bed." He knew Yoshio went to church on Sunday mornings. He had confided that he was Buddhist but that he enjoyed the ritual in the other church as long as he didn't listen to the words.

"Ward." Sandra pushed the door open, waiting for him.

"Hi, Trinket."

"I waited and waited for you. I thought you cared about me." She was naked and crying, Kincaid's robe wrapped carelessly around her slender body. "I know you didn't invite me here or anything, but I needed to talk to you." Her long blond hair was loose around her shoulders. Her eyes were red and swollen. She looked so pitiful that he didn't stop to wonder what had unsettled her so. His words were gentle, meant to be consoling.

"You were playing with fire. I had to stop you. Dallas Younger is mean in a way you can't even comprehend. He isn't playing games, Trinket. He plays for keeps."

"Liar!" She jerked away from him, screaming that word from the very depths of her, her teeth bared, her movements violent. "No! You bastard! You rotten bastard! You tricked me! You're just like all the rest! Tricking me! Using me! I know what you're trying to do! You're like my father, like all those sanctimonious self-righteous bastards who try to keep me from finding happiness. You make a thousand rules so that no one can remember them all and then punish a man for nothing." She sobbed angrily for almost a minute before she started again, this time jerking free of the hand he put out to restrain her, to pace back and forth shouting and waving her arms.

"Life is a joke! You know that? All I want, all I ever wanted, is to be happy! To have someone who wants me! Me! Is that so much to ask!? To have someone of my very own! Someone who wouldn't push me away." She fairly spat the words.

"Hey, I haven't lied to you..." He reached for her, to gentle her the way he would a riled-up horse, and she leaped at him, her nails curved into claws. Pain flashed like fire through his cheek. He slapped her hard, then pinned her arms before she could rake his other cheek with her nails.

"What the hell has gotten into you? Stop this nonsense, dammit, or I'll turn you over my knee. I care about you, or I wouldn't have even bothered with you. I meant what I said. You stay the hell away from Younger. He's a dead man anyway, as soon as I get him on my turf instead of yours," he growled, holding her struggling, naked body.

She changed instantly, like a child who gratefully accepts her punishment and then, relieved of both the guilt of the misdeed and the pain of the scolding, is reborn in innocence. "Do you really care?" she asked, snuggling against his chest, slipping her arms up to cling around his neck. "Can I stay with you? I need you, Ward. Please? I'm sorry about your face. I didn't mean to..." New tears flooded her swollen eyes. She sounded like a child. Looked like one with her clenched fists pressed tightly against her trembling lips. He let his guard drop, pulled out his handkerchief to wipe his cheek. Blood stained the whiteness. What the hell had gotten into her?

"I'm a working man, Trinket. I'm leaving town now. I won't be back for at least a week," he said gently, trying not to show the impatience he felt. "Behave yourself, and stay away from Younger."

He disengaged himself, took her small hand in his, and led her to the bed. She followed eagerly until she realized he wanted her to dress herself.

Ignoring her, he strode purposefully around the bedroom he had used, gathering his few personal belongings. Sandra, fully dressed now, watched with baleful resentment. His mind was miles away. He was eager to bring this job to a quick conclusion. He had most of what he needed now—men he trusted at his back. It was just a matter of time and a little luck. All they had to do was catch Younger and some of his men with stolen cattle.

Sandra couldn't read his thoughts, but she didn't need to. She could tell what was important to her—he had forgotten she existed—if he had ever known it…Her face, if he had bothered to look at it, was a mask of betrayed femininity.

He stopped to survey the room, checking to see if he had forgotten anything. He pulled out his handkerchief and wiped at his cheek where blood was trickling.

"I'd like a cigarette," she sniffed, wiping her eyes.

He rolled one for her, lit it, and passed it to her.

"Thanks," she said, inhaling deeply.

He watched, fascinated. He'd rarely ever seen a woman smoke. She did it with perfect ease.

"Did you have something on your mind tonight?"

She shrugged. "I don't know. I just didn't want to be alone. Before, I just pretended with everyone. They all think I'm pretty and stupid. I hate it," she said with sudden vehemence, curling in on herself, like a flower closing. "I just want someone to love me for myself."

Ward reached out and touched Sandra's bowed head. Buoyed by Leslie's magic, he felt magnanimous toward the world, especially the pitiful, lost girls. "That's what we all want, Trinket," he said gently. "It isn't easy to find."

Sandra shook her head. "How can you say that? Every woman in town is in love with *you.*"

Ward grinned. "That's not real. I'm a novelty to them— nothing more."

Sandra frowned. "A rugged western bad man who looks smashing in a dinner jacket?"

Ward shrugged. "That's all it is…"

"Do you love Leslie Powers?"

His blue eyes darted away. "I've got nothing to offer a woman," he said grimly, meaning it.

"You do love her," Sandra said knowingly.

"The timing is all wrong." He knew exactly how important timing was. He had seen perfectly planned train robberies turn into disasters because of timing that was off a few seconds one way or the other. Timing was everything.

He had a debt to pay to society that might take years. Leslie wouldn't wait for him while he moldered in some prison.

"That is the dumbest reason I've ever heard of. If you love her, you love her. You'll just have to find some way to overcome the bad timing."

Was this the same girl who had just raked her nails down his left cheek? He put questions about Sandra's strange behavior out of his mind. Just as he should Leslie if he didn't want to risk the sort of pain he had suffered when Simone died.

"You said that Younger might kill me...Was that just to keep me away from him?"

"No, it's true."

"Can you prove it?"

"No, I can't," he said, turning to look at her.

She searched his eyes, saw the level honesty there, and shrugged. "So could you be wrong about him?"

He nodded. "I could be, but I doubt it. Just do me the favor of keeping away from Younger until I know, okay?" he asked.

Her eyes skittered off to one side, unable to meet his. He sighed. "Then try to protect yourself at least. Don't be alone with him."

Her eyes were enormous in her face. "I'm not sure I can promise either, Cantrell."

"Well." He sighed. "At least you're honest."

Sandra smiled shakily. "Surprised me as well," she admitted. Something flickered in her gray eyes. She took off the necklace she wore and put it in his hand. "Keep this."

"Hey, I don't wear necklaces," he protested.

"I know, but I don't want to be forgotten. If you have to keep it, it's always going to be in the way, so I know you won't forget me."

"You've got that right," he said ruefully.

"Will you keep it?"

"You sure ask a lot."

"I need a lot."

"All right," he said grimly.

"Just tell her it's from a friend. She'll understand," she said, reading his mind. Smiling, she picked up her coat and turned to leave.

"I'll walk you home," he said.

"No thanks. I can walk myself. Besides, if my father saw me coming in at this hour with a man, he'd have a conniption."

Ward was tired enough that he wanted to accept the out she had given him, but his conscience wouldn't let him. "I'll walk you as far as your yard. He won't see me."

"You shouldn't be nice to me. I don't deserve it," she said, her gray eyes clouded with something akin to remorse.

The moon had set and the sky was dark except at the horizon, where it was turning murky pink. Stars looked like tiny pinpricks of light overhead, already fading. The wind was chill and dogs howled occasionally. Sandra sneaked in the back way, through the kitchen.

"Coming in sort of late, ain't you?" the cook asked, looking up from where she was lighting the tinder in the wood stove to begin her Sunday baking.

"Don't nag me! I'm sick and tired of everybody in the whole world always telling me what to do!" she snarled viciously but quietly, for fear her father would hear and come down. "If you say one word about this, I'll get you! You hear me, you old witch?"

Mary Freake, a pale woman with a tiny pointed chin, backed away from the venom in her mistress's face, nodding in acquiescence. She needed this job, and she'd heard stories about what happened to people who carried tales to that nice Mr. McCormick. "Yes, ma'am. No offense intended, ma'am."

Sandra didn't stop to acknowledge her victory. The servants weren't people to her—they were battlements hired by her father to protect him from her. They came with the house, like furniture. She slipped up the stairs, thinking her angry thoughts. All she had to do was walk back inside this house and she filled up with rage, as if it leaked into her from the air here. She could feel the rage bubbling in her veins.

She fairly flew up the stairs. There was nothing she could do until tonight. Then she would show her father. She would show all of them!

Sandra slept all day Sunday, only getting up at teatime to bathe and dress herself for dinner. She could get away with almost anything as long as she was pretty and charming to Daddy's dinner guests.

That brought a bitter smile to her young face. How long had she known that? Forever it seemed, but she'd learned it a little at a time. Beginning when she was very young. Her first conscious memory of her father was when her mother died.

"Daddy, Daddy…"

"What is it? What do you want?" Sam McCormick asked impatiently, fighting his way back to the surface. He'd been drowning in his own bitter thoughts, reliving that last hour when the woman he loved, who had promised to love him forever, abandoned him to this grief. "Maramee! Oh, God, Maramee, please don't leave me! Please! I love you! I need you!"

Tears had welled in her gray eyes. "I'm sorry, Sam," she whispered.

"Please don't leave me…" He was crying, great silent sobs that were tearing his insides apart. Her hand was so cool. So cool. How long had he been crying? He looked up suddenly and knew she was gone. His whole world ended that day—that moment. Except that the remnants of their life, their world, wouldn't leave him alone.

"Daddy…Daddy…"

"Sandra—please—go play."

"I don't want to play, Daddy. I want to help you. What are you drinking? Can I have some?"

"Of course not. You're not old enough. Now run along. Daddy wants to think."

"I'll help you think, Daddy. I'll be good and quiet."

"If you want to be good, go outside and play."

"I'll just sit here beside you, okay, Daddy? I just want to sit with you."

"Margaret! Margaret! Would you come get this child!" he yelled to the housekeeper.

Margaret came rushing in.

"Naughty girl! Why do you keep bothering your poor daddy? Doesn't he have enough problems? I'm sorry, Mr. McCormick. I didn't realize she was bothering you again."

"No, it's okay. You can't watch her every second. Maybe I should get a governess for her."

Margaret had picked her up, and she had cried all the way up to her room. She had cried all afternoon and she didn't even know why she did. But she had slowly learned not to bother her father. She had a whole houseful of women to remind her what a busy, important man he was.

Sandra had learned her role well, so that she had become almost invisible. Tonight she suffered graciously and smilingly through the Sunday dinner and after-dinner rituals and then kissed her father's cheek and asked to be excused.

"Of course, dear. Good night," he said absently, turning back to his guests.

Sandra glided smoothly up the stairs until she was out of sight, then ran the rest of the way. She changed her evening gown for riding clothes—a buff-colored silk blouse and a divided riding skirt. She shrugged into a long, full coat and slipped out the back way without being seen to walk the short distance to Tim Summers' house.

"Sandra!" he said, a quick frown knitting his brow. Wariness and calculation clouded his black eyes as he pulled her inside. "Did anyone see you leave? Are you alone?"

She walked slowly into the middle of the large, sparsely decorated parlor, wondering if she had made a mistake coming here. "No one saw me," she said petulantly.

"Did you see Cantrell?"

"Yes."

"Did you do as I told you?"

"Yes," she said sullenly, feeling the dark ugliness of remorse. Cantrell had tried to be her friend.

"Would you like a drink?" he asked, his voice becoming cordial.

"Yes, please," she said, grateful that he wasn't treating her like a bothersome child. Maybe it would be all right after all.

He poured two drinks and led her to the couch. He sat down beside her and looked her over while she sipped gingerly at the drink. She had changed since that night at the river. Before she had been a pretty, if somewhat vapid, young woman. Now, with her breasts swinging free beneath the thin silk blouse she wore, she was very desirable.

"I don't know you very well," she said softly, flushing at the truth in her words even though he had taken liberties with her that still caused a dull ache of shame when she allowed herself to think about it.

"But you can trust me."

"Can I?"

"Absolutely."

"Why did you tell me to invite Dallas Younger to stay and dance the other night?"

Tim hesitated, watching her eyes and the particularly glazed look when she mentioned Dallas Younger's name. He had expected her to ask why she was told to mark Cantrell's face. Since the party, he'd had an opportunity to reappraise his plan, and it had not come up wanting in any serious respect. Except that if Sandra turned up dead, Cantrell might have an alibi and it would be harder to place the blame on him. So Sandra would disappear. Blame would be more easily placed on Cantrell, with no definite time frame to worry about. A hundred men could be deputized to track down Cantrell and hang him. With claw marks on his face and Sandra's locket in his possession Cantrell wouldn't be able to convince an angry lynch mob of his innocence, would he?

He moved closer to her, his eyes darting from her half-opened mouth to her eyes. "Dallas Younger wants you," he said softly to distract her from any more questions.

"He does?" A heavy pulse started in her throat.

"I told him he didn't have a chance."

She frowned, not understanding. "What?"

"Well, you're in love with Cantrell, aren't you?"

Sandra swallowed miserably, remembering Ward's rejection of her and her own duplicity. She shook her head.

"You're not in love with him?" he asked, looking surprised. "Then there is some hope for Dallas?" Tim lifted Sandra's drink to her lips and watched her obediently sip the straight whiskey he had poured into her glass. "That makes more sense, though, when I think about it, since Cantrell has asked Leslie Powers to marry him..."

"He asked Leslie?"

"You didn't know that?" he lied smoothly.

"I thought Leslie was going to marry you."

Tim sighed, looking hurt. "So did I." He waited for the impact to hit her, then he proceeded. "So we've both been rejected, haven't we?" The rest of his plan was clear now. Even if Sandra were found alive, which was unlikely, she was so stupid and gullible that she would think she *had* run off with Dallas Younger. With their agreement, she wouldn't mention him even if she did realize it was his idea.

Pain was bright and sharp in her smoky gray eyes. She was really quite lovely. He set her drink on the floor, put his arm around her, and pulled her close. "Poor baby," he crooned. "Poor sweet Sandra..."

She was completely pliant in his arms. His eyes darting from her glazed eyes to the rapid rise and fall of her rich breasts, he reached out slowly, deliberately, and began unbuttoning her blouse. He slipped his hand inside, cupping the silky, heavy swell of her breast, feeling the warmth and the tumultuous pounding of her heart.

Sandra moaned and turned her face away, shamed by the look in his glittering black eyes but unable to stop him.

His fingers moved slowly, insistently, playing with the tiny bud until it was rock-hard, stroking and teasing the sensitive flesh until she could no longer think coherently.

"Stand up and take your clothes off for me," he whispered against her ear.

Sandra was in an agony of wanting, but there was something about Tim Summers that discomposed her. She had taken off her clothes with men before, but then it had been playful or teasing or because she wanted to. With Tim it had to be because he ordered it, and there was something humiliating in obeying him, in watching the twisted, ugly expression in his eyes while she did so. She still had some pride…

"I think I'd better go," she said weakly.

He didn't answer her in words. He caught her hair at the nape and pulled her head back, forgetting himself, forcing a cry of surprise and pain from her half-opened mouth. "I need you, Sandra," he whispered urgently against her cheek. "We need each other. Don't disappoint me."

"You're hurting me," she whimpered.

Tim relaxed his grip on her hair, reminding himself that he had to go slow until he had her where he wanted her.

"Sorry, but you're so beautiful," he lied softly.

"Why are you doing this to me?" she whined, stalling.

"Because Dallas wants you. And because we are alike, you and I. If you insist on meeting Dallas as he wants you to, I might be willing to help you."

Bemused, Sandra gazed into his eyes, the shame slowly dissipating, being replaced by the needy ache that deadened everything else for her. "Please don't hurt me," she said softly.

He helped her up and walked her into the bedroom, his hands possessive and rough around her waist.

CHAPTER THIRTY-SEVEN

Sunday morning was quiet around the Kincaid household. The family had eaten a late breakfast. The children were upstairs playing in the nursery.

Chane and Jennifer were relaxing in the library before a cozy fire that had been built to take the early November chill out of the air. He was reading the newspaper while she read a book she had started two days ago. They were lost in an easy and companionable silence. Jennie lay curled up on the sofa with her bare feet pressed against Chane's thigh.

Malcomb came to the end of the sofa, gliding on noiseless feet. "Ahem," he coughed.

Chane scowled. The man moved so silently he could never tell where he might appear next.

"Yes, Malcomb."

"The sheriff is here to see you, Mr. Kincaid."

Jennie gave a low cry and sat up. Malcomb closed the door behind him. "Oh, no, could it be Peter? You don't suppose…"

"Your brother is fine. We just saw him last night before he left town," Chane reassured her, folding the paper to put it on the table beneath the electric desk lamp with statuary base—an alabaster water bearer surrounded by crystal teardrops hanging from the lampshade. Chane walked the long way around the sofa so he could touch Jennie's shining crown of sleep-tousled curls. Neither of them had gotten much sleep, but she looked cuddly and fresh-faced in spite of it in a purple velvet dressing robe that complemented her wide purple eyes.

"Something could have happened to him," she said, uncomfortably.

His hands closed around the soft warmth of her upper arms. "You worry too much about him and not enough about me."

"No one has a price on your head," she whispered, and there was fear and pain in her eyes, shimmering there.

"Jennie, love, he's fine. More than likely Tatum wants to tell me that more of my cattle have been rustled."

"You're probably right," she said, sighing and putting her head on his broad chest.

"If you press your body against me like that, neither one of us will ever find out what Sheriff Tatum came here to say to me," he warned, his voice turning sensual.

"Then go! Please, and hurry back," she said.

Chane found the sheriff waiting in the entry hall. "Morning, Sheriff Tatum. What can I do for you?" he asked, steering him into the dining room.

"Morning, Mr. Kincaid. I'm here on business, to see Miss Powers."

Chane was instantly alert for all that it didn't show on the surface. "You're here to see Leslie?"

"Yes, sir. About her uncle. Guess you haven't heard. He was found dead this morning about nine o'clock in the livery stable. Found him behind one of the stalls."

"Horse kick him?"

"No, sir. Throat been cut. Dallas Younger's swearing it was Ward Cantrell. He claims Miss Powers lied about Cantrell not being the one who kidnapped her. He's also saying that Cantrell and Miss Powers are lovers. That maybe Cantrell did this so's he could marry her and own the Powers spread." He paused. "This does leave her full owner now."

"Sheriff, I can assure you Miss Powers would not be a party to murder no matter what she stood to gain by her uncle's death."

Tatum flushed, staring at the delicate pattern in the plush carpet beneath their feet. He didn't have nice things himself, but he could appreciate how the brick red pile complemented the rich shine of the mahogany table and chairs.

He did not feel comfortable arguing with a man of Kincaid's stature, but he did have a job to do. "'Fraid I'm going to have to talk to her anyway," he said, looking Kincaid in the eye.

Chane knew Tatum was a good man trying to do a difficult job, but he wasn't sure Leslie could face Younger's accusations if she had succumbed to Cantrell's lovemaking. She was level-headed and full of spunk, but she was far too honest.

He made a quick decision. He'd seen Tatum in action on other occasions and hadn't been disappointed in any serious respects. Tatum already knew a little about the circumstances leading up to Cantrell's original release and that he had personally arranged it.

"I guess I'd better level with you, Sheriff. Have a seat. Let me take your jacket. Would you like a cup of coffee?"

"Coffee's fine," he said, taking the chair Chane nodded at. When Malcomb had come and gone with the coffee, Chane told Tatum the truth—that Cantrell was Jennie's brother and a rich man in his own right. Coupled with Tatum's prior knowledge that Cantrell had been sworn as an Arizona ranger, the explanation seemed sufficient.

"I'm a reasonable man, Mr. Kincaid. You know that. I'll look elsewhere for the killer, but frankly, it won't help much, my knowing. There must be a hundred men that Younger's talked to since this morning. Any one of them could take a hankering to shoot Cantrell on sight. Seems to me if you want to protect your brother-in-law, you'd better make an announcement or something."

Chane knew the man was right. They'd considered that. But Ward Cantrell was only wanted in Wyoming for working on the wrong side in a cattle dispute. Peter Van Vleet was wanted in Kansas for almost a dozen counts of murder.

"I know your advice is good, Sheriff, but we can't do that yet. We'll just have to pray he stays out of their way."

The sheriff left, and Chane sent Jennie, armed only with the information that Powers was dead, upstairs to break the news to Leslie. He wanted her prepared and composed before she had to face any questions from anyone. Her open, sunny disposition was prone to bantering, teasing, and blunt truths. She might admit her interest in Cantrell, and that could lead anywhere, depending upon the mood of the mob.

Leslie was stunned by the news. She hadn't known Mark Powers at all three months ago; then she had tried to like him and ended up hating him, but she hadn't wanted him dead. Even hearing that she was full owner of the Powers ranch had no meaning for her.

"I could never live there," she said, frowning at Jennie. "Not as long as Younger is..."

Jennie saw the frown and understood. "But you can fire Younger now, disband his riders," she said, patting her hand.

Leslie looked stunned by her new power. "I can, can't I? Then I will, immediately." But she knew she still wouldn't feel safe in that house. There were too many memories, and no assurance that Younger wouldn't come back.

Jennie left Leslie to dress and found Chane in the library, holding the paper absently, as if he had dropped into deep thought. He reached up and patted her hand. "Is she all right, dear?" he asked.

Jennie sighed and sat down beside him on the sofa. "She's fine. But I've been worrying. Do you suppose they could blame Pe—I mean Ward?"

"Don't go looking for trouble," he said gruffly, feeling a moment of guilt that he hadn't told her everything, but he didn't believe things were out of control to the point where he and Ward couldn't handle them. "I'll keep my eye on things. Ward's pretty damned good at taking care of himself, you know."

"I know," she sighed, "but I just couldn't stand it if something happened to him."

Her eyes were darkened with pain and worry. Chane cursed the circumstances that kept her in constant fear. Her love for her brother had been a constant threat to their happiness, and he was feeling that threat more each day, not less. He stood up and pulled her into his arms.

Jennie pressed herself against the length of his hard, masculine body. "I love you so much," she whispered, her silky voice barely more than a whisper. They had made love the night before, and she should have been sated with it, but his clean-smelling masculine scent aroused her again.

His warm hand stroked her face. His thumb teased lightly over her lips and then lifted her chin. His mouth was warm and adhesive against hers, clinging softly.

He meant to kiss her lightly, teasingly, but the spark that was always between them caught fire and leaped into brilliance. He took her there, on the sofa, with only a closed door between them and the rest of the family, and her lovely legs wrapped around him, holding him tight against her. She should have protested, but she wanted him with a fierceness that frightened her.

He brought them much too quickly to fulfillment. When he lifted his dark head from her breasts, her lashes were dreamily closed, her carnation-white skin was flushed pink, and her silver blond hair was fanned out on the sofa. She was so appealing to all his senses—he ached with desire to possess her completely, even now, when the proof of his possession was still between her legs. There were times when he felt mad with desire for her. The only time he possessed her completely was when he was making love to her, and those times were too short, even when they made love most of the night. The rest of the time, Jennie withdrew into her own interests: her music or her ballet or their children. For the most part he appreciated her individuality, but part of him still wanted to possess all of her.

"Treacherous little trifle, aren't you?" he asked huskily, using banter to hide the clutch around his heart. "What shall I tell the servants when they discover us like this? That you couldn't keep your hands off me? That I tried, but you were too strong for me?"

"Liar! I daresay one of us is a mess," she said, becoming aware of the warm moisture between her legs. She didn't relish the thought of explaining to Malcomb what the new stain on the sofa might be.

"I love you, Jennie," he whispered, the teasing banter completely gone. "I love you so much it scares hell out of me..."

Jennie pulled his head down to hers, sighing with the happiness she felt. "I love you, Chane. I have never loved you as freely as I do this minute. It's so wonderful, I feel free to really love you now that Peter is back with us. And safe..."

Something must have flickered in Chane's eyes. Alarm showed in her wide violet eyes, and a small frown puckered her usually smooth brow. "He will be safe? You wouldn't lie to me about that, would you?"

"He will be safe," he said with far more certainty than he felt. She sighed and held him close. Chane closed his eyes, listening to the beat of her heart against his ear. There were times during the last eight years when he had actively resented Peter's intrusion into their happiness. Now, by her own words, Jennie admitted that if anything happened to Peter, it would sabotage their happiness. Chane couldn't help but be resentful.

Chiding himself for his selfishness, he sat up, retrieved the nightshirt from the floor, and pressed it between her legs, enjoying the way she dragged in a ragged breath and closed her eyes as if expecting more. "If you are trying to tempt me, it's working," he said softly.

"Oh! You...you...*man*! You are tempting me!" she said, slipping the gown under her hips.

Thus freed, he put on his robe and stood up. He was feeling a pressure to walk downtown and see just how bad things were.

"Is everything all right?" she demanded.

He cursed the closeness of the bond between them at times like this; it was too hard for him to fool her. He reverted to a ploy that always worked. He turned her over and slapped her on the bottom. "Listen, wench, if you don't stop trying to seduce me, I'm going to call Malcomb in here. Now get dressed." He fled the room before she could recover and figure out his real motives for leaving the house.

Tim rushed to Leslie's side as soon as he heard the news about her uncle. He was loving and solicitous. Common sense dictated that Tim was by far the more suitable choice for a husband. She enjoyed his company; he was a thoughtful person and a good conversationalist. Later that afternoon he came by again to take her riding.

"You need to get out of the house. It'll do you good, darling."

"Thank you, Tim. I feel a bit confused. I don't remember Uncle Mark from my childhood. And we didn't get along very well when I was staying at the ranch."

"Don't feel guilty, darling. Relatives are like historical monuments— it's nice to know they're in place, but they're best enjoyed from a distance."

They rode out in Tim's elegant little surrey, Leslie admiring the scarlet and gold of the early-November landscape. Orchards on either side of the road were alive with color. The afternoon air was cool. Soon winter and snow would mantle those northern mountains.

They passed the last farm, and the landscape grew rougher, the thickets beside the rutted road more dense and impenetrable. Clouds, like fat cottonballs, scudded across the blue sky, threatening to bring rain. Except that she had learned they practically never did. Trees in an orchard on their right were tipped with vibrant red and other bright touches of color, proving that even though it was warm during the day, the nights were cold enough to slow the sap in the trees.

"You look beautiful, Leslie," he said, glancing at her as he held the reins loosely in his capable hands.

"Thank you," she said.

"You look exceptionally lovely for a girl with a headache," he smiled.

"I don't still have a headache," she said, looking at him coolly, not liking his insinuating tone.

"Did you sleep well?" he asked.

"Very well, thank you."

He tilted her chin up and kissed her lightly, ignoring her instinctive withdrawal. "It shows, darling."

Leslie thought she must have imagined that momentary change of tone. The rest of the afternoon Tim was charming and entertaining. She enjoyed his anecdotes, laughing frequently. It felt good to be so carefree.

They stopped beside the river to walk. He took her hand. She glanced at him but didn't take her hand back. She was still under the influence of Ward's lovemaking and hadn't decided what role to play with Tim. Could they be friends? Or would he want her to declare her feelings for Cantrell? She almost laughed. She would be glad to do that, if she knew what they were.

Undecided, she did nothing. Tim was possessive and loving, and while he let her know that he loved her and wanted her, he exerted no pressure on her. He was so unlike Ward in that regard. At times Ward's mere presence was an almost unendurable pressure. She felt disloyal riding and chatting with Tim, but Ward hadn't made any commitments to her or asked for any from her. They walked to a grassy knoll under a tree and paused. Tim smiled into her eyes, his pale face handsome. "So here you are again, in the center of a maelstrom."

"What?"

"Your name is on every tongue in town. Surely you knew."

"No, I didn't know. What are they saying about me?"

Tim closed his eyes in remorse. "Kincaid is protecting his womenfolk, isn't he? And I...Oh, Jesus!"

"You might just as well tell me. Otherwise I will have you take me home so *they* can tell me."

Tim looked miserable. "They are saying that you and Cantrell are lovers. That he killed your uncle so that the two of you will be full owners of the Lazy P."

The color drained out of Leslie's cheeks. "Do you believe that?"

"Of course not! If I thought for a second that you have a lover who kills everyone who gets in either of your ways, would I be standing here?"

"Why are they trying to blame this on Cantrell?"

"Because your uncle's throat was cut. That is Cantrell's trademark, my love. That's the way he killed a number of Younger's men."

"He's also a gunfighter. Does that mean that every man who is shot was killed by him?"

Tim laughed. "You don't need to convince me, love. I am convinced he's innocent, just as I am equally convinced that he is *not* your lover. I happen to know that Sandra McCormick spent the night with him last night. And I told the sheriff as much this morning when this whole thing got started. God knows I have done all I can to help the man."

Tim took her home at five o'clock, and his kiss was short but ardent.

"I have to go to Tucson on business tomorrow morning, but I'll be back Tuesday, latest. I'll miss you dreadfully, my love. Try to think of me," he said, kissing her again.

Too bad she couldn't respond. It would certainly have simplified her life if she could have felt the tumult of passion when Tim kissed her instead of Ward.

It wasn't Tim's fault that by the time he arrived at any stage in their relationship, Ward Cantrell had already ruined it for him. Comparing Ward to Tim was ludicrous. Like comparing a race horse with a plow horse, a Renoir to a child's drawing, a lying, cheating bastard to a decent and honorable man!

CHAPTER THIRTY-EIGHT

Monday morning, when John Loving reached the feedlot, the sharp, heavy smell of cattle assailed his nostrils. There was a crowd—actually two distinct crowds—facing one another in grim silence, waiting for him. He was reminded of the adage that the mob has many heads but no brain. All John Loving could see for sure about the men waiting on the edge of the maze of pens and cattle runs was that they were armed to the teeth and potentially explosive.

The feedlot foreman, Will Wenton, was lined up with Simon Beasley, opposing a cattleman by the name of Hank Morrissey. They were standing at the entrance to the loading chutes, below the ramps that climbed up to railroad car level. A train was waiting, chuffing its black smoke into the air. Cattle lowed and bawled.

John walked into that fearsome crowd like Daniel going into the lion's den. There was no way he could win this. The messenger's words still rang in his ears.

"Mr. Loving, you'd better come quick! There's trouble down at the feedlot! Hank Morrissey's been waiting ten days, and he says his steers'd better move out today or else."

"So why don't we accommodate him?" John asked quietly.

"Because Mr. Beasley bought Aaron Wellman's herd, and he wants to ship today."

"Wellman's cattle have been in the feedlot four days, haven't they?" John said. It wasn't really a question. He knew they had. He also knew that Beasley from Consolidated Can Company was a snake, but that Summers had ordered him days ago to allow Beasley to ship his herds on a priority basis.

"All right, I'm on my way." The acres of pens where the cattle were held for fattening before shipment were two blocks south of the office—two long blocks.

When Hank Morrissey saw John Loving, he left the others and came forward. He was about thirty-five, wiry from hard work, with a clean-shaven, weather-beaten face. Beasley and Wenton exchanged smug looks, but they stayed where they were. They knew Loving had been carefully instructed by Summers.

"I've been waiting to ship for ten days, Mr. Loving. I got a hundred head here, and I'm losing money every day they stay here. A couple more days and I'll have to give that herd to Beasley just to stay outta debt!"

John stopped, a light dawning slowly. It cost him something to keep his face impassive, but he managed it.

"Did Beasley make you an offer for your herd?"

"Sure! Two dollars a head cheaper than I can sell them for in Chicago, even with transportation and normal feedlot costs! The bastard!"

"I guess I'd better hear both sides," John said uneasily. They walked to the edge of the two factions. Men grumbled low, threatening remarks, but they moved back to let him pass.

"What's the trouble here?" John asked.

"No trouble. I have a reservation to ship a hundred and fifty steers today and Morrissey is protesting."

"Is that right?" John asked Will Wenton, who was looking belligerently at Morrissey.

"That's right," he said smugly, rocking back on his heels. "Had that reservation a week, he did."

Morrissey swore vehemently, and the men behind him began to mutter threateningly. "That's a damned lie! He couldn't've had a reservation, 'cause he just bought that herd yesterday."

John considered that for a few seconds. "Can you explain that, Mr. Wenton?" he asked reasonably.

Wenton, a man with a protruding stomach that made him look more pregnant than fat, glanced uneasily at Beasley. Simon Beasley, a swarthy heavyset man with an expensive frockcoat and diamond-studded cravat, chewed on a half-eaten unlit cigar and grunted. His small eyes glittered at Loving.

"I can," he said smoothly, mouthing the cigar. "I have a contract to ship a certain amount of beef on certain days of the month. I reserve my boxcars ahead of time like any good businessman would."

"That right?" John asked Wenton.

"Yes," he said smugly.

John turned to Morrissey. "You heard. It's our policy to honor reservations. I'm afraid there's nothing I can do except guarantee you personally that you can ship tomorrow."

Wenton and Beasley exchanged glowering looks.

"You can't do that!" Wenton exclaimed.

"Why not?" John asked, his look reminding Wenton that he was still the boss.

"Why, because you cain't! That ain't your job, for one thing. And Mr. Beasley has those cars reserved for tomorrow, too."

"What is he shipping?"

Morrissey spat angrily into the dirt at Beasley's feet. "He thinks he's shipping my herd! But I'll starve before I'll let him have 'em!"

Beasley motioned his men forward, and John saw the signal and faced Beasley squarely.

"You cause any trouble here, Beasley, and I'll change my mind and see that Mr. Morrissey ships today—not tomorrow," he said firmly.

Beasley's swarthy face took on a dusky red hue. "You're overstepping yourself now, Loving. Your boss ain't gonna like it when he hears about this," he said grimly.

John Loving knew Beasley was right about that. He'd had too many close calls with Summers already. This would cost him his job, but he didn't care. It would be a relief to be rid of it. The Texas and Pacific wasn't run like the rest of Kincaid's operation. Maybe there was something about the political infighting that always accompanied railroads that had brought out a streak of greed. But that wasn't his problem. Not after today or, more particularly, not after Tim Summers got back from Tucson tomorrow night. Morrissey would ship tomorrow if he had to personally load those cows across Wenton's and Beasley's fat carcasses.

"But that will be too late to help you, won't it?" John Loving asked quietly, enjoying the incredulous look that came into both their eyes.

Beasley considered Loving's ultimatum, finally shrugged. He could ship today, see Summers tonight, and ship tomorrow, too. This snot-nosed kid was just trying to placate Morrissey and save his own ass.

"All right," he growled. "We'll do it your way, for the time being."

Morrissey's riders were grumbling to themselves, not sure yet if they were going to back down or not.

"You guarantee we ship tomorrow?" Morrissey demanded.

"You have my word," John said.

Morrissey dragged in a frustrated breath. "All right," he said, signaling to his riders to disband.

Wenton gave the signal to start loading Beasley's herd, then spat into the dirt at John's feet. "You're asking for it, ain't you? Summers ain't going to like this."

"He won't be back until tomorrow night. Shall we take the problem to Mr. Kincaid and let him settle it?"

Wenton paled and lowered his eyes, looking from side to side. "Naw, we'll do it your way. You're the boss," he said grudgingly.

"Where's Morrissey from?"

Wenton's eyes narrowed. "He's from Pleasant Valley."

That figured, John thought. If he were local, he'd know enough to complain to Kincaid personally, but Wenton and Beasley were probably careful not to pull this guff on local ranchers. He had half a mind to go to Kincaid and tell him, but he knew he wouldn't. He had to play it out now.

John Loving was at the feedlot before seven o'clock the next morning. Morrissey and all his hands were there, too—armed to the teeth—but it wasn't necessary. Beasley didn't show his swarthy face.

When all his cattle were loaded, Morrissey relaxed and turned to John, his clear gray eyes level. He stuck out his rough brown hand. John gripped it.

"Thank you, Mr. Loving."

"You're welcome," John said, feeling slightly foolish. A man shouldn't have to go through this kind of rot just to ship a herd, but his hands were tied. He'd spent a bitter night; he finally decided he didn't want to work for Kincaid anymore. He was either crooked or blind, and either one was inexcusable. He'd written out his resignation before he'd gone to work. It was on Summers' desk.

Morrissey frowned. "Are you going to lose your job over this?" he asked, squinting into the sun that was just coming up.

"No. I quit."

"I'm sorry."

"I'm not. I can work other places," he said, meaning it.

"I'm sorry for the railroad—not you. You'll do all right anywhere."

"Thanks."

Hank Morrissey went to the Bull Whiskey Saloon to wash some of the residue of frustration out of his system. He had been in town almost two weeks, so he knew some of the faces by now.

"Howdy, Hank, name your pizun. I'm buying." Sam Shibbel slapped the bar.

"Whiskey, Sam, and thanks."

"Did you get rid of that herd, or should we have the biggest damned cookout this side of Austin?"

"I got rid of it, but it's the last time I'm shipping Texas and Pacific," Hank said grimly.

"They got you there. Ain't another railroad till you get to El Paso."

"How the hell can they get away with this?"

Shibbel shook his head. "I've known Kincaid, the feller that owns most of the T and P, for nigh onto six years, to speak to, and he didn't seem like the type. Shoulda known better. All them hightone swells is crooked as the day is long. That's how they got rich," he said disgustedly.

Morrissey downed his drink and turned to leave. "Give him my regards—the bastard!"

Shibbel laughed. "We ain't that close."

Riding in the Kincaids' heavily sprung brougham toward the church at the west end of Van Buren Street, she felt weighted down and hot. God! How she missed her Massachusetts. The town of Wellesley was spread on a carpet of green. Trees would be brilliant with autumn, and the wind would be cool with smells of wood smoke and burning leaves.

Sweltering at ten o'clock in the morning, on her way to a funeral, Leslie lifted the black veil and dabbed her perspiring face, hating the formality of mourning clothes. She felt like a hypocrite in the borrowed black gown, with its low bustle and its too-full skirt that ballooned out over her hips. She had left her acceptable mourning gown at home, never guessing she would need it again so soon.

The street they were on was lined with a shallow fringe of two- and three-story buildings. There was a depressing conformity of style in the way the gaunt, squarish buildings each had a door and two windows and a porch roof or awning that jutted out like bulky eyelashes demurely lowered.

The brougham swayed around a corner, and Leslie got a glimpse of the road ahead of them. It was a ribbon of glistening dust-colored sugar flowing between the clapboard false-fronted buildings whose weathered wood was fading even as they passed.

The desert seemed more hospitable than this town. She imagined people staring at the sleek Kincaid carriage, thinking angry, accusing thoughts about her. She unconsciously pulled her veil down, straightening it protectively. She even hated the thought that they had occasion to think about her.

In passing all this hodgepodge of shabby buildings, only the Bricewood West, with its French Second Empire version of the palazzo style, showed a very unPhoenixlike dignity. There was something so incongruous about the way it sat so smugly, as if it knew something about this town that no one else knew. Gazing at it now, as the carriage rocked past, she had the feeling she had never really seen it before. Maybe she hadn't seen any of Phoenix before.

They reached the church a few minutes before ten. Mrs. Kincaid walked with Mrs. Lillian and Annette, while Chane escorted Leslie to the gravesite, where the clean, precise pine box already waited beside the open grave. By now, Leslie knew about making arrangements, having been forced to cope with her mother's death, but she was grateful to Chane for taking care of these for her. He had arranged for the church sexton to dig the grave, the local carpenter to build the box, and the livery stable owner to deliver the body in a horse-drawn glass-sided hearse. On the whole, the arrangements were far more primitive than her mother's, but embalming had not spread to the West on a large-scale basis yet.

She saw faces she recognized: Tim Summers, Winslow Breakenridge, some riders from the Lazy P, Dallas Younger, some cattlemen whose names she did not remember, and a few merchants.

Mr. Kincaid had engaged Reverend Abercrombie from the First Presbyterian Church to officiate at the burial. He had paid a formal call on Leslie the day before. He came forward and greeted her warmly, with ceremonial solicitousness that made her grateful now for the black veil that covered her face.

The words spoken were few, and it was apparent that Reverend Abercrombie had never met Mark Powers. The last time she went to a funeral, it was her mother's; it had been followed closely by another death, her father's. Was this funeral again only a prelude to another disaster?

Tuesday afternoon at four o'clock, only six hours after Mark Powers's funeral, four riders from Happy Slocum's Sleepy S found a stranger hanging from an oak tree on their land. There was a fire nearby and a running iron still hot. They cut the man down and found a note stuffed in his vest pocket. It was a warning to all rustlers to clear out of the territory, that Ward Cantrell was taking over the rustling of cattle in the Salt River Valley and that there wasn't room for competition. It was signed tersely: Cantrell.

Word reached town by five o'clock, and rumors were flying. Cattlemen feared that rustling was being organized like crime had been in large eastern cities for years. Men were coming in singly and in groups to ask the governor to deputize a special posse to hunt Cantrell down. Losses to rustlers had instantaneously doubled, at least in their minds.

Sandra McCormick, missing and presumed kidnapped, only added fuel to the fires that were burning. She had been gone since no telling when; the maid had found her bed unslept in on Monday morning. A thorough search of the town turned up nothing. Sam McCormick was convinced Ward Cantrell had taken her. He announced a reward for her return and the capture of the person or persons who had taken her. The town buzzed with excitement.

Elizabeth Cartright made a special trip to see Leslie on Wednesday while Debbie was visiting. Elizabeth, with her penchant for gossip, could talk of nothing else.

Brightly gowned and stylishly coiffed, the three girls made a striking picture to Chane as he strode past the library, looking for Jennie.

"Well, frankly, darlings," Elizabeth said, smiling knowingly, archly, "I think I was wrong about one thing in this whole little episode."

Debbie shot Leslie a weighted look. When Elizabeth Cartright admitted she'd been wrong about something it was a red-letter day.

"I think Ward's little flirtation with Jennifer was a trick to make Sandra jealous."

Leslie shook her head wearily. Debbie's lips curled into a patient smile, and she glanced at Leslie. No sense trying to stop her. When Elizabeth wanted to say something she would say it. Arguing with her would only give her more opportunities to snipe and speculate.

"Apparently it was Sandra he was after all along. The thing with Jennifer"—she whispered her name, looking at the door guiltily—"was just to upset Sandra, to remind her she had serious competition."

"*Serious compet*—?" Debbie couldn't help herself.

"Of course, darlings, don't you realize? A married woman is *the* most serious competition a single girl can have. Why, heavens, I thought everyone *knew* that! She's older, experienced, and best of all, she's safe. Even if he gets her in trouble, she has a way out—she's already *married!* What could be better than that? All fun—no fear!"

"I'm sure there must be *some* drawback—else why would a man ever chase an unattached female? They do, you know," Leslie reminded her dryly.

"Of course, darlings, of course they do. When they decide to settle down. Maybe, just maybe, Sandra and Ward have eloped—no—no—not likely. More likely he has taken her into the hills to continue their affair without interruption. Can you imagine that? Mistress to the chief of a rustler gang! Think of the *experience* she is having! If it all weren't so *sordid*, I would probably envy her. After all, he is a very *attractive* outlaw."

"Are you disappointed that he didn't take you?" Debbie asked.

"Heavens! What a question! I'm as outraged as anyone over the whole sordid mess! I simply find it fascinating, that's all! It is one of the most exciting things that has happened since Leslie was kidnapped and ra—" Elizabeth clapped her hand over her mouth in horror. "Oh, Leslie, *darling*! *I'm sorry*! I would rather bite my tongue off than remind you of your unfortunate experience!"

"I'm sure you would," Leslie said smoothly. *I would rather you had, too. Had Ward really carried Sandra off?*

Tim came over after dinner with his own ideas about Sandra's abduction.

"I don't think she went with Cantrell."

"You don't?" Somehow that surprised her. She hadn't expected Tim to rush to Cantrell's aid again.

"No, not really. But you saw what an impact he had on her. She changed overnight." He laughed. "I mean *overnight.*" He grinned admiringly. "I wouldn't mind having that kind of an impact on a woman."

Leslie stiffened.

"Can you imagine what he does to cause all these girls to fling themselves at him the way they do?" Tim asked, smiling warmly, leaning forward to brush a kiss on her cheek. When his black eyes were lighted with warmth it was hard to tell what might be going on behind them...

Tim lifted her chin, brushed a kiss on her parted lips. "I'm glad *you* aren't one of his Trinkets," he said, his black eyes still narrowed with smile crinkles. Did she only imagine it, or had the sable warmth of a second ago been replaced by cool impervious ebony?

Feigning pique, Leslie lowered long silky lashes and lifted her chin provocatively. "Why, Mr. Summers, I do believe you are beginning to take me for granted. Was that a left-handed compliment or an outright insult?"

Tim grinned and the warmth was back as if she had imagined that tiny flicker of emotion. "I could just be counting my blessings, couldn't I? After all, I didn't lose my girl. It wasn't *you* he carried off."

Smiles were getting harder to come by. This one took its toll. Thank goodness he pulled her close to kiss her. Too bad she couldn't stop thinking. *Respond. Don't think.* But she did.

"Tim, please, people are still dropping in to pay their respects. The funeral was only yesterday."

"I'm sorry, darling," he said contritely. "I forgot you're still in mourning."

Any excuse, even a phony one, was better than nothing. She accepted her reprieve gratefully.

Sandra McCormick waited two days in Powers' fortress for Dallas Younger—two of the longest days of her young life. The Mexican women who still ran the place as if Mark Powers would walk in any moment were cordial and accepting, having become accustomed to Younger's and Powers' women. To them this one was no different, except younger and fresher-looking. Most of the white women who came to the ranch were plump, brassy, and laughed too loudly. This one still had the bloom of youth and the nervousness.

Younger rode in on Tuesday night about ten o'clock. Sandra's heart began to pound wildly. What would she do if he sent her away again? She'd been secretly infatuated with him since she had seen him in town three years before. She had pursued him in the same fashion she had Ward Cantrell, except she'd only been sixteen then, and Dallas Younger had laughed at her and sent her away. "No, dice, sweetface. I know a hanging tree when I see one. Your daddy's too big, and you're too little. Come back when you're all growed up," he had drawled, his slate gray eyes mocking her.

Well, here she was. Would he think her grown-up enough now? Had he told Tim he wanted her, or had Tim only told her that so he could misuse her? She still carried bruises from Tim's lovemaking. He had said terrible things to her and worse things about her. At the time it had heightened her excitement, but she hadn't been able to look at him afterward. She had almost refused to go to Younger after that. What if Ward was right about Dallas?

She could see him at the foot of the steps, hear his men greeting him, hear his heavy step on the porch, feel the flush of embarrassment. Her bravado, that dazed sort of mindlessness that allowed her to function, almost failed her completely. What if he laughed at her and sent her away? After all she had done to get here. She hadn't left a note for her father, hadn't told anyone. She must have been insane to let Tim drag her off that way.

The yearning and dreaming over Dallas Younger's dark, handsome, virile image all those years must have made her crazy. Damn Ward anyway! If he hadn't disappointed her...

Younger—tall, broad-shouldered, almost as lean-hipped as Ward, but harder-looking—stopped just inside the door when he saw her standing there. His dark brows formed a heavy ledge of disapproval over his bold eyes and hawklike features. His sensual lips quirked up at one corner, as if he were chewing a toothpick.

"Hi, Sweetface. What y'all doing here?" he asked gruffly.

Sandra thought her heart was going to stop. It lurched crazily, then thundered on. She couldn't think of anything to say. "I came to see if I'm all grown-up," she said thickly, her lips trembling so she had to bite them.

"You alone?" he asked, looking around suspiciously, his eyes narrowed now, watching her intently.

"I've been here two days, waiting," she said expectantly.

"I thought you were Cantrell's girl," he said harshly. "He bring you here?" He had heard the rumors about Cantrell's kidnapping her. He'd gone to Powers' funeral and, being a practical man, he knew he wouldn't be working for the new owner. He had stopped to pack some things, take any cash Powers had left lying around, and head up into the hills to take over the rustling operation firsthand. Since he couldn't use Powers' backing and the ranch as a base, he expected he'd be moving on soon anyway. Talk in town was that rustling, with Cantrell making his brags and the furor that caused among the honest ranchers, wouldn't be easy work anymore. He and Cedar Longley had talked about that on the trip out.

He stamped his feet as a matter of habit and began to take off his gloves. She looked terrified, but he had to admit that she was a pretty little doll, nervous as hell, but determined. He'd recognized her type years ago. She wanted a big daddy. Well, he thought, smiling, she'd come to the right place, if she was on the level.

He walked into the center of the room, took off his Stetson, his gloves, his coat, and threw them at the sofa.

"Come here," he growled.

She walked into his arms blindly, her blood a deafening roar in her ears. She was on fire even before his harsh mouth found hers. His powerful arms crushed her against his hard chest, and after a few seconds of measuring what he thought of as her sincerity, his hands found her breasts and began teasing and tormenting them while he kissed her.

When he finally lifted his dark head, she was limp and shuddering with ecstasy, her blouse gaping open, pulled down at the shoulders, exposing her full, round, thrusting breasts. He lowered his head and buried his face between the silky globes.

"I reckon you'll do," he growled, picking her up to carry her into his bedroom.

CHAPTER THIRTY-NINE

Wednesday morning Kincaid saw John Loving in the tobacco store. The store reeked with the roguish smell of fine tawny tobaccos artfully blended. John was leaving as Chane paused, momentarily blocking the narrow doorway.

"John! How are you?" Chane asked, smiling warmly.

Loving looked at him with uncustomary coolness in his intent gray eyes. "Fine, thank you."

"I talked to Jennie about that dinner we discussed; can you come on Saturday? She's looking forward to seeing you. You know how Jennie loves to talk about New York." While it was true he and Jennie had discussed John's coming to dinner, Jennie had not agreed that it should be this Saturday. She was taking Ward's new troubles hard. It was his idea, upon seeing John, that it would do Jennie good to entertain someone who would get her talking about New York, take her out of herself.

A muscle bunched and writhed in Loving's jaw. He couldn't believe Kincaid was so out of touch with what was going on in his own town. "No, sorry," he said politely. "Give my regards to Mrs. Kincaid, though." Loving nodded coolly and stepped around his former employer.

Frowning, Chane watched him walk stiffly away. A cloud of dust at the south end of town caught his eye. It looked like a dozen or so riders in a big hurry. Other men stopped to watch. Within minutes the center of the wide, dusty road was filled with rearing, milling horses and shouting men.

"We've found Cantrell! We've found that bastard, and he's got the girl!"

Chane pulled one of the men aside. "What's happening?"

Red Barnett wiped his sleeve across his face and spat into the dust beside his horse's feet. "Cantrell and about six, seven men are in Buckeye. Beasley is offering a reward for any man who rides in there and takes Cantrell."

"Beasley?" Chane demanded. "What the hell does the Consolidated Can Company care about Cantrell?"

"Don't know," he said, spitting a long arcing stream of tobacco into the dust. "But you add his reward to McCormick's and they've got my full attention," he drawled.

"Did you actually see the girl?"

"No, but Beasley did."

"If he said he saw Cantrell with Sandra McCormick, he's lying!" Chane shouted, trying to be heard over the din. "Cantrell is a sworn officer of the law."

"A lawman! Bullshit!" a man beside him interjected. "That's like leaving a grizzly to guard honey! Stanton fell for that un, he's gettin' senile!"

Others joined in the laughter. Chane spent an hour going from man to man, making sure they knew that Cantrell was a sworn officer of the law and that there would be penalties for interfering with him, but there were too many hot heads, too many men who shouted him down, repeating the cant that had been bandied about ever since Powers's death, Sandra's disappearance, and Cantrell's unfortunate departure.

Jennie and the children were waiting lunch for him. He kissed Jennie and knelt to hug the children. Jennie was distracted. Worry clouded her lovely eyes. He had kept as much from her as he dared.

He was agitated about the events of the morning, but only one seemed acceptable to discuss with Jennie. The coolness and strangeness of that encounter with John Loving was too unusual to ignore. "I ran into John Loving at the tobacco store this morning. He refused my invitation for dinner Saturday."

Jennifer frowned. "He did? Did he seem all right otherwise?" she asked, taking her place at the table.

"No," he said, seating her and then the children.

"Do you suppose things aren't working out for him at the office?"

"I don't know. I haven't been near the place to speak of in weeks. I'm concentrating on the revisions to the blueprints for the hotel we're building in San Diego. You know how I am when I have an opportunity to be creative. I've been so engrossed with that project..."

"Chane, I think you should talk to John. Find out what's wrong."

He scowled. "I guess I'd better."

"Have you heard anything about Ward?"

"Nothing from him directly. Just the usual rumors started by people who don't have anything better to do."

Leslie joined them at that point, and Chane was grateful for the diversion. In another moment, Jennie would have begun to question him.

To Leslie, looking at them around Mrs. Lillian's charmingly set table, all seemed serene. The fragrance of fresh flowers, grown with painstaking care by the Kincaid gardener in a small greenhouse beside the stable, mingled with the rich smells of warm bread, ham, and coffee. China and crystal gleamed. Jennifer was cool and lovely in a crisp yellow batiste morning gown. Her usually warm smile was subdued.

The children greeted Leslie gaily; she hugged them and then sat down.

"Good morning." She smiled, taking her seat at the table. Leslie wore dark blue in deference to her uncle. Chane sat at the head of the table. Jennie had once said laughingly that wherever he sat, that *was* the head of the table. Jennifer sat on his right, Leslie on his left, nontraditional but very "Kincaid" seating arrangements; Amy sat next to her mother, and young Chane next to Leslie.

But before the meal could begin, Malcomb was at the door to the dining room. "Excuse me, sir. Governor Stanton is here to see you."

Chane cursed inwardly at the fresh wave of pain that darkened his wife's eyes as she tried to gauge the seriousness of Stanton's news from the tone of Malcomb's voice. "Relax, love," he said, squeezing her cold hand.

The men went into the library and Jennifer sighed. "Another high-level conference about Ward Cantrell."

"What do you think they will do?" Leslie asked, sipping her coffee, trying not to show her concern.

Eyes haunted, Jennifer shrugged. It would please her tremendously if Leslie would admit she was in love with Peter—Ward, she corrected herself. Then they could suffer together instead of apart, both trying to pretend only an acceptable level of polite concern. She wanted to tell Leslie the truth. Leslie wouldn't tell anyone. But Chane was so adamant, telling her that Ward's life could depend on her silence.

The devil in Jennifer couldn't resist testing Leslie's reactions. "The Cattlemen's Association is threatening to offer a rather sizable reward for Cantrell—dead or alive—I heard." It was only a rumor, and one that Chane had managed to squelch, but it served its purpose. Leslie looked properly stricken in spite of her attempts not to. Leslie trusted Ward's competence to evade capture, but the thought of another reward, dead or alive, added to the other two, frightened her. Jesse James had been shot in the back of the head by his best friend for ten thousand dollars only a few years ago.

A cold heavy lump formed in Leslie's chest. He wouldn't stand a chance. Too many people would want that money. Someone should warn him. He could ride away…be safe.

"Chane said he's absolutely sure Ward had nothing to do with either Powers's murder or Sandra's disappearance. I've known Ward a long time. I know he is a man of honor…"

Leslie barely heard her. Jennie didn't know the same Ward Cantrell she knew. He had killed Younger's men, kidnapped and seduced her, and had spent the night with Sandra after spending the day making love to her. The part of her that wanted to believe in him was starved for details that would repudiate the damning evidence against him, but they were not forthcoming.

Chane came into the room before she could reply. Jennifer turned her attention to him. "Was it bad news? Is Ward—?"

"He's fine, as far as we know."

"Were you able to talk him out of the reward?"

"Yes," he said firmly. "We're calling another meeting of the cattlemen tonight. I'm sending a rider out to the ranches to let the owners and operators know. I'm sure Ward's been framed. It's unfortunate that he left town at the same time all hell broke loose. He'll be fine, I'm sure," he said, forcing an optimistic demeanor. "But with murder and kidnap charges being bandied about, even Stanton is nervous, and I vouched for Cantrell."

Jennifer's face drained of color. Things must be more serious than she'd thought. She knew by Chane's look that when he said, "I vouched for Cantrell," he had told Stanton that Ward was her brother and that it was barely enough to sway him.

"At least they are going to hold off until tonight," she said worriedly. "Will that be enough time?"

"Not unless the sheriff finds Powers' killer, or Sandra reappears. The town is hanging mad, and Ed is first and foremost a politician. He's not going to go against public sentiment.

"Word just reached town that Cantrell has taken over the town of Buckeye. They're talking about an alternate plan now—a big posse to ride in there tonight, rescue the townspeople, and bring Cantrell and his men to justice." He had softened that considerably for the women's benefit. The mob he saw, which apparently was still growing, would not bother to bring anyone they caught back to town for a trial.

Wheels began to turn in Leslie's mind. Winslow Breakenridge had assured her that if she needed money, she could draw on her uncle's bank account. He had arranged it with the bank.

After lunch, she rode into town with Chane, who said he was going to the railroad office to talk to Summers about Loving. Chane suggested she stay home and let him take care of her errands for her, but she insisted.

The town was strangely quiet. He was grateful that the streets were cleared of lynch mobs—probably because the eager vigilantes were home preparing for their big ride.

They parted on Van Buren Street.

Leslie went directly to the bank and sought out Harvey Aspen, the president.

"Well, good afternoon, Miss Powers." He smiled. She was, since her uncle's death, one of his biggest depositors. "What can I do for you?"

"Good afternoon. I want to find out how much money I can withdraw from my uncle's...my...account."

Harvey Aspen's prim banker's face puckered into a frown. He didn't like withdrawals, especially by women, but unfortunately he couldn't prevent them.

"How much would you like to withdraw?" he asked cautiously.

"Ten thousand dollars," she said tentatively. "Is that much available?"

"Haarrumph. Well, uh, yes, there is..."

"Good! That should be fine. I would like large bills, please." She smiled, breathing a sigh of relief. Apparently Winslow knew exactly what he was doing.

"It's dangerous to carry that much money in cash."

"I'm not going far," she reassured him smilingly. "I'm going to invest it, so please don't say anything."

"Invest it? Here?"

"Mr. Kincaid is letting me buy some stock."

"Ahh! A wise investment! We can make a simple transfer."

"And spoil my fun? Oh, no, I want to do this personally. Miss Freeman always told us if it was worth doing, it was worth doing personally. In money matters, she said, it is best to handle those very personally."

"Who is Miss Freeman?" he frowned.

"A very dear friend and president of Wellesley College. You wouldn't know her, I'm afraid. But there was some scandal about her having a love affair with the president of Harvard. Sort of a long-distance, mail-pouch type of affair."

She chattered incessantly, so that by the time the transaction was finished, he was glad to see her leave even though a good portion of "his money" went with her.

Financing arranged, her next stop was the railroad ticket office. She avoided the central administrative offices, where Tim worked, and studied the ticket schedule.

"May I help you, miss?"

"I'm new in Phoenix," she said, smiling prettily. "How much does it cost to go to Tucson?"

"Five dollars."

"How far is Tucson?"

"A hundred and thirty miles by rail."

"Could I see that on a map?"

"Course you can, ma'am. One thing a railroad ticket office always has is a map," he said proudly, glad he could so easily impress this pretty girl.

He brought the map out, and Leslie spotted Buckeye immediately. It was about twenty miles downriver on the north side of the Gila, the same as Phoenix. That should be easy to find, even for her. She thanked him profusely, and then rushed home to change into riding clothes.

Her uncle had sent the rest of her things before he died. She was surprised, but realized he was probably glad to be rid of them.

The weather was decidedly crisp for Arizona. Perhaps there *would* be a winter clime. In Wellesley, horseback riding had been popular for both sexes. She had all the winter-weight paraphernalia. She chose her favorite riding habit—London smoke-colored cloth with beige cambric jacket, long sleeves, a full skirt over petticoats and riding trousers, to allow her to ride astride. No lady would ever be seen in just the trousers—too unfeminine! Around her neck a brooch secured a rich brown stock that complemented the beige of the jacket. Over her right breast was an embroidered horseshoe and the initials LMP. Dark patent-leather boots with silver spurs, a beige felt tophat trailing a long flowing veil of pale beige, and brown leather gauntlets completed the ensemble. With a warm cashmere coat behind her saddle, full enough to cover her legs in case it got colder before she reached Buckeye, she felt prepared for anything.

She wrote a short note to Jennifer, took a fast horse from the stable, and left without seeing or talking to anyone.

Kincaid's office in the Bricewood West could well have been described as chaste in its furnishings. The major piece of furniture in his office was a conference table twenty feet long, which he used to spread his drawings on. Next in importance was a drafting table, then a large, cluttered desk, and lastly three large, comfortable leather chairs.

At the moment Kincaid and Brian Perry, his chief architect, were in a huddle over drawings they were working on in the center of that long table. A loud knock on the door, which had been left open, brought Kincaid's head up.

Ed Stanton stuck his head in the door and rapped again.

Kincaid straightened, wondering if it was more bad news.

"Come in, Ed. You know Brian here, don't you?"

The three shook hands. "I just stopped by to see if you have a couple of minutes to spare," Stanton said jovially.

Brian Perry gathered up three of his tools from the scatter of papers. "I'll be next door figuring those cubic feet of air space requirements."

"Thanks, Brian."

"I won't keep you long," Stanton said as Kincaid closed the door after Perry and motioned him to a chair.

"No problem. I needed a break, and so did he. Looks serious."

Stanton frowned. "Could be. Could be nothing, but I thought you would want to know. A rancher by the name of Hank Morrissey is talking real bitter about the treatment he got from the Texas and Pacific."

Kincaid let his breath out slowly. He had feared worse—much worse. If he weren't afraid of insulting his young brother-in-law, he would have ridden out himself to bring him in. Tell him to call off the whole thing. This was no time to try to solve something as simple as cattle rustling when the whole countryside was up in arms, ready to shoot him down on sight. It still amazed him how this whole mess had come about. A week ago everything had been fine. Now...God only knew how it would all end.

But apparently Cantrell was not what was on Stanton's mind.

"What happened?"

"Seems your people held him up in the feedlot eight or ten days, letting other herds that arrived after him ship out, charging him for feed until he was about bust. Reckon the last straw came when Simon Beasley bought a herd that had only been in the pens four days and shipped 'em right out. There was almost a shootout. Wenton says if he hadn't been doing some tall talking, there would have been bloodshed."

Chane scowled thoughtfully, his green eyes narrowed. "I guess I'll pay a visit on Summers. Get his side of it. Was that all you heard?"

"Yes. I knew you'd been tied up with the rustlers and your other business interests." He didn't mention that he was also feeling a little guilty about not being as helpful as he could have been regarding Jennifer's brother, but business was business.

"Thanks, Ed. I appreciate it. Did you ride over?"

"Walked. Dr. Matt says I have to *walk* my ulcer, not nurse it with milk and whiskey."

"Good. I'll walk to the office with you."

When Tim Summers came back from lunch Kincaid was waiting for him.

"Afternoon, Tim."

"Good afternoon, Mr. Kincaid!" Tim smiled warmly, his face lighting with pleasure. "What can I do for you?"

"Information."

"Let's go into my office. Have you time for some coffee?"

Chane waited until they were both seated with their coffee cups before he continued their conversation.

"What's our current policy for getting herds in and out of the feedlot?"

"We've found that we have the best success in shipping steers that have at least four, five days to rest after a drive. Gives them a chance to get back the water they lost on the trail and cuts down on losses by death. Their weight is better, too. Everyone benefits."

"Do we ever hold up a herd longer than that for any reason?"

Summers frowned, his black eyes filling with indignation. "Not on purpose," he said grimly, "but I had a problem with my new assistant."

"What kind of problem?"

"Nothing deliberate—I don't think. Mostly just inattention to detail and an inability to follow simple instructions." He paused, looking apologetic. "I had to fire him. He caused a serious problem with a man named Morrissey. There was almost a range war from what I heard," he ended in disgust. "But let me assure you, Mr. Kincaid. I'm not trying to pass the buck. I take full responsibility for my entire staff. I called him in as soon as I got back from Tucson, as soon as Wenton told me what had happened. I hope this hasn't embarrassed you too badly. I had a feeling I should have sent someone else to Tucson, but I like to do the important things myself. And I knew you felt strongly about hiring a good manager for the Tucson branch office."

"You did fine." Chane nodded. "We don't keep anyone's cattle over five days?"

"No, sir!" Tim said crisply. "And that only to increase their chances of surviving the trip."

Kincaid stood up. "Good, Tim. Thanks for the coffee."

"My pleasure, Mr. Kincaid."

CHAPTER FORTY

A cold November morning slowly turned into a warm afternoon as the hooves of Leslie's horse thundered over the dry, hard earth. She rode parallel to the watercourse, keeping the wide silver-gray shimmer of the river in sight. Galloping at a comfortable pace, she admired the tangle of alfalfa that grew along the river banks, so different from either the ocotillo, cactuses, tumbleweed, or orchards or farms she passed.

She had made her decision precipitously and regretted it at least a hundred times in the last two hours. She was making a fool of herself. He would probably take her money and use it to keep his mistresses! What if she found him with Sandra? *Hello, Ward! Just rode over with a wedding present for you two—and to let you know there are six hundred angry men coming here to kill you.* The sight of Sandra clinging to Ward would probably bring such a hot flush of rage that she would kill him herself. *Good afternoon, Ward! Should I rip out your throat first, or would you prefer I mangled some very vital parts of your arrogant young body, you bastard?*

Buckeye was barely a settlement. There were four buildings, mostly lean-tos. She didn't see anyone, but there were six horses standing in the shade of a weathered two-story building. A faded sign whispered *Hotel*. The paint, when the sign was new, had been black; now it was hardly darker than the gray wood. A shaggy, long-haired red dog dozed on the porch.

She reined Kincaid's powerful racy Arabian to approach the building with the horses and the dog slowly, realizing afresh how insane she must be. What if he wasn't there and a pack of bandits raped her and stole her money?

Damn! Why did she have to care what happened to him? He hadn't given her any commitments. A day of love, a few tender words, some lingering good-bye kisses, and here she was, making a blessed fool of herself! Why?

Only because she couldn't bear to see Jennie suffer so grievously? Or did part of her still nurture the hope, blind and pitiful as it was, that Tim was wrong about Ward and Sandra?

At some point a woman gets tired of asking herself questions she can't answer. Why shouldn't she come if she wants to? In any event, she was here! She gave herself a good talking to—about cowards dying a thousand deaths—but it didn't help. Her heart was still hammering madly in her chest, and she felt like a foolish child.

Ward and Dusty rode into Buckeye late Sunday morning. The wide dirt road was deserted except for a Mexican woman driving an oxcart away from the small store. She was broad and swarthy, with a flat, unemotional face that reminded Ward of Mama Manuela and revived the empty ache in his chest.

They tethered their horses in front of the only two-story building in the settlement. There were two *vaqueros* lounging at a table just inside the door and one man behind the bar, sleeping, his feet up, his sombrero pulled down, the wide brim reaching all the way to his fat belly. It smelled of cigarette butts and whiskey.

The scrape of their boots on the rough wooden floor stopped the snores and brought the man's hand up to shove the sombrero back, revealing a round face with small deep-set eyes, thick lips, and a heavy mop of stiff black hair. When he saw Ward his eyes came alive. *"Señor,* Ward! Welcome!"

Grinning, Ward exchanged greetings with the beaming man. Dusty watched in silence, not understanding the rapid Spanish.

"It has been a long time!"

"Yes, it has, friend. Too long!" Ward agreed.

"Mama! Come! Señor Ward has come!"

A short, smiling woman with a face that glowed with perspiration and pleasure shuffled out of the kitchen, wiping her hands on her apron. *"Señor* Ward!"

They hugged, and the woman clasped his face in her two hands, smiling at him. "You're too skinny. You need some good home cooking. What is Manuela doing? Starving you? Or are you chasing the girls too hard? Is that why you carry these marks on your face, *hombre?"*

At mention of Manuela's name, Ward's smile faded, and he straightened. Carmen Castenada looked from Ward to her husband.

Ward sighed. "Manuela is dead," he said gently.

Quick tears sprang into Carmen's eyes. Ward told them about the Mendozas and what he suspected of Powers' involvement. When he finished, Cruz, who was patting his wife's shoulder, spoke.

"You will stay here. I can get *vaqueros* to ride with you. Powers must not go unpunished for this!"

"We can't stay here. We don't know what to expect from Younger and his gang. They may run—they may come after us. I'm not going to endanger any more people than I have to."

"Then what will you do?" Cruz asked.

"We don't have a plan. Except to get Younger—whatever it takes."

"Make this your headquarters. We have many contacts that will be of use to you, *Señor* Ward."

Ward looked at Dusty. "What do you think about using this as our base?"

"Suits me fine. No one could get near here without our knowing about it."

Ward frowned. He didn't like bringing war to a friend's home, but Cruz was a smart man and a valuable ally.

"We can try it," he said slowly. "If things get hot, we can stay away from here—pull any pursuers off to the north toward the yellow pine country." Dusty agreed.

"Good! It is settled! You, Señor Ward, will sleep in Juanita's room. She is gone to Sonora, married to a wealthy *haciendado*," he said proudly. "Your friend can have the room next to Juanita's."

They ate Mama's excellent rice, beans, tamales, and corn cakes, and Ward caught up on news of the Castenadas and their mutual friends.

When the rest of Ward's men rode into Buckeye, the welcome they received was vastly different from the one they had gotten the day before. The welcome mat was out.

Doug Paggett, who had accepted this opportunity to earn a pardon, was grinning when he took Ward aside.

"Hey, *compadre*! You should have been here sooner. We got the full treatment yesterday. Cool courtesy and hot chili! I mean *hot*! Today— we're family."

Ward grinned. "I'm glad you came."

Doug shrugged. "What the hell? 'Lowed I've tried everything else— don't work out—what'd I lose? A couple of weeks."

Ward didn't mention the small matter of survival. "None of the others wanted to try it, huh?"

"Naw, my mama didn't raise no lunkhaids. This boy knows better. Without you they'll end up as tree ornaments. But they don't know that. Nate sees as how he's the brains. I'm happy to be out of it."

"Did you learn anything while I was in Phoenix?"

Doug took off his hat and ran his hand along his ear, which had collapsed at the point of an injury, so that the top half-inch of it flopped over. "Larned myself not to stick my head up."

"Christ! How'd you get a gotched ear?"

"Ran smack into six riders herding about sixty cows into a ravine. Lookin' guilty as hell. Opened fire right off. Low-down ornery galoots stampeded that blamed herd practically right over us. Felt a tolerable amount of gratitude to make it back here with my pelt intact."

Ward looked disgusted. "They got away?"

"We were lucky not to get killed!" Doug protested. "Hope you didn't sprain your back humping all the girls in Phoenix while we were busting our asses," he said bitterly.

"You complain more than a woman," Ward said, shaking his head.

"Figures you'd know that. It's been so long I almost cain't remember what they're like."

Ward cuffed him lightly as Dusty joined them.

"Good chow," Dusty said.

"You shoulda been here yesterday. Chili—Montezuma's revenge!" Doug said dryly, grinning ruefully.

"Did you get a line on how many riders Younger has?" Ward asked.

Doug frowned, becoming serious. "Hard to tell—maybe twenty, but they keep moving. Looks like they're pulling back into the mountains. Looks like something's fetching it to a close. We saw tracks going north. Not too many coming back. They ain't exactly deuce high with me."

"What are we going to do?" Dusty asked, watching Ward.

"I want to catch Younger or some of his men with some cows that don't belong to the Lazy P. Any cattle moving north?"

"Yeah, some, I reckon." Doug nodded.

"When was this?"

"Yesterday morning."

"What'd you do today?"

Doug looked disgusted. "I was feelin' kinda low-spirited about how I hadn't been doin' enough, so we checked on that train—to see if it was makin' any runs."

"Was it?"

"Naw," Doug drawled. "Looks like they're aiming to see the deal through to the last turn of the card, but I don't know. If they're using the blamed railroad to move 'em, they should be shipping some ever' danged night."

"You're right. Unless something happened to their contact in the Texas and Pacific."

"You didn't find nothin' going through them books?"

"The only thing that would seem to support our theory is that earnings didn't go up this year. Units transported went up, overhead went up, but not profits."

Dusty nodded. "That makes sense. The Texas and Pacific is absorbing the cost of transportation. What does it cost to ship a steer back east?"

"Two dollars a head."

Doug grinned suddenly. "Maybe the old Devil's Canyon Gang had somethin' to do with that. Payrolls were up forthwith—paying all them special agents to ride around on his trains pretendin' they knew what they was doin' when they didn't know any more than a range bull."

En masse they spent two and a half days scouring the countryside for any sign of illegal activity but found nothing. About noon they saw the agreed-upon smoke signal from Cruz. He was waiting for them on the porch.

"Bad news, Señor Ward," Cruz said, pursing his heavy lips. "You have wasted much time because my lazy friend whom I depended upon was drunk. *Señor* Powers is dead. *Señor* Younger stayed in Phoenix for the funeral. He and his men left only last night."

"That explains a lot," Ward said grimly. "How did Powers die?"

"His throat was cut, cheeeech."

"They know who did it?"

"I think not, *mi amigo.* You are the one they look for."

Ward frowned. "There's more?"

"*Sí.* Word among the *gringos* that you are taking over rustling. That you hanged another rustler for working in your territory, *Señor* Ward. The townspeople are forming a *muy grande* posse to ride you down. And"— he paused significantly—"a beautiful *señorita* is missing and they think *secuestrar ella.*"

"I kidnapped who?"

"I did not find out her name, but apparently she was to be your *novia.*"

Cold bands clamped around his chest. That could only mean that Younger had Leslie. Either Younger or the mysterious head of that gang—the name Younger's man would not divulge, even with a knife to his throat. The thought of Leslie at the hands of the man or men who had killed Isabel chilled his blood.

"Sounds like we've been framed," Dusty growled.

Doug nodded. There was general agreement among the others who had clustered around, listening in silence.

Dusty spoke first. "I say we ride north into the mountains, find their rabbit hole, and wipe 'em out. I think we've wasted enough time."

"There are only six of us," Ward said. "I think Younger has forty, fifty men—all told."

"Forty? Jesus!" Doug exclaimed.

Dusty grimaced. "Let me repeat myself. I say we ride south into the desert and give them Sonora *señoritas* a run for their money."

"Layin' up in Charlie Tarbell's Eagle Hotel in Tombstone ain't exactly the same as facing Dallas Younger and his pack of wolverines," Doug drawled.

"Don't sound like the same idee to me!" Boisterous men howled their agreement.

Ward ignored the good-natured exchange. "I don't think rustling is their only source of income. I think if this mountain hideaway exists, one man could ride in there, but not six."

"One man! Who?" Dusty demanded.

"Me," Ward said quietly.

"Whew! I was afraid he was volunteering me," Doug drawled, dragging his hand across his brow.

"And what are we s'posed to do in the meantime?"

A commotion out front caused all heads to turn.

"Hey, boss! One rider coming in!"

The men exchanged looks and strode quickly to the window. Ward and Dusty recognized her at the same time. Dusty motioned the men back to the bar.

Ward was a master at hiding his emotions from others, but he couldn't ignore the leaping in his blood at sight of Leslie Powers riding into his camp. Relief that she was safe flooded through him first and then pride. She was so fetching, so alive, and so singularly female. In that fancy riding habit and tophat with her hair twisted up into a wind-whipped topknot beneath it...and her cheeks flushed from riding...she was incredibly lovely. There was a hungry reaction all through his lean frame. But why was she here?

CHAPTER FORTY-ONE

Cantrell stepped out into the slanting sunshine on the porch and moved forward to lift Leslie down from her mount. And once she was in his arms, it was only natural that he kiss her half-parted lips, stilling whatever utterance she'd been about to make.

All her fears and doubts dissolved in that warm, strong embrace. When his tawny head finally lifted she was weak and breathless in his arms.

"Leslie, love, what the hell are you doing here?" he asked huskily.

"Could we talk somewhere?"

"Sure." He led her into the dim interior. It was ordinarily a combination saloon, dining room, and hotel. Now it was an armed fortress—guns, rifles, hard-faced men in various positions. No one seeing that room of desperadoes could miss the tension and the deadly coolness of their demeanor. They were armed and ready to do battle. She recognized Dusty Denton, cool and sturdy with a level, piercing gaze. There were others like him—all young, lean, determined. How had they come to this end—waiting here to die? But they wouldn't die until they had killed a number of their enemies—faceless men who would leave behind wives and daughters to weep and wear their widow's weeds. She could have wept with the sudden sweep of emotion that rose up in her. How futile it all was!

Ward's room was at the top of the stairs to the right. It was the logical place to take her. She followed silently, thinking her riotous thoughts, resenting him for being so willing to expose himself to danger and death. Angry, selfish thoughts trembled on her lips, seeking release, but he pulled her inside, closed the door, and she was engulfed: lost, drowning, and suddenly not caring. His mouth closed over hers, demanding and reclaiming everything: her will, her body, her soul. There was no chance to protest. He undressed her and took her there on the bed that stood alone in the middle of that forlorn shabby room, with soft breezes flapping the cheap windowshade and gold sunlight yellowing the floor and his hair.

And somehow, making love in an armed camp, to a man who would very likely be dead tomorrow, reduced everything to basics. There was no need now to pretend she didn't want him, no need now to hold back.

Urgent. Fierce. Tender yet savage. They were both hopelessly caught up in each other's spell.

Remembering the tension she'd felt until she'd been recognized brought it all home to her. He knew the risk he was running! Why did he stay? Nothing he had ever done made sense to Leslie—except this. But even this couldn't go on forever. Even the wildest, sweetest flame, once it had flared into brilliance, burned down.

Snuggled safely in his arms, with a glorious flush still tingling through her, she could almost forget.

"Leslie," he whispered.

"Hmm?"

"I can't let you stay here. We're moving out soon."

"I came to warn you. There's a posse forming to run you down. They're coming tonight to free the town and hang you."

"What for?"

"For rustling and because they think you killed Mark Powers and kidnapped Sandra McCormick."

"How did Powers die?"

"Someone cut his throat, and Younger told the sheriff it was your trademark. I don't think they believe me anymore about your not being the one who kidnapped me—the sheriff looks at me funny..." Her voice trailed off.

"Why do they think I'd kidnap Sandra McCormick?"

"She was your girl..." Leslie stammered.

"When did she disappear?"

"Her father said she had dinner with him and his guests Sunday night, went to bed early, and was gone the next day when the housekeeper checked. Not a trace."

"When did Powers die?"

"They found him Sunday morning at the livery stable. His body was in the stall your horse had been in—at least that's what Elizabeth said."

"You came to warn me?" he asked softly, so amazed that he forgot to mention that he hadn't been keeping his horse at the livery stable.

She couldn't answer him in words. "I brought some money. I thought if you...if..." She couldn't say, "I'm trying to bribe you to run away with me." Even she had too much pride for that. "I mean—it's too dangerous for you to stay here." Her voice trailed off. He hadn't even tried to help her—hadn't uttered a single word to make it easy for her.

Ward was stunned. The woman he had kidnapped and robbed of her virginity, leaving her vulnerable to every wagging tongue in the Territory, had come there to save him. Not even knowing for sure that he hadn't killed her uncle and run off with another woman. Not even asking.

Now, when she would have moved away to dress herself, his hands stopped her, pulled her close to him, kissing her eyes, cheeks, forehead, lips...nuzzling tenderly at her neck. "Leslie, my love, my own sweet love..."

Did she only imagine that husky whisper?—skin to skin, his hands on her face, holding her as if she were the most precious thing he had ever touched?

Trembling, she gave herself up to this new experience. Allowed him to immerse her in tenderness, her body moving in perfect counterpoint. He made love to her again, and this time his touch was a balm, a drawing-out of old pain, a healing. Tears wet her cheeks, and his lips found them. He gave her the assurances she needed with his body. No matter what happened, she would have this hour, this day, to remember. A warm, soft, perfect moment...encapsulated in time, memory, flesh.

Did she sleep? Or only lose track of time? The sun, slanting in at the window, had sharpened its angle. Alarmed by the approach of sunset, she remembered why she had come there.

"Ward, you must get away. A posse is coming to hang you," she whispered against his cheek.

He didn't answer. He was immersed in joy, first that she had come here at all and second that she would run away with him.

"What could be more important than your own survival?" she persisted. "Those men are not going to give you a chance to deny anything. Don't you see?" She sat up, her sense of urgency returning. "They'll take you any way they have to. They'll shoot you or hang you, whatever they have to do. There's a reward for you, dead or alive."

Ward rolled onto his back, frowning. He had lived as an outlaw for six years. For the first time, he had an opportunity to start over. If he ran away there would be no life worth living anyway. No Leslie. He had no choice. He could either die now, fighting for his and her future, or he could run away and die by degrees, as he lost first her concern, her respect, and then her love.

Ward's silence was deafening. What was he thinking now? What a fool she was? Probably. She bit her bottom lip and let her eyes rove around the room they shared. There was a bureau on one wall and a small table with a lacy shawl draped carelessly so that it hung down halfway to the floor. Cream-colored lace that would look very pretty over long black hair. Leslie could feel a coldness settling into her lungs. It spread out, making her breath tingle and ache in her throat. He made love to her in the room he shared with another woman!

Leslie couldn't look at him, couldn't even speak. Mutely, she turned away, fumbling with the clothes he had nearly torn off her body moments ago, feeling her nakedness painfully, and remembering the fears she had suppressed riding into this dust-whipped little town. She could almost laugh now. She expelled a shuddering breath, ignoring the warm hand that caressed the curve of her back—or tried to ignore it. How could he look so relaxed? Didn't he care that by tomorrow he'd probably be dead? She had a sudden vision of him on that big black horse, bare-headed, riding straight into that pack of shouting, shooting men. No one knew better than she what a reckless hellion he was. Or what a rotten cheat! But this, making love to her in his girlfriend's bedroom, was going too far!

She was determined to be as cool about it as he was.

"They are mad enough to hang you on sight. Rustling can't possibly pay all that well. I brought some money. If you leave now, you can be away from here before they arrive."

"Does anyone know you came here?"

"No."

"Whose cattle did I rustle?"

Leslie looked at him sharply. "Don't you know?"

Apparently even Leslie believed that one. He shrugged. "Seen one cow you've seen them all. How did they find out it was me?" he asked instead.

"I guess it was the subtle way you issued that challenge to all the other rustlers to clear out of your territory. Hanging one of them didn't help your image any. I don't know all that much about rules of conduct for rustlers chief, but it seems you have outraged everyone—ranchers, rustlers, even the little old ladies."

"Those are the ones to watch out for," he said wryly, "the little old ladies. They'll get you every time."

The cold ache was gone now. All she felt was a strange sense of numbness. He wasn't interested in running off with *her* even if she paid him. That much was clear!

Leslie stood up and began reaching for her clothes. Ward watched her, completely entranced with the delicious sight of silky skin—creamy white all the way to the bone—and that luxurious mass of midnight-black hair cascading halfway down her back. Perfect cone-shaped breasts with rosy red nipples that he could almost feel against his lips. He would like to spend the day making love to her but…

He frowned. He had to somehow get free of this neat little frame someone had constructed for him. He hadn't issued a challenge. Who would gain by killing Powers? Or kidnapping Trinket?

His mind was a hundred miles away, Leslie could tell by the look in his eyes—they were smoky blue in the shabby room. White pitiless sunshine streamed in the undraped window. A shade pulled halfway down was flapping gently in the afternoon breeze.

She straightened and walked to the vanity, picked up the shawl to feel the texture of the lace, and saw Sandra McCormick's locket lying on the dusty wooden table. Ward stretched, languorously, and she noticed the scratches on his face, the ones she hadn't bothered to ask about when she arrived, because she'd been too caught up in her overwhelming response to him.

The intricately engraved Chinese dragon on the gold and enamel locket seemed to glow with a perfect, terrible light.

He *had* lied to her! Perhaps only indirectly, since she didn't ask questions…but surely allowing her to believe he didn't know about Sandra's disappearance…She picked up the locket and walked to the bed.

Eyes closed, he was still sprawled like some pagan lord, his lean body completely relaxed. Words trembled on her lips, but she dared not speak. How could he answer her? He would either lie or tell the truth. If he said yes, it is Sandra's, then she would know he had taken her. If he said no, it wasn't Sandra's, she would know he was lying to her. Either would be equally damning, because neither was acceptable to her. The room was suddenly cold and tawdry-looking, like she felt. A great place for a quick, meaningless encounter.

Trembling, she cautioned herself to take her lead from him—to keep it light and get the hell out before he inspired her to do anything else stupid.

"Well, sir, was that satisfactory?"

Ward frowned, his eyes narrowed, and one corner of his mouth pulled down. How did he manage to look so damned reserved and sensuous at the same time? It had to be his mouth, the way it could look so kissable and yet so insolent—like now.

"Very," he said softly, watching her intently.

"Good," she said briskly. She had finished dressing, but her hair was still loose. It swung in a fragrant, heavy mass when she leaned across the bed to pick up a small reticule he hadn't noticed before. He picked up a tress of her hair, trapping her there within easy reach.

Leslie forced one of those sunny smiles Chane and Jennifer raved about, leaned forward, and kissed him very quickly on the nose. "Excellent. Then this should take care of it." She let the money sprinkle down on his thighs. "I have to go now, love. I'm sure you will agree I have kept my part of the bargain. There is ten thousand dollars there. You can live like a king for a long time on that—almost anywhere except Arizona." She laughed.

His hand fell away from her hair. He seemed to go still all over as if he were turned to stone. He didn't move—didn't change expression. He just looked at her without speaking, and she could feel the pain spreading out in waves around her throat and chest and knew she had to get out of there fast.

He picked up one of the hundred-dollar bills, then a thousand-dollar bill. His impassive mien didn't change, but the look in his eyes did. The blue cooled inexplicably, turned opaque, unresponsive. He lifted one eyebrow questioningly, and she forced a little trill of laughter.

"I'm defining a new market for myself. That's a new term I learned listening to Tim talk. We're—getting married soon. I really can't continue being your mistress—but you deserve to be compensated. A deal's a deal." She shrugged as if money matters always embarrassed her.

"Thanks, but as you can see"—he gestured casually to the shabby room—"I have everything I need."

He was right about that anyway, she thought bitterly. She ached all over just looking at him—Apollo—sprawled in naked abandon.

She turned away, a smile curving her lips, shrugging. "Well, keep it anyway. I don't need it. As Tim's wife I will have everything I need. Who knows? You said once, maybe you could go straight. Why don't you try it? You might even like it."

"I tried that once," he said softly. "People won't let you up—once you're down." Did she detect bitterness in that husky quiet voice?

She was at the door now, and he was still on the bed, naked, his left arm folded under the back of his head. A ray of sunshine hitting the window just right sent a shimmer of brightness across the bed, backlighting his still form so that he was only a silhouette: Apollo, the sun god, framed in gold.

She paused, knowing better but unable to help herself, and her mind was filled with craziness: "A lighted chamber, a darkened court." The phrase "Chambre Ardente" flashed into her head from some forgotten history lecture, and she could see the Courts of Cardinal Lorraine, in those dark ages before the Revolution, where prisoners were tried in torchlit chambers, the judges' faces carefully hidden from the hapless men and women they judged. Those people had known instinctively, as she did now, that you could expect no mercy from a judge who hid his face from you.

It reminded her of the way Cantrell had always hidden his real self from her. Or had she only refused to see?

"So long, Cantrell."

Ward picked up one of the bills and blew her a kiss.

"Thanks, hellcat."

CHAPTER FORTY-TWO

Leslie was home by dinnertime.

"Did you have a nice ride?" Jennifer asked, smiling at her wind-flushed cheeks. "It was a lovely day for it."

"Beautiful," Leslie said, forcing a smile. She had resented all that autumn splendor because it didn't suit her mood. But maybe, she conceded, there wasn't a climate anywhere that would satisfy the needs of a woman who had just been ravished, impoverished, and rejected.

Jennifer was sensitive enough to catch the insincerity in her less than jubilant reply.

"Are you all right?" she asked, looking at Leslie closely. Leslie sighed. "I don't know," she admitted wearily.

"Would you like to talk about it?"

She shook her head, and even that negative response was a lie. She did want to talk about it—desperately—but there was no one she could turn to.

Jennifer might be one of his mistresses. How could she know? Even Chane, whom she trusted instinctively, was off limits because she might slip and incriminate his wife. Even Debbie was suspect. She had gone out with Ward, but fortunately she didn't brag. Certainly Tim wouldn't appreciate hearing about her love or hate relationship with another man.

Tim came after dinner that night and took her for a ride, and this time when he kissed her she responded exactly as he wanted her to. She couldn't lie, but she snuggled closer into his arms, and that was answer enough. He wanted her, and she needed someone who wasn't just using her. His love was a soothing balm, at a time when she desperately needed comforting.

"Leslie, please say you'll marry me," he pleaded.

The instinctive denial rose, but Leslie stifled it. She had already told Ward she was going to marry Tim. She could do a lot worse.

"All right," she said softly.

"Do you mean it?" he asked incredulously, holding her away from him to let his black eyes burn into her.

"Yes, of course," she said weakly.

"Oh, darling, you've made me the happiest man in the world!"

When he took her home he made a big production of asking Chane for her hand. Chane's warm green eyes jolted her like a physical shock when he turned from Tim to her. She felt exposed—the whole facade she had erected to hide behind peeled away under that piercing look.

"So you've made your choice?" he asked gently.

He knew! She felt like a traitor now. What was he asking her? Since Ward is in trouble, you've chosen Tim? Her chin lifted defiantly. Let him think it! He didn't know Ward—not really. But she writhed inwardly under his scrutiny. Was he really as disappointed in her as she imagined?

"Yes, I think marriage is still a valid choice," she murmured, smiling.

"Well, if you're sure, then of course you two have our blessing," he answered smoothly, graciously, bending down to kiss her cheek. "I'll find Jennie. She's going to be thrilled at the prospect."

The announcement of their engagement did not need to appear in the newspaper. Word was all over town instantly. Everyone knew! And she was wearing a one-carat diamond solitaire.

"It's beautiful, Tim, but it looks so expensive."

"I've had nothing to spend my money on before. All I ever did was work and save it. Now I have you, my darling. I want to dress you like a queen, set you in a beautiful mansion, frame you like the rare masterpiece you are, show you off to all my friends."

He went on, but she wasn't listening. Why did she suddenly feel like a possession?—the most prized treasure of all, but still only an acquisition?

Dusty Denton watched the lovely black-haired creature rush out of the hotel, her cheeks flushed with color. He waited patiently for Cantrell to come down. In two minutes Ward was coming down the stairs tying his guns down, one on each thigh as he strode into the room.

"Get ready to ride out," he said flatly as Dusty came to his feet, his gray eyes watchful.

Dusty nodded to the others and they began to comply.

Ward passed on what Leslie had added to what they already knew.

"What's the plan?" Dusty asked when he had finished.

"I want you and the rest of the men to gather up as big a herd of mixed brands as you can in three days and drive them to that point where the rustlers load 'em onto the railroad cars. By the time you get there, I should have something arranged. I'm going to pay a visit on Younger."

"Alone?"

Ward grinned. "You're not afraid, are you? I realize it gets scary out there at night, but if you all stay close together…"

"Graduated from Radcliffe, didn't you? You know what I meant." He grinned.

Ward had already dismissed him from his thoughts. There was a mood of controlled brutality that he was going to work off on someone. It might as well be Younger. He didn't need a sorceress to tell him where Trinket had gone. She'd be lucky if she wasn't dead.

Dusty interrupted, still trying to stop him from going it alone. "Boy, she must be some girl—spends two hours up there and turns you into a one-man army."

"You should see what I've done in the last three days," Ward said dryly.

"Just hearing about it was enough to scare hell out of me."

"Me, too."

Ward left, and Dusty joined Doug Paggett at the bar.

"What the hell is he up to?" Dusty asked.

"I don't know. Did he look like he'd been shot or anything?"

Dusty scowled angrily at Doug.

"No," Doug said, shaking his head, "I'm not joking. The last time he got real quiet and cool like this and took off all by himself we found out later it was because he took a bullet in the back when we were running from a posse. We didn't see him again for months. He almost died. Hadn't been for an old Mexican woman finding him in the desert he would've."

"Why do you suppose he did that?"

Doug looked at the tiny dust cloud that was all they could still see of Ward Cantrell.

"He couldn't keep up. I guess he didn't want to slow us down."

"You suppose it was the same woman I heard him telling the Castenadas about? He asked them to send a priest to bless the grave."

"I don't know. I didn't know she was dead."

• • •

That mood of bitter passion still menaced Cantrell—growing darker and more vicious as he rode toward the Powers spread. Dusty hadn't wanted to separate, but they knew each other well enough now so that he had accepted Ward's mood and his decision as final.

Fate played strange tricks. Dusty Denton had grown up with him and graduated from Harvard in the class Ward had been expelled from. This was the third time his and Dusty's paths had crossed. They rode with the Jackson Hole Gang in Wyoming at the same time, and now they were both trying to earn a pardon.

Dusty's story was almost as bizarre as his own. He had inherited a ranch in the Texas panhandle about a year after he got out of school. He and his cousin took a trip to Lubbock to look over his holdings. He didn't intend to stay, just to find out how much to sell it for, but his cousin got into a fight—a simple fistfight over a girl who smiled at him once too often. The other man drew a gun and shot Jonathan Denton in the chest. Jon was unarmed. When Dusty found out he went to the sheriff and demanded that justice be done, but there was a mob on the other side, and the sheriff was too timid to buck it. So Denton issued his own challenge for the other man to meet him in the street—Texas-style—even though he had never worn a gun around his waist. He bought a gunbelt, gun and bullets, and spent less than an hour practicing his draw before the showdown. He was a practiced marksman with a hunting rifle, and he discovered he was just as good with a handgun. He wasn't as fast on the draw as the other man, but his opponent's first shot missed. By then Dusty had his gun out. He fired one shot, and Red Dooley fell—dead before his head hit the ground.

The Texas rangers chased him out of Texas, and he couldn't go home because the sheriff wired the police in Boston. He discovered that nothing spreads faster than bad news. The only solution was to travel in places where there was even less law than Texas.

Dusty hadn't been a close friend of Ward's at school or in Wyoming, but he was developing into one now. If they both managed to survive this...

Ward stopped himself with a frown. He was no Jack Hays, ranger hero. He was more a Poggin, the kind to die with his back against the wall, both guns smoking and only one bullet left in the chamber. When he took this job he hadn't expected to survive it—just to die in a manner more of his choosing. He wasn't a coward or a quitter; if he could survive it, he would. But survival hadn't been a condition then, and it certainly wasn't one now. He hadn't gotten emotionally involved with a girl since Simone, and now that he was, he felt the loss as frustration and fury: frustration because he was trapped by circumstances that made it impossible for him to pursue her and fury that she was too eager to grab the gold ring!

He pushed the big black relentlessly, and the exertion of a wild, heedless ride brought all the muscles in his lean frame into play. The exercise and the rhythmic pounding of hooves flying over the desert finally worked its magic, and after an hour he slowed the horse, finally beginning to relax.

He settled down to a ground-eating pace that was more comfortable for his mount. The killing mood—the cold, deadly passion of the gunfighter—was in him now, and he knew it. He had felt the icy flicker of foreboding too many times—before too many confrontations— not to recognize it now. But always before he had resisted it. Now he welcomed it—goading the horse forward when it slowed its pace across the desert, ignoring the splendor of the sunset that was turning the sky into a panorama of coral and purple.

Dusk found him on the hill overlooking Powers's fortress. The same controlled rage that had brought him there in headlong flight, cooled his nerves, now that he was in sight of his goal, hardening them with grim purpose. He rode the rest of the way slowly, deliberately, expecting Younger to be waiting for him. To all outward appearances he rode coolly, casually, but to a man familiar with his type, the very coolness of his demeanor was warning enough.

He stopped at the gate to Younger's walled sanctuary, drew his gun, and fired twice into the air. He could hear the scuttle and yell of men in startled awareness and then a voice:

"Who goes thar?"

"Cantrell."

"What the hell do you want?"

"Younger."

"He ain't here anymore. Picked up his things and left last night."

"Then you won't mind if I come in and look around, will you?"

There was a short conference and then the gate screeched open on rusty hinges. The man doing the talking looked like any honest range rider. He wasn't one of the men who rode with Younger; and he wore no gun. Most cowboys didn't, though.

"Come ahead."

There was a man in the lookout tower with a rifle trained on Ward as soon as the door swung open. It followed him all the way to the house, and

Ward knew it would be there when he came out, if he came out. If these men believed he had killed Powers, they weren't showing any signs of it. He didn't believe Younger was gone, but it was possible. Younger knew exactly where he stood with the new owner. At the porch he stopped, dismounted, and faced the man who had greeted him at the gate.

"Did Younger have a girl with him when he left here?"

Slim Whitman watched the man's eyes—cool, merciless blue—and was suddenly glad he wasn't Younger. "Yeah. A pretty, blond girl. She waited here two days for him to come from Phoenix, then they grabbed a few things and hit off for the mountains."

"Talk in town has it that I killed Powers and made off with the girl," he said, watching the man's face for any sign.

"Reckon they must be wrong, then," the man said coolly.

Ward considered the answer and then nodded—much to Slim's relief. "Did he take any men with him?"

Slim felt no special loyalty to Younger. He'd had his own doubts about the gun-toting foreman and his special riders. "You want to set a spell? About dinnertime," he said laconically, waving to the man in the tower to lower the rifle.

"Thanks."

Ward shared the simple fare with twenty or so cowhands, and then he and the man who had finally introduced himself as Slim Whitman moved out to the porch to enjoy the whir of crickets and the trill of a few birds before the cold night winds made it too unpleasant.

They talked about numerous things, all seemingly inconsequential, but in short order Ward had gotten a picture of an operation similar to the robber baron Cheseldine's some years back. Slim was perceptive. He was one of the spread's regular hands, not privy to any crooked deals, but he had sharp eyes and a quick mind, and apparently he had sized Ward up and made his decision. Else Ward could have gotten a bullet from that tower without warning. When Ward stood up to go, Slim put out his rough hand, and Ward took it. A grin spread across Slim's lantern-jawed face, then quickly disappeared.

"I never shook the hand of a gunfighter before."

"What makes you think you have now?" Ward asked, flashing a grin of his own.

"I know. Plumb smooth, like satin. Can tell you don't rope steers, mister. And I reckon it ain't like that from wearing gloves."

Ward hadn't worn a glove on his right hand in six years. The man didn't expect a reply, and none was offered.

"Younger and the girl left alone. The other men who worked special for him rode off a day earlier—heading for Morristown. They didn't say that, but that's the direction they always go. We hear 'em talking."

"Much obliged."

"My pleasure, Cantrell."

Ward started to leave, paused. "When is your new boss taking over?"

"Reckon not for a week or so. Younger said she's planning on marrying some hotshot railroad man in a few days—probably don't know a cow from a gelding," he ended disgustedly.

"So long, Slim, and thanks for your hospitality."

CHAPTER FORTY-THREE

Sandra and Younger arrived in Morristown Wednesday afternoon. It was barely more than a settlement: a dozen buildings and a few shanties. From a distance, with gusty winds whipping up the dirt into sheets to throw against the weathered walls and a shutter banging insistently, it looked like a ghost town. Only the horses, standing patiently in the cold mountain air, added a touch of life.

Younger led her past gaunt buildings where she saw shadows of faces peering through the water-stained, dust-coated windows, to a wood-frame house at the northernmost edge of the village. They dismounted; she had to fend for herself. Dallas bellowed an order, and a raw-boned, slow-moving red-haired man ambled out and took the horses around back while they went inside.

There were four men inside, playing cards and drinking. A tired-looking woman in a shapeless gown was cutting vegetables for a stew.

Sandra felt her face flushing as every eye in the place roamed over her body, even the woman's. Sandra was wearing the silk blouse and riding skirt, but no undergarments of any type. Dallas wouldn't permit it. Said he didn't like nothing getting between him and what was his. She had the feeling they all knew. A muted throbbing in her loins quickened her breath.

The men were seated at a table that someone had thrown a rough blanket over. Cards and money were scattered around. The blanket hung down crookedly, almost touching the floor where it wasn't impeded by someone's lap.

Dallas waved a careless hand at her. "Boys, meet my little sweetface." He turned back to her carelessly. "What's your name, sweetface?"

"Sandra."

"That mean-eyed cuss thar is Cedar Longley. The man to his right is Pick Sitwell. His brother was the one who took our hosses when we came in. The sleepy one thar is Bass Wimer and the big burly lady's man is Texas Jack Jones."

Sandra nodded. Cedar Longley, she'd heard that name before. He was Younger's second lieutenant. Pick Sitwell had sly, furtive eyes that made her want to see if her blouse was buttoned. He was lanky and raw-boned like his brother. Bass Wimer had a dull, listless look in his eyes that didn't look like it would last. He might burst into some act of violence if he ever came fully awake. Texas Jack Jones had bold black eyes that made her belly feel strange and tight, like it did when Dallas touched her. Even when he resumed his lazy-lidded concentration on his cards she could still feel that stirring in her belly.

"Y'all be good to this little sweetface, ya hear?"

There were various comments, some lewd, as to exactly how good they would like to be, and Sandra reddened painfully. She had been raised a lady, and knew the exact degree of her own shame. No lady would be where she was now. Leslie Powers, who looked the epitome of a gentlewoman, except for the flashes of spirit that bespoke a fiery temper, would never allow herself to be paraded in front of such crude range bums. But Leslie Powers did not have her problems or her needs.

There was scraping and rearranging of chairs as Dallas sat down, and then the card game resumed. No one noticed that Dallas had forgotten to introduce the woman, Bass Wimer's wife, who turned away in disgust. Sandra was forgotten as the men became engrossed in sporadic conversation. She wandered over and asked the woman if she needed any help.

Cold gray eyes flitted over her. "Don't reckon the likes of you would be able to do anythin' I'd find tolerable, much less helpful."

Sandra flinched and wandered around the room, ending up behind Younger. She was an outsider; even that tired old hag had something that made her belong. She reached down and began rubbing Dallas's shoulder. He responded, so she pressed close to his chair and let both hands rub his shoulders and chest. That took her mind off her loneliness, and he seemed to enjoy the attention. The stew smelled good, but Sandra had lost her appetite. The ache in her loins was throbbing insistently. She could see the men letting their bold eyes stray over her body. Part of her realized how crude these men were in comparison to the men her father expected her to associate with, but she was too needy to take her shame seriously. Shame was an almost necessary part of getting what she needed from men.

Lightheaded from the rush of events, Sandra started having visions of herself naked among these six rough-looking men, doing their bidding, being the center of attention, and by the time the old hag served the stew, she barely touched it. The playing seemed to go on and on. Sandra stayed at her post caressing Dallas and accepting the looks of the other men until she was in agony. She leaned down and whispered in his ear.

"Dallas, honey, can we go to bed soon?"

She ignored the derisive snort from the man next to Dallas.

"I'm winning, sweetface. I cain't leave now."

"Please, honey, I need you," she whispered desperately. "Please."

"Please, honey," someone mocked her. "Please, Dallas honey." Dallas cuffed him lightly, and they all laughed. Play stopped and the one across from Dallas swore crudely: "Hey, Dallas, take her in that room and give her what she wants, then come on back. We'll still be here."

"Hell, yeah! We'll listen—yell if you need any help."

They laughed. Dallas stood up and yawned elaborately, joining in the fun. Sandra didn't look at anyone, especially the other woman, as she turned.

"Reckon I could use a nap. Come on, sweetface. We'll give the boys a break. They been losing long enough."

Sandra was on fire. She ignored the cacophony of crude remarks and followed Younger into the small bedroom that was separated from the main room by a curtain. Her hands trembled on the buttons and almost tore the skirt off. He only slipped his guns and pants off and they fell across the squeaky bed. She wanted him inside her—hard and big and rough—but he was teasing her, only pressing between her legs, refusing to go inside while he kissed her hungry mouth and squeezed her breasts. Soon she was groaning, pleading with him.

"What d'ya want, sweetface?"

"I want you," she gasped, writhing beneath him.

"You want Dallas?" he prompted.

"Yes, yes, I want you, Dallas!"

"Say it, baby."

"I want you, Dallas."

"Say it louder, baby. I cain't hear when ya whisper."

"Oh, Dallas, Dallas! I want you!"

"Louder, baby, who d'ya want, sweetface?"

"I want *you*, Dallas."

That was loud enough to bring a chorus of ribald remarks and a crude cheer from the other room, but she was too far gone to notice.

Dallas kept Sandra at fever pitch for twelve minutes while the men in the other room made bets about how long it would go on. Pick Sitwell won the bet when they heard her orgasmic gasps and cries exactly nine-twenty-three by Bass Wimer's watch.

"Ride 'em, cowboy!" Pick yelled triumphantly while the others cussed, becoming even cruder with their remarks.

Younger came out in three minutes, and Bass won that bet on both counts: that it would be under five minutes and that he would be alone.

Dallas took his place at the table amid back-slapping and more raucous remarks. The initial uproar died down slowly because the men were steamed up. About midnight the talk grew more serious.

"Heard anythin' from the boss?" Pick asked Younger as he dealt.

"Naw. He's keeping low for a while. We're jus' gonna round up all the steers we've got hidden in them ravines and drive 'em down to the pens so's they can be loaded and shipped."

"Hell, don't sound like you need us for that," Pick snorted.

"Probably don't, but it's something to keep you from drinking, gambling, getting on one another's nerves, and killing one another," Dallas said.

Pick looked to the others defensively. "We been gettin' along fine, ain't we?"

"You always get along fine for the first three days. Then the trouble starts. You're worse'n a box full of locoed gnats! I cain't leave you alone for longer'n that. You always get into trouble. Remember those goddamned Mendozas!"

"Hell, that wasn't our fault. We was jist doing what the boss wanted us to."

Younger threw down his cards, a scowl turning his handsome face dark. "Wal, you done a damned sloppy job of it, too! I took the rap for that with Powers. That was about the stupidest piece of bad work—leaving that gunfighter alive and killing off the women, the old man, and the kid!" That had rankled for a long time. "Stupid goddamned bastards!"

Pick dropped his cards. "We didn't know about the gunfighter. We'd a got him fust off if'n we did."

"Stupid damned bunch!" Younger growled, letting his eyes rip over them. "We been fighting that bastard ever since!"

"Hell, you're jist upset cause it's you he's after."

"'Twarn't our fault anyway," Bass Wimer interposed. "We coulda handled that more convincin'-like, 'cept the boss was horny for thet gal. He likes it when they're crying and scared. Things jist kinda got outta harness after that."

."I reckon you could say that, all right!" Dallas growled, deciding to drop the subject. "I'm moving up to the camp at dawn. Y'all be ready to ride out."

"Shucks, boss, we figured you was gonna leave us here with the filly," Bass whined in pretended or real agony.

"Aw, hell!" Dallas growled. "'Sides, you got yourself a woman. Cooks a right good stew, she does."

"Man don't live by stew alone," Bass grumped.

They played one hand in silence, then Texas Jack Jones, the big burly Texan, leaned back in his chair and eyed Younger. Texas Jack had a deep, sonorous voice and usually spoke slowly and carefully. Because of his reputation for a quick gun and a short temper, when he spoke, men listened.

"Wal, now, Dallas, I reckon if that hongry yelling went on much longer tonight you woulda had a problem on your hands."

Dallas leaned back, grinning. "What might thata been?"

Texas Jack kept a straight face. "A couple more minutes of that pretty little filly yelling about how good you was and I was gonna go in thar and let you hump me," he drawled.

They roared with laughter.

CHAPTER FORTY-FOUR

Sandra was treated like a celebrity when she appeared for breakfast. The men made a big show of making room for her at the table and taking care of her needs. For the first time in her life she felt important in her own right—not just because she was Sam McCormick's daughter. She didn't mind the crude remarks. It was all part of belonging.

They left together in a cohesive pack just as the sky was turning from gray to pink. The cold was bitter, and frost was everywhere, covering the hills with white. As Dallas Younger's woman, she rode at the head of the pack, beside her man. There was a new confidence in Sandra now. She had a man who was really a man, and he treated her like a woman. Two days' growth of beard only added to his attraction. He was rough, and he looked it, but when he caught her look and grinned, there was a hint of pride mixed with the desire that burned between them.

They were going deeper into the mountains now. The sun slowly melted the frost that crunched under the horses' hooves, and the ride became more bearable. Dallas had found her a coat like the men wore, and only her legs were cold. "We'll fix that when we get to camp. Little Doug has some pants that should fit you right fine."

They stopped at a wide, shallow stream. They dismounted and drank upstream from the horses. The men wandered off to relieve themselves, and Sandra did likewise.

Everyone came back except Bass Wimer, so Dallas yelled for him to get his butt back so they could leave.

"I found something," he yelled, the booming voice that had earned him his nickname echoing and bouncing off the surrounding mountains.

Dallas shook his head in irritation. "Damn fool! He's gotta be the stupidest son of a bitch west of the Pecos!"

"He's hauling a short load all right," Texas Jack drawled, spitting in disgust at a rock.

Bass Wimer came out of the trees, carrying a long slender pole. It was two inches thick and almost symmetrical, as if it had been planed by a carpenter.

"Ain't that purty?" he asked proudly.

"What the hell you gonna do with a stick ten feet long?" Younger demanded, raising a disgusted eyebrow.

"Make things," Bass said defensively.

"Shit, put that thing down and let's ride."

"Aw, dammit, Dallas, let me keep it. It cain't hurt anythin', and I need it."

"Jesus Christ!" Younger shook his head. "All right, but you see to it."

"Thanks, boss."

Sandra looked back several times to see how Bass and his stick were faring. He carried it like a lance for a while, then across his saddle like a tightrope walker she'd seen once. He did whatever he had to do to keep it.

As the trail grew rougher and narrower, Sandra fell back until she was riding in front of Bass. All went well until they broke out onto a wide grassy meadow. The group was in single file with Sandra and then Bass and his stick, carried across the saddle like a balance pole.

Dallas held up his hand and turned in the saddle. Did he see something? She couldn't tell. He was too far ahead for her to read his expression. Bass stopped, pulled out his red paisley handkerchief to mop his brow, and was almost unseated when his horse reared. Bass heard the whirring rattle of the snake, but he never saw it. The horse came down and lurched forward into a dead run. There were too many things happening at once. The horse to control, the handkerchief in his hand, the stick across the saddle. He didn't make it in time. The stick caught Sandra across the middle of the back. She screamed and fell to the side, one foot caught in the stirrup. Her horse caught the stick on the back of the head and bolted, dragging her along.

Pick Sitwell, the closest one to Sandra, lunged off his horse but couldn't reach her in time. Texas Jack was on the wrong side of Sandra's horse. If he thundered up beside her runaway mount, his horse would trample her. Dallas could see the problem instantly. He got into position and was there when the big speckled gray came by. He caught the reins and jerked the horse viciously until it stopped. He held the head down. "Get her foot outta there!" he yelled.

Cedar Longley reached her first, freed her boot from the stirrup, and dragged her out of reach of the horse's hooves. Dallas turned the horse over to Pick and rushed to Sandra's side.

She was unconscious but breathing. He made a hasty examination, his hands feeling for broken bones, crushed places.

Bass Wimer ran up, panting. "She all right?"

Dallas couldn't remember later what happened then. Something snapped inside him, and the next thing he remembered, Texas Jack and Cedar Longley were pulling him off Wimer's limp body. He vaguely remembered hitting him, and his fists were both scuffed and sore, but he had no recollection of Wimer's response. Did he fight back?

Sandra came awake, groaning, and he went to her.

"You all right, sweetface?"

"What happened?" She looked around in a daze. Wimer was limp and bloody; the horses and men were all scattered above her. Had they been attacked?

"Is everybody all right?" she asked.

"Bass and his damned stick! He hit you, sweetface, and then your horse. The horse bolted and dragged you."

She looked around wonderingly. There was real concern in Dallas Younger's eyes—in all their eyes. They really cared about her! She felt tears well up in her own eyes and saw the response in his eyes, and it gave her a sense of power she hadn't felt since the time she had scarlet fever and everyone spoiled her because they thought they had almost lost her.

"Did you do that?" she asked softly, taking his hand and kissing the scuffed knuckles.

"I reckon. I thought he'd killed you. I musta hit him a hundred times, the way my hands ache." He shot a grim look at Wimer, who was beginning to groan and roll over. "He ain't going nowhere, though. I can get him again later. He'll be around."

Younger spoke so matter-of-factly that Sandra nearly beamed. He really cared for her! Now she rode the rest of the way beside Dallas. If she couldn't keep up, they slowed down. She was in heaven. All she had to do was grimace and she could bring the tightening into his handsome face and the anger back into his eyes.

Sheriff Willie Slaughter opened the letter with the Phoenix postmark on it slowly. He read it and sat frowning, gazing out the window of the jail aimlessly. He stared at the livery wagon standing in front of Barnard Bros. Photo Graph Gallery.

"I'm going to King's place," he said to the deputy, who lounged in a chair across the narrow room, his feet up, reading the morning newspaper.

"Be gone long?"

"Naw."

Slaughter put on his hat and walked carefully across the wide, deeply rutted main street of Dodge City, sidestepping a wagon and then a buggy with a man and woman perched precariously on the narrow seat.

The interior of the Oriental Saloon was dim until his eyes adjusted to the difference. He could make out Frank Lovell and Wyatt Roundtree playing the faro bank, Frank keeping cases while Wyatt socialized with the dealer and the lookout. Men slouched at the bar over their social glasses. He heard one man joshing his friend about checking to see how come the end of his neck was all haired-over like that. The man did have a very impressive head of hair. Slaughter always admired that, since his own hair had disappeared, leaving only a ring of fuzz around his neck and ears.

Three boys were piking at a monte game, and ten drovers sat around a long table eating together, one of them complaining about the cost of yardage at the feedlot. He could hear the righteous indignation in the man's voice: "I'll not ship any more cattle to this town until they adjust their yardage costs. Listen! For two bits I can get myself a room with a nice clean bed in it, plenty of soap, water and towels, and I can stay there for twenty-four hours. And their stockyards are way the hell out there and they want to charge me twenty cents and let my steers stand out in the weather."

Slaughter stopped at the far end of the bar where Jack Fuller was standing, wiping absently at the bar.

"Morning, Jack."

"Morning, Will, you drinking this early?"

"Naw, I came to see your boss. He in?"

"In the back." He nodded toward the bead-covered opening that led down a narrow corridor and then out into the alley.

Slaughter found the office he was looking for, a large room on the left side of the corridor that looked like a lawyer's office or some rich politician's office instead of just the owner of a Dodge City saloon. He'd been in this office many times, collecting his share of the take off the gambling tables. It was customary. He kept law and order, and King gave him a cut. Saved them both some time and trouble.

John King was something of an enigma for Dodge City. He was the richest man in town, the best dressed, and black as the ace of spades.

He owned the Oriental and three other establishments in town. The Oriental was one of the fanciest saloons in the territory. The bartender, Jack Fuller, had been imported from one of those fancy hotels back east, and he could make any mixed drink a man could ask for, as long as he had four bits to pay for it.

Today King was dressed in a very expensive fawn-colored suit that few other men could have afforded. The finest wool, soft as a baby's bottom, and impeccably cut. He was a massive man with thick neck, burly arms, but narrow through the hips. Store-bought clothes would have been ridiculous on that enormous frame. Slaughter could imagine buttons straining and popping off to leave gaping holes where that shiny black skin would glare out. King's face was as much an enigma as the rest of him. The features were brutal, heavy, reminding Slaughter of a prize fighter who had been brutalized once too often, but the eyes—there was no explaining them. They could have belonged to a teacher, someone smarter than he ever met. And there was no doubt John King was tough. He had made a place for himself by sheer brute force five years ago. He had stuffed this town's pride and ignorance down its own throat. He no longer had to prove himself or apologize for his color.

He looked up when Slaughter tapped on the doorjamb.

"Yes?" he asked curtly, his intelligent brown eyes jolting Slaughter with the reminder that they did not belong in that taciturn, brutal face.

Slaughter cleared his throat self-consciously. "I got a letter today about that outlaw you've been looking for—Ward Cantrell."

Impatience was replaced by interest now.

"Oh, where is he?"

"Phoenix, Arizona."

"Are you going after him?" King asked politely.

"Me? Hell, I'm no gunfighter. I ain't never faced a man like Cantrell." Slaughter paused, feeling foolish. "There's a big reward for him. Fifteen hundred dollars. I thought that was why you wanted to know."

King didn't reply. His brown eyes watched Will Slaughter as if he were not seeing him anymore.

Slaughter shifted uncomfortably. He didn't understand what was going on. He had expected King to be grateful, but now he looked like he was remembering something it would be better he didn't remember. He wouldn't have come, except years ago King asked him to let him know if Cantrell or word of him turned up. He worked for the man, so he remembered that request.

John King had been the most feared bounty hunter in five territories but had given that up after he amassed enough money to buy his first saloon. A number of fugitives were damned glad he had, too. He brought back every man he ever pursued. Mainly because King was a bloodhound on a trail. His massive frame never tired, and he would not give up. He had a reputation for being fast with a gun, and people suspected he had an abiding hatred for white men. He never went after blacks, Mexicans, or Indians. It was said he could track a snake over granite. People claimed he was really the devil, pretending to be a black man to trick unsuspecting white men into crossing him.

"Are you going after Cantrell?" Slaughter asked.

King dragged in a deep breath. "How much is that reward?"

"Fifteen hundred. Dead or alive."

It would not be worth the trouble for so little money, to disrupt his life here, his business, leave his woman. But he had a personal score to settle with Cantrell. He stood up heavily, weighted down by his thoughts that had taken such a bitter turn.

"I will go, but I don't want any competition."

"You got my word."

King was towering over him, broad and stalwart. Slaughter had the urge to back away or hold up his hands, but the man did nothing.

"When does the next train leave here for parts south?"

"Twelve noon. You gonna be on it?"

"Yes."

CHAPTER FORTY-FIVE

Ward rode through the bitter cold without feeling it, made camp ten miles north of the Powers spread, but found after his long, eventful day that sleep did not come. He was coiled like a spring inside, ready to meet and kill Younger.

He stared at the stars, traced the passage of clouds blocking the view, and watched the moon rise above the horizon. He listened to the yip and howl of coyotes off in the distance.

I'm defining a new market for myself. That's a new term I learned from Tim. We're getting married soon....

He should have followed his instincts and slapped that condescending smile off her face. What a little hypocrite she was! One minute she made love to him wildly and with such abandon that he was half mad with desire for her, and then, for no reason, she changed into Winslow Breakenridge.

Ward closed his eyes. The thought of Leslie married to Tim Summers was unbearable. Why had she ridden to Buckeye and brought him money if she didn't love him? And if she had ten thousand dollars, why did she need Summers? If security were so damned important to her, why would she give it away?

He could see her long black hair fanned out on the pillow, framing her pale face. Her lime-green eyes half-closed, her seductive, kiss-swollen lips were provocatively parted. Her slender body beneath his own was enough to drive him mad.

He forced himself to stop seeing her, but he was outraged that she could spend such a long time making him love her so she could prove beyond doubt that she felt nothing for him. He had the terrible feeling that he would live the rest of his life alone, remembering her, married to Tim Summers.

Angrily, he closed his fist around a rock and threw it. To hell with her! And to hell with the governor's damned amnesty agreement.

Bookkeeping was their problem, not his. He didn't give a damn whether they wiped his record clean or not. He could live in England or Europe under any name he chose. All he needed was money, and he had more than enough if he lived to be two hundred years old.

The only people who needed his services were the Mendozas, and theirs was the only debt he cared about paying. He had killed eight of the men who slaughtered them, and he was going to kill the last four.

He tried to concentrate on that goal, but kaleidoscopic flashes of memory haunted him. Was she as frankly sensual with Tim Summers? Did she take her pleasure as openly and as joyously with Summers as she did with him? Why had she waited naked in her room that night after the party? Could anyone be that highminded? That she would sacrifice herself for a friend's reputation? Or ride twenty miles to repay what she considered a debt, and stay to give herself wholeheartedly, with wild, sweet abandon, before sprinkling her money on him?

Try not to hurt Younger. I may have to marry him. A day later she refused to leave when he tried to release her. She was a mass of contradictions. Even her actions today: first the melting, then the ice. Had she come to save him or only to buy him out? "As Tim's wife I will have everything I need," she'd said.

There was a certain sureness in the outcome of his life now. He couldn't expect to ride into Younger's camp, kill him, and ride out again—not alive anyway. He would die tomorrow, and Leslie would get married and live happily ever after.

He lay back and closed his eyes. Regrets accomplished nothing. At least tonight he didn't have to write any farewell letters. He'd said his good-byes this afternoon.

Sleep came at last and then dawn. The sun crept over the horizon and lit a bank of thunderheads from beneath with brilliant color, turning them and the sky a fiery orange and red. Ward saddled his horse and headed north. There had been good forage. Blueberry felt good. His stride was powerful, rhythmic, impatient. Ward gave him his head, and the stallion stretched out for a good long run that suited Ward's mood perfectly. He was ready for action—tired of waiting.

Morristown nestled in a steep-walled, bowl-shaped ravine formed by two mountains. A stream, barely more than a trickle, cut through the notch. The buildings were east of the almost barren watercourse, probably because spring snows swelled that trickle to a torrent. The residents had apparently learned respect for the river's path, avoiding it scrupulously.

As the sun set, Ward tethered Blueberry near tall grama grass and climbed the rock-studded ridge that overlooked the settlement. He watched from a vantage point on the slope of the mountain west of the small hamlet. There was no activity to indicate Younger was there. He rejoined Blueberry and rode boldly in.

The saloon was a run-down shanty, but it was in better shape than most of the other buildings. It smelled of wood smoke, bourbon, sweat, and cigars.

"Evenin', stranger." The bartender wiped the glass in his hand mechanically.

"Evening. Whiskey."

"Kinda off the beaten track, ain't yuh?" he asked after Ward downed two drinks slowly, appearing to be deep in thought.

"I don't pick where I work—just who I work for."

"And who might that be?"

"Don't reckon that's any of your business," Ward said noncommittally, smiling to soften the rebuke.

The man nodded, accepting that. He could tell he was one of Younger's men, but he must be new, since he hadn't made a beeline for Bass Wimer's place on the north end.

Ward finished his drink, paid the man, then paused, smiling sheepishly. "Younger leave this morning?"

"What's it to you?"

"Just trying to decide how much hell I'm gonna catch for making him mad."

"'Bout twelve hours' worth."

Ward grimaced in pain. "Much obliged."

CHAPTER FORTY-SIX

"Oh! It is so exciting! A real wedding at last. We haven't had a formal wedding in eight months. Can you believe that?" Elizabeth Cartright gushed. "Eight months!"

Leslie believed it. She felt nothing but envy for anyone who wasn't getting married in a few days. But she would die before she let Elizabeth know it. She had never been willing to submit her innermost thoughts to public scrutiny. Fortunately Elizabeth didn't require an answer, just a listener.

"Think how exciting it will be. You will be a young matron! That opens all sorts of doors! You'll share secrets with other young marrieds, and learn all about their secret affairs, who belongs to whom, so to speak. Oh, how I envy you! Tim is so *handsome*. I *adore* fair-skinned, black-eyed, black-haired men. They look so *intense*, don't they? And he has such a *nice* smile. It is obvious he absolutely *adores* you."

Leslie fretted over the pretty bouquet she was supposed to be making as a pew decoration and finally put it aside. Wedding preparations were tedious, boring, and a bloody waste of time. She was too nervous to work on trifles. She needed something—maybe a ride. And here she was, trapped with Elizabeth. A person could die listening to her talk about how wonderful everything was. Why didn't she let each person decide for herself what was wonderful and exciting about her own life? The way Elizabeth gushed, it was no wonder denials sprang into Leslie's head faster than she could stifle the flow.

Tim *was* going to be a good husband: considerate, loyal, faithful. He *was* handsome. It was just that his black eyes only looked friendly when he smiled, and too often he stared and then they looked unaccountably cold and unfeeling. It wasn't his fault, though. He had a lot on his mind. Kincaid kept him extremely busy. Leslie caught herself before she could follow that thought with *thank goodness*. In one week she would be married—how incredible! It had seemed so right, telling Ward Cantrell of her decision, but trying to live it was another matter altogether.

Damn you, Cantrell! Damn you!

A day's ride beneath low-hung, slow-moving thunderheads was endured before Younger's party reached the secret camp. Sandra was pale and weak. She had a bruise on her back that jarred each time the horse put a hoof down.

The string of tents trailing down the mountainside from a weathered gray house with a steep roof was a welcome sight. She was half-frozen, tired, in pain. Dallas lifted her off and carried her inside.

Men seated at the table playing cards stood up, scraping their chairs on the wooden floor. "She hurt?"

"Yeah, where can I put her?"

"There's a cot in the bedroom thar."

Dallas carried her through the main room while the others came stomping in, taking off their coats, exchanging greetings with the three men inside the house. They were more of the same rough lot that were becoming so familiar to Sandra: gunslingers, outlaws, range mavericks—trail trash, her father called them.

He put her down on a cot in the bedroom that opened onto the right side of the common area that was used as kitchen, parlor, and dining room. Tired as she was, she couldn't sleep. Dallas rubbed her back with horse liniment cut with butter. With her head on his arm, snuggled against his warm body, her last thought before sleep claimed her was that no one had *ever* been so good to her.

"Dallas, Dallas, wake up…"

Younger opened one red-rimmed eye and glared balefully at Pick Sitwell.

"There's a messenger here from the boss. Won't talk to anyone but you."

"All right," he growled, disengaging himself gently from the sleeping girl and coming easily to his feet. He pulled his boots on and ran his fingers through his disheveled black hair, moving purposefully now that he was awake.

The messenger was Slim Parker, a tall stringbean of a man Dallas had seen many times before in that role. Neither of them acknowledged the other. Dallas appeared at the door; the messenger started off walking, and Dallas fell in beside him. It was habit. They didn't need to appear casual here in the midst of Dallas' own camp, surrounded by his men.

"The boss wants you to come see him."

Dallas hid the angry reaction that came instinctively to him and shrugged. "I thought I already had my orders. I was going to drive the herd down to the pens so we could ship 'em."

"He said he wants to talk to you—alone. He didn't mention any other plan."

Dallas cursed to himself. It would take a day to get down there and a day to get back. "All right," he growled. "Get yourself a fresh hoss and grab a bite to eat. I'll be with you in a minute."

The sun was just coming up, turning the sky near the eastern horizon misty rose. Clouds were gold on the bottom, like the leaves of aspen trees on the canyon floor. Dallas found his second lieutenant, Cedar Longley, pulling on his pants.

Dallas respected Longley in a way he did few men. It was Cedar who had led Younger into this old Apache stronghold; Cedar who placed the lookouts. Longley, son of an old Indian agent, had been raised on Indian reservations till he was twenty. His father was present at the signing of the Guadalupe Hidalgo Treaty, which made the U.S. government responsible for keeping the border Indians under control, and Cedar could tell surprising stories about the Apache as the feudal robber barons of the Southwest. He had watched them take regular and ritualistic tribute from settlers who chose to buy their safe passage rather than fight for it. For fifty years the Apache controlled the passes and looked with contempt upon the white tillers of the soil who lived in their wattled stick houses, plastered with mud and roofed with sticks and branches in the style of the Indian and Mexican arbors.

Younger's tone conferred that respect now. "I gotta go back and see the boss."

"What for?"

"Don't know."

Longley's face was dark, his cool blue eyes speculative. "You think he's getting cold feet?" he asked.

"Could be. Things are getting tolerable warm in these parts, what with Cantrell and his riders harassing our men and making brags that are firing up the ranchers. Hell! We ain't stole half as many cattle in the last two months as we been used to, but loose talk is causing so much hell ranchers are exaggerating like crazy."

Longley frowned and stood up. "We ain't had a chance to talk, what with the girl being hurt and all, but I guess now's just as good a time. The boys ain't going to take it lightly if he's figuring on going straight and leaving us out in the cold."

Younger nodded. "I reckon the boys won't be alone. I'm not taking kindly to the idea either. Ain't no reason why we couldn't continue just like usual once we kill Cantrell."

Longley nodded. "We're of a mind, then," he said with satisfaction.

"Drive 'em to the pens jest like we planned. We'll ship this herd whether he likes it or not."

While a man readied his and the messenger's horses, Younger drank coffee and ate bacon and biscuits.

"Tell Sweetface for me," he said, swinging into the saddle.

"Sure thing, Dallas, and you tell him for us."

"You betcha."

CHAPTER FORTY-SEVEN

The sun was shrouded behind pale, cloudy vapors. The air was chill but dry and bracing. A horseman rode into Younger's mountain camp, the horse's hooves kicking up dust and eliciting angry shouts from men trying to shave along his path.

Cedar Longley, from his vantage point at the table, recognized the man as one of the sentries posted along the trail. He stood up. By the time the rider reached the main building he was on the porch with his hat on.

"Rider coming," the man yelled, jerking his horse to a halt. The animal stamped and pawed the ground, kicking dust into the air.

"Alone?"

"Yeah."

"How's he moving?"

"Real casual-like, but he seems to know right where he's going."

"What's he look like?"

"Packing two guns, slung low. Blond dude—looking relaxed as hell."

Cedar Longley grunted. Ward Cantrell—it could be no other. An uneasy vibration raced through his lean frame. Cantrell was here to meet Younger and the last three survivors of the original band who had participated in the raid on the Mexican family—Bass Wimer, Pick and Rand Sitwell. Bass was just stupid. He could be led anywhere by anyone, and once he got caught up in the excitement, he would do anything. Pick and Rand were just plain mean. The two raw-boned twins had probably enjoyed every second of it.

Longley had been an outlaw since he was twenty-one, but he had never raped or murdered women. He had the real gunman's intolerance for needless cruelty. He would kill, but only in self-defense. And like all gunmen he knew the names and faces of all the really dangerous men: King Fisher, Sam Bass, Dusty Denton, Dallas Younger, Lance Kincaid, Ward Cantrell, Ben Thompson, Bat Masterson, Clay Allison, Wyatt Earp, and Temple Houston. At least half of them were already dead. Cedar didn't know any old gunfighters. Even the best of them met their match sooner or later. He'd heard about Cantrell first-hand because a friend had ridden with the Jackson Hole Gang the same time Cantrell had. According to Cedar's friend, Cantrell had split the gang down the middle. He was a born leader and when he stood up to their chief over a deal he wouldn't be a party to, half the men backed him. They woulda seen the bloodiest shootout in history if Cantrell hadn't convinced him that he was fast enough to kill him and three of his men before any one of them got a shot off. He was backed by Dusty Denton and a dozen others almost as good. Denton was greased lightning on the draw too. Rumor had it he could put three holes in the Ace of Diamonds—never missing that big diamond—from twenty paces.

Longley expelled a heavy breath. "Let him come."

"I'll pass the word."

"Do that." Longley, a big, rangy, solid-looking man, was famous for his eyes. They were dark blue and shot daggers that effectively discouraged opposition. He was a Texan, like Younger and Texas Jack Jones, with the Texan's inbred sense of fair play. He wouldn't condone having a man like Cantrell shot from ambush any more than Younger would if he were there.

He went inside and strapped on his guns.

"Hey, boss, what's up?"

"I reckon Ward Cantrell's on his way in here."

"Well, hell! Stop him!" Pick Sitwell came to his feet, almost knocking the table over, spilling coffee everywhere. "He ain't got no right riding in here in broad daylight like he owns the damned place!"

"Won't hurt to ask him his business then, will it?"

Rand Sitwell left the room and came back with his own gun. "Reckon we know what he wants," he said grimly, tying the holster down with a slender rawhide around his right thigh.

Pick and Bass Wimer were already wearing their guns.

"How many men with him?" Rand asked.

"None."

That should have been reassuring, but somehow it had the opposite effect. Pick Sitwell paled two shades, leaving the freckles standing out like tiny cherries floating in milk.

"He's crazy riding in here alone. Ain't no way he can get out alive. We got forty men here."

"Maybe he ain't worried about getting out. Reckon he's just interested in paying a call on the men that killed his friends," Longley said significantly.

"I don't reckon I like your tone, Longley. We was following orders, same as anyone in this gang follows orders. Jest doing what we were told."

"Then you won't mind explaining that to Cantrell. He looks like the understandin' sort."

"Like hell he does! I saw him once in Cheyenne—the day he met and killed Mad Dog Masters. He only understands one thing and that is that he don't brook no opposition."

"Reckon you got a problem all right," Cedar drawled.

"What!" Pick growled, coming over to glare into Longley's face. "I got a problem? I thought we were in this together."

"I don't hold with killing women and kids—nor even old men waiting 'round to die. You pick your work and you pay the price. I'm a rustler, and I've been worse, but I got limits," Longley said quietly, inexorably.

"Well, ain't you something! All of a sudden, with one of the deadliest guns in the Territory riding in, you got scruples! Shit! You're scared— same as us!"

"I ain't denying that. I'm just warning you, the three of you are on your own."

"You yellow bastard!"

"Practical, maybe. He's got no business with me or any of the others."

Pick grabbed a chair and threw it at the wall, smashing it into a dozen pieces. "Bunch of fine friends you turn out to be." He faced the other five men in the room. "Y'all feel like this two-bit rustler here?"

Their silence spoke for them. They knew the raids on the honest ranchers, like the one on the Mendozas, were on a volunteer basis. Even among the hardest bunch of outlaws, most of them wouldn't participate in wiping out families. It spoke badly for this gang that twelve of the original fifty men had been willing to do it.

Ward had ridden hard the previous day and made up some of the twelve-hour lead Younger had on him. By the time the sun was up an hour he could see the rustler camp. A half-hour later he was there.

He rode slowly and casually, using the opportunity to observe the rustlers' hideout. It was cleverly hidden, comfortable and secure. If he hadn't been following fresh tracks, he wouldn't have found it. Fears that Denton would stumble into the camp and take on Younger's gang were permanently laid to rest.

Younger, or someone, must have had some army experience. The camp was laid out like a military encampment, with one main building and a string of tents straggling down the mountain. It was set in a ravine that branched off in four directions, like a well-planned rabbit hole—plenty of exits, but only one comfortable way to approach, and that well guarded. He had been aware of the sentries for the last five miles.

The house was old and weathered, and Ward guessed that that was where he would find Younger and his pack of killers. The thirty or so men who stepped away from their tents to watch his slow passage looked like run-of-the mill outlaws, little different from cowhands except that they lived by the gun now.

Ward saw signs that this was only a summer camp. First snow would find this bunch on the move, probably heading down into Sonora.

Riding slowly, he appraised every face along that tent-strewn route, recognizing some of them on sight. They were all of a breed not vastly different from himself. A couple of them nodded when his narrowed blue eyes caught theirs and held for an instant. He recognized three men from the Lincoln County range war, one from the Pine Tree outfit.

He passed the last tent and turned his attention to the weathered gray house and its occupants. When he reached the steps to the porch, he dismounted, dropping the reins.

No one came out, so he went up the steps, his hands brushing the gun on either thigh. Only the scrape of his boots sounded in the stillness. Even the birds had stopped singing, as if they too were anticipating danger. He stopped at the open door and pushed his Stetson back with his left hand.

There were nine men in the small cabin in sight and a possibility of more behind the two closed doors. He almost smiled at that. They must have me overrated, he thought ruefully. Nine men should be able to do the job.

Longley saw that flicker of amusement in the steady blue eyes and felt something of what Cantrell must be feeling now. He stepped forward slowly. No one was making any sudden moves. "You got business here, Cantrell?"

Ward nodded. "With the slime that killed the Mendoza family."

Boots scraped as men moved out of the way, leaving three men alone in the center of the room. Ward hid his surprise that it had been so easy to single them out. The two raw-boned redheads and the fat one with fresh bruises on his meaty face had ridden in the parade, but he wasn't sure he could have picked them out. Apparently no one was covering for the three, exposed by the move toward the far walls.

"I got business with them," he said. "And Younger."

"Younger ain't here."

Ward accepted that. If he were here, he'd be where the action was, not hiding in a bedroom. "He take the girl?"

"Naw, she's still sleeping." Longley nodded toward the room on the right.

His questions answered, Ward turned his attention back to the three he came for. "You want to do this outside?"

"We ain't going to fight you, Cantrell. I ain't no gunfighter."

"I didn't come here to *fight* you. I came to *kill* you. Don't matter that you don't fight back—can if you want to—it ain't a requirement of mine."

Pick sputtered. "You mean you'd just shoot us down like mad dogs."

Cantrell nodded, watching them coldly, no sign of mercy in those pitiless blue eyes. "Just like you handled the Mendozas," he said flatly.

Pick nodded. "All right," he said, expelling a heavy breath. "Outside, then." Cantrell would either have to back out or turn and walk out. If he turned...

Longley knew Pick too well to turn his back on him, but apparently Cantrell didn't. He turned; Pick and the others clawed for their guns. Cantrell's turn changed into a full circle, and somehow by the time he was facing them again, both guns were smoking. The explosions rolled one on another until only Cantrell was standing. The floor was littered with the three men he had come there to kill. The sharp, piercing smell of gunpowder was strong.

Cantrell crouched in a posture of readiness, his guns pointing now at the others. "Who's in charge here?"

Longley stepped forward. "Reckon I am."

"I'm taking over this outfit. You got any objections?"

Longley thought about that for a moment. Younger was already talking about moving on to greener pastures. He knew Cantrell's history. He was a good man to ride with. Planned his jobs carefully, executed them well, didn't kill people in the process; no one died in his train holdups.

Longley shook his head. "No objections from me, but maybe some from Younger when he gets back."

"Good." He looked at the others now. "Which one of you do I have to kill to make this stick?"

Texas Jack Jones was the first to break the spell. He stepped to the side and picked up his hat. "I ain't never been too partic'lar who I work for. I'll go tell the boys."

With his exit, the tension began to relax.

"When do you expect Younger back?"

"Two days at the soonest."

"Pass the word. We're moving out in two hours, with the herd you're holding in that blind canyon," Ward said tersely.

Cedar Longley looked askance. Cantrell was crazy. It was one thing to ride in there past forty armed men to kill three men he wanted, but another thing entirely to ride out as the leader of that gang. The man had more guts than good sense. Or he didn't give a damn what happened to him.

Longley shook his head slowly. His eyes were clear—respect mingled with disbelief. Reckon your cards are about dealt out. Cain't hardly wait to see how this turns out. Your life ain't worth a white chip as it is…Out loud he said, "Will do, chief."

Ward nodded and holstered his guns. He knew exactly how long that was good for—until Dallas Younger returned. And he knew that Cedar Longley knew it also.

"Is the girl all right?" Ward asked, starting toward the bedroom.

Longley nodded. "You taking that over too?"

"You have any objections?"

"None atall."

The train pulled into Phoenix at eight o'clock Friday morning. John King stood and picked up his satchel. He stopped beside the conductor.

"Which way to the jail?"

"Down that street. You can't miss it."

Sheriff Tatum was not a small man, but he felt small next to the massive black man who stopped beside where he was tacking up another wanted poster.

"You're the sheriff?" The voice had a cultured eastern accent that didn't look like it belonged on a big strapping black man with the battered face of a professional fighter.

"That's right," Tatum nodded.

The big Negro held out his enormous hand. "My name is John King. I'm from Dodge City."

Tatum looked at the hand, then at the man's eyes. He slowly held out his hand.

"Matthew Tatum." He'd never shaken hands with a Negro before.

He resisted the impulse to wipe his hand on his pant leg. "What can I do for you?"

"I'm looking for Ward Cantrell. You know where I can find him?"

A light dawned in Tatum's eyes. Now he knew why that face looked vaguely familiar. There had been a story about John King in one of those fancy eastern magazines. The man was a bounty hunter. He was the one who hounded the Shiner brothers until they killed themselves rather than keep running or be caught by King. The man was implacable.

"Everybody's looking for Ward Cantrell," he said heavily. "Half the town is out right now. If they find him first, maybe you can cut him down and take him back."

"What did he do?"

"I don't know that he *did* anything, but folks think he kidnapped a girl, murdered a wealthy rancher, and rustled some cows."

"How come you're not with the posse?"

"They got seventy men. That ain't a posse. It's a lynch mob. They don't need me," Tatum said flatly.

King nodded. "I'm staying at the hotel I noticed on the way here—the Bricewood West. I'd appreciate it if you'd let me know if you hear anything that would be helpful to me." He took out a fifty-dollar bill and stuffed it in Tatum's vest pocket.

Tatum pulled the neatly folded bill out and looked at it. That was a month's wages for him. He shook his head and gave the money back.

"You'll hear before I will," he said tiredly. "This town ain't got any secrets, especially about Cantrell."

John King thanked him and headed back toward the hotel.

Sheriff Tatum finished nailing up the posters and then got his jacket and walked over to see if Chane Kincaid was in his office.

CHAPTER FORTY-EIGHT

"What time is the boss going to meet me?" Dallas asked.

"Ten o'clock tonight—the usual place."

Younger and Slim Parker separated at the river. Younger rode into town alone just after sunset, stabled his horse, Maverick, and walked to the Red Eye Saloon to kill time and listen to the talk. Friday nights were lively. There was the usual stir when he entered. He had admirers and those who carried grudges, but there were few men who would publicly denounce him—he had survived too many gunfights for that.

The gossip was about Cantrell: his challenge to rustler gangs, his kidnapping of Sandra McCormick, and how mad everyone was because the governor hadn't appointed a special cadre of rangers to hunt him down. Whole ranches had stopped normal operations to join unofficial posses. Everyone was outraged. If they caught him, they would hang him first and ask questions later. Or shoot on sight. Younger grinned at that—his sentiments exactly, except in his case it was a necessity.

Younger ordered a steak and sat down at a table alone with his back to the wall so he could watch both entrances. He was halfway through the steak, listening idly to the talk around him, enjoying the gaiety and the stimulation a crowd provided, when a pretty, young dark-haired girl approached his table.

"Howdy," she said tentatively.

"Howdy yourself," he replied, grinning appreciatively.

She was young and fresh-looking, not brassy or belligerent like some of the older women were.

"You in the mood to buy me a drink?"

"Set yourself down and we'll see." He nodded to the bartender for two drinks and leaned back, grinning. "Don't recollect seeing you here before."

"I ain't been here long—about a week." Her eyes roved over him, lingering on his broad, furry chest. "You sure are a good-looking dude," she said admiringly.

"You like 'em big and rough, do you, sweet thing?"

She giggled and tossed her hair. "My name's Peggy. What's yours?"

"Dallas Younger."

Her eyes widened. She cocked her head at him. "You one of those dangerous Texans I been hearing so danged much about?"

"Who you been hearing about?" he countered.

"Oh, you and Ward Cantrell."

"Cantrell ain't no Texan. He's no Texan—none atall!"

"How come you say that?"

"I know a phony Texas accent when I hear one, sweet thing. He can drop it and does too damned often for it to be real."

"He's a phony gunfighter, then?"

Dallas shook his head. "I didn't say that either. The men he's killed are just as dead. I reckon he's a gunfighter all right—he just ain't from Texas."

"I thought all the really dangerous men was from Texas," she laughed.

"That's 'cause those damned Texas rangers hound a man until he has to leave or hang. You didn't sit down here to listen to my life story, did you, sweet thing?"

"I sat down here to do whatever you wanted me to. If you want to talk"—she shrugged—"well, that's fine by me," she said, smiling archly.

"And if I want to go upstairs?"

She laughed breathlessly, and he tossed a coin on the table and took her arm.

Peggy enjoyed Dallas Younger thoroughly. He was exactly what he appeared: a simple man who took his pleasures when and where he found them. No fancy stuff for him. His loving was as straightforward as he was.

At nine-thirty, Dallas disengaged himself and dressed.

"You don't forget me, Dallas, honey," she said, fingering the twenty-dollar gold piece he had tossed onto the bed. "Next time you're in town ask for Peggy, you hear?"

"Right, sweet thing."

Younger sauntered through the saloon, waving and nodding to acquaintances. He left the noisy saloon, but the raucous sounds of laughter, piano music, and loud talk followed him halfway to the livery stable where he had left Maverick.

The stable boy was asleep or gone. Younger walked through the big barn, lit now by one kerosene lamp hanging from a support post, to the stall where his horse waited.

"Howdy, Maverick. You enjoy that grain, did you?" He reached for the saddle that was draped over the gate, and just as he did, a noise behind him, like the crunch of straw underfoot, brought his senses surging alert. He threw himself sideways, using the momentum of the saddle swinging down to help. He fell, rolled, came up with his gun in his hand, only to hear the sound of footsteps running into the dark alley.

He holstered his gun, cursing himself for not getting a look at his would-be assailant. He took the lamp off the post and looked around the barn floor for footprints, hoping he would recognize some peculiarity. But the straw that had probably saved his life didn't provide footprints. A gleam of metal led him to a buck knife half-hidden by straw. He picked it up, tested the blade, and flinched when its razor-sharp edge nicked his thumb. Probably the same knife that had killed Powers. He stuck it in his boot, saddled Maverick, and led the horse outside before he mounted him.

Summers was waiting for him beside the old line shack. "You're late," he said testily.

"Had a little problem."

"Anything serious?"

"Naw. What's up?" Dallas demanded.

"Slight change of plans. We aren't going to be moving cattle over the Texas and Pacific anymore. Too risky now. I want you to drive this herd to El Paso and ship them on Crocker's line."

"El Paso! That's eight hundred miles."

"I know how far it is," Summers said caustically. "Do you have a better idea?"

"We're rustlers, not drovers. Mexico's closer if you don't care what kind of price you get for them."

"Mexico's fine. I'm through with rustling. When this is over, scatter the gang."

"What if they don't want to be scattered? We've had a pretty comfortable set-up here for a long time," Dallas said.

"Then kill them! I don't care how you do it—just do it!" he said vehemently, his pale face reflecting his intensity.

Dallas kept his face impassive, but he was remembering that Powers had been killed when he was no longer useful. Now that Summers was marrying the Powers girl, he didn't need the gang anymore—or Dallas. Dallas started to point this out to Summers, but the sound of a rider approaching at a rapid rate brought both their heads around.

"Did anyone know you were coming here?" Summers demanded, his eyes like black pearls in the moonlight.

"Only Parker—he told me to be here."

"I can't afford to be seen with you," Summers said angrily. He moved into the abandoned line shack, and Younger stepped away from the door and moved to stand in the shadow of the building. The rider was only Parker, but he looked agitated, riding the horse almost into the side of the shack before he could stop him.

"Whoa, dammit, whoa!" he shouted, swinging down. "Dallas, it's me, Slim!"

Younger stepped around the corner, putting his gun away. "What you all lathered up about?"

"Hell to pay up at the camp! Texas Jack sent a rider down to let you know what happened. Smoky said Cantrell rode up there and killed three men: Rand and Pick Sitwell and Bass Wimer. He's looking for you, Dallas. And he's taken over the gang. They're driving the cattle down to the pens starting first thing after Cantrell got there. Smoky almost killed a hoss getting here! I found you as fast as I could," he panted, sagging against the wall.

"That worthless two-bit bunch of bastards!" Summers swore, coming out of the building. "Forty goddamned men up there and they let him ride in, kill three of their friends, and then start giving orders! I don't want those cattle at the pens! I want those pens destroyed! Not a trace!" he said vehemently.

"That don't solve our immediate problem," Dallas drawled, watching Summers.

"Go on," Summers said grimly.

"Looks like Cantrell has decided to be your new partner—cutting me out. Don't look like he wants to be told to take those cows and stuff 'em."

Summers controlled his fury with an effort. "If you have an idea, now is the time for it," he said grimly.

Dallas grinned. Summers was an arrogant bastard. He was enjoying seeing him sweat. "Cantrell is in one hell of a precarious spot. He's got almost forty men behind him, driving five hundred head of stolen cattle, and he's all alone. Soon as I show up—don't matter what he's doing—those men are mine. I take him on, and it's open season on Cantrell. He's a dead man."

"Are you absolutely sure of that?"

"Hell, yes, I'm sure. They're a good ole bunch of boys, but there ain't a leader in the lot. I step back into the picture, and they'll follow me."

"I'm going with you. I want to be sure Cantrell is dead. No slip-ups this time."

Younger raised one eyebrow, but he resisted the urge to remind Summers that he was the one who made the mistake that put Cantrell on their backs in the first place. "When d'yuh want me to brace Cantrell?"

"Soon as possible. I want this behind me. I'm getting married in a few days, and I want that bastard dead! I'm tired of him messing around in my business."

"We can cut 'em off about sunset tomorrow, before they move out of the brakes, if we leave first thing tomorrow morning."

"All right, I'll meet you outside of town at six o'clock in the morning."

Friday night and not even Tim was around to help her fight off the doldrums. Monday the creamy white lace Jennifer had ordered would arrive and they could start work on the wedding gown, but now…

Jennifer came into the parlor where Leslie was putting the finishing touches on a sketch of the mountains to the north.

"Where's Tim tonight?" She had just come downstairs from tucking the children into their beds. Jennie had changed drastically in the last week. Her lovely purple eyes were haunted, forlorn, filled with worry, pain, fear. She had faint blue circles under her eyes, like bruises. It was almost physically painful for Leslie to look at her. She felt embarrassed, as if she were prying into family secrets.

Jennifer was able to hide her pain for brief social intervals, but it came back quickly, stronger than before, as if the poor thing were crumbling under the strain.

Leslie saw this as proof that Cantrell had lied about his relationship with Jennie. Had he also lied about how he fell into outlawry? Not that it mattered any longer. She was finished with him, but she hated being taken in by a cheat.

"Tim had a business meeting. He left at eight-thirty. He said if we were up, he would stop afterward."

Jennie sighed and slipped into a chair, depression showing in the uncharacteristic lethargy that seemed to have seeped into her very bones. "I don't see how you do it," she sighed. "Every time I look at you you're doing another painting, or finishing a sketch. Don't you ever get moody?"

Leslie grimaced. "Moodiness is a luxury. People with few interests are moody. Those of us with work we love experience different degrees of tiredness." She stifled the urge to remind Jennie that she used to be one of the busy ones, before her obsession with Cantrell.

"I guess you'll be waiting up for Tim then. Would you like to play gin rummy? Chane won't be back until almost eleven. He had another meeting with the governor about the rustlers. I know I'll never be able to sleep," she said nervously.

"I'd love to play rummy," she lied. She would do anything to help Jennie. She owed her so much, both her and Chane. In truth, she had lost interest in painting as well. But she continued out of desperation. It was easy to hide behind her work. There were times when she did enjoy it. There were other times when she took her rage out on the canvas. She worked because not to work was unthinkable, because she knew that this too would pass, and when it did, if she had worked hard, she would have something besides her scars to show for it.

They moved to the table. Jennifer brought out the cards and shuffled them. She dealt each of them ten cards and turned a ten of clubs face up. "You go first," Jennifer said.

They arranged their hands, and Leslie drew a card from the stack, pretending to concentrate. "Any news about Cantrell?" she asked casually.

Jennifer looked thoroughly miserable. Her hand trembled as she took a card. "Only bad news so far. Sam McCormick has increased the reward. He wants Ward tarred and feathered *before* they hang him," she said bitterly.

"Why is he so sure Ward took her? She's a big girl. She could have just run away." Since leaving Cantrell in a jealous fury, she had thought of six ways he could have gotten Sandra's locket.

"I guess because she chased him so. She was so infatuated with Ward. Anyone could tell."

"She looked just as infatuated with Dallas Younger to me," Leslie said defensively. She had gone over that scene at the hotel in Buckeye a thousand times. She watched Ward's reaction over and over, and she still could not be sure he had taken Sandra. Wouldn't he have looked guilty? Wouldn't he have tried to hide Sandra's necklace? Unless he hadn't expected her to follow him there—and of course he hadn't. If he *was* innocent, where did he get the scratches? She always came back to that.

Jennifer's lips tightened into an angry line. "I know it wasn't Ward. I've known him too long. He's not a sneak thief. If he wanted a woman, he would announce it to the world."

Leslie lowered her eyes, embarrassed and miserable for her friend. Had Jennie forgotten that Cantrell had kidnapped her?

Jennie saw Leslie's expression and stopped. "You think me batty, don't you?"

"No, of course not," she said gently, biting back the urge to say, "But I don't see how you can be so sure he's innocent."

"He had a good reason for taking you," Jennie said, as if reading her mind. "Those men killed four people he loved!"

"What?"

Jennie stopped, alarmed that she had blurted a secret they had agreed needed to be kept until this business was settled. "I guess there's no help for it now." She sighed and told her the story of the Mendoza family's murder.

"I never knew..." Leslie whispered when Jennie, eyes brimming with tears, ended her recital. "He never told me."

Jennie patted Leslie's hand. "To retell it is to relive it. He told Chane because he had no choice. They were going to hang him."

Leslie bit her tongue to keep from replying. She was moved to tears by the story of the Mendoza family, but that did not change the major issue between the two of them. She could forgive many things, but infidelity was not one of them. It was an unforgivable crime between a man and a woman. She was immovable in that regard. Ward Cantrell could be champion to any number of Mendoza families, honest in every other respect, but if he could make love to another woman after that day at Aravaipa Canyon...

Confused and frustrated, Leslie covered her face with her hands. "Why can't he just stay away from women?" She didn't realize she had spoken aloud until she heard Jennie.

"She chased him!" Jennifer said, instantly angry. "You won't see too many men who toss aside beautiful women who throw themselves at their feet. Most men will allow a woman to make as big a fool as she wants of herself." Jennifer laughed suddenly, a brittle, tinkly sound that bordered on hysteria. "You'll think me foolish," she said, new tears welling in her eyes, "but I really think Ward is in love with you."

Lime-green eyes widened, and the last vestige of color drained out of Leslie's cheeks.

"Oh," Jennifer said, "I know he isn't like Tim, always showering you with attention, flattery, and gifts, but I could see the reaction in him the second he saw you, or someone mentioned your name. I'm equally sure he was careful not to let you know, but he can hide very little from me. I've known him too long. He acted very much like Chane did when we were in love but our problems were keeping us apart."

Jennie sighed, responding to the implacable look on Leslie's face. "I'm sorry. It's just that I am so worn out from worrying about him. It seems I've worried about him so damned long." Tears began to stream down her cheeks, and she buckled forward, covering her eyes with her trembling hands.

Alarmed, Leslie moved around the table and put her arms around her. "There, there," she whispered, feeling helpless.

Jennie huddled against Leslie's shoulder, sobbing. After a time, the gasps turned into sniffs and then into shuddering indrawn breaths. At last, she raised her head and smiled weakly. "I know he didn't take her."

Contrarily, Leslie remembered his response when she asked him if her lovemaking had been satisfactory: that husky-quiet "very" and the look in his suddenly opaque blue eyes, as if he were expecting a twist of the knife. Well, she hadn't disappointed him, had she?

Leslie was suddenly trembling. She stood up. "I'm tired. I think I'll take a bath and go to bed, if you don't mind."

"Of course, dear. We both need rest. There won't be much time next week with shopping and fittings and then the wedding and honeymoon, will there?"

Unfortunately sleep did not come. At eleven-thirty she finally got out of bed, wrapped a blue silk dressing robe around her, and started down the stairs only to be stopped by masculine voices coming from the first floor, from the direction of the library. She was at the top of the stairs. The library door opened, and she stepped back into the shadows. She was in no mood to see anyone now.

Chane and Tim stopped in the entry hall.

"When will you be leaving for Tucson?" Chane asked.

"Early. My business should be completed in two or three days and I'll catch the first train back."

"Don't rush. These family things come up. Take your time. You've earned a vacation."

"Thank you, Mr. Kincaid. I really appreciate all you've done for me."

"Nonsense. You work hard. I'm going to hate losing you."

"Well, maybe we can still be useful to each other, even after I take over the ranch."

"I'm sure we can be. Then you'll be a customer, if all goes well."

Tim laughed. "Of course. I forgot that." Then his voice sobered. "Unless Cantrell has already stolen all my cattle," he said grimly.

Chane, a scowl darkening his handsome face, held out his hand.

"You'll tell Leslie for me, won't you?" Tim asked.

"Of course. Have a good trip. Give your aunt our regards."

"Thank you, sir."

The front door closed, and Leslie slipped back into her bedroom, the urge for a glass of milk forgotten. Tim was going away on business—a family problem. Relief swept over her. She had no problem going to sleep after that.

CHAPTER FORTY-NINE

Leslie woke long before dawn. She lay quietly, listening to the sounds of birds coming awake. Her window was half-open and she shivered slightly, wondering if the cold had awakened her. The sky was a luminous gray, becoming lighter in a cloudless dawn. Yesterday's clouds, which had looked so threatening, were gone, leaving the air crisp and fresh. She felt good, like a weight had been lifted off her shoulders. She stretched and rolled around in the bed, enjoying the freedom and the delicious tingle of good health. Too bad her head was still so confused.

Maybe a ride would straighten that out. It had worked before. She got out of bed and dressed in a simple buckskin skirt that Jennie had given her for riding astride—it had been her sister-in-law's. Apparently Angie didn't cotton to all those fancy riding habits most women wore. With a pale green cambric blouse and the cashmere coat—why not? No one would see her anyway. Mrs. Lillian was in the kitchen. She stopped for muffins and bacon, even stuffing some in her pockets for later.

"Tell Mrs. Kincaid I'm going for a ride. I'll be back before lunch."

"You be careful, dear. Remember what happened to that other young lady."

Leslie smiled. I should be so lucky, she thought.

"I'll be fine. Mr. Kincaid insists I take one of the guns from the stable with me. Don't worry. He taught me how to shoot it."

Leslie chose the big white Arabian again because she liked his gait and he was in a stall instead of loose in the corral.

Saddled up, with the gun in a holster hanging from the pommel, she headed north. Even with Dallas Younger no longer around—he was gone, Tim said, probably in New Mexico or Nevada looking for work—she still wouldn't ride west toward her ranch. She enjoyed riding toward the mountains. It gave her a special sense of freedom, and today she was glad to be alone.

The sky turned clear blue and it was warm enough so that she rolled the coat up and put it behind her saddle. Two hours of the big horse's rhythmic stride and her absorption in the ride burned away her strange mood.

She turned the horse back toward Phoenix about to kick him into a run when she saw a tiny speck between her and the distant town. She stopped, leaning forward to stroke the horse's sleek, wet neck.

She had good eyes, but the riders, if the speck was riders, were too far away: just a tiny cloud of dark vapor, but something flashed a warning at her.

"You be careful, dear. Remember what happened to that other young lady." She looked for cover and found it less than a hundred feet away. There was probably no need for this but...

She stifled her doubts. It would cost nothing but a little time to be careful. She waited a half hour before they came into sight. Recognizing them, she stiffened in surprise and rushed to cover her horse's mouth so he wouldn't snort and draw attention to her.

Dallas Younger and Tim Summers! What an unlikely duo! Especially since Tim had told Chane he was going to Tucson about family problems! Tucson was the other direction.

Her heart was pounding, a heavy ache in her chest. She was afraid, stunned, but she didn't know why she should be. Tim could have a perfectly reasonable excuse for riding north into the mountains with Dallas Younger.

Could she follow them and find out what they were up to? She waited until they passed out of sight, and followed at a pace calculated to keep her well behind them. The tracks were plain in the soft, sandy loam. It should be no problem to follow them as long as they didn't see her.

By sundown the cattle, stretching back as far as Ward could see, had begun to settle down to the drive. It would take time before they adjusted fully, and the drive—four days—would be over before they made it. Cedar Longley was in charge. He was the closest thing this bunch had to a trailwise drover who knew where they were going.

Ward didn't stay in one position long. He rode lead and then drag and then rode ahead to see if the cook had found a suitable place to stop for the night. The heavily laden chuckwagon was already camped.

Dinner was simmering over the cook fires and Sandra lay on a pallet under a tree with blankets pulled up under her chin. When she saw Ward she came up into a sitting position.

"You can't hold me prisoner forever," she said angrily.

Ward dismounted and poured himself a cup of coffee. "I don't intend to. I'm taking you home, where you belong." He hunkered down between his horse and the campfire.

"I don't *belong* at home! I belong with Dallas. He isn't anything like you said. He's nice, and he loves me."

"After you explain to your father that I didn't kidnap you, you can go anywhere you want, with anyone you please," he said flatly.

"That's all you care about, isn't it? That's all you ever cared about! You never cared about me—just your own skin!"

Ward grinned. "It has been on my mind."

"Don't you dare laugh at me!" she yelled, coming to her feet. "You won't think this is funny when Dallas gets back! He'll kill you! He's not going to let you get away with this! Even if you did kill him, which you can't, 'cause you're not good enough, the others would kill you."

"Got it all figured out, don't you, Trinket?" he asked, still grinning.

"You're crazy. You can't possibly survive this! Why aren't you worried? Why don't you just ride away before Dallas comes back, and save yourself. I don't really want to see you die," she said, her eyes dropping away from his.

"I am worried," he said evenly. "I think you've got it figured right."

"Then why are you smiling?"

"Why not?" He shrugged. He stood up, reached into his saddlebags, and tossed her the necklace he was carrying for her. She frowned at him, fingering the chill necklace until a light dawned in her eyes. He was giving it back so she could give it to someone who would survive her. Someone who would be around to remember her. But now that Dallas loved her she no longer felt like she was going to die. She felt invincible.

Slowly, still looking into Cantrell's eyes, she fastened the necklace around her throat. They didn't talk anymore. Ward finished his coffee and rode back to rejoin his herd.

The sun had just slipped beneath the horizon, and the sky was ablaze with gold, red, and purple clouds when Dallas Younger spotted the herd milling around as the riders tried to drive them into a blind canyon to hold them overnight.

"Whoa," Dallas said softly. "Whoa, Maverick."

"So, we finally come face to face with Cantrell," Summers said, a feral light glittering in his black eyes.

"No holds barred," Dallas said grimly, checking his gun. He spun the cylinder, broke it, and added one bullet where he usually carried only five. It was a safety precaution to keep an empty chamber under the hammer when he wasn't expecting trouble.

"What are you going to do?" Tim asked.

"Wait till they settle them steers down and most of 'em are around the cookfires eatin'. I reckon that'll be as good a time as any to face him."

"Your men behind him and you in front of him." Summers grinned with satisfaction. Younger was a better man than he had thought. Too bad he didn't need him any longer. He chuckled. "Too bad I can't watch firsthand."

"I thought you were riding in with me," Dallas said, a frown pulling his straight black brows down.

"You know I can't afford to have that many people know who I am," he said testily, looking at Younger as if he weren't too bright.

Dallas Younger's cool dark eyes swept over him. "What did ya come along for?"

"To make sure Cantrell is dead. I told you that once, and I don't like repeating myself," Tim said, his tone harsh, cutting.

Dallas grunted to himself, thinking, or to finish me off if I survive killing Cantrell? Ever since Powers's death he had been thinking like that. Last night when someone had tried to cut his throat—the same way Powers died—his suspicions had multiplied.

Since Cantrell had killed every member of Summers's special troops, only Slim Parker and he knew who the real head of the gang was. It would be no problem for Summers to get rid of the trusting Parker. With himself and Parker dead, Summers would be in the clear for good. No one could tie the murders or the rustling back to him. He could marry Leslie Powers next Saturday and be a rich and respectable man.

Dallas settled down to wait for the right time. Dusk came, the sky turned smoky gray, and the riders wandered in one by one to the cookfires that burned like three beacons in the distance.

Finally Dallas stood up and mounted his horse. Summers maintained his stance by the oak tree he was leaning against.

"Mount up," Dallas said tersely.

"What did you say?" Summers shot him an incredulous look, his pale face mirroring the disruption Younger's insolent command caused in him.

"I said mount up. I'm taking you with me. If you're worried about your reputation, you can go in as my prisoner. No one will know except me that you're not."

"This is ludicrous! You don't need me," he protested, fighting for control. He was furious, but this was not the time to vent that fury. He would settle with Younger later—after the man killed Cantrell.

"Mount up," Dallas said softly, inexorably, drawing his gun smoothly to aim it at Summers's chest.

Tim hid his venom behind his usual calm mask as he strode to his horse. He mounted. They rode boldly down the incline into the camp. There was still enough light so that one of the men, looking up from his bowl of beans, yelled: "Hey, it's the boss!"

Dallas heard Sweetface give a glad cry, and grinned before he settled down to business. He singled out Cantrell and decided how he was going to proceed.

No one made a move to slow their progress. Summers rode in front like a hostage. There was complete silence when they stopped beside the cookfire Cantrell stood in front of.

With the fire between them, Younger and Cantrell faced each other.

"Welcome back," Cantrell said quietly.

Younger trained the gun on Cantrell's broad chest and grinned. "It's good to be back." Then, without taking his eyes off Ward, he said, "Hey Cedar, you here?"

"Over here, boss."

"Good. I want you to take all the boys and get that herd moving again."

"What?" Tim asked incredulously, turning on Younger.

"You better learn to keep quiet," Dallas growled.

"What do you think you're doing?" Summers asked vehemently, ignoring Dallas's warning.

"The boys are going to drive those steers to the railroad so I can settle my business here and join them," he said coolly.

Cedar Longley looked at Dallas, saw that he meant what he said, and shouted an order for the men to get moving. There was a scramble of activity, some grumbles about the change, as men put down their bowls and coffee cups and began to run for the remuda and their horses.

Sandra came forward from the shadows. "Dallas, honey, I'm staying with you, aren't I?"

Dallas frowned. He had forgotten her momentarily. "I reckon," he said finally. "Don't move, though. Stay outta my way." She was behind Cantrell, between him and the chuckwagon but far enough to Cantrell's right so she was out of the line of fire. "Summers, go stand by Cantrell so I can keep an eye on both of you without straining too much."

Tight-lipped with fury, Tim complied. They waited like that while Longley and the others saddled up and moved out to start the cattle moving again. The cook started to move the wagon, but Dallas told him to leave it. He nodded and ran to find himself a horse. Soon they were gone, leaving Tim, Sandra, and Cantrell waiting silently across the fire from Younger, waiting for him to make his move.

CHAPTER FIFTY

Ward turned and grinned at Summers. "You can relax now. No one can hear you anymore."

"What do you mean by that?" Summers asked, contempt showing in the oily glitter of his black eyes.

"You're Younger's boss. It was a good ploy, but no longer necessary. I knew two days ago. I just didn't realize I knew until you Came riding in here."

"How did you know?"

"You're the one who had something to gain by killing Powers and framing me, and you were the one in Kincaid's office with the pull to cover your tracks."

"Too bad you found out too late, isn't it, Mr. Cantrell?"

Ward shrugged. "Better late than never."

"Not in your case," Tim said, his voice taut with fury. He turned to Younger. "Kill him," he snarled.

"Not until you tell him I didn't lead that raid on the Mendozas," Dallas said.

"What the hell difference can that make to a dead man?" Summers demanded angrily.

"It makes a tolerable difference to me, Summers," Dallas drawled. "I don't go around killing helpless women and kids. I got my pride. It happens to be important to me."

"Shit!" Summers sneered. "You're a killer. What difference could three or four more make to you?"

"I don't reckon you savvy gunfighters, Summers. I ain't never killed an unarmed man," Dallas said stubbornly.

"He's helpless. That's as good as being unarmed," Summers sneered, pointing at Cantrell.

"I ain't killed him yet," Dallas said significantly.

"Well, what the hell are you waiting for?" Summers snapped.

"For them to get good and gone," he said, nodding toward his riders. "Or did you forget, we're still protecting your image? Might as well have a cup of coffee. We'll be here a spell."

Ward backed up slowly and leaned against the chuckwagon. All these weeks he was after the wrong man. Dallas Younger was exactly what he appeared to be: a thoughtless ruffian and a gunfighter-turned-rustler, but not a murderer. He should have known. Summers had left clues. He hadn't seen them because he was thinking of him as Leslie's lover. That was reason enough to hate him; apparently it clouded his mind as well.

In his mind's eye he saw Leslie, slim, proud, defiant. *As Tim's wife I will have everything I need.* She was unaware of her lover's complicity. He knew that without question. Leslie Powers could not condone dishonesty in anyone associated with herself. She was a victim like the others.

"Hey, Trinket. Who took you to the Powers spread?"

Sandra's eyes widened in surprise at being addressed. She looked mesmerized by events. "Why, he did," she said, pointing to Summers.

Ward laughed. "I guess Summers is going to have to see to it that none of us gets away from here alive."

"Don't listen to him, Dallas. He's trying to confuse you," Tim said, shooting a reassuring look at Younger.

The herd was moving now. Conversation stopped. The rumble of hundreds of steers running was like thunder, loud and continuous, moving closer. They were almost a half-mile away, but sound traveled far in the clear mountain air.

Leslie stopped at the foot of the hill, ready to turn back. Dusk had come too soon and she lost their trail. Even by continuing in a straight line, she didn't find them. She felt frustration and anger at herself for staying too far back. If she weren't so timid...

She turned the horse, unwilling to continue the search. A low rumble, like distant thunder, stopped her. What on earth? She turned the horse and forced it to climb the hill. She could see from there if it wasn't already too dark.

The hill was little more than a hump between mountains, but once she gained the uppermost hummock she saw a black mass of cattle, shaped like a triangle, moving slowly, at a safe distance. In the foreground, a covered wagon stood tall and ghostly pale beside three fires. She recognized Sandra, Tim, and Younger, but cursed the encroaching dusk, wondering if that lean tawny-haired figure beside the fire could possibly be Cantrell.

There was a sudden urgency in her. She had to know the meaning of this bizarre meeting. She spurred her horse and rode boldly down the hill. The wagon was at least two hundred yards away. They couldn't hear one horse over that growing rumble. She rode within fifty yards of the wagon, then dismounted, remembering to take the gun. Leaving her horse with reins dragging, she walked the rest of the distance, to come up from behind the wagon.

She thanked the noise of the herd for covering her clumsy attempts to be stealthy. She was panting by the time she reached the tall covered wagon Kincaid had called a Conestoga.

She took a few seconds to catch her breath and bring the gun up into position. Then she peeked over the seat. At first all she saw was Dallas Younger with a gun, facing her. She moved slowly to the other end of the wagon, slipped around to the front, and peered over the edge of the low wagon bed. This time she saw Ward, Sandra, and Tim. Sandra was facing her, wearing the necklace she had admired at the dance, the same one she found on the vanity in Ward's room in Buckeye.

She stepped back, trying to still the sudden pounding of her heart. Ward Cantrell *had* run off with Sandra! What a monumental liar he was! Or an excellent evader. She hadn't asked. He had pretended innocence and she had fallen for it. Fool! Idiot! Now Younger was probably going to kill them—even Tim. Poor Tim. Of all the people who might deserve to die violently he certainly was not one of them. He was gentle, dull, and boring—the perfect administrator and bookkeeper.

Leslie leaned against the wagon, trying to get control of her pounding heart and shaking hands. She *had* to save them. Before she lost her nerve, she dragged in a ragged breath, lifted her chin, and stepped around the side of the wagon.

"Drop your gun, Mr. Younger," she said firmly, both hands gripping the gun as hard as she could to keep from trembling.

CHAPTER FIFTY-ONE

"Drop it! Or I shoot!"

Dallas Younger considered the alternatives. If he turned toward her Cantrell would draw. If he shot Cantrell she would shoot him. Could she hit him at twenty paces? She sure lord looked like she thought she could.

He dropped the gun into the dust at his feet.

"Tim, get his gun!" Leslie yelled, moving away from the wagon so she could cover the others.

Summers moved swiftly to comply. When he had Younger's gun in his hand he waved it at Younger. "Get over there with the others," he said tersely. He motioned Leslie to his side, drew her trembling body against him with his free arm and gave her a hug. "Thanks, darling, you just saved my life," he said gratefully.

"What are we going to do now?" she asked, turning in his embrace to face the three in front of the wagon.

Summers considered that for a moment in silence, reassuring her with the warmth and pressure of his body. He would kill all three of them, but he mustn't let her see it happen. She was idealistic and trusting now, but if she thought him a rustler and murderer, her stupid ideals would turn her against him. She must keep thinking of him as a model of perfection—at least until after the wedding.

"Leslie, darling, I want you to go for help."

"I can't leave you here…with them," she protested.

"Darling, it's necessary. I can take care of everything now." He gestured with the gun at Cantrell, and Leslie dared to look at him for the first time. "Throw down your guns, Cantrell. Do it!" he said vehemently, with barely controlled viciousness. "Do it or I'll drop you where you stand!"

In the firelight Ward's eyes were in shadow, but Leslie saw the flexing of smooth muscles in his cheek as his left hand unbuckled the gunbelt at his narrow hips. Even knowing all she did about him, the life force in him—so vital and commanding, so resolutely masculine—urged her toward him. She shuddered at her own weakness. His eyes were probably spitting hate at her. Thank goodness she couldn't see them!

"Hey, Dallas," Ward drawled, "how long do you think he'll wait to kill us after she leaves?"

"Reckon about five minutes," Dallas said, "until she gets out of earshot."

Summers felt Leslie stiffen in his arms and cursed savagely to himself, That smart-aleck bastard!

"Don't listen to them, darling. They think all men are as vile and corrupt as they are," he said smoothly.

"You aren't going to kill them, are you?" she asked, searching his face for any sign.

"Of course not. I'll hold them here until help comes. But you must go, darling. I'm counting on you to bring help."

"I lost my horse. I don't know if I can find it again," she said, stalling for time.

"Take mine."

Reluctantly, Leslie walked to his horse and mounted, still holding the gun she had forgotten she had. She rode up beside Tim, he smiled to reassure her, and she slowly walked the horse around the end of the big Conestoga.

Summers heard the horse break into a gallop and breathed a sigh of relief. As obedient as she was beautiful. A few more minutes to give her time to get out of earshot and then he could kill them and end his problems forever.

The rumble of the herd diminished to a low roar. They had stayed a quarter-mile away at the nearest point. Now the bawl and moan of the cattle was almost gone. None of the others knew him as Younger's boss—only these three.

Younger could tell by the oily glitter of Summers's eyes that he was almost ready. Younger had faced at least as many men over a gun as Cantrell. He shot a look at Ward and saw that he knew too.

"Hey, Cantrell, if I rush him, do you think you can drag one of those guns up in time to kill the bastard before he kills my baby?"

Summers laughed softly. "Don't waste your time. I'll shoot Cantrell first, then drop you like a pole-axed steer. You may be big as a bull, but you can't survive a bullet through the forehead."

Dallas shrugged. "Reckon he's got us dead to rights."

"Looks like it," Cantrell drawled.

"Where the hell did you learn to sound like a Texan?" Dallas asked suddenly.

"I studied a little French in school," he said, grinning. "Anyone who can learn a French accent can master a Texas drawl."

"I'll be damned."

Summers sneered. "You two going to hell as friends?"

"You ready to send us?" Ward asked. "You think Leslie is far enough away by now so she'll never know? What are you going to tell her, anyway?"

"That you tried to rush me, of course."

"How are you going to explain killing Trinket?"

"A stray bullet," Tim said smoothly. "A terrible, tragic accident."

Sandra began to whimper and moved closer behind Younger. "That's okay, Sweetface. He's gotta go through me first," Dallas drawled.

Summers sneered. "Now aren't you gallant? I'm going to shoot Cantrell first. I've been waiting a long time for this." He aimed the gun at Ward's broad chest and began to squeeze the trigger slowly. There was a look of triumph in his cold black eyes. His lips lifted in a smile.

"Say good-bye, Cantrell."

Ward dived for his gun. Dallas charged toward Summers. There was a crash of gunfire just as Ward's hand reached the smooth handle of the Colt, and he knew he was too late, but strangely he felt no pain.

He continued the motion, came up into a crouch, ready to fire. Summers toppled forward as if he had broken in two at the middle. Younger stopped, as startled as Ward.

They both turned at the same time and saw Leslie, her face pale and glowing, her eyes wide and staring, before she crumpled forward in a dead faint.

Ward walked over and turned Summers with a kick of his booted foot. With the gun trained on Younger now, he knelt and felt Summers's throat for a pulse. Finding none, he took Younger's gun out of the dead man's hand and stuck it under his belt. He slowly straightened, facing Dallas.

Dallas Younger took a deep breath. He and Cantrell had been working up to this meeting for a long time. He kissed the girl and put her away from him. It was time to die, and he didn't relish waiting around for it.

"Cantrell," he said softly, contemptuously, "you know if I was holding that gun, you'd be dead by now."

Ward grinned. "Well, you're not holding the gun, are you, Dallas?" he asked softly.

"What's the matter. Cantrell? You too yellow to shoot me? Or just too vain? Don't want folks to know you killed an unarmed man?"

There was admiration in Ward's blue eyes now—and respect. The man had more guts than he'd expected. Maybe those stories about Texans and their courage weren't just tall tales after all.

"Well," Ward drawled softly, "I have an extra gun here." He tossed Younger's gun at him. Dallas caught it smoothly, his handsome face breaking into a grin. He looked at Ward, then down at the gun, fondling it slowly, almost lovingly, brushing the dirt off before he slipped it into the empty holster on his right hip.

Cantrell, gun under his belt, walked to where his gunbelt lay, leaned down, and dragged it up. He strapped it around him, holstered the gun and then faced Younger, his stance seemingly relaxed, his right hand hanging casually at his side.

"I'm waiting, Younger," he said quietly.

Sandra's hand flew to her mouth to stifle a sob. They were crazy! Both of them! Only moments ago they were chatting quietly, conversationally, about joining forces to take Summers; now they were facing each other coldly, their eyes narrowed and glittering with their intent.

The tension was too heavy, too stifling. Sandra couldn't move—could barely breathe. "No, Ward, please," she stammered. "No, Dallas, honey, no, please," she pleaded.

"Hush, Sweetface," Dallas said softly, holding up his left hand in a signal for her to stop pleading. His eyes never left Cantrell's eyes. That was where the first sign always showed—not in the hands.

They faced each other tensely for long seconds, then Ward dragged in a slow breath and relaxed visibly, straightening only slightly, but it was enough. Younger saw the change and knew what it meant. He too had the gunman's instinct to kill, but the moment had passed. There was relief mixed with regret. Now he would never know who was faster. Too late for regrets, though. Younger dismissed Cantrell, turning abruptly to face the girl who was frozen in fear.

"You coming with me?"

Sandra looked at Ward, then at Dallas. There was the slightest hesitation before she nodded.

"Well, come on, Sweetface. Let's get the hell outta here."

Ward grinned. "I wouldn't go south if I were you. There's a posse waiting for that herd."

"Much obliged," Younger said, taking the girl's arm.

Ward watched them leave. He sighed. He'd never make a good ranger. Kincaid would be disappointed.

CHAPTER FIFTY-TWO

Leslie woke up slowly. Her eyes blinked, then focused and she could see. Stars floated like diamonds in an inky black sphere; the rhythmic sound of the horse's hooves against the earth drummed in her ears, and cold wind whipped her feet. She slowly became aware that she was on a horse, being carried across the saddle, wrapped in a blanket and cradled like a babe in strong arms. Her cheek rested on a rough vest that smelled of dust, leather, and sweat, but through all that she recognized the man who held her. There was a scent: a faint, salty, lemony, musky smell that had an irresistible appeal for her. It seemed to pervade her senses—even her ability to think.

"Ward…"

"So you're awake at last."

"Where are you taking me?"

"Into the mountains. You're a hunted outlaw now, just as I am."

"Ohhhh!" That pitiful little cry constricted his heart.

"Then I…killed him?" she asked softly.

"Yes."

Leslie groaned and turned her face into his chest, burrowing there as if to hide from that terrible truth. She had killed the man she was going to marry to save an admitted killer, kidnapper, train robber, and probably rustler.

The enormity of it staggered her. But fearing that Tim *was* going to kill Sandra, Dallas, and Ward, she had dismounted, slapped the horse into a run, and hurried back to the wagon. She had watched and heard everything until she had mustered her courage in time to pull the trigger and send that bullet slamming into his body. Remembering the stunned disbelief on his pale face when he looked at her with the knowledge of his own death full upon him…She would never forget that…

Shuddering, she turned her face and burrowed it into Cantrell's warm body. Ward held her close against him while she fought the revulsion and sickness that came with realization, but he knew that struggle well, and that no one could share it with her. He pulled the blanket closer around her and brushed a kiss on her smooth forehead.

Far off thunder rumbled, and finally Leslie wriggled around until she was riding astride in front of him. Pulling the blanket tight around her, she watched the sky and the sparkles of lightning. How long did she ride thus, shuddering with the memory of her evil deed?

They rode until almost dawn, Leslie alternately sleeping and struggling with her conscience and Ward watching the trail for signs he recognized. At dawn, when the sky was slowly turning pale gray, he found what he was looking for: a small one-room cabin he'd built two years ago when he was in need of solitude. It sat on a level shelf halfway up a mountainside, almost hidden by tall trees. He dismounted and helped Leslie down to stand beside him.

"Where are we?"

"Mountains north of Phoenix. If we get lucky and those clouds dump some rain, we'll be safe from pursuit. No one will find us except by accident. We'll be safe until spring."

"Spring?" she asked incredulously, looking from the lowering black clouds to Ward's face. He was serious. She had never seen him more distant. She could tell by the bleak coldness of his eyes that she could never go back. She was a hunted outlaw now, just as he was. His expression confirmed the finality of it.

Why did she do it? She knew what Ward Cantrell was. She knew he expected to die a violent death. She knew it when she walked through that armed camp in Buckeye. She had sensed it in him when he had first kidnapped her. She shivered in the cold, knowing it would be easier to say why she kept breathing. She could no more allow Tim to shoot Ward than she could hold her hand over flaming coals until it burned off.

Ward led the horse behind the cabin. Dawn changed the gray to blue above the towering pines and firs. A grove of aspen trees surrounded by gold, silver, and red leaves carpeted the mountain with warm color; lofty blue-green firs soared upward to be obscured by swirling blue mists, damp viridescent spears piercing the sky. The air was cold, thin, moist. Pine trees scattered pine cones like acorns. The air was redolent with the resiny smells of pine, fir, sage; the earth beneath her feet was spongy with dead pine needles—brown and slippery. The horse snorted from behind the cabin, and it was an eerie, heavy sound in all that stillness. A bird answered from high overhead and Leslie shivered again.

"Come inside. I have a fire started," he said gently, taking her arm. She was still in shock; it showed in her eyes and the way she moved.

Leslie looked up, her eyes solemn. "Why are you doing this? Helping me escape?"

"You saved our lives. Why not?"

Leslie gasped. She had forgotten the others. "What happened to Sandra and Dallas Younger?"

"They escaped."

"But Sandra...Why did you let him take her?"

"It was her choice."

"She chose it? She wanted to go with that animal?"

"'Fraid so."

"How could she? He's so rough, so...so...crude!"

"Some women like their men rough," he said quietly.

"But...she can't possibly find happiness with a man like that! He'll never be true to her; he'll never be able to give her anything."

Ward shrugged. "Maybe that's enough for her." He turned and walked into the cabin. Leslie followed slowly, wondering what he was thinking about.

Ward was wondering if Dusty and Doug had cut off Cedar Longley and the herd, if Kincaid would get the note he left on Summers' body, and if that would be enough to save Leslie and himself. Summers was a respected man in Phoenix. Would anyone, even Kincaid, be willing to believe that Summers was a crook? This paralleled too closely the events in Dodge City. Was that why he had carried her into the mountains instead of returning to Phoenix? Was history about to repeat itself? This time at Leslie's expense? Or would they assume *he* killed Summers?

"Ward?"

"Hmmm?"

"What are you thinking about?" she asked.

"Nothing."

He spread the blankets on the floor in front of the fire and told her to lie down. He covered her with more blankets and then carried in the saddlebags and began unpacking utensils and food to make a meal. Apparently he had raided the chuckwagon. He had everything he needed, and soon she smelled bacon, coffee, and biscuits.

They ate in silence. Leslie had to force herself to take the first few bites and then her appetite came alive and she was ravenous. She'd had only muffins since breakfast yesterday and was half-starved. She ate until she was embarrassed.

"It's a good thing I cooked plenty," Ward said, grinning.

That was the first real expression she'd seen on his face. He was unusually quiet and thoughtful. He seemed to be waiting, locked away with his own thoughts. Was he remembering when they had been together in Buckeye? Immediately afterward, when she was safe at home, in her room, surrounded by friends who cared about her, alone and miserable nonetheless, she had remembered the tension in that armed camp, the grim faces of the men, and wondered if that flash of hardness she kept seeing was bitterness. But why should *he* be bitter? Why should his cool blue eyes look as bleak and cold as a winter snowscape? What did he want from her?

She shook her head miserably. He had never offered her anything. He had tricked her and taken advantage of her—what did he expect?

Ward caught himself frowning into the fire and forced his muscles as well as his face to relax. This wasn't going to work. His instinctive reactions—so deeply distrustful of authority—had sent him off into the mountains instead of back toward Phoenix, where she belonged. Except he wasn't sure he could go back there, ever. Would they believe him about Summers? The town so far hadn't been exactly receptive to ideas of his innocence. It was only their word against Summers' reputation as a leading citizen. Even with Leslie insisting she had shot Summers, they might not believe her. They could conveniently assume it was another attempt on her part to protect him. He knew the way they'd slandered her after that confrontation in the jail.

"What are you thinking?"

"Nothing."

"Yes you are."

"What would you like me to be thinking about?"

"I don't know." She shook her head sadly and then lifted her chin. Her green eyes flashed with the richness and depth of emeralds. "You know what I would really like?"

Ward shook his head. With her eyes sparkling and midnight-black hair foaming out around the pale oval of her face she was Leslie Powers, the imperious lady again—not a trace of shock left to pale those sweet-curving cheeks.

"No, what?"

"Just one time, Ward Cantrell, I want you to tell me the truth."

His face looked grim and purposeful, as if he could walk away from her and never look back. But part of her didn't care. It felt reckless, willing to say anything and take the consequences.

Clutching the blanket around her, she faced him defiantly. "All right! What's on my mind is that I thought you loved me. Then I went to Buckeye and you made love to me in the bedroom you shared with Sandra."

"Is that why you?…"

"I saw her necklace on your vanity. And tonight she was wearing it!"

His voice was low, expressionless. "She gave me the necklace in Phoenix because she was convinced she was going to die. She said she wanted me to keep it so someone would remember her after she was gone. I gave it back to her because it looked like I had the lifespan of a snowball in hell."

His husky words sobered her. "She wasn't with you?"

"That's right. She was with Younger. Your damned lover took her to Younger."

"Tim?" she asked, frowning. "Why would he do that?"

"To frame me. So you and everyone else would believe I kidnapped her. He wanted me dead. Summers killed Powers and the Mendozas."

"Ohhh…Tim?" She felt weak suddenly. Weak and stupid. But she had to know everything. "But there was another girl in Buckeye. I saw her shawl…"

"If there was a shawl there," he said gently, "it belonged to Juanita Castenada, the owner's daughter. She was married last month…before she moved away."

Pale and lovely in the firelight, Leslie was supremely doubtful of Cantrell's motives, his integrity, probably even his parentage, and yet, in spite of her misgivings, he felt compelled to protect her splendid, brave spirit. Even though she obviously didn't trust him, he was determined that he wouldn't let her make a fool of him again. He reached out and touched her cheek. "There was no female in that room or any other with me except you."

Cantrell's touch weakened Leslie's resolve against him, and she resented that it should be so. She didn't reply. She was watching his eyes, wishing she could read them more clearly. Part of her was vibrating to his nearness and his restrained anger. But another part of her was equally determined to get at the truth. She was tired of worrying and waiting. "Were you lying to me about Jennifer Kincaid?"

"Which time?"

"How many times did you lie to me about her?" she demanded angrily, clutching the blanket around her. "When you said you were not romantically involved with her!"

"That's the truth."

"But there were other lies?"

"You accused me of some things that weren't true and I allowed you to believe they were. I don't think you can blame me for that."

"Will they hang us?" she demanded suddenly.

He poked at the fire, a grunt of laughter escaping from him in a gust. "I suppose it depends on who we run into first, but with Summers out of the way, maybe the mob will lose its steam."

"Ward?"

"Hmmm?"

"I can't run away," she said softly. "I'm going to have to go back and face whatever has to be faced."

Without warning he pulled her into his arms, holding her as if the sheriff were already trying to pull her away from him, and Leslie knew she was in love, and the knowledge that it had come too late filled her with sadness and unshed tears.

"What's wrong?" he asked, his lips nudging her cheek.

She laughed. What could she say? The man I love is an outlaw! A killer. Wanted by the sheriff. And I'm about to hang for murder...

"Hey!" That half-hysterical laugh told him volumes. He shook her and then folded her in his arms again. "I'm not going to let them hang you," he said huskily.

"What about you?"

"Me either."

"I have to go back, you know."

Ward's heart felt like it would burst. He pulled her closer, cradling her face in the crook of his neck and shoulder. She was insane, insisting on her right to be hanged. But insane or not, she had bewitched him from the very beginning with her passionate pursuit of her noble ideals. Her courage and honesty and spirit had shattered his defenses and played havoc with his unwillingness to fall in love.

"Then we'll both go back," he said.

"No, Ward! You can never go back there. I have a chance. You have none." She clung to him tightly, trembling in spite of his warmth. "They'll hang you."

"Would you care?" he asked, holding her away from him so he could search her eyes. His own were strangely dark.

"I would die," she said.

"Then stay with me here...for one week."

"Why?"

"One week to remember and I'll tell them I shot Summers."

"No!"

"Why not? It won't make a difference for me. I've killed other men."

"No! I will not permit it. Never!"

"Because you don't want to spend a week with me?"

"No," she whispered. If she were going to prison or to hang, she would still want that week.

"Will you stay one week?"

"If you promise not to try to stop me from turning myself in."

"I promise," he said, burying his face in the fragrant black mass of her hair.

The week slipped past like a butterfly flitting from flower to flower, sampling the sweetness of the nectar until pleasurably sated. They teased and played and made love, pretending they had forever, and Leslie only fretted occasionally about the future. At those times she watched Cantrell closely, but if he was aware he lived under a cloud, it was not discernible. Except for a moment after he had saddled their horses for the long ride back. His blue eyes—so clear and untroubled this whole week—darkened as he lifted her into the saddle. In that second she felt the reluctance and tension in him, but no shirking. A lump rose in her throat. Cantrell would face whatever had to be faced, but she hated the fact that their future was now beyond their control.

CHAPTER FIFTY-THREE

"Leslie, wake up, dear. The sheriff is downstairs. He wants to talk to you."

Leslie covered her head and groaned. The sun streaming in the window hurt her eyes. She opened one eye and squinted at Jennifer, who was smiling delightedly at her.

"Oh, no! I'm such a mess," she groaned.

"You look wonderful," Jennie said, smiling as if she meant it. "The sheriff will wait, but you had best be up and dressing."

Leslie's heart constricted with fear and alarm. "Where's Cantrell?" she demanded.

"He's downstairs with Chane and some gentleman."

Leslie struggled upright in the bed, looking so confused and scared that Jennie pulled her into her arms and hugged her. "I'm so glad you're safe!" she said. "We were so worried about you. Except I knew he would save you."

Annette came in with a rustling of petticoats and excited exclamations in mingled English and French that went on the whole time Leslie bathed and dressed. Jennie withdrew, probably in self-defense, promising they would talk later.

"Have you seen Mr. Cantrell?" Leslie asked when Annette finished putting the last pins in her hair.

"*Oui!* He is so handsome! *Magnifique, no?*"

"Where is he?"

"Downstairs! With him!"

"Him? Who?"

"Him! John Loving. He's here. In ziss house!"

Leslie grinned in spite of her fear. "So you finally got him here?"

"*Oui!*"

"Well, what are you doing up here wasting your time with me?" she demanded.

Annette shrugged. "He was busy with Mr. Kincaid, zee sheriff, zee governor, and some man I do not know. He scare me *so* bad."

"Scared you? Who?"

"*Oui!* I opened zee door, expecting somezhing ordinary, and *he* is zere! Staring at *moi* with zee meanest face I have evair seen. Like he as soon shop off my head as say hello." Annette shuddered.

"Who is he?"

Annette shrugged. "John King."

"Where's he from?"

"I do not know...Such good English...unless...Is Canvas a place to be from?"

"Canvas? Kan...sas?"

"*Oui!* Kan...sas! That is good, no?"

"No," Leslie said grimly, cursing herself for coming back here. They had him! There was no turning back now. She was regretting so many things suddenly. And remembering what Ward had said when she railed at him for refusing to give her his seed. When she said that man-made laws couldn't take away her right to have his baby: "They can take everything," he'd said quietly, inexorably, "even my right to live."

Her heart was pounding so loudly she could feel it in her toes. Annette stepped back to admire her handiwork, and Leslie stood up. Her heart fluttered at the base of her throat. She might never see him alone again, never feel the warmth of his skin against her own.

"Ready, *mademoiselle?*"

No! No! She wasn't, but she nodded calmly in spite of that nerve-end jangle that threatened to betray her.

At the top of the stairs, she paused. Deep masculine voices were coming from the library. *Here goes. Please, legs, don't collapse. If he can face this, I can too...*

She negotiated the stairs in a sort of breathless daze and stopped at the door of the library, watching them before they became aware of her presence.

They were clustered around the fireplace, sipping from coffee cups and looking pleased with themselves. She found Ward instantly. Annette was right. Clean-shaven, wearing a dark blue shirt and dark trousers, he was Adonis incarnate. Just the sight of him, leaning against the far side of the fireplace, his mouth set in that look of sensual reserve that she knew so well, was enough to double the force of that pounding in her breast. He hadn't seen her yet. He was watching Kincaid and a strapping, well-dressed Negro man, warily, it seemed. Annette was right about the man. He had the most terrifyingly brutal face she had ever seen. Her heart almost stopped.

The governor and the sheriff were there also. But her eyes went back to the Negro. There was something ominous and frightening about him.

Ward glanced at the door and their eyes met. His seemed unusually dark and unreadable—without the slightest trace of sardonic amusement. Her eyes moved down that lithe familiar form and widened. He was not wearing a gun. Did that account for the unusually solemn cast of his handsome features? But why shouldn't it? Ward Cantrell was a warrior, and a warrior should not be stripped of his weapons without a fight. Leslie writhed inwardly with the knowledge that he had laid down his guns and submitted to this civilized form of humiliation for her. Because he loved her. The realization that she had taken the man she loved and reduced him to this, that he should die or be imprisoned like an animal for deeds he could not help, was more than she could bear. The pain spread out in ever-widening waves until her chest ached and her throat felt rigid with anguish.

Ward saw the pain reflected in her wide green eyes. "Let's get this over with," he said to Kincaid.

Chane came forward to take her arm. "Leslie, join us, please."

They paused in front of the governor. "Leslie, you remember Governor Stanton, Sheriff Tatum, Reverend Abercrombie. Frank Johnston is president of the local Cattleman's Association. Doug Paggett and Dusty Denton are friends of Warden's. I'd like you to meet John King, from Dodge City, and John Loving, the new manager of the Texas and Pacific Railroad."

Leslie glanced quickly at Ward, but he was concentrating on his coffee cup, his eyes averted from hers.

"Yes, there've been some changes taking place while you were away," Chane said, smiling at John Loving.

Loving's face broke into a glad chipmunk-cheeked smile of greeting to Leslie, but John King only watched her impassively. She forced herself to nod at each of the men. She wanted to go to Ward, touch him, reassure herself that he was all right, but Chane had a firm grip on her hand.

"Ahem!" Sheriff Tatum cleared his throat, looking around the room at the other men. "I guess since Miss Powers is here, we might as well begin. Would you like to sit down?" he asked solicitously.

"May we offer you tea or coffee?" Chane asked.

"No, thank you."

"Very well," he said, nodding at Tatum.

The sheriff asked a great number of questions, and she answered them honestly, casting glances at Ward to see if somehow she might be saying things that were damaging to him; but he only watched her quietly, his eyes as unreadable as before.

When she felt dizzy with so many questions, Tatum sighed with satisfaction and Governor Stanton stepped forward. "Miss Powers, it gives me great pleasure to present you with these checks for capturing Sandra McCormick's kidnapper and the leader of the rustlers that have been preying on honest ranchers hereabouts for the last three years."

Horrified, she looked from the governor to Chane. "You don't understand," she said, "I didn't capture Cantrell—he saved me! I killed Tim Summers to keep him from killing Sandra, Cantrell, and Younger…"

"That is correct," the governor said, smiling at her.

Leslie sighed. "No, you don't understand…I killed Tim because he said he was going to kill them. I didn't capture Cantrell!" she insisted.

Governor Stanton smiled. "Perhaps an explanation is in order. Chane?" he asked, passing the buck.

Chane grinned. "Leslie, you are a heroine. Tim Summers *was* the head of the rustler gang."

"But…but I thought Cantrell was the…"

The governor smiled benignly. "Mr. Cantrell is an Arizona ranger, Miss Powers. His job along with Dusty Denton, Doug Paggett, and the others was to smoke out the real rustler chief."

Chane took her hand. "When we discovered you'd ridden off Saturday, Sheriff Tatum and I took a posse out looking for you. We came upon Denton and the others the next day after they had recovered the herd from Summers' and Younger's men. We saved the herd, but most of the rustlers escaped over the border."

Leslie barely heard him. She was stunned. An Arizona ranger! Ward knew from the very beginning she wasn't going to hang for killing Tim! He knew *he* wasn't in any danger of hanging either! Rage bubbled in her veins. What a monumental liar he was! She would kill him with her bare hands!

She turned on Ward, her eyes spitting fury, poised like an angry tigress, but he came forward and caught her hands before she could spring at him.

"Wait, Leslie. There's more. We might as well get this all out in the open," he said grimly.

"That happens to be more than enough!"

"I have to go back to Dodge City to stand trial for murder."

Anger forgotten, her eyes went to John King and stayed there. She could feel her insides collapsing. Her hands dropped to her sides.

"They'll hang you…" she whispered, fear squeezing so tight she almost could not speak.

The man named King stepped forward. He nodded. "There is hope, Miss Powers, else I wouldn't be taking him back."

"Hope? How can you say that?" she gasped.

"The men Captain Van Vleet killed murdered my brother-in-law, the captain's friend, and his wife. The captain only killed after gross provocation, Miss Powers. He only killed in self-defense. I have…um, you might say…encouraged two witnesses to come forward who will testify to his innocence."

Leslie closed her eyes and covered her face.

Ward sighed. "We should have talked this morning, but you were so tired…" Ward's jaw clamped shut, and she could see the muscles in his lean cheek writhing as he decided how to proceed. The thought of him standing trial again, possibly going to prison and hanging, was insupportable.

Chane took her hand. "He'll have good counsel, Leslie. He'll have the support of his family and Mr. King this time. We think that will be enough to tip the scales in his favor."

"What if you're wrong?" she demanded.

"We have to start somewhere," Ward said softly.

"I think we'd best leave these young people alone," Kincaid said, herding the others out of the room.

Leslie barely noticed them. Her eyes were riveted to Cantrell's face. Ward nodded at her, his eyes filled with that sharp light that dazed her. His fingers closed around her arm, above the elbow.

"You were a ranger this whole time?" she whispered.

"Since the day after my trial."

"You knew you wouldn't hang."

"No. I didn't know that. If I failed…"

"Why didn't you tell me about Tim?"

He shrugged. Bitterness flickered in the blue depths. "Would you have believed me?"

She was watching him intently, her eyes riveted to his. "There's more, isn't there?" she whispered.

Ward took a deep breath. This *could* get him killed.

"You remember when I told you that I wasn't romantically involved with Jenn?"

Leslie could feel her heart slowing down, like an engine preparing to stop. She looked quickly at Chane, but he was closing the door behind him. They were all gone except Ward.

She shook her head. There was cruelty and cruelty. To tell her now that he lied about loving her…

She backed away from him, her eyes spitting, cat green. "Don't touch me! I don't want to hear about the other women in your life."

She backed slowly away, and he followed, stalking her the way he would an animal he meant to kill.

"Leslie, didn't you ever wonder why I kept punishing you?" he asked softly, inching closer.

"No! I don't want to hear it."

But he was determined that she would hear it. His face was set in grim, unwavering purpose. She backed into the wall and gasped. She was trapped! But what had she done to bring out this streak of implacable cruelty in the man she loved? Why was he determined to tell her he loved another woman?

"Leslie," he said softly, "Jenn is my sister."

She couldn't speak. Her jaw dropped. Her head began automatically, involuntarily, to shake from side to side, denying what she would not hear.

The clock on the mantel ticked loudly in the sudden stillness. Everyone had left the room. It was only the two of them now. "You tricked me!" she said incredulously.

"I didn't mean to. I pretended to accept your noble sacrifice to punish you for not believing in me…I never meant to collect on that bargain. I was going to tell you at the dance, but you left. I only came here that night to tell you I was leaving Phoenix."

"Oh! What a liar you are!" She jerked her arm free and grabbed one of the books off the shelf beside her and hit him with it. "You beast! Oh! How I hate you!"

"Ow! Leslie, stop it!" he howled, ducking.

She was like a panther, darting and striking at will. He was helpless against her. The only alternative was to run, so he did, with her behind him, screaming invectives.

Jennifer heard the loud commotion and left the children with Mrs. Lillian. She had wanted to be with Chane when they told Leslie the truth, but a cry of pain from Amy had sidetracked her. Little Chane had tripped Amy, and she cut her lip. He was almost as upset as Amy was. It took both women to get them calmed down and patched up.

When she could leave them she sought out Chane.

"What happened to Ward and Leslie? I thought they were going to…"

Chane grinned, his hazel eyes filled with mischief. "I guess that will have to wait until *after* she kills him."

Jennifer laughed, a low, sultry gurgle that still sent tingles up Chane's spine. "Was she very angry?"

"Well, just a little," he said. "Nothing Ward can't handle, I'm sure."

"I hope he's as humble as you are."

"I didn't notice any humility as he ran past here—only a well-developed survival instinct."

"Do you think she'll catch him?"

Chane grinned, his warm green eyes twinkling. "I'm sure of it. He ran for her bedroom."

CHAPTER FIFTY-FOUR

Leslie ran to the door of her bedroom and stopped, panting from the wild run up the long, curving staircase. The room looked empty. Hadn't she seen his leg and boot disappearing into this very room?

She walked slowly inside, looking quickly from side to side. The sound of the rug being compressed under a heavy foot brought her whirling around.

"Oh!"

The door slammed shut. He was between her and the door, coming toward her slowly, his blue eyes reflecting a strange satisfaction, as if now *he* had *her*.

Unthinking fury surged up, blocking out reason. She lunged at him, her nails curved into talons.

She would have scratched him too, if his hands hadn't caught her wrists and forced them down behind her back. He pulled her hard against him, taking both wrists in one hand so he could use his other hand to capture her head and hold it still.

She felt like a crushed rose. Furious, she squirmed and twisted, trying to get loose, but she was helpless. He leaned down and set his mouth over hers.

Leslie was determined that she would not respond to his kiss. He had tricked her again. Lied to her, laughed at her, held her up to public ridicule. What had Jennie thought? Knowing everything?

But the hard pressure of his lips, burning into hers, pressing her mouth open, forcing her head back...her anger was dissolving into heat, her body coming alive, as if his touch stripped away her protective covering—leaving her exposed to him, to his hands, his lips, his will...

No fair! How could she ever get an accounting from him for his outrageous actions when fear for his safety left her so needy for him? He kissed her endlessly, until she forgot everything except her love for him.

He relinquished her lips. Panting, she pressed her face into his shoulder and felt the scar tissue from the injury he had received the last night she was his captive. She kissed him there, breathing the warm, manly fragrance into her nostrils.

So many memories...They crowded into her head, blinding her. She could see him on the corn husk mattress in the small hut after she had taken the bullet out of his shoulder—unconscious, with his face turned away from her, the sturdy column of his neck tempting her. How could a man so strong, so enduring, look so vulnerable?

She had reached out to smooth that tawny thatch of silver-streaked flaxen hair off his forehead and ended by pressing her lips there. Finally, losing all control, she had held him blindly, helplessly, until he stirred.

A vision of his lean form hanging limply between Younger's men as Younger pounded his face into raw meat, brought a helpless groan from deep in her throat. He'd had tinges of those bruises in jail...

And yet he had let Younger go.

She hadn't expected to see Ward again after the jail. Certainly not dressed in the height of fashion, framed against the sumptuous background of the Kincaids' *sala grande*, looking negligently at ease while her heart pounded so loudly she feared she would shake apart from it.

Remembering the confused impulses of fear and pride she'd felt, seeing him beside the fireplace, across the library, a prisoner, she'd thought, a warrior disarmed and waiting to be executed...only to find out he was Jennie's brother—why hadn't she guessed? She'd had clues. The way Jennie couldn't quite bring herself to turn loose his hand. Jennie's instant recovery so soon after her brother's death. Chane's look of rapt pride and happiness when Ward and Jennie danced together. She'd been blind.

But he helped blind her. The unselfconscious way he held Jennie in his arms that day...She could see herself. Heavens! How foolish she must have seemed to him, going to the house on Barton Street, asking him to give Jennie up.

It *had* been bitterness in his husky voice when he taunted her: "I only care about myself. That's what you said. Why should I deprive myself of a choice female like Jenn?"

When she tried to leave, he stopped her with that look in his blue eyes and the warm pressure of his hand on her arm. In her extremity she had called him an animal, accusing him of any vile thing she could think of, and that strange light flared in his eyes, darkening and then lightening the blue before he said, "I want you." By the time his hand tangled in her hair, pulling her close for that terrible, punishing kiss, everything inside her was collapsing: pride, stubbornness, courage.

But...she hadn't been honest with him either, had she? Maybe if she'd told him why she went to Buckeye...Later, up at the mountain cabin, if she had admitted she was afraid to go back to Phoenix...

She jerked away from him, as far away as she could get in the steely circle of his arms.

"Now what is it?" he asked, recognizing the look in her defiant green eyes.

"You could have told me a week ago that neither one of us was in any real danger of hanging."

"Not me. I didn't believe it. In case you don't remember me, I'm the one with no excess of trust."

"You could have told me you were a ranger."

"To what purpose? When things don't work out, people have a way of conveniently forgetting their promises. Stanton is a practical politician. If the mob chose to believe Summers and Younger over me, he wouldn't have had the guts to tell them I was working for him...I didn't know *what* to expect when I got here. They could just as easily have been waiting to hang me."

"You didn't know?"

"On my sister's honor," he said solemnly.

"Jennie's your sister?"

"All my life..."

"There was no girl at Buckeye?"

"Only you."

"Why didn't you come here right away? Didn't you want to know if everything worked out?"

"Desperately. Unfortunately I wanted us to survive more. I thought a week would give things a chance to settle."

She gazed out the window, remembering the low, deliberately expressionless tone of his husky voice the day he told her about Simone and his friend Snake. No, he wouldn't have an excess of trust that all those angry townspeople would believe him just because he was innocent.

"How did John King find you?"

"Someone wrote a letter to the sheriff in Dodge City, describing and naming me. King said he had guessed years ago that Ward Cantrell was really Peter Van Vleet...He had asked the sheriff to keep an ear open for word of me."

"Tim..."

"What?" Ward asked, frowning.

"Tim may have been the one..."

Ward's lips tightened. "Could be. We'll never know." He was silent a moment. "I'm glad this worked out for Doug and Dusty and the rest of the men who agreed to help me. Stanton was so pleased he pardoned all of us." Leslie murmured her agreement, and they fell silent.

Sounds filtered into her consciousness. Two birds were arguing back and forth in short, raucous spurts of sound. She heard voices outside, in the garden. A horse whinnied and another answered. A dog barked.

"Cantrell?"

"Yeah?" Did she detect wariness in his reply?

"I love you." Her voice sounded taut, strangled, not like her. He held her away from him and saw the tears streaming down her lovely cheeks. Her eyes were dark, the pupils dilated, welling with new tears.

"Leslie, Jesus..." He pulled her into his arms and held her tightly, feeling hers and his own pain keenly. She sobbed against his shoulder, her arms moving up to cling around his neck. "Leslie, love, please don't cry...Hey, I can't stand it when you cry...I love you. Don't cry... Everything is going to work out."

She was trembling uncontrollably. "I was so mean to you! You were so brave...You could have been killed. You could have died."

"It's all right now. Hush. I love you."

"I never trusted you. I was going to let him shoot you...I almost did..."

"But you didn't. When it mattered, you came through for me."

She kissed him softly, breathing him in.

"Don't worry," he whispered. "We'll find some way for you to make this up to me."

"Ohhh! You are incorrigible. Now that I know your type..." she began threateningly.

"It won't help. I trick you every time."

She laughed, her tears forgotten. "I might get smarter as I get older."

"Lord, I hope not," he growled ruefully.

"But then I would have to, wouldn't I?"

Laughing, he cut her off with the only weapon he had, kissing her into forgetfulness. He undressed her and came into her slowly, groaning her name.

"Leslie...I love you so..."

She held him close, reveling in the sensations of love: his husky voice murmuring love words, his body dissolving into hers, her bones melting into fiery liquid. She couldn't remember hating him, only loving him. And she would do it all again for him. For this.

MORE FROM JOYCE BRANDON

THE LADY AND THE LAWMAN

Life on the Western frontier in the 1880s is filled with risks and danger—a fact Angie Logan quickly relearns upon arriving back at her family's Arizona ranch, home from college back East. To help quell the riots against Chinese immigrants that have settled in Durango, Angie relies on her education and wits in appealing to the governor for assistance. The governor sends help in the form of Lance Kincaid, a charismatic gentleman who became a ranger to avenge the murder of the woman he loved. While working to resolve the current upheaval, Lance catches the trail of the murderer. Nothing will stop him from catching the killer and bringing him to justice, except perhaps Angie, the mysterious woman who looks eerily like his lost love.

THE LADY AND THE ROBBER BARON

Jennifer Van Vleet is a woman who knows what she wants out of life and won't let anything stand in her way. She's dedicated herself to the art of ballet and becomes the prima ballerina for her company. When her costume catches fire during a performance, Chantry Kincaid III—a rakishly charming Texan builder whose family has as many enemies as it has properties—saves her. Jennifer finds herself drawn into a whirlwind romance with Chantry, where the passion between the two is undeniable, until she learns of the Kincaid family's hand in her parents' deaths years ago. Now she has a decision to make, one that will decide whether she can let go of the past and move forward from tragedy.

ADOBE PALACE

After the deaths of her parents, Samantha Forrester was raised with the Kincaid children. She fell in love with Lance Kincaid as he protected her from childhood bullies. Now they've both grown up and Lance has married another. When the devilishly charming Steve Sheridan rides into Samantha's life, she sees her chance to build the house of her dreams, save her son's life, and claim Lance's heart for her own. But life doesn't always go according to plan, and fate will take them all on a journey as wild as the land they live on.

AFTER EDEN

Teresa Garcia-Lorca was raised as the favored daughter of "El Gato Negro," the infamous Mexican revolutionary. She lived in sheltered bliss until the day the truth of her paternity comes out, and her former "father" becomes furious. Teresa and her mother are forced to flee for their lives to escape El Gato's murderous rage. Her only hope lies in the home of her biological father, Bill Burkhart, but nothing could have prepared her for the treachery of gringo/white greed. Her new-found father's bastard daughter, Judy Burkhart, has had everything—and every man—she's ever wanted. Her indulgent world shatters when Judy learns she's been disinherited in her father's will. She and Teresa must learn to fight for all they have lost—and only one of them will end up with the man they both love.

Printed in the USA
CPSIA information can be obtained
at www.ICGtesting.com
JSHW031706140824
68134JS00038B/3541